The Death and Life of Edward Reed

The Death and Life of Edward Reed

Dawn Hogue

a novel by

Dawn Hogue

This is a human made work of fiction. References to historical events, places, and persons are used in service of the story and are represented as accurately as possible. All other places, events, and incidents are either the products of the author's imagination or are used in a fictitious manner and resemblance to actual persons or places is purely coincidental.

ISBN: 978-1-952526-32-9

Printed in the United States of America

Water's Edge Press LLC
Tucson, AZ
watersedgepress.com

Cover and book design by Water's Edge Press.
Images are licensed through AdobeStock and VectorStock.
Fonts are licensed through Adobe Fonts.

A Water's Edge Press First Edition

for everyone who wonders
and for my mother and father,
who always believed in me

"Rien ne se perd, rien ne se crée, tout se transforme."
"Nothing is lost, nothing is created, all is transformed."

— The principle of conservation of matter, Antoine Lavoisier

"Oh, earth, you're too wonderful for anybody to realize you. Do any human beings ever realize life while they live it? – every, every minute?"

— Emily Webb in *Our Town*, by Thornton Wilder

PART ONE

Chapter 1

August 1927, Chicago, Illinois

Edward Reed had often wondered how his life would end. When his brother Richie died of appendicitis, fifteen-year-old Eddie wondered if it would get him next. Then in 1918, when influenza took his mother and father and some of their neighbors, Eddie figured his time was up, but his case had been mild and he recovered. A few years back when J. Edgar Hoover's boys started cracking down on bootlegging operations, even small ones like his, Eddie figured one of them would get him. He and Nelson and Bear were always on the lookout for those bastards, and that made a guy nervous as hell. Thinking someone was after you could make you careless. But it wasn't his appendix, or the flu, or the G-Men. It was fear that got him.

Eddie's constant state of apprehension began the night someone, they figured it had to be Capone's boys, took out his boss, Mick Sheridan. Sheridan had taken his new wife to Martinetti's on Saturday night for a spaghetti dinner, and that's where they got him, right there on the sidewalk under a wine-colored canopy that said *Ristorante*. It was awful. Mick's pretty young wife in her mink coat, spattered in blood, just standing there, screaming. At least that is how it was reported in the paper. "Gangland Killers Terrorize Restaurateur," the headline read. After describing the gory scene and the wife's ordeal, the reporter played up how distraught Martinetti was, saying the murder would put him out of business.

As soon as he heard the news, Eddie went to Nelson's sister's place south of the stockyards. It was where they met up when things got hot.

Nelson was at the kitchen table, his empty plate covered in egg yolk and toast crumbs.

Bear was at the table, reading the latest article about the murder.

"Sit down Ed," Nelson said. "Edna'll fix something for you."

Eddie smiled at Edna and said he wasn't hungry. "Thank you just the same, ma'am." Eddie had always felt a bit sorry for Edna. The boy she was going to marry had been killed in Italy during the war, and ever since she had lived alone. If it weren't for the way her shoulder blade jutted out, she would be a nice looking woman, Eddie thought.

"It's just a sob story about the restaurant owner, how the slaying will hurt his business," Bear said, moving the paper over to Nelson. "Nothing about an investigation."

"They're not going to look into a thing and you know it," Nelson said, looking up after reading the article for himself. "One less bootlegger is a win for the cops. And I wouldn't worry about Martinetti's business. He's going to be loaded with creeps who wanna see where Sheridan got bumped off."

Eddie agreed. He did not care one bit about Martinetti. He was worried about himself. And Bear and Nelson, of course. "What's our plan, Boss?" Eddie asked.

Nelson jerked his head toward Eddie. "No siree," he said emphatically. "I am not the boss. I'm not stepping one foot into that trap."

Eddie understood. Guys like them were secondary targets. Bosses were the ones with bullseyes on their foreheads.

That afternoon, Bear went back to the city to assess the situation. What he wanted to know would not be in the papers. Entering the alley door of McGinty's Diner, Bear tromped down the back stairs to the cellar, passing shelves loaded with flour sacks, lard, and canned vegetables. Bear imagined Tommy, McGinty's hired man, washing tables and sweeping the speakeasy, getting ready for that evening's crowd. Bear used their coded *rat-a-tat-tat* knock, and the door opened. Instead of Tommy, Bear found Declan McGinty himself.

"You shouldn't be here, Bear," McGinty said, looking over Bear's shoulder as if someone were right behind him. "Things are hot."

"Yeah," Bear said. "But we need to know how hot. And who we're up against."

McGinty told Bear what he knew. "Wish it was more. I only hear things, you understand."

"It's enough, Mac. It can only be one guy and you know it."

McGinty agreed.

"Thanks, Mac. And watch your back." Bear slipped a fifty into McGinty's hand before heading out.

"I don't think it was Capone who went after Sheridan," Bear told the boys that evening. "Mac heard that Loughlin was bragging about rubbing someone out. It had to be him."

Moose Loughlin swooping in to claim Sheridan's territory was a gutsy move and one that would get him killed before long, but old Moose was not the brightest guy and probably had not considered what it would mean to overstep his boundaries. That didn't mean he wasn't a threat. What Moose lacked in brains, he made up for in ruthlessness.

"We're gonna have to split up," Nelson said. "He'll be after us next."

Bear nodded. "My thoughts exactly." After a short pause, he added, "unless we take out Moose ourselves?"

"And start a war?" Nelson shook his head. "Not happening."

Edna set a bowl of mashed potatoes and a platter of fried chicken on the table. "Eat up boys," she said. "Then you need to be on your way." It was clear from her tone that she had gleaned the gist of their conversations.

When his sister was back in the kitchen, Nelson said, "I don't know where you boys are headed, but I'm going to *May-he-co*. Going to find me a señorita or two."

"It's my brother's hunting cabin in Wisconsin for me," Bear said. "What about you, Cowboy?" Bear asked Eddie. When they had first partnered up, Bear had started calling Eddie "Cowboy" because, Bear said, the kid looked just like the Western movie star, William S. Hart. "Where do you think you'll go?"

Eddie shrugged. He had loved their time in Florida, managing Sheridan's hotel and running rum for a while, but it wasn't safe. Everybody in Miami knew Sheridan's boys. "California, maybe?" California had been his brother's dream, and it was farther away. "Sure can't hang around here."

As the chicken disappeared, then later a peach pie, the three men talked about their futures, away from this life. Bear said he might open a shop and sell little animals and toys, as he was getting good at carving things from wood. This fact came as a surprise to Eddie and Nelson, who didn't see Bear as having more genteel qualities.

Nelson, true to his character, spoke only of his female conquests, but when pushed, he argued he could open a cantina if he needed some dough. "I hear they don't care so much about their liquor down there," he said. "If McGinty can do it, so can I."

Eddie, because he did not really believe in his dreams, had no idea what he would do, *if* he made it out west. He was a cowboy in nickname only. When the others asked him what he'd get up to out in Hollywood-land, he just shrugged. "Find me a movie star, of course." His answer amused Nelson and Bear and they catapulted into a speculation of movie star life.

"You maybe could find your look-alike," Bear said.

"Better yet," Nelson said, "you can go to swanky places and say you're him. Betcha they won't let you pay for your drinks or even your dinner. Gotta work at least a couple of times."

The light banter, which only erased the surface of their anxiety, continued until dark, when they agreed it was time to be on their way.

Outside on the front porch, the three companions embraced as if they would never see one another again. "It's been a riot, hasn't it?" Nelson said, his voice on the verge of breaking.

When Nelson's eyes glistened with tears, Eddie about called him an old softie, but thought better of it. No man wanted to hear something like that. Instead he said, "Best of luck in Mexico."

Bear coughed, then pushed his hand out to shake Eddie's.

"All right, kid," he said. "Get going. I don't know how, but they seem to be two steps ahead of us, so stay low and be careful."

Eddie nodded, then he stepped out into the night.

Chapter 2

Tuesday, August 23, 1927

They got to Bear first. Bear. The best of them. Got him in his car, while he waited at a red light just south of Racine, the paper said. The face in the photo was bloodied, but Eddie still recognized his friend. That was three days ago. This morning a photo of Nelson lying in a pool of blood on the sidewalk outside his brownstone appeared on the front page. "Gangland War Escalates! Terrorizes the Public!" the headline read. Eddie felt the hairs stand on the back of his neck. He'd be next.

This morning, Eddie was stretched out on his bed, staring at the ceiling, imagining various scenarios. They played like little movies in his head. The more he thought about what could go wrong, the more his *character* got killed in the end. He tried to quit worrying, but the more he tried, the worse it got.

Today would be a long day of waiting. Right now the house was quiet. Out his bedroom window, he heard only the usual neighborhood noise. Dogs barking, birds chirping, kids calling out to one another in their games. Around 2:00 p.m., Eddie heard the squeak of the brass letter slot. Only the mailman, he thought reassuringly. "Stay calm," he said to himself. "Just gotta hunker down a while longer."

So far things were going to plan, and if he made it to the middle of the night, he would be able to get away. Eddie doubted anyone would come after him in broad daylight in an ordinary neighborhood like his, but these days he knew better than to count on what ought to make sense. Eddie was almost ninety percent certain that Loughlin didn't know where he lived. But that was only because Eddie had gotten good at ditching tails over the years. And he rarely went home the same way twice. What really worried Eddie was that Moose wasn't as dumb as people said he was.

Eddie also worried about his rucksack. It was not hidden well, only tucked under the back porch so he could easily grab it when he made his getaway. Any nosy kid could find it. But there had never been a time when a nosy kid had ventured into Eddie's yard. Inventing improbable outcomes helped nothing.

Yesterday, Eddie had packed the rucksack with a clean shirt, his knife, an old toy canteen filled with water, and for reasons he still didn't understand, the little toy soldier Richie had stolen from Joey Crandall. Most important was the envelope he'd give later to some lawyer and his three bankrolls totaling $6,000. Those were banded tightly and tucked into the sleeve of a shirt, which was folded at the bottom of the bag. Twice he had fought the urge to creep downstairs to make sure the bag was still there. Then, finally he had given over to sleep.

Since leaving Edna's, Eddie kept mostly to his bedroom and the adjoining bathroom. He hoped from the street the house looked like no one was home. He had brought up enough food to get him through, and yesterday made sandwiches. Those were out in his rucksack too. Eddie planned to leave tonight at 2:00 a.m. while most of Chicago slept. He would creep out, retrieve his knapsack, and make his way to a train yard somewhere west of the city, where he would wait to hop an early westbound freight. At that time of night, Moose and his boys, if they stayed true to form, would be passed out from a night with a bottle of rum. Eddie was counting on that, but he did not like thinking that his safety depended on Moose Loughlin's bad habits.

After sunset, Eddie pulled out his pocket watch. He could barely make out its face in the moonlight. Quarter past eight. Seven more hours. The endless waiting was always the hardest part. His heart, mimicking the watch, ticked every second. Aw, quit complaining, he thought. He and Nelson had spent longer than that on surveillance operations, but when you were with a guy, time went faster somehow.

Eddie stretched. His legs ached from disuse. He couldn't believe how tired he was. He did a few push-ups to snap the sleep out of his brain. "Better not use up my strength," he said, then he laughed, remembering how Ma would sometimes talk out loud when no one was around to hear.

Remembering his mother at this moment brought Eddie a profound sense of grief, not just for her absence over the past nine years, but for how he had disappointed her. She had never said so, but he knew. And Pop had made the fact clear enough—Eddie hadn't measured up.

Eddie checked his watch again. 11:45 p.m. Just about two hours to go. In his business, guys got whacked all the time. But not his guys. When Bear and Nelson got it, Eddie felt the lens of his own life closing. That's when he knew something had to change. Not just the scenery either. If he could get away, he would start fresh. Change his name. Leave all this underworld stuff behind. First though, he had to get out of Chicago. He should have gone last night after the rucksack was packed. But something in him said lay low one more day.

Seconds later, the folly of that decision was made clear when Eddie heard the sound of a fist pounding on the front door. Then came the familiar hoarse croak of Moose Loughlin's voice.

"We know you're in there, Cowboy."

Out in the hallway, Eddie stayed close to the walls and made his way towards the stairway. If it were December, the street light would be shining through the bare limbs of the trees out front lighting up the living room and parlor, but it was August and the rooms below were pitch black. He could be out back in seconds, but he had to go now. It was only the next sound that halted his progress.

"Open up!" said a deeper voice.

"Jack," Eddie said in a panic. They didn't call Jack "Cutter" for nothing. Instead of a pistol, Jack carried a long pointed blade in a leather holster. Eddie had seen for himself the damage that thing could do.

"Oh, Cowboy," Jack's voice sang out again, a sinister tune.

Eddie heard nothing for a moment, then the sound of metal clicking against metal, like someone were trying to start a dead engine. Then Eddie remembered the other thing Jack's dagger could do. Open locks. Eddie took a deep breath and stepped out of the hallway.

Then he misjudged the first step.

Moose Loughlin peered through the lace curtain of the sidelight window into the dark house. "You in there Cowboy?" he said menacingly. Then Moose heard the satisfying click of Jack's dagger. "Not for long," Moose said, then he turned the knob. When he tried opening the door, it hit an impediment. Figuring Eddie had set up some kind of barrier, Moose pushed against it until he could step inside. That's when he almost tripped over whatever lay on the floor. "What the?"

"Get the lights, Jack," Moose ordered.

Jack squeezed past Moose and fumbled along the wall for the light switch. Then they saw him.

"Jesus Christ," Jack said, recoiling at the sight of Eddie's body, the head twisted as if it had been taken off and put on backwards. "That's unnatural, is what that is."

"Check him," Moose said. "He could still be breathing."

Jack hesitated, then he kicked at Eddie's body, which shifted silently before falling back into repose. "Nobody could survive—having your neck twisted like that," Jack said.

Moose grunted. He passed his gaze over the living room, then let his eyes settle back on Eddie's body. "All right," he said. "Turn that damn light off, and let's get the hell out of here."

On the street, Curly waited for them in the jalopy. As he pulled away, the car backfired.

Seconds later an upstairs light went on at the house next door. The loud bang had woken Esther Crandall. Wrapped in her robe, she went downstairs and out onto the front porch, where she looked up and down the street. A cat crossed under the streetlight about four houses to the east, but nothing else appeared out of order, so after one more look to be sure, she went back to bed.

When Esther woke at six the next morning, the noise from the night before was still worrying her, so instead of fixing Joe's breakfast in her nightgown and robe as she usually did, she got dressed and went outside to look around.

Charlie Alford waved from across the street, where he was watering his geraniums before the day got hot. "Morning, Esther," he said. "Everything all right? I don't usually see you out this early."

"Did you hear it?" she said, crossing the street.

"Hear what?"

"Last night. A gunshot. I swear that's what it was."

Looking incredulous, Charlie asked, "Are you certain?"

She shook her head. "No. And I wouldn't know the sound of a gun except for the radio shows, but it sure did sound—" Abruptly, Esther went silent.

"What's wrong?" Charlie asked.

She pointed to the Reed house. "Look. The front door's open." Without saying another word to Charlie, Esther Crandall marched purposefully across the street.

Just as Charlie got his hose turned off, she screamed.

PART TWO

Chapter 3

December 1914, Celestia

Precisely at 8:00 a.m. on the first of December, as he had been instructed, Adi Fattoré presented himself to a scribe named Soraya, who was to be his mentor.

"Good morning," he said, "I am Adi Fattoré. Lord Malach—"

"I know who you are. What I do not know is why Malach always gives me the trainees," Soraya said brusquely, as if something about Adi was glaringly amiss. She shook her head.

Perplexed, Adi wondered if there was something wrong in the way he looked. Granted, he had not thought to change into Celestia's current fashion, an ankle-length, cap-sleeved shift and sandals, somewhat reminiscent of Ancient Greek garb. The costume was worn by both men and women, adapted as one pleased. Soraya's shift was sleeveless and gathered at the back of the neck for full-flowing effect. Adi was still dressed as a working man from 1914—gray wool trousers and suspenders over a collarless shirt. As Earth's fashions changed, Adi adopted them. It was less jarring for the newly dead to meet someone who appeared to come from their own time. When Adi died in 1347, he wore a velvet doublet over a linen tunic and cotton hose. It was a fine look, and he hated to give it up, but over time, he realized he appeared comically outdated.

On Earth, Adi's job as a spiritual guide was to work with those who had been granted an opportunity to atone. It was challenging work at times, but he enjoyed it. Now he would be doing nothing but clerical work, far beneath his abilities if he were honest, though he would never express such a thought to anyone. World War I was to blame, the First Battle of

Ypres to be specific, for it was that event that brought Lord Malach to the conclusion that Celestia needed Adi's skills more than Earth did.

"Malach says you are a highly skilled but—and I am quoting here—*sometimes arrogant guide*," Soraya said.

Adi extinguished the spark of ire he felt growing within him, as this was not the time for anger. He would also not say, however true it was, that there were few in Celestia more arrogant than Malach himself.

"I assume you have read the manual?"

Adi nodded, but Soraya was already walking away, expecting him to follow. "Yes," he said. Then before he realized her question had been rhetorical, he repeated himself in case she had not heard him the first time. Why this young woman—a girl really—made him feel foolish, he did not know. It was as if he were a young man again, awkward in the presence of beauty. For as much as she seemed aloof, Soraya was beautiful. Dark-eyed with clear olive skin, her long black hair hung down her back, plaited with an ivory ribbon. As she walked, her slender arms moved without effort, and the scent of jasmine followed her everywhere.

Soraya took Adi to Celestia's main administrative center, a sprawling white stone building fringed in deep green cypress trees. Inside they made their way down a corridor of immense wooden doors, their wide lintels four feet above Adi's head. His gaze continued up to the cloudless blue sky. Except between the floors of multi-storied buildings, there were no ceilings in Celestia's edifices, only the firmament of Earth itself. Celestia's sky was Earth's sky, for Celestia was not a place above Earth, but a place with Earth, existing everywhere upon the crust and beneath the heavens of the planet itself.

Tonight the denizens of Celestia would have an unobstructed view of the galaxies—that is, if they remembered to look up. While Celestia enjoyed the best of Earth's skies and operated by its diurnal rhythms, it was not impacted by Earth's weather. Celestia's perfectly temperate atmosphere was one of the only advantages of being in Celestia, Adi thought. He hated the rain. Illogically, for Adi could no longer feel its effects, but despite knowing it was his vestigial human stubbornness that made him feel the way he did, Adi had no intention of altering his opinion of rain. I may be stubborn, he thought, but I am not arrogant.

This morning, as he followed Soraya down the hallway, Adi took notice of the intricately carved scenes on each door, each one a unique vista, all replicating some of Earth's most majestic landscapes, scenes that did not exist here, for Celestia had vistas of its own. But in honor of Earth's natural beauty, the doors featured mountains, enormous cliffs rising up against the ocean's shore, and waterfalls, among others. The door Adi stood before now, number twelve, presented a forest of ancient trees, whose roots began at Adi's feet and whose canopy nearly met the sky above. How lifelike it all appeared, as if the woodcarver had been able to make his vision of the forest appear in the wood without wielding a single blade.

Adi peered closer. He was about to touch the bark of the foremost tree, when he saw movement. A stag had begun to emerge from the forest, but then it retreated quickly. Had the stag seen him? Or was Adi's imagination running rampant as usual? Probably there was no stag at all. He looked back hopefully at where he thought he had seen that broad splay of antlers. This was Celestia after all, and the stag could have been real. But when he looked again, all Adi saw through the trees was darkness.

Soraya took an iron key from her pocket and clicked the lock open.

"What need is there for separate rooms?" Adi asked.

"Organization and order," she said as if the reason were obvious. "Otherwise, no need. This is where Oswald, my clerk, and I work. It is where you have been assigned. Our day begins at nine each morning, and you are expected to arrive not one second later."

The room was sparsely furnished with a rectangular wooden table and two chairs as intricately carved as the door had been. At the rear of the room, twenty or so feet from the table, was another door over which the words *Omnes Unum Sunt*, all are one, were carved.

Coming into the room now was a man who greeted Soraya with a cheerful "Good morning."

"Good morning, Oswald," she said.

For a moment Adi thought he recognized the man. He looked so much like a merchant he once knew in Rimini that Adi nearly addressed him as such. Instead Adi nodded a wordless greeting.

"What is in all the other rooms?" Adi asked. "More offices?"

"Of course. I could hardly manage all of the world's souls by myself. There are many scribes, many clerks." Then Soraya proceeded with a review of the role of scribes. "Our job is more than simple paperwork," she said. "We determine each soul's worthiness for continuing on in life's progression. Or if we deem a soul is pure—" She paused and looked at Adi as if she wanted him to hear her clearly. "Rare, by the way. Very rare. But if we do, we can recommend passing them into aeternum.

"Why are you and the others called scribes if your role is to judge?" Adi asked.

Soraya narrowed her eyes, as if his question were impertinent. "It is because we sign our names, I imagine," she said. "I really do not know. Nevertheless, we do what we do. We do not question."

Adi felt chastised. Surely he had not been called to be a drone. Despite his annoyance, he did not voice the obvious truth that they did much more than sign their names, and such a job required intellect, discernment, even wisdom.

Soraya continued with her monotone instruction. "While few are pure, most are virtuous souls, or if not, souls who came to their deaths in the full knowledge of their faults and weaknesses and were thusly sorry for them. Due to the war, many will have fallen in battle or died later because of their wounds. Disease is taking many. And there are still those who die of old age, in childbirth, from a fall, or a common act of violence apart from the war. The ways humans have found to die are innumerable."

Adi thought Soraya said this as if she believed humans were responsible for their own deaths.

"But we will treat each soul kindly," Adi said.

"Yes," she said. "Coming into afterlife is a bewildering experience. It is best if we make the transition as tranquil as possible." Soraya held out her hand to a Oswald who handed her a rolled parchment. "Oh, do sit down," she told Adi, sounding exasperated. She pointed to the chair next to her.

Adi sat as instructed and watched Soraya unroll the parchment. "The record of each soul is kept on a scroll exactly like this. We have clerks called scriveners who record the details, and our job, after we verify worthiness, is to sign the newest entry of record," she said.

"An entire life is recorded on a scroll?" Adi asked.

"An entire sequence of lives," Soraya corrected. "It can be helpful to know a soul's histories."

"We judge them on their present life only, or most recent one, that is. Correct?" Adi asked, remembering chapter three of the manual.

"Yes," Soraya said with hesitation. "But if I feel compelled to recommend someone for aeternum, I like to go on more than intuition. Typically, we do not start considering aeternum until a soul has lived at least fifty lives. However, that is not a rigid measure."

“What is aeternum, exactly?” Adi was aware of the general concept of eternity, but in the kind of work he did, used to do, hoped to do again, eternity was not his concern, so he wanted to hear Soraya’s definition.

“Rest, essentially. Forever peace. When you are designated for aeternum, you are relieved from the burden of rebirth and ensuing lifetimes.”

Adi had so many questions. “And what about those who are not so virtuous?”

“Fortunately, they are not my problem. The flagrantly unrepentant are generally sent back in time, instead of forward. Into a reversed timeline, that is. Theoretically, such a move confuses consciousness and increases the chance that in a new life, a soul will be less influenced by any hereditary memory of their errant ways. Some call it the Nautilus Loop.”

Adi expressed confusion.

“Like the shell, I imagine,” she said. “The way it—”

“No. I understand the reference. I am wondering if the practice works. That is, sending a soul back in time.”

Soraya shrugged. “There is still evil in the world, is there not? It is not for me to say, but the world would be a better place if evil souls could be extinguished, forever. Annihilated.”

Adi nodded. “Nothing is destroyed, only transformed?”

“I took you for a dull wit, Adi, but here you are stating a universal truth.”

Adi laughed. “It seems you underestimated me.”

“Be that as it may, the point is, such matters typically do not concern us,” Soraya said. “Most of the souls you and I meet were good people, most of the time. It is their records we keep. I see it as a privilege—helping to maintain the human parts of their spiritual history.”

Adi sensed the pride she felt in her work, but he saw little point in all this record keeping. What did it really matter? A life ended, a future life would be born, and the link between the two was thinner than spider’s silk. “Is this process even necessary? If all things are known?”

Soraya smiled. “Not known to you or me, until we unroll a scroll. This process makes all things transparent,” Soraya said. “And it keeps us honest. The more pitiable a death, the more likely you are to assign virtue without proper circumspection.”

Adi felt certain no one could beguile him.

“And to keep them honest.” Soraya warned Adi to keep a close eye on anyone who looked like they might want to slip back to Earth. “Some are wily, even in death.” She leaned over to Adi to whisper what she said next.

"It is rumored that Malach once let one get away. A not very nice fellow from what I have heard."

Adi's eyebrows rose. "And yet—" he began, then stopped. He was remembering his own death and how desperately he had fought against it. If he had been able to summon the will, had he been able to go back, he would have done it. It seemed to Adi that if someone was not ready to die, who was he, or Lord Malach, for that matter, to interfere. "That is," he continued, "I do not think I have the right to make that kind of life-or-death decision," Adi said.

"You may not want to, but you might have to," Soraya said. "Also, and this is rarely the case, you can send someone back, if you judge the situation warrants it."

Adi knitted his brows. "How is that possible?" he asked.

"If their passing is obviously an error. A mistake. A glitch in time and circumstance."

A glitch in time and circumstance? How would he know—? Adi realized in that moment that this job required more even skill than he originally thought it did, so for the remainder of the day he watched his teacher work, paying rapt attention to the lessons she imparted.

After several days, Soraya deemed Adi was ready to handle cases on his own, so she had a table brought in for him, placing it adjacent to hers. She also assigned an experienced clerk to work with Adi, a man named Thomas that Oswald had recommended.

At 9:00 a.m. sharp, Soraya said, "Time to get to it," Adi Fattoré. "Do not let me down." Then she laughed as if she enjoyed her role as Adi's master. "In a moment, you will be too engaged in work to cause me any trouble."

The first soul to come before Adi stood at the edge of the table, trembling. The man—a boy in years—held his belly that had been cratered by a hand bomb.

Thomas handed Adi the man's scroll.

"Do not fret about your wound," Adi said, unrolling the document. "It will be healed momentarily. Already you feel no pain. Am I correct?"

The soldier nodded, his mud-crusted face expressing a small smile.

"Good," Adi said. "Soon, all of this horror will be nothing more than a faint awareness deep within your soul's consciousness. It is very likely that in your next life, you will remember nothing of this cruel war." The sentiments were not his own. He had heard Soraya express the same thing yesterday, to a young man nearly identical to the one who faced him now. Adi ran his finger up the long sheet of parchment. "I see that this so-called 'Great War' was not your first."

The young man looked quizzically at Adi.

"You fought in—. My goodness, wars too numerous to name, but may I say, I hope your days as a soldier will now end." Adi signed the newest entry, then rolled up the scroll, tying it with a length of sisal string, before handing it to his clerk. "I only mean to convey my hope that the misfortune of your previous lives will remain as motes of memory deep within your soul and will not cause you future pain."

The boy nodded, and Thomas escorted him to the door at the rear of the room, a door Adi had learned was more symbolic than functional, for even before a soul passed through, they were already on their next journey.

Soraya turned to Adi with a sympathetic look. "The soldiers break my heart," she said. "War is so—" A low growl escaped her lips. "Senseless. No. Worse. It is shameful."

Adi said he agreed. He was about to say something else, something she might find profound, when he noticed another soul waiting for Thomas to escort him to Adi's desk.

"Also," she continued, "I find it confuses already bewildered souls to go over the details of their past lives. That poor boy had no idea he had lived and died before. But now, because you planted that idea in him, in years hence, he might one day wake from a dream and wonder if it was possible that he had been a soldier of the Great War. How unsettling such a thought would be," she said. "Or do you think otherwise?"

Adi nodded. "No. I understand. I will stick to a review of each soul's latest existence from now on."

Soraya was inscrutable, Adi thought. Not easy to please, but he was determined to earn her esteem.

Chapter 4

1920

Adi had been working alongside Soraya for six years. The war that had sent him to Celestia had been over for two. A month after Armistice Day, Adi had gone to see Lord Malach to request a transfer back to Earth, but Lord Malach turned down his request that day and twice more since then. If it were not for Soraya, Adi knew his daily work would be even more tedious. And yet, this sometimes tiresome work was important. It was just that he missed Earth terribly.

Thomas appeared with a wizened woman, her blue eyes defiantly bright. Adi accepted her parchment. "Old age," Thomas said, stating the woman's cause of death.

Adi nodded deferentially. "Peace, sister," he said. She smiled in reply, revealing only three crooked teeth. Adi wondered how the woman had managed to take in sufficient nourishment. Likely not well, her gaunt frame suggested.

Adi unrolled the scroll and perused the details of the woman's life. A French lace maker. Widowed twenty-seven years. Lived with and cared for by her unmarried daughter, a skilled seamstress. The two had lived meagerly, but were known to give alms to those less fortunate. How effortless it was to determine this woman's worth, Adi thought, so with no hesitation he certified her document.

"I hope you will endure less hardship in the future," Adi said. If she were to endure another life. Such decisions were not Adi's to make.

"L'adversité vous rend plus fort," the woman said. Then she pulled her face into a broad, concave smile.

"Hard times make you stronger," Thomas said, translating for Adi, who had the gist of the phrase on his own. It was a generous thought. Adversity made some people bitter, and the worst of those sometimes inflicted their pain upon others who had no part in their misfortune. Cruelty, Adi knew, was often born of feelings of inadequacy or the sense that one had been treated unfairly. But this woman was far above all of that.

When Thomas took the woman's hand to lead her away, she squeezed it. "Vous êtes très gentil de m'aider," she said.

This time Adi understood her. She said you are very kind to help her.

Thomas nodded his appreciation and led the woman to the rear door, where he handed her off to one of Celestia's many attendants, whose job it was to ferry souls from one existence to the next.

What a remarkable woman, Adi thought. He had witnessed too many souls behave imperiously towards his clerk, expecting to be served. But this woman who had nothing, had expected nothing. She was humble and grateful and generous. As we all should have been in life, he thought, thinking of his own transgressions.

"Pitiable," Soraya said. "The aged—some so decrepit you wonder how they managed to get from place to place." She took a new parchment from her clerk, but paused before unrolling it. "Whenever I register someone so old, I feel privileged to have died young."

"You cannot mean it," Adi said.

"But I do. You saw how hunched over she was. Her hands as gnarled as an olive tree. How painful every day must have been for her."

"But her pain is gone now," he said.

"Yes," Soraya said, impassively, before she turned her attention to the man who waited before her, adding nothing further.

Adi found Soraya's commentary perplexing. Soraya was not an uncaring soul, but her forthright manner could sometimes seem callous. Maybe her demeanor was a consequence of dying young. Soraya did not intend to be heartless, but she had a rather simplistic way of thinking at times. Adi had once tried to persuade her that humanity's greatest gift was empathy. People's ability to see their interconnectedness was one of their greatest strengths.

He remembered her saying that if people cared so much for each other, why were they always causing harm. It was a good question, but when he tried to get Soraya to consider the complexities of human frailty and understand there were reasons, sometimes subconscious reasons, people faltered, she said it sounded like he was making excuses.

It was nearly sunset when Thomas handed Adi the final parchment of the day, and a man with bushy salt and pepper whiskers more reminiscent of the past century than current times walked hesitantly towards Adi's table. As there was no one behind the man, Adi did not try to hurry him along. He could see the man was a soul afraid of the unknown.

"Peace, brother," Adi said. At the sound of his words, Adi saw the man's tense shoulders sink into relief.

Alfred, his name was, and he had been a man of letters, a teacher, a good man overall. There was no question Adi would send him on to his next life.

Adi signed the scroll and beckoned to his clerk.

Alfred bowed, then said, "As virtuous men pass mildly away, I whisper to my soul to go."

A familiar expression, Adi thought, but how did he know it? The answer did not come easily. "Are your words from a poem?" he asked.

"*A Valediction: Forbidding Mourning*," Alfred said, then he let himself be led away.

Alfred's departure left the room silent.

"John Donne," Soraya said a moment later, sensing that Adi still could not remember.

Adi nodded. "You know Donne?"

"You are not the only one who reads," she said.

It was true that Adi had seen her in Celestia's vast library, home to all of humanity's greatest works. He had not, until this moment, thought of asking her what books she enjoyed most. More than a lapse of courtesy, he had missed an opportunity to get to know her better.

Adi looked up and saw the first stars begin to twinkle. The candle in his lantern was growing shorter. He looked over at Soraya, who was sketching something on a flattened a scrap of parchment. A face. A woman of refined features, not dissimilar from Soraya's own.

"You are an artist," Adi said.

"I would not say so," she said, but obviously flattered, she held up her drawing for Adi to see more clearly. "It is my mother, or a likeness to my memory of her."

"She is beautiful," he said.

Chapter 5

1927

“No more for us tonight?” Soraya asked Oswald, who shook his head. “Time to go then, Adi.” She smoothed back the hair along her temples, then motioned for him to join her.

For nearly a year now, at the end of their work day, Soraya and Adi walked back to their rooms together. It began the night he had seen her sketching, the night he told her she was an artist. And although they worked side by side all day, Adi looked forward to their evening walks home, for it was only then that Soraya left behind the seriousness of work and allowed herself to be the woman Adi had grown so fond of.

“You once asked me about my life, Adi,” she said when they exited the office building. “Is that still a story you want to hear?”

Almost unable to believe what he was hearing, Adi said, “You would honor me.”

Soraya gave a little laugh. “I do not know about that, but I will tell you my story nevertheless. I was born on earth in 536 BC but lived only a short while,” she began. “When a baby dies, its soul is automatically exalted to aeternum, taken from the burden of having to live again. Or it is supposed to. Mine was reborn again in 535, and this time I lived. When I was ten, Persia conquered Egypt and my father was killed in battle. My mother was taken by a wealthy man and made a servant. He made me his wife, one of many. I was only thirteen when I died in childbirth.

“When I arrived here after my second death, I stood before a table very much like ours while my story was revealed, a life unremarkable in many ways, except for one startling thing—I was able to remember my first life and death. I knew details no infant could know. Some here called me a mystic. I should have been sent into another life, but someone made the judgment to keep me here, in Celestia.”

“This explains why all this time you remain a child,” Adi said.

“In appearance only. In wisdom I am over two thousand years old.”

“Why were you not designated for aeternum?”

Soraya smiled. Then she touched Adi’s arm and imparted a warm glow to his entire being. “I was. But all that ease and freedom did not suit me. I wanted to be useful. *Busy* as they say now.”

"You astonish me," Adi said. "I thought aeternum was each soul's ultimate desire. Rest, eternal peace. No worries. No pain."

"Perhaps. But my life on Earth was so brief. You died a young man, yes, but you were educated. You had experiences. And in your afterlife, you have seen so much of the world. I had none of that. For me, eternal rest was unsatisfying. Can you understand?"

Adi lifted his shoulders. "I imagine it gives you satisfaction to do well by others?"

"As it does you," Soraya said. "Guiding your souls as you do. You find it gratifying. Even peaceful?"

"But would there not be that same peace in aeternum?"

"I can go there any time it pleases me. But I like my work here, so I stay. I experience life, in some small way, through the story of each passing soul."

They reached La Casa Tranquila, informally known as La Casa, a cylindrical stone tower that housed Celestia's scribes and their clerks. Scriveners, messengers, and other servants were housed in a separate building, and magistrates and lords had their own palatial homes.

Five floors of fourteen rooms encircled La Casa's central courtyard. Even though no one actually needed it, a stairway, which began at perfect north, curved along the inside of the tower like a Fibonacci spiral, breaking to allow passage at each floor. Each of the tower's seventy rooms had two doors. The front, or main door, was accessed from the veranda overlooking the courtyard. Each apartment's rear door opened to a small balcony overlooking some version of the area beyond the building.

Adi's room on the third floor had a view of the Moss Mountains, so called because they appeared, from a distance, to be covered in moss. Celestia had many mountain ranges, all separate entities from those on Earth, but the Moss Mountains were Adi's favorite.

Soraya also had a view of the Moss Mountains, but because her apartment was on the top floor, she had something Adi did not—an open view of the sky. How magical it must be, Adi had often thought, to lie in bed and stare up at the stars. He refused to be envious, however. Soraya deserved all good things.

Adi and Soraya passed through an open portico into the courtyard. In the center, bordered by beds of jewel-like flowers, a large bower arched over a pond. Sometimes at night, when Adi was restless, he would sit by the pond and watch the little orange fish in the moonlight.

"Do you—" Adi was about to probe further into Soraya's life, when a small man wearing the crimson-belted, green robe of a messenger appeared.

"Yes?" Soraya asked. "What is it?"

"Lord Malach requests a visit from Signore Fattoré," he said. "Tomorrow. 11:00 a.m. At the Azul Romana." The messenger handed Adi a card, the details of the meeting calligraphed in deep violet ink.

Adi nodded and the messenger left.

"What have you done now?" Soraya snickered. "And the Azul. How lavish."

"Maybe he is sending me back," Adi said. "To Earth." He saw Soraya's shoulders fall slightly and wished he had sounded less enthusiastic.

"I know you are anxious to go," she said, "but it will not be the same around here without you."

"I have not left yet," Adi said. "Besides, we do not know what he wants." The truth was, Adi was not as eager to leave Celestia as he once was. More than a small part of him hoped Malach would say Adi's Earth days were over, that they could not possibly do without him here, now that they were used to his presence. And yet he did miss life on Earth. It was only Soraya who made him hesitate.

"I think we do. You are needed elsewhere." Soraya smiled. "You know, Adi, when I first met you, I thought you were a bit insufferable."

"I remember," Adi admitted. "When I first met you, I was a bit afraid. You can be fierce, you know," he said with a smile. "However, I have come to admire that and everything about you."

She laughed. "And you, Adi Fattoré, are a fine and decent soul. If I were selfish, I would make sure you were never allowed to leave." She winked and lifted her heels and kissed him on the cheek. "Now go to bed. Tomorrow, find me, and let me know what the old man had to say."

Chapter 6

Azul Romana, 1927

"Adi!" Malach exclaimed when he saw Adi emerge from Azul Romana's wide-arched main portico. Malach stood some thirty yards away, near a pair of chaise longues on the right side of large, rectangular Roman bath. "Over here," he called to Adi. "I have reserved this spot for us."

Reserved, Adi muttered with a laugh. There was not another soul in sight. Adi's previous meetings with Malach had been held in the magistrate's austere marble office, so his entry into the tropical paradise before him was somewhat astonishing. Before Adi, the deep stone pool was framed by enough chaise longues for a hundred bathers. At each corner of the pool, marble columns crested with intricate acanthus carvings gave the illusion that they held up the sky. Along the windowless perimeter walls, palms and flowering hibiscus spilled out of hip-high terra cotta pots.

Adi greeted Lord Malach with some reservation, as he now saw the magistrate was dressed in a short robe that exposed the old lord's knobby knees.

"Come. Sit." Malach eased himself into a chaise longue, expressing a deep sigh of well-being.

Adi complied with the order, though as he lowered himself to the cushion, Adi he could not seem to conjure the sensations that Malach could.

"What is this place?" Adi asked. He was accustomed to Celestia's magnificent sights, beauty taken in through the eyes, but this place—built to soothe the physical body apparently—was singularly Earth-like. It seemed odd. Illogical. While a spiritual mind could replicate all the physical movements of the living, it took exertion to replicate physical pleasure. By the looks of it, Malach had practiced well.

"This is all quite recent," Malach said. "Is is not wonderful? I could spend aeternum here."

"Quite—uh, Baroque," Adi said.

Malach lifted a small brass bell from the glass topped table at his side and rang it. "Do you think so? Perhaps. Did you see the fresco on the underside of the portico as you came in—frolicking naked nymphs? Certainly puts one in a certain state," Malach said.

Adi's eyes widened. He knew too well what state Malach referred to, but hearing a chief magistrate allude to such things was unsettling. Celestial beings did not replicate that sort of physical pleasure. At least Adi did not think so.

A serving girl was at their side now, balancing a tray that held two gold-filagreed goblets filled with a pale green liquid. She handed one to Malach and the other to Adi. Then she bowed and went to the far end of the pool, where she disappeared under another arched portico. Adi wondered what painting might meet her upward gaze, and for a brief moment, he worried about the girl's innocence.

Malach took a sip. "Hmmm. Delicious. It is made with limes and something called agave," Malach said.

Adi sniffed at his, then set it on the table next to him. "I assume you have a new soul for me," Adi said, more assertively than he had rehearsed. He had meant to ease into the topic.

Malach took a long drink, bits of ice clinking against the goblet. "Maybe I value your current work so much I have decided to keep you here indefinitely."

"But I thought the arrangement was—"

"Calm yourself, Adi," Malach laughed. "Would I be so heartless? Yes, yes. A new soul. A small time thug in Chicago, Illinois named Edward Reed. He seemed destined for the Nautilus Loop, but his mother interceded, so—" Malach emptied his glass, prolonging the moment. "Soon, he will be all yours."

Adi exhaled a wistful, bittersweet sigh. He was to go back to his old life, America this time. He had not been in America since the seventeenth century. And while he had kept up with the country's history, he had never been to Chicago. Chi-*ca*-go. It sounded exotic, like archipelago. "Will I be getting his profile report soon?"

"You are in a hurry." Malach rang the brass bell again, signaling for another drink. "In a moment, yes. But—"

But what? What scheme did Lord Malach have in mind? Adi had to admit that all this poolside banter had made him suspicious. After all, he and Malach were not friends. And Adi was quite certain only lords and magistrates were allowed access to Azul Romana. Adi was there as a guest, nothing more. On Earth they called such ostentatious hospitality buttering someone up.

When the girl arrived with the tray, Adi smiled at her. She returned his smile and set a second goblet on his table next to the first one, which now glistened with water droplets.

Malach took his goblet from the girl, and thanked her, before waving her away. He took a sip. "Marvelous. And yet, you have not touched yours?"

Drinking intoxicating beverages, no matter how evocatively green, did nothing for spiritual beings, just as a Roman bath did nothing. Ethereal life did not depend on the food and drink of mortals, nor their comforts, but Adi conceded that pleasurable elements of Earth life were sometimes too tempting to let go of, even in a place like Celestia. An exclusively spiritual life had its downsides. Adi lifted his glass and sipped. "Yes. Marvelous," he said, mimicking Malach, who seemed to take Adi's close-to-irreverent tone in good humor.

"Now, Adi, before I give you your assignment, I do have a small—a trifle really—," Malach said, hesitating. "Just an minor addition to your duties, once you are back on Earth. It should not cause you too much trouble."

By now Adi was certain whatever it was would definitely cause him trouble. "What is it?" he asked, knowing there was no way he would be able to talk Malach out of the additional task.

"I would like you to detain and return a fellow named Viggo. He is a rogue soul of mine and—"

"He is the one you allowed to escape," Adi said. He had not meant to blurt it out like that, but now that he had, maybe he would get the story he had been curious about for so long.

Malach frowned. "I see the rumor mill continues to grind away at the grist of my ignominy."

Adi said nothing, but wished Soraya were here to see this. He could not wait to tell her about it.

"Yes. Viggo. I let him get away," Malach said with a great sigh. "For the record, I am not the only one who has made that error. But because I am the senior-most official to have let a soul escape, my faux pas seems endlessly spoken of. However, the situation is not as bad as it sounds. You must understand, Viggo is a—a unique case. Orphaned at the age of twelve, Viggo was sold by his uncle to a sheep farmer in Jutland, who took in such children with the premise of giving them 'a good Christian upbringing.' The man did preach the Bible on the sabbath, but the rest of the week he worked those children to the bone. If that were all, it would be bad enough, but when it suited him, that farmer used those children to satisfy his *urges*. Mostly the girls, but sometimes the boys as well." Malach leaned close to Adi. "I think most of us in Viggo's position would have found it easy to envision taking a knife from the butchering shed and thrusting it into the farmer's chest. Most of us would not, however, have had the courage to act upon our vision. Seventeen-year-old Viggo did, and for that he was hoisted up the gibbet."

"I can see why you sympathize with him," Adi said, "but—"

"You will say murder is murder, and right you are, but yes, I pitied the lad. Beyond that, I saw something in him. Something inherently good. I was prepared to sign him into his next life when the rascal vanished. It was that moment of pity that did it—I created the space for him to take advantage of me."

"When was this? I understood this happened nearly a hundred years ago. How has the man not died?"

Malach shifted uneasily on his chaise. "This is the troublesome part. As I am sure you know, sending someone back into their life must be accomplished within close proximity to their last breath on Earth. We can rewind time a bit, but I had hemmed and hawed so long about what to do with the lad, that he had already begun his transformation as a spiritual being. Then he sensed that keyhole, and he was gone before I could lift him from his present life."

"So he's a spirit on earth, like I was?"

"Hmm," Malach said as if he were avoiding an uncomfortable truth. "Not exactly, no. His role is, well, complicated. He is a spirit with just enough human left in him to make him unpredictable. He can appear in human or spirit form, as the situation, or lately his mood, dictates."

"How is that even possible, for a spiritual being?"

"As I said, he still retains some of his human life force." Malach waved the thought away, as if he did not want to discuss it further.

Adi resisted the urge to upbraid Malach over his negligence. Why had he waited so long to remedy this situation? What was in it for Malach? Adi glanced at the green drink at his side, the ridiculousness of this place altogether and thought Malach did not deserve so much deference after all. "And all this time, you never slipped into Earth to bring him back because— Why exactly?"

"I suppose it was because I thought he was doing some good. Viggo likes to rile up the wicked, which can have a balancing effect. But—" Malach laughed, "If I am to be honest, I hesitated because Viggo's creative justice can be amusing."

Amusing how? Adi wondered. And was that reason enough to leave a "rascal" at large on Earth? "So why now?"

"I have been told it is time." Malach lowered his chin. "And this is an order I cannot refuse."

"My next question is how will I find him?"

"It will all be in his dossier, but as you bring it up, most recently in the American Midwest, Chicago and elsewhere."

Adi grinned. "So convenient to send me there now, I see."

Malach waved off the comment. "Please, just sip your drink and relax while we take a look at your new man—Edward Reed."

Malach snapped his fingers. Seconds later, one of Malach's assistants set up an easel near the chaise longues. On the easel he placed a large gilt frame. Instead of a painting, the frame presented a swirl of white clouds against a gray blue sky. In moments, the clouds cleared, and Adi saw a tree-lined street.

"Chicago, Illinois, 1904," Malach said.

The frame was focused on a well-kept two-story house, where Adi saw the face of a small dark-haired boy staring out the parlor window. Another boy, almost identical in looks, but a few years older, scampered down the front porch steps to meet a friend who waited for him on the sidewalk. The older boys were off to school. It was springtime. A swath of yellow daffodils bloomed in two flower beds on each side of the porch steps. On the porch was a swing, suspended by chains. Pale leaves had begun to sprout from the branches of an elm tree that grew between the sidewalk and the street. Overhead, clouds darkened, promising rain.

"Is that him?" Adi asked. "Edward Reed? The school boy?"

Malach shook his head. "The one at the window."

PART THREE

Chapter 7
April 1904, Chicago

Four-year-old Eddie Reed watched through the parlor's lace curtains as his older brother Richie scrambled down the porch steps and headed up the sidewalk with his friend Billy on the way to school. Eddie would go to school next year, and he couldn't wait. Richie, who was seven and in second grade, was always telling Eddie about school, how he and his friends were kings of the jungle gym and the big slide, and how Richie won all their foot races.

At home with Mama, Eddie had no one to play with and he was still expected to lie down for a nap each afternoon, as if he were a baby. When Mama was not busy with laundry, mending, or dusting, she was cooking. Eddie liked baking days best, as he was often the beneficiary of one or two misshapen cookies.

Mid-morning Eddie stood beside his mother, holding the clothespin basket for her as she took the wash off the line.

"This shirt is not quite dry," she said, "But I don't like the look of those dark clouds. I think it's going to rain."

As soon as the last shirt was laid in the basket, a big splotch darkened the ground at their feet. A loud crack of thunder sounded, and heavier drops began to fall. "I guess you were right, Mama," Eddie said. He ran up the porch stairs and held the door open for his mother.

Once they were inside, Naomi laughed. "I guess I was." They stood at the door for a moment and looked out at the downpour, which had intensified so quickly Naomi worried about the cellar flooding. Already the ground under the clothesline was beginning to puddle. "You will have to play inside today, Eddie," she said. "After I finish the ironing, I will make lunch."

Eddie went to his room and dumped his rubber farm animals onto the floor. He set up the fences for the sheep pen first, then the cattle, then the pigs. Around the outside of the pens he placed the cats, then he took up the little brown and white dog and pounced him around the perimeter, calling out "bark, bark." He pretended it was raining on his farm too and laid the pigs on their sides to play in the mud, which he had heard they like to do. He would have moved the sheep into the barn, but Richie had ruined the little metal barn last year when he had held it over Eddie's head, teasing him to try to get it back. Even on his tip toes, Eddie had strained to get the barn away from Richie. Then, laughing, Richie had run out of the room with it, holding it like a football. When Eddie caught up to him in the hall, he smashed against his brother and the barn bent almost flat under Richie's weight, leaving a nick in the wallpaper. Eddie had cried and taken the barn to show Papa, who had held it up unsympathetically. "This is what happens when you boys play rough," he had said. But it wasn't Eddie's fault at all. And instead of trying to fix it, Papa had thrown the barn out in the trash. At the memory, Eddie sighed, then he knocked over his little farm in one sweeping motion before picking it all up and putting it back in the box.

When Eddie went down to the kitchen, his mother was still ironing. "Why don't you stay here with me for a while?" she said. "I like your company. I'll get your crayons and tablet."

Eddie nodded in agreement, but knew that meant an alphabet lesson, which he was not eager to do.

"Here," she said now sitting at the table next to Eddie. "Let me get you started." Naomi wrote A B C D E in capital letters down the left side of the page.

Eddie's job was to replicate those letters. Even staring intently at Mama's examples, Eddie's B's and D's often faced left. He didn't recognize there was anything wrong until she pointed it out, and then he felt ashamed. At least Mama was kind. She told him that everyone makes mistakes when they are learning. Father was less patient. Richie called him dumb. But Mama never did.

On the C Mama had made, Eddie drew ears and a nose. Then long whiskers. He was trying to make it look like a cat. Eddie liked drawing animals. It was easy for him to remember pictures from storybooks and remake them in his mind, but he couldn't yet make very good likenesses appear on paper. He liked drawing and wished he was good at it.

"I like how you made a cat from that C," Naomi said a while later. "Because "cat" starts with a C?"

Eddie bit into a cookie. "Because I like cats."

"You know we don't talk with our mouths full," Naomi Reed said. She took his crayon and paper. "Finish your cookie, and I will show you."

On a clean page she drew a column of four "C's." After each one she added more letters, speaking each word she made as she went along.

"C-A-T spells cat. C-A-P spells cap. "C-L-O-W-N spells clown," she said. If you copy these words two times, you can have another cookie."

Eddie wasn't sure he wanted another cookie that bad, but copying the words would make Mama happy, and he liked it when Mama was happy.

"Okay," he said, trying not to sound sullen. Papa did not like sullen boys.

Mama leaned over and kissed him on the top of his head.

When Eddie completed his task, he slid his papers over to Mama for her approval.

"Good work, Eddie." She gently squeezed him arm. "You still need to get your P's right, and that L is missing its leg, but if you keep practicing, you might be able to write the whole alphabet before you go to school." She tore out another sheet of paper and wrote only the letter P down the left side. "Practice a few more P's," she said temptingly.

"I just want to color," Eddie whined.

"Just this page, all right? Then when you are done, we will eat lunch."

He nodded obediently.

"You know, when you are in school, you will be busy with letters and numbers all morning long."

Eddie looked at her with a stunned expression. "What?"

Mama frowned. "What did you think school was for?"

"Jungle gyms and foot races."

"There will be time for those things too, but mostly you and the other children will be learning to read and write and do your sums, all necessary to be successful in life."

Eddie scrunched his face in frustration. Mama and Papa were always talking to him and Richie about success in life.

"I don't want to go to school," Eddie whined.

"Oh, hush," she said. "That's just silly."

Eddie's stomach felt sick. This news about school was bad. Richie had only talked about the fun things he did. Eddie saw now that school was going to be hard, not fun. He took up a black crayon and wrote one P before trying to turn the next one into an animal face, but his mind was empty of everything but worry, so the connection between imagination and his fingers was broken.

"All right. Put that away now," Mama said kindly a few minutes later. "You've done enough for today." She set a plate of leftover meatloaf and mashed potatoes before him, and the sight of his favorite meal lifted Eddie's mood a bit.

They ate silently, and when they were finished, Naomi cleared their lunch plates and set them in the sink to be washed later. "Time for our nap," she said.

Dejected, Eddie allowed his hand to be taken, and they climbed the stairs. Naomi swung the bathroom door open. "Watch your aim in there," she said with a wink. "And use soap when you wash your hands. I'll wait right here."

When Eddie emerged, he padded dutifully down the hall to the bedroom and climbed into bed. Mama untied his shoes and set them under his bed. Then she unfolded his little blanket and held it in her arms until Eddie got settled. Then she covered him.

"You are a lucky boy, do you know that?"

"If I was lucky, I wouldn't have to go to school."

"When I was your age, my father thought little girls did not need to go to school. He thought it was better to stay home and learn how to keep house and sew—things like that. But my mother thought differently, and she kept fighting for me. Finally, when your uncle Stanley was ready for school, I was enrolled the same year, even though I was two years older. At first I was placed in a classroom with younger children. I caught on to the lessons quickly because my mother had taught me to read and write at home. Soon I was learning along children my own age. I enjoyed school. I was so eager to learn all about the world, especially exotic places like ancient Egypt and Persia. When I was thirteen, I had to quit school. It was the saddest day of my life."

"Why'd ya have to quit?"

Naomi shrugged. "That is sad tale for another day. For now, believe me when I tell you that it is a privilege to go to school. Many children are not as lucky as you. Some don't go to school at all, and others will go only a few years before they are put to work."

Eddie's eyebrows raised. "Like Papa's work?"

"Not even as nice as Papa's work. Boys like you and Richie, whose mama is home each day to cook and care for you, who have nice warm beds and books and toys are fortunate. No, Papa is not a rich man, but he gives us everything we need and more." She patted his leg and sighed. "You will not be my little boy for much longer, will you?"

"I'll be tall as Richie soon," he said.

"Do not worry about school, Eddie. It is still months away. For now, try to sleep. I know you don't want to, but Mama needs to rest."

Chapter 8

September 1905

Being in school was not as bad as Eddie feared it would be, though his teacher, Miss Armstrong, was stern. She was tall and thin and wore her graying hair behind her head in a tight bun. She wore her glasses on a gold chain, and when they were on her nose, she often glared over them at children who misbehaved. Children who could not control their impertinent mouths were forced to stand in the corner facing the wall instead of going out for recess. Bertie Bromsted had been sent to the corner one morning, and just as the other children were returning to their desks, his knees buckled and he fainted. Everyone laughed until Miss Armstrong said in a voice that had stung Eddie's ears, "That's enough!" By mid October, not a single one of Eddie's classmates dared to speak out of turn.

Eddie was placed in the first desk of the center row. He did not like being so close to Miss Armstrong's desk. He was so close he could smell her perfume. It reminded him of baking day at home, of the brown liquid Mother put into cake batter and cookie dough.

To one side of Eddie sat Anton, a thin, sickly boy who sniffled most of the day. His fingernails were dirty, a fact that Miss Armstrong said they would have to remedy. But Anton was a friendly boy who said he wanted to be Eddie's friend. Lena Nowak sat in the desk behind Eddie. She had long braids and light brown eyes. She had greeted Eddie on the first day by clasping his hand in hers, a gesture that shocked him. He had never touched a girl before.

"Goot mornink," she had said loudly. "I em Lena. Do you heff a dok or a cat? I haff a leetle dok."

Before Eddie could answer her, Miss Armstrong told them all to sit down and face the front of the classroom.

At lunch that day, Eddie told his mother about Lena, saying she was a nice girl, but she talked funny. Mama had given him a harsh look.

"You must always be kind to everyone, Eddie," she said, setting his lunch plate before him.

Eddie nodded, but he thought Mama's comment was unfair. He had been kind to Lena, and Eddie liked hearing her talk. When he found out some time later that Lena could draw, even better than he could, he admired her all the more.

Each morning when Miss Armstrong released the class for recess, Eddie spilled out onto the cinder playground as gleefully as everyone else. The girls huddled with the girls and twirled their skirts or skipped rope. They sometimes took the set of smaller swings the older children had abandoned.

The kindergarten boys kept to themselves as well, and they eyed the new jungle gym with envy, hoping for their turn. Only now and then when the playground supervisor told the older boys to get down and let the little ones have a chance were Eddie and the other boys able to climb the big steel dome.

Then Anton lost his grip and fell, splitting his lip open. After that, the kindergartners were barred from using the jungle gym. "You will have to wait until you are in first grade," they were told. Eddie didn't think it was right that everyone was being punished. It was only Anton who had slipped.

The kindergartners were also denied use of the big slide and swings, as those were claimed by older children, so Eddie and his playmates were left with tag and running foot races. Eddie discovered he was the fastest boy in kindergarten. For a time he lorded over the other boys with this fact, until a tough kid named Archie told Eddie it wasn't nice to brag about stuff, not if he "didn't want no enemies." So Eddie stopped gloating. But no one could take away how winning made him feel, or how, when his legs were pumping hard across the school yard, he forgot all about the frustrations of sounding out words written in chalk on the blackboard.

It was the last school day before Thanksgiving, and that morning the kindergartners had made turkeys out of brown and orange paper. They traced around their hands to make the turkey's fanned-tail.

When they were gluing little felt eyes onto their turkeys, Lena told Eddie that her family did not celebrate Thanksgiving.

"Whaddya mean?" Eddie asked. "Everyone celebrates Thanksgiving."

"We don't," Lena said. She shrugged and went to the sink to wash the paste from her hands.

Afterwards, Miss Armstrong read the children a story about how the Indians had been good neighbors to new European settlers called Pilgrims.

When they had first come to Massachusetts, these Europeans knew very little about farming in New England, so the Indians had taught them how to plant a dead fish with their corn. Even so, the Pilgrim's first harvest was meager, and with winter coming, the settlers worried about starvation.

Miss Armstrong read that part dramatically, then laid her book in her lap and wrapped her arms about her, pretending to shiver. "Can you imagine, boys and girls, how dreadful that was? Can you imagine what it would be like to be without enough food to make it through a bitter winter? Well at least they had their warm woolen clothes and plentiful firewood."

"My ma ain't got a coat," Anton whispered to Eddie. "Only a shawl to wear in the winter."

"Boys! Hush," Miss Armstrong said, before returning to the story. She read about how the Pilgrims invited their Indian neighbors to sit down with them to share the first Thanksgiving feast, which was not like ours, but consisted of roasted venison, fish, squash, and corn. "This, children," she said, closing the book, "is why we give thanks each year for all our blessings."

"And eat turkey," Bertie Bromsted blurted out.

Miss Armstrong didn't scold Bertie. Instead she laughed. Eddie could not remember ever hearing Miss Armstrong laugh.

At noon, dressed in their coats and caps, the children lined up at the door as usual and waited to be dismissed. "Everyone have their turkey?" Miss Armstrong asked. In response the sound of paper turkey feathers filled the room. "Now before I let you go, I have something else for each of you." From a large basket, Miss Armstrong took small paper bags filled with caramel corn that she had made and handed them to the children.

"Hoo boy," Anton said. "Thank you, ma'am."

"You are welcome, Anton. Now, boys and girls, I hope you all have a happy holiday with your families."

Outside the classroom door, Eddie stood as still as a statue and stared at the bag of popcorn in his hand. Lena said "Goot by," and other children raced around him on their way out, but Eddie didn't move. When the hallway quieted, Eddie brought the little bag to his nose and smelled the warm scent of popcorn and caramel. In that moment Eddie decided he would eat his treat on the way home, and he would not tell his mother that Miss Armstrong had done a nice thing. He would not tell Papa or Richie either. He would keep this confusing truth to himself.

Chapter 9

June 1908

On the first Monday of summer vacation Richie and Eddie were up early enough to see their father before he left for work.

"Be good, boys. And keep out of your mother's hair. She needs her rest. I don't want you two giving her any grief."

"They will be fine," Naomi said. "Now, off with you. I don't need you in my hair either."

Eddie looked at Richie, and the two boys giggled.

After Delmar left, Naomi asked, "Oatmeal or a bacon sandwich for breakfast, boys?"

"Bacon," Eddie and Richie said simultaneously.

"Just enough for my hungry hooligans," Mother said, placing two strips each on slices of buttered toast. "Now sit down, and don't gobble."

"Why does Papa say you need rest, Mama," Eddie asked.

Naomi wiped the grease out of the iron skillet with wadded newspaper.

"Because I'm going to have a baby. I guess there's no harm in you knowing now, but I want you to keep this news to yourselves. No one else needs to know. Not yet."

"A baby brother?" Eddie asked.

"Maybe," Naomi said, "But I am hoping it will be a little girl. Wouldn't that be nice?"

"Aw gee, Ma," Richie said. "What'll we do with a sister?"

Naomi wagged her finger at her older son. "That's what I said when you were born. I saw your little red face and said, *now what will I do with this squirmy little thing*."

"N'ya n'ya," Eddie taunted.

The minute Mother's back was turned, Richie gave Eddie a sharp jab in the chest.

Eddie glared and quietly quipped once more, "n'ya n'ya," before racing out the back door away from Richie's fists.

Mid-morning Naomi came outside with her knitting and was about to settle in her wicker rocker on the back porch when she noticed her sons crouched down near the alley gate looking at something in the dirt.

"What have you found?" she called out.

"A dead bird," Eddie answered.

Naomi walked out to see for herself. "It's a mama robin. Poor thing," she said. "Richie, get the shovel and scoop it up and toss it in the burn barrel. If you leave it there, it will draw maggots."

It was Eddie's idea to dig a grave for the bird instead. While Richie fetched the shovel from the garage, Eddie stroked the bird's glossy feathers. Its black eyes seemed to be staring into the sky. Where were her babies? Eddie wondered. Were they orphans? Or did they still have a father? How would they feed themselves?

Eddie's school friend Martin had become an orphan this year, when his father was killed in an explosion at the foundry where he worked. Eddie had not known that Martin's mother had already died. "Such a tragedy," their teacher said when she told the class why Martin was moving to Cincinnati, where he would live with his uncle and aunt. The class held a goodbye party for Martin on his last day. The teacher had baked sugar cookies, and all the boys and girls gave Martin the cards they made for him. Eddie remembered he had felt envious of Martin. Later, that feeling grew and Eddie almost wished he could be an orphan too. All the kids would tell him to be well and have a fun trip on the train. All the girls would cry and tell Eddie how much they would miss him.

Naomi anxiously watched her boys clamber up the old sycamore tree. Richie had been up in that tree more than the birds, but until today, Eddie had refused to follow. Richie, who was always reading adventure stories and acting them out, had finally wrangled Eddie into one of his imaginary plays. Richie had declared himself captain of a ship that was going to sail to a far-away land. He had made himself an admiral's hat out of newspaper. The big tree in the back yard was the ship.

"Look up there, mate," she heard Richie say to Eddie. "That's the crow's nest." Richie pointed up to a strong limb above him. "You gotta take this spyglass and climb up there to get a better view." Richie handed his brother the imaginary telescope.

"I'm not going up that high," Eddie said.

"Then you'll walk the plank," Richie said, pointing to a weathered, bark-less limb that stretched nearly to the garage roof.

Naomi laughed. "Walk the plank," she muttered to herself. The captain was not quite twelve, and he had begun to think himself quite grown up. She wasn't sure she liked how domineering he'd become, but Delmar said it was a sign that Richie would make a good leader one day. Maybe that was true, but Delmar wasn't home all day, and he didn't have to cope with the aftermath of Richie's leadership when Eddie fought back.

"Darn," Naomi said. She had lost count of her stitches. She turned her attention to her knitting and ignored the boys while she carefully recounted.

"You go first," Eddie said.

Richie pushed his brother toward the weathered limb. "Captains don't walk the plank," he said. "It's the plank or the crow's nest."

"This is a stupid game," Eddie said. "I'm going down."

Richie clamped his hand on Eddie's arm. "I said walk the plank."

Eddie narrowed his eyes and gritted his teeth. He was in a tough spot. To fight off Richie and reorient himself for a climb down, he'd have to let go of his grip on the branch that gave him safety. His stomach bubbled, sick with nerves. For the moment he did nothing. His breath grew heavy.

Richie let go and maneuvered past Eddie. "You're a baby if you think this is scary." Using the limb above for stability, Richie stepped out onto the thick, old limb. "Easy," he sneered. He let go of the branch and balanced imperiously with his hands on his hips.

Eddie had no intention of following his brother out on the "plank." Now that Richie was out there a couple of feet, this was his chance to get down. He didn't think they'd climbed that high but looking down now made his stomach lurch. Eddie sucked in his breath and drew his hand off the branch above to reach the one behind him. As he was about to move away, Richie grabbed his wrist and pulled. Eddie felt his stomach rise into his throat. "I said I'm not doing it!" Then he wrenched his arm away before giving Richie a shove.

Richie tottered and nearly lost his balance. "Now you're gonna get it," he growled and pounced towards Eddie who clung to the trunk.

Naomi heard the crack and threw her knitting to the floor. She saw Richie clinging to the overhead branch, his feet dangling in the air, the old limb shattered on the ground.

"Help him Eddie!" she cried. "Give him your hand."

Eddie worked his way back around to Richie's side of the trunk and set his foot on the stump of the old limb, its torn edge frayed like a rope. But just as he was about to reach out for his brother, Richie was moving hand over hand back to the trunk. Eddie got down quickly after that, and the moment his feet touched the ground, he thought he was going to be sick all over his mother's shoes. He sat and put his head between his knees and took short, sharp breaths until the feeling passed.

Richie was on the ground now too, his dark eyes glaring at his brother. Eddie wouldn't look at him. Naomi reached out and touched Richie's shoulder. "Are you all right? I was so frightened."

Richie pushed her hand away. "Holy—. Ma. I'm fine," he said.

Eddie wiped his hair from his eyes and got to his feet. His face was red and damp with sweat. Richie glared at him, his mouth curled into a sneer.

The expression did not escape his mother's eyes, and she glared a warning in return. "Never," she said, with her fist on her chest. "You will never climb that old tree again!"

Naomi pulled Richie's chin toward her. "Do you hear me, Richard?"

"Yes," he said, pulling away but subdued by her tone.

"Edward?"

"Yes." The answer was easier for him. He hadn't wanted to climb the stupid tree in the first place. Richie had goaded him, called him a baby. He was no baby. Eddie felt about to cry, but he sucked in his hurt and swallowed it. He didn't like it when his mother was angry, but at least this time, she was angrier with Richie than she was with him.

By dinner time, Naomi had let her anger dissipate. It had been more fear than anger, but anger was the only way she knew how to express what she'd felt when she thought Richie was going to fall. Terror was more like it. She put the boys to work setting the dining room table while she finished up in the kitchen. Then she called them to carry out the platter and serving dishes and told them to set them carefully on the trivets.

When they were all seated, Richie nearly threw her back into a fit.

"Pop," he said. "Tell Ma it'll be okay for us to climb that tree."

"Your mother knows best, Richard."

"Aw, Pop," Richie said. "We weren't in any danger."

Delmar looked down his nose at his son. Richie understood his father's meaning and chewed his food quietly after that.

Naomi asked about her husband's day, and he said it was nothing out of the ordinary.

"May I have another biscuit?" Eddie asked.

Naomi looked to her husband for his implicit permission. He shrugged. "What if I break this one in half for you and your father?" she said.

"Give him the whole thing," Delmar said. "You're not going to follow your brother up that tree again, are you son?"

"No, Pop," Eddie said, his face turning red. Under the table, Eddie kicked his brother's shin. It was no playful kick, but Richie did not retaliate.

"As for you Richard," Delmar said, "you must remember Eddie does not have the judgment you have. He looks to you as his older brother to make good choices."

Eddie's chin dropped to his chest. Pop wasn't being fair. Eddie had known better from the start.

"Jeez, Pop," Richie said, now returning the kick. "We wouldn't a got hurt."

Delmar looked seriously at his son. "We never think anything bad will happen. And then, bang, it does."

After dinner, the boys were sent upstairs for their baths. Delmar went to the kitchen and took a clean towel from the drawer to dry the dishes.

"They were just—being boys, my dear," Delmar said.

She shook her head and scrubbed at the frying pan, working to dislodge a bit of hardened chicken fat. When the dishrag wouldn't budge it, she took a knife and scraped it away, then submerged the pan in the dishwater again before rinsing it. From the sudsy mist came a feeling that hit her now and then no matter how she tried to suppress it, a feeling that only a woman who has lost a pregnancy could understand, a feeling that came from the knowledge that life can be taken in an instant.

She laid her hand on her belly and thought as hard as she could, "You stay in there little one. Stay as long as you can."

Chapter 10

August 1908

"It's so goddamned hot up here," Naomi screamed from upstairs.

Eddie, who had come inside to steal a molasses cookie from the jar, felt his ears burn. His mother never used such language. He supposed she had a right to be upset. She had lost her baby a few days ago, and when she came home from the hospital yesterday, Pop took her straight up to bed, where the doctor ordered her to stay for a few days more.

Eddie had not understood what it meant to lose a baby, and when he asked his father what it meant, Pop had only confused him more. They kept saying the baby had died, but that's all they would say. After Eddie remembered Grandfather Fletcher in his casket, he asked if there would be one for the baby. Would they kiss the baby like they had kissed their grandfather? Would the baby be cold too? But Eddie got no answers. Pop had only sighed and shook his head. "When your mother comes home, she needs rest. Questions like these will only hurt her. Do you understand me, Edward," Pop asked in a stern voice.

He had not understood, but he didn't want to make his mother feel bad.

"Richie? Eddie?" Naomi called. "Anyone down there? I need you."

Eddie felt the back of his neck prickle with apprehension. He wished his father were home. He wished he had not come inside from riding his bike up and down the alley. He wished Richie was not at Billy Jensen's house. Eddie felt helpless. He imagined trying to help his mother to the bathroom, as Pop had done, and in a panic, he went out the front door and up the street where he called loudly, "Richie!" After several failed attempts to summon his brother, Eddie realized he would have to go to Billy's house, which he did not want to do because Mrs. Jensen was a snoop, always pinching his cheek and asking about his mother. If she answered the door, she would batter him with questions, but he would have to brave it out. He needed his brother.

Eddie knocked then stepped back on the Jensen porch. The smell of onions and meat cooking permeated the air. The door opened to his brother and Billy, who both laughed at Eddie when they saw him. "Whaddya want?" Richie said.

"You gotta come home. Ma needs us."

"We're busy. I'll come later."

"Now. You gotta come now," Eddie said with the authority of one much older.

Richie shrugged and told Billy he'd see him later.

They raced down the street.

"Beat ya, again," Richie gloated.

Eddie ignored him and walked toward the house.

"Don't be a sore loser," Richie said.

"You—" Eddie searched for a comeback, but could think of nothing. Instead he said, "You would think that kid was your brother the way you are always over there."

"Guess he's just more interesting than you, you dope."

"Guess he's just more interesting than you, you dope," Eddie said back in a mocking tone, edging his way into the house first.

Richie let the back door slam behind him and cried out, "We got any root beer, Ma?"

"Shut up," Eddie said. "She's all on edge."

"What for?"

"You're the dope, you know that?"

"What do I have to do with it?"

"Boys!" Naomi called. "I need you."

Eddie glared at his brother, then motioned for him to follow. Upstairs in her room, they found their mother drenched with sweat, her nightgown clinging with revealing detail to her body. She was trying to open the window wider.

"Damn thing's stuck," she said, slamming her palm against the window.

"Ma! Be careful," Richie said. "You'll break the glass." He took her by the arm and led her back to the bed. "Here, just sit down."

Richie wiggled the sash. Humidity had swelled the wood, but he worked it up at last. The open window made little difference.

"It's so hot I can't breathe."

"I'll get you some water," Eddie said, making his way to the door.

"Wait. I want you to help me downstairs. I want you to make a bed for me out on the back porch. It must be shady out there by now."

"A bed?" Richie laughed. "Outside?"

"Yes, Richard. Is that too much to ask?"

Eddie shook his head at Richie, then started to take the sheet off his mother's bed.

"Eddie, just the top sheet. And both of my pillows too," Naomi said. "Richie, go get that little mattress off the bed in the nursery. Then come back and help me downstairs."

Eddie gathered the bedding and followed Richie down the stairs.

"You be careful, Eddie," Naomi called after them.

On the back porch, Richie dropped the mattress that had wanted to spring out of his arms all the way down the stairs. "I'll go get her," he said. "You can fix this up."

By myself? Eddie thought. But he didn't complain. Richie was always calling him a baby as it was. He moved the two chairs and a potted geranium off the porch into the yard. Then he swept the floor before dragging the thin mattress over to shadiest spot on the porch. Its length hung over the edge, so Eddie folded the other edge to make a kind of bolster. Best as he could, he arranged the sheet, then placed the pillows at the head of the little bed. With everything set, he looked around feeling satisfied. It was much cooler out here, and lying there Ma could look out over the yard, see all of her flowers.

Moments later, Richie was down with their mother. "Oh my," Naomi said, stepping out onto the porch. "This is wonderful, Eddie."

The boys helped her down to the mattress. Eddie was glad to see she had put on her summer robe. He went inside and filled a glass with water. When he handed it to her, she smiled.

"You need anything else, Ma?" Richie asked.

She shaded her eyes and looked up at him. "No. Nothing." A cloud covered the sun, and a light breeze cooled her sweat-soaked skin. She sighed. "This is the best gift you could ever give me. Bring those chairs back up and sit with me for a while," she said.

Eddie and Richie stayed with their mother until she fell asleep, and then they sat in uncomfortable silence until Richie whispered he had to pee. When Richie left, Eddie sat there, but he was embarrassed to watch his mother sleep, just as he had been embarrassed to see her in her clinging nightgown. And yet, he thought he ought to guard her. Some minutes later, when Richie had not returned, Eddie got up anyway and went inside.

"Richie?" he called up the stairs. The quiet house did not answer. Eddie shrugged and knew his brother had slunk back to Billy's house.

Back in the kitchen, Eddie saw the day's dirty dishes on the counter, so he ran the faucet and washed them. It felt odd to be in the house alone, doing a chore he had only helped with before now. As he dried the last bowl and put it in the cupboard, Eddie felt good about what he had done. No one had told him to clean up. He had just done it. Like a grown up would have done.

"Boys?" came Ma's voice through the screen door.

"I'm in here. I'll be right out," Eddie said, hanging up the dish towel.

He carried out a plate of cookies and a glass of milk and set them on the floor near his mother. She lifted the glass and drank. "Mmm. That is good." She looked past her son. "Where's Richie?"

"Don't know. Billy's maybe."

"Well then. It is just you and me." Naomi sighed and smiled at Eddie. Then she lifted up a cookie and bit into it.

It seemed like an hour of quiet passed between them, and Eddie was reminded of those days before he'd started school, when he and his mother could pass the entire morning without saying a word. While Eddie copied letters, drew animals, or played with toys, Ma would sometimes hum tunes as she went about her work. But on most days, all he heard were the sounds of the house—Ma's shoes on the floor, the oven door squeaking open and closed, a wooden spoon whipping at a bowl of batter, the thump of her iron hitting against a shirt on the board.

"It is getting late," Eddie said. "Maybe you should come inside."

She shook her head. "Not yet."

Eddie took a cookie from the plate and sat cross-legged on the floor facing his mother. Seconds later a thought that had been pushing itself forward in his mind escaped his lips. "What does it mean to lose a baby?"

She smiled. "You are too young to understand."

"I'm eight," Eddie said, as if eight was old enough to take on the world.

Naomi put her hand alongside her face, peering into her son's face. Then she sighed and let her hand fall to her lap. "Eight. How does time get away so quickly?"

Eddie shook his head.

"The baby was too sick and too little, so it died before it could be born. It is almost as if there was no baby at all."

"That's sad."

Naomi wiped the corners of her eyes. "Very sad. And now you will have no baby sister—or brother."

"Can't you get another baby?"

"No. The doctor did an operation. I am too old for babies, he said, and your father agreed."

Eddie nodded as if all of this made sense to him, even though none of it did. But his mother had told him straight. She had not tried to hide the truth, as Pop had. "Do you want more milk? Or I could make you a jelly sandwich."

Naomi's chest heaved and she sounded as if she were going to cry. Then she caught her breath and settled herself. She shook her head. "You are a sweet boy, my little Eddie."

Eddie thought he had never felt her love more strongly than in that moment, and he imagined for a second that if Pop never came home, if Richie could die or go away somehow, he and Ma could live here by themselves and he would take care of her. No one would call him baby or say he was dumb or wonder why he couldn't read or learn, and he wouldn't feel bad about any of that. Then the alley gate squeaked open and Richie came through, waving up at the porch, and Ma, smiling widely waved back, and Eddie's fantasy vanished.

The house was quiet when Delmar arrived home from work at six. He hung his hat on the coat rack by the front door. "Boys?" he called to no answer. He went through to the kitchen and set a bag of deli sandwiches on the table. He was about to get a drink of water when voices through the open door drew him out to the porch.

"What on earth?' Delmar said, when he saw Naomi reclining on the floor.

"Hey, Pop," Richie said.

"Like my new bed?" Naomi said. "The boys made it up for me." She answered his confused look with the story of that afternoon.

"I'll be darned. I guess they're a couple of good lads after all," Delmar said, patting Richie on the back.

Eddie felt dejected. It had been him. He had been the one to take care of things. He had been the one to hear his mother's cries. He had made Richie come home. Eddie wanted his father to know he had been the one in charge. But he felt his chest tighten and knew if he tried to say one word, he would start to cry.

Chapter 11

December 1908

What's the news, boys?" Uncle Stanley said, as he came inside and handed Richie his overcoat. Stanley took off his scarf and gloves and gave them to Eddie, who peered around his uncle as if looking for something in particular.

Stanley rubbed Eddie's head. "Don't you worry little man. There are presents in the car. I'll bring them in later."

"Stanley!" Naomi said, appearing from the kitchen. "You made it. The roads were not too slippery?"

"You just can't drive too fast is all. And it's Christmas Eve. Sensible people are home."

"I cannot believe you didn't take the train. How on earth did you stay warm?"

"Mind over matter, dear sister. Besides, I wanted to see how my new motorcar would do on a long journey."

"Still, in winter. It's madness," she said disapprovingly. "Well you're here now. And safe. That's what matters, isn't it boys?"

Naomi told Richie to hang Stanley's coat on the hall tree, then said, "Let's go in the parlor."

"Where's the old man?" Stanley asked.

"He should be along shortly," Naomi said. "I sent him to the butcher shop."

"Hey, Uncle Stanley," Eddie said as if a brilliant idea had just risen in his mind. "The old man next door died. You could buy his house and then you wouldn't have to drive at all to come visit."

"That would be fine," Stanley said, "but who would do my job back in Peoria?"

Eddie's crestfallen face soon turned to anger when Richie socked him in the shoulder. "Yeah, dummy," Richie said. "Who would do Uncle Stanley's job?"

"Stop it, boys," Naomi said sternly. "Uncle Stanley just got here, and he doesn't need to see you two at it."

"They're all right. Boys can't help being boys." Stanley gave Richie and Eddie a look that said, "Better behave though."

Naomi was about to offer her brother a cup of tea when Delmar came through the front door, stomping the snow from his shoes on the rug.

"Got the largest turkey the butcher had, dear," Delmar said. "I think that young man is sweet on you."

Naomi waved him off. "Richie, take the bird from your father, and put it in the kitchen."

Delmar hung up his coat and hat, then greeted his brother in law. "Good to see you, Stanley."

"And you, old boy."

"The neighbors are going to think we are entertaining royalty with your automobile parked in front. There is space out back in the garage."

"As it looks to keep snowing, I'll gladly get it under the roof. You could drive it around first, if you like."

Delmar looked surprised. "I would not want to be the first one to put a dent in your fender."

Eddie shook his head in amusement. Pop driving an automobile? That would be something to see. "Can we come?"

"Your father is not going to drive Stanley's motorcar," Naomi said in a way that ended the possibility.

Eddie thought he saw a glint of disappointment in his father's eyes.

"All right," Stanley said. "Let's all go for a little drive. Then I'll park in the garage and each of you can help me bring in the presents."

Naomi turned down the invitation by saying she was needed in the kitchen. "I hope you will not get silly in that contraption," she said. "Tea will be ready when you return."

Dinner that night was a simple meal of toast and buttered cream of wheat. Tomorrow Naomi would be up early preparing the Christmas feast. She had baked that morning, and the stollen and pumpkin pie were in the pie safe. Delmar had put up the tree the day before, and the house smelled of pine, cinnamon, and roasted nuts.

Stanley's gifts were strewn around the tree. His offerings overtook the Reed's few wrapped boxes. Her brother had gone overboard as usual, Naomi thought. Last year he had given the boys a little pine bookcase he had built. No matter what, Uncle Stanley's gifts were the boys' favorites, so Naomi used Christmas as a time to give Richie and Eddie the things they needed, like new pajamas, scarves, and mittens.

The family were in the living room now, sipping hot cider. The tree lights cast their warm glow over the quiet scene. Outside dandelion puff snowflakes fell slowly to the ground. Naomi could barely keep her eyes open. She hoped everyone would be ready for bed soon, but it would be poor manners to make the suggestion, so she sank into her chair and put her feet up on her little needlepoint stool and listened to Stanley and Delmar talk about automobiles. Delmar wanted one desperately, but they had both agreed that there was no money to spare for that kind of luxury right now.

Eddie stood by the tree and peered at the tissue-wrapped packages as if he were X-raying their contents. Naomi could feel his excitement. She was glad that her nine-year-old was still a baby in some ways. She was not ready for Eddie to be grown up. Not just yet.

Richard was different. He had lost his baby ways too soon. Naomi did not always like the way he acted towards Eddie, as if he were the parent, but one could not change a child's character. Richie was assertive. Eddie the opposite. Eddie would grow up to be a sensitive soul. He was artistic, like his uncle Stanley. True, he had a temper, but she saw his outbursts as evidence of the frustration he often felt in school, or from unfair comparisons to Richie, who was a natural and quick learner. While Delmar worried that Eddie would struggle in life, Naomi thought it might just take him longer to find his place. He would find it though.

Richie yawned loudly and rubbed his eyes. His yawn nearly repeated itself in Naomi's lungs, but she stifled it. "All right boys," she said. "Up to bed now."

"Aw, Ma, I don't want to," Richie whined.

"You heard your mother," Delmar said. "Besides, the sooner you get to sleep, the sooner you will know what's under all that tissue."

Stanley waited until he saw the upstairs lights go out before he handed his sister a bit of folded newspaper. "It's not good news, I'm afraid," he said. "But it is news."

Naomi studied her mother's death notice from *The Atlanta Journal.*

> Marie Rose Fletcher died November 2, 1908 at her home in Sawyerville. She was employed as a textile worker at Rockvale Mills. Miss Fletcher had no known surviving relatives.

Naomi handed the obituary to Delmar.

"My," Delmar said. "I'm sorry to read this."

"I am shocked," Naomi said. "How—?"

Delmar handed the clipping back to his wife. She read it again. "How did she end up in Georgia? And who found you?"

"So many questions, aren't there? I don't have all the answers, but according to her landlady, Mrs. Green, Mother had been in Sawyerville for five years. Before that, no one knows."

"How did Mrs. Green find you?"

"When she was cleaning out Mother's room, she found a small copy of the Psalms and inside was written our names and our address in Peoria. Since I still live in the family home, it was easy to track me down."

"I wonder what she died of," Delmar said.

"Mrs. Green thinks tuberculosis. She found bloodied handkerchiefs."

"She kept our names in her Psalter, but all this time she never wrote. What horrid children we must have been for her to want to abandon us," Naomi said bitterly. "You were only eleven at the time."

"We were not horrid, and you know it. Mother was not well," Stanley said. "You know that too. Don't think it was anything you, or I, or Father did to make her leave."

Delmar got up and poured the three of them a small glass of brandy. Naomi, who rarely imbibed, took the offering gladly. "I honestly thought she would have died long ago, an unknown pauper," Delmar said. "But your mother had the strength to live some kind of life, simple as it was. If she was as—disturbed—as you say, it took a lot of will for her to keep going. Many in her shoes would have taken matters into their own hands."

"Mrs. Green sent this, along with the Psalter," Stanley said, and handed a small box to Naomi.

"What is it?" Naomi said, taking the paper box with some hesitancy.

"Her only treasure, it seems. Besides her clothing, everything else in our mother's furnished room belonged to the landlady. Just her copy of Psalms and this."

Naomi opened the box and lifted out a fine gold chain bearing a locket. She gasped when she opened the clasp. "It's us. Why, we're barely more than babies in these photographs."

"I think I was four, maybe five," Stanley said. "I remember Father taking us all to have our photograph taken and how afraid you were of the man who hid his head under the black cloak."

"I was seven or so? Why don't I remember this?" Naomi handed the locket to Delmar. "Can you imagine I was ever that young?"

"You have not changed so much that I would not know you from this picture."

"He's being kind—overlooking my graying hair," Naomi said to her brother.

Delmar handed the necklace back, and Naomi looked at it once more before closing the locket and placing it back in the box. When she handed it to Stanley, he said, "You keep it. I'll take the Psalter."

Naomi nodded. "I have no daughter to pass it on to. Boys don't care for such things."

"But young men marry women who may appreciate such things," Stanley said.

Naomi laughed.

"What do you find amusing?"

"You never married. You've never even courted as far as I know. A bachelor for life, I guess. Though maybe someday still?"

"I'm too set in my ways, Sister. No woman in her right mind would have me now."

"A nightcap, Stanley?" Delmar asked, rising from the sofa.

"I wouldn't mind just a splash since you're offering."

"I'm off to bed," Naomi said. Before heading upstairs, she laid her hand on her brother's arm. "Well, now we know," she said. "Some of it anyway."

Eddie and Richie scampered into their room and into bed before they could be caught eavesdropping. Eddie lay on his back, staring at the ceiling, listening to his mother's footsteps going down the hall to the bathroom. He dared not even think about everything he had overheard until he heard the telltale squeak of her bedroom door. Then it was Richie who broke the silence.

"We had a grandmother," Richie whispered, "and Ma never told us. Whoo boy, what a secret."

"Yeah. What a secret," Eddie said.

"Pop said she was disturbed. An even worse secret."

"Is that what terbercalosus is?"

"Nuh uh. Disturbed means loony in the head."

Eddie gasped. "Like old Mr. Kent?"

Oliver Kent was their widowed neighbor. One morning last winter Naomi went out to get the milk, and she saw him sitting on his front porch in only his nightshirt. When she questioned him, he said he was waiting for Ella to come home from the market. His wife Ella had been dead for ten years. Not long after, Oliver was moved to a home for the aged. And only a couple of weeks ago, they found out he had died.

"No. Not like that. Mr. Kent was just old. Disturbed means something worse, like—"

"Boys!"

Pop's voice startled Eddie so much his heart pounded in his ears.

"I thought you were told to go to sleep," Delmar said.

"Yes, Pop," Richie said.

Then, when they heard the bathroom door click shut, Richie said, "I'm going to sneak a look at that locket tomorrow. Wanna come with me."

"But what if we get in trouble?"

"Aw forget it. Go to sleep."

Eddie wished he had said yes. He wanted to see the pictures too. That old locket was like a secret treasure. "I'll come. I promise I won't say nothing either."

"That's more like it," Richie said.

Then, with their conspiracy settled, they quieted and went to sleep.

Christmas morning began with Delmar Reed shouting up the stairs at his sons. "Boys, Mother has breakfast ready. Let's hop to it."

Eddie arrived at the table first with a barely concealed grin, and Richie, right behind him, sat down with a thud, trying to avoid everyone's stares.

"Normally you two are down before everyone else," Naomi said, passing a plate of pastries to Eddie, who took one before handing the plate to his brother. "What's going on?" she asked. "You look like the cat who ate the canary."

"Nothing's going on," Richie said.

"Yeah. Nothing's going on," Eddie echoed.

"Well, at least you're not two tomcats at it in the alley as you usually are," Delmar said. "That's something to be grateful for."

"There certainly are a lot of cats with us this morning," Stanley said, which made them all laugh.

After breakfast, Delmar turned on the tree lights and Stanley invited the boys to sit next to him on the sofa. Knowing her gifts of hand-knit socks and mittens would be nothing after whatever Stanley brought, Naomi passed her packages to the boys first.

When Eddie tossed his socks aside, Delmar said, "Your mother worked hard on those. Thank her, young man."

Eddie did as he was told. Richie didn't wait to be told.

"Is there a pair for me, Naomi?" Stanley asked. "Or are the boys the only lucky ones."

Naomi mouthed "Thank you" to her brother. "I'm happy to knit you a pair. Of course I will."

Richie handed his mother the gift he had made for her in school, a wooden jewelry box with "Mother" carved in script on the lid. Eddie's gift was a drawing of her favorite flower, a tulip. He had found a frame for it in the second-hand shop.

Naomi's praise of her sons' gifts was effusive. Eddie blushed and mumbled, "you're welcome." Richie's expression was a bit more haughty. "I knew you would like it," he said.

"Now it's time for Uncle Stanley's gifts, isn't it boys," Delmar said. And just as if the treasury vault had been opened to them, Richie and Eddie dove to find the matching gifts with their names on them: Along with realistic U. S. Marshall costumes, including cowboy hats, the boys got holster and pistol sets. Uncle Stanley also gave them a copy of Frank L. Baum's newest Oz book, *Dorothy and the Wizard of Oz*.

When Eddie gave a disappointed look, Stanley said, "I'll read it to you this afternoon, if you like, boys."

Eddie smiled. Uncle Stanley was his favorite person in the world. "Are you sure you don't want to buy the house next door, Uncle Stanley?"

Stanley smiled. "If only I could, Edward. If only."

Chapter 12

June 1909

Eddie and Richie were in quarantine, both with a case of the measles. Naomi had been keeping them fed with chicken broth and saltine crackers, brought on trays up to their room. Their fevers had spiked and then abated the day before, but they were still coughing, and that rash was awful to look at. At least it wasn't itchy like the chicken pox had been. Eddie had a scar on his wrist from scratching open one of those blisters.

This morning after they'd eaten their breakfast of hot bowls of cream of wheat with sugar and milk, their mother tucked them back in bed and told them they still needed to rest. But they were feeling better by noon and were anxious to be outside. It was summer and neither one wanted to spend all day in bed.

Besides, there was a lot of action at the house next door. The Crandall family had moved in the day before, and Eddie and Richie were curious about the new kid. Ma had spoken to Mrs. Crandall over the fence, so she knew all about him. He was eight, and his name was Joey. "Poor thing," their mother had said. "He walks with a limp, due to polio."

"Hey, look," said Richie, on his knees by the window. "It's him. Joey."

Eddie climbed out of bed and went to the window.

"Scootch down so he won't see you," Richie said.

There were no curtains on the neighbors' windows yet, and they could see right inside the upstairs room. "That's his room, I bet," Richie said. "It's probably just like ours. You think he's a dummy?"

"Why do you say that?"

"He's a gimp and wears glasses."

"He doesn't look dumb to me."

"You seem to know a lot about dummies, Edward."

Eddie socked Richie in the shoulder. "Shut up."

"Eddie knows a lot about dummies—" Richie sang, holding Eddie's fury at bay.

"Boys!" Naomi said at their doorway. Her arms were loaded with a wash basket. "I told you to stay in bed."

They stared back, their eyes wide and waiting.

"I mean it!"

The boys scrambled quickly back into bed and lay there wiggling their toes under the covers until they heard her footsteps going down the stairs. Then they went back to the window to stare at the new boy.

"When I get better," Eddie said, "I'm going over there to say 'hi' to him."

"Not me," Richie said. "I don't wanna be friends with a gimp."

Chapter 13

July 4, 1909

On Independence Day, the Reeds took a picnic to the park and laid their blankets out near the bandstand. While Naomi got things situated, Delmar wandered over to where another family was standing, and he was engaged in conversation with them. Richie noticed Billy Jensen and said he'd be right back.

"Before the band leader takes the stage," Naomi said with a stern look, "you will be back here."

Eddie stayed with his mother, but she could see him scanning the crowd for his friends. "You will keep your Ma company, won't you Eddie?" A few minutes later, she felt sorry for him and told him to go. The joy with which he scampered away broke her heart. How quickly her babies had grown away from her. And away from each other too. Her boys, who had once been the best playmates, now seemed always to be at war.

Their latest squabble over who owned more territory in their shared bedroom had pushed Delmar to the limits of his patience. But this time, her husband had defended Eddie. Even he could see it was Richie who was the instigator in the battle. So one night with both boys in their pajamas, Delmar began to strip the bedding off of Eddie's bed.

"How would you like the back bedroom all to yourself, Edward? Wouldn't that be nice?"

Eddie's eyes widened in amazement. "Where will Uncle Stanley sleep?"

"In the room next to your mother's and mine. Now, don't just stand there," Delmar said. "Help me."

Eddie took his blanket and pillow from his father and sneered triumphantly at his brother.

Naomi had nearly laughed at her older son, who stood statue-like with his arms crossed over his chest. She knew he wanted the back bedroom for himself, but Naomi had always said no. Now Delmar had removed the decision from them both, and she was just fine with that. In the end, Naomi thought Eddie got the better part of the deal, for his room looked out over the back yard, with a door to the airing porch. Were she still a girl, it would be a place she would convert as her own play space. She had done her duty as a mother, however, and warned Eddie not to go out there to play, saying it could be dangerous, even though she knew it was not as dangerous as climbing trees.

“Where are the boys?” Delmar asked, jolting Naomi back to the present. He didn’t wait for an answer but lowered himself to the blanket.

“Off with friends of course. Would you like some lemonade?”

“Yes. Thank you, dear.”

“Who are those people you were talking with?”

“Jakub Dvorak. My right hand man and his family.”

“Oh yes. Of course. How are they enjoying the day?”

“You know, I think they love this country more than we do. It seems that way for most immigrants.”

Richie and Eddie were back now, rummaging through the picnic basket.

“We may just take all of this for granted,” Delmar continued, waving his hand over the scene. “Jakub, on the other hand, counts his blessings each day.”

The band leader took the stage and bowed to the crowd who applauded and cheered. Then he turned to the musicians, raised his baton, and the first notes of “Stars and Stripes Forever” spread over the appreciative crowd.

The stirring tune always brought a lump to Naomi’s throat. As did this day, with all of the flags and pageantry, the pride she felt to be an American. So despite her sons’ ongoing rivalries, Naomi Reed knew she had many blessings to count as well. The difference between her and Mr. Dvorak, Naomi thought, was that she sometimes forgot that. Today reminded her that gratitude was a virtue.

Chapter 14

September 1909

For Naomi, September brought the first week of school and a welcome respite from a contentious summer. Let the boys' teachers manage them a while, she thought. No doubt the other neighborhood mothers felt just as she did.

The only exception was her new neighbor, Mrs. Crandall. By midweek, Naomi saw the Crandall boy out in the yard with his mother, helping with the wash, then later tossing baseballs against the wall of the garage, an incessant, annoying sound. He could be ill, Naomi thought. But he didn't look ill, and by the next Monday, the child was still at home.

"That boy should be in school," she said to no one as she lie on her bed that afternoon, a cold rag over her pounding forehead. The headaches that had begun after her hysterectomy last year had worsened lately. Along with the pain, some even made her sick to her stomach, incapacitating her for hours. Delmar had bought her a bottle of little liver pills, said to cure headaches, but she had found no relief from them at all. Oddly, what did help was Coca Cola, but there was none in the ice box today, so she hoped a nap in the dark would ease her pain, at least a little. The more she worried about things, the worse her temples throbbed. She tried to ease her mind, but it was difficult. There were shirts to iron and the kitchen floor to mop, but none of that was in her control at the moment.

After the grandfather clock chimed two, Naomi felt her pain begin to diminish at last. Then, only moments later, just as she felt herself about to nod off, she heard the sound of Joey's baseballs thunking against the garage.

Two weeks later, Richie and Eddie were in the back yard with their heads over a new ant hill. Naomi had sent them out with a cup of Borax, enough to take care of that colony and more. If the ant hill had emerged back by the garage, Naomi would have told the boys to leave it alone, but since it was under her wash line, it unnerved her.

"When you're done with that big one," she said, "see if you can find any more around the house." She watched them sprinkle the white powder over the hill with a spoon, as she had instructed, and felt satisfied they were doing a good job.

Then she turned her attention to the spice cake she had made to see if it was cool enough for icing. The cake was a welcome gift for the Crandalls. Naomi's true motive for baking the cake, however, was not quite neighborly. She was determined to find out why Joey didn't go to school, and the cake was her way into having a chat with Mrs. Crandall. She had chosen this Saturday morning because Delmar wouldn't be home from work until mid-afternoon, so he wouldn't be able to talk her out of it. She was sure he'd say the neighbor boy was none of their business. Naomi transferred the layers from their cooling racks onto her second-best cake plate and slathered them in vanilla frosting. After lunch, she would take the boys with her to deliver the cake.

Naomi expected Mrs. Crandall to answer the door when she knocked, so she was disappointed when Mr. Crandall opened the screen door with a terse hello. Naomi smiled and held onto the cake plate hoping Mrs. Crandall would appear soon. When Mr. Crandall held his hands out for the cake, it was too awkward not to hand it to him. He uttered a gruff thank you before disappearing into the house. Delmar would never have done such a thing. Kitchen gifts were exchanged between the women of the house. That was the unwritten rule.

Moments later Joey was at the door staring through the closed screen at them. He smiled brightly and said, "Hi."

"Hello," Naomi answered. "You are Joey, aren't you?" The boy nodded. She smiled at him, somewhat sadly. He was a beautiful child, sandy blond hair, hazel eyes, a spattering of freckles on his bright cheeks, but all were overshadowed by his physical impairments. A moment later, Naomi chastised herself for the thought. What did it matter. If he was a kind child, that's what mattered.

"Good afternoon," said Mrs. Crandall, now at the door. "Can I help you?"

Naomi thought the cold greeting felt odd as the two had met briefly before. Maybe Naomi had interrupted something. She hoped not.

"She brought us a cake, Esther," Mr. Crandall shouted from inside.

Mrs. Crandall still appeared confused, so Naomi explained. "Yes, I made you a spice cake. I wanted to welcome you to the neighborhood properly."

"Oh, goodness," Mrs. Crandall said, sounding relieved. "You didn't have to go to all that trouble." She opened the door and pushed Joey out onto the porch before her and motioned for him to go out into the yard, where Richie and Eddie stood like two short stone pillars. "Those boys came to see you, Joey."

The boy bounded out to where Richie and Eddie stood tentatively. "Where are your manners?" Naomi said. "Shake Joey's hand, boys." Her sons faced Joey Crandall as if they were afraid he would bite. With a glare from Naomi, Eddie reached out first. Then Richie.

"I've got a fresh pitcher of iced tea, if you would like a glass."

Naomi nodded and said thank you.

When Mrs. Crandall emerged with the tea, she told Naomi to take a seat in one of the porch chairs, before handing her the glass.

"Joey's got a new ball and glove," Mrs. Crandall said to the boys. "You could play catch."

"That would be fun," Naomi said. She told Richie to go get their gloves. He didn't move. Then she glared at him, a look that had its effect.

Eddie and Joey stood as still as toy soldiers, until Joey asked if Eddie liked baseball.

"I like the White Sox," he said.

"Me too," Joey said. "I have a pennant in my room. Want to see it?"

"Some other time," Eddie said, thinking his mother probably wouldn't want him going in the house. By then Richie was back with their gloves.

"Cyril's already cut himself a piece of cake. My husband has an insatiable sweet tooth, so I'm sure he is grateful to you."

The comment was not quite a thank you, but Naomi took it as one nevertheless. "You're welcome, Mrs. Crandall. I should have done it before now."

"Call me Esther."

"And call me Naomi. Are you settling in, Esther?"

"Pretty well," she said, then she offered no more.

A long paused lingered before Naomi went on. "It takes time, but before long, it will seem like you have never lived anywhere else. At least that's how it was for me when we moved here."

Esther Crandall only nodded. A cardinal called and Esther looked in the direction of the Reeds' sycamore tree. "Isn't that the loveliest sound," she said, and Naomi agreed.

While the women sat on the Crandalls' shady back porch, the three boys tossed a baseball between them. Richie played as if it he would face punishment if he refused. Naomi's own situation was not much different. Another "cheer, cheer, cheer" from the cardinal animated Esther who told Naomi about a robin's nest.

"We found it in that tree there," she said, pointing to a spindly ash near the alley.

When Naomi joked about not needing an alarm clock when baby robins woke at 4:00 a.m., Esther looked as if Naomi had insulted the entire bird species. "Because they are so loud," she explained, but the nuances of her comment elicited only a shrug.

"Shall I cut us all a piece of cake," Esther asked a short time later.

"No. Thank you," Naomi said. "It is too close to dinner for us." This comment also seemed to insult Esther Crandall somehow.

In the quiet space, Naomi listened to the boys, who had given up their game of catch and were now sitting nearby in a shady spot. Joey was telling Richie and Eddie about the book he was reading, something about a magical bird called a phoenix. Joey became animated and excited, lifting his arms as if they were wings. Richie, who was a reader, listened to the neighbor boy with interest, while Eddie stared at the ground, scuffing over a bare spot with his ball glove.

"Esther," came an urgent call from inside the house.

"Now what does that man want?" she said in a subdued voice. "Is your husband so demanding, Naomi?"

Naomi did not know what to say. There was no good answer to the question, and she was certainly not going to discuss her marriage, so she just smiled and decided Esther must have meant it rhetorically.

"We should go home," Naomi said, rising from her chair. "It's time to get my chicken in the oven."

Esther smiled. "Yes. Of course." She stood and shouted indoors. "Cyril. They're leaving."

A moment later, Cyril Crandall appeared, but he did not come outside. "Good of you to come over," he told Naomi through the screen door. "Thank you for the cake."

"You're welcome," Naomi said, suppressing the urge to smile at the man, who seemed not to understand social graces at all.

"Joey, it's time to say goodbye," Esther said. "Shake hands with your neighbors."

Not new friends or the boys. *Your neighbors*. These people were so odd.

Eddie and Richie shook Joey's hand then preceded Naomi out the alley gate. It almost broke Naomi's heart the way Joey waved at them when they left, as if he couldn't bear for them to go. Naomi thought the boy's demeanor probably had more to do with being isolated from playmates than from anything wrong with him. If Esther and Cyril Crandall did not get him in school soon, he could grow up just as maladjusted as they appeared to be. Naomi heard Delmar's voice in her head. *None of our business.* Still, Naomi could not help feeling motherly towards Joey, as any decent woman would.

At dinner that night, Naomi told Delmar about the visit to the Crandall's before the boys gave him their version. "Joey seems so bright," she said. "I still can't believe they teach him at home. At least that's what Esther told me. I haven't seen much evidence of lessons, except he can obviously read. Otherwise, that boy is outside alone almost all day."

"I thought kids had to go to school," Eddie said. "If Joey doesn't have to, I don't want to go either."

"Don't get your hopes up," Delmar said, putting an end to Eddie's complaint.

Eddie's head fell and he went back to his dinner.

"They probably don't want other kids making fun of the boy," Delmar said to Naomi. "Perhaps they will send him to a special school."

"There's nothing wrong with his brain, Delmar. I don't think he needs anything like that."

Delmar grunted then changed the subject. "Richard, I met a man on the trolley today. A city planner, which is kind of like an architect. Doesn't that sound interesting? I told him about you."

"Aw gee, Pop. What for?"

"Never too soon to start thinking about your future," Delmar said, "and with your abilities, a career in architecture would be a fine choice. One that would take you far in life. You don't want to end up at the post office like me, do you?"

"Delmar," Naomi said with an exasperated tone, "Postmaster is a perfectly respectable profession, and you know it. Besides, the boys have plenty of time to consider their futures."

"Did you tell him about me too, Pop?" Eddie asked excitedly.

Delmar shook his head. "I don't see you in—in a career like that, Eddie."

"Yeah, dummy," Richie said, kicking his brother under the table.
"That's enough!" Naomi said. "Richie, apologize to your brother."
"Sorry," Richie said reluctantly.
"Eddie," Naomi said softly. "Your father meant to say that he did not mention you to the man because of your age. He doesn't see you as a working man yet. Isn't that right?" Naomi glared at her husband.
Delmar cleared his throat. "Yes. That's right, Edward. But don't worry. You will soon be old enough to think about what you want to do in life."
"And until that time," Naomi said, "all you need to think about is being a good boy and doing your best in school."

A week later, Naomi did something she would always feel guilty about. She sent a letter to the school. Identifying herself as Mary Jones, a neighbor, Naomi reported a case of truancy. A child named Joey Crandall. Soon afterwards, Eddie and Joey began walking to school together, a situation that Naomi also orchestrated, telling her son that since he and Joey were nearly the same age, they would get along well, adding that since Joey had never been to school he would need a friend. That part, at least, was true.

Chapter 15

June 14, 1910

Naomi's intervention in Joey Crandall's education had more than one positive effect. It brought a sense of normal life to the Crandall house. Whereas Esther had once seemed aloof, she was now friendly, at times more convivial than Naomi was prepared for. It was as if some secret shame she had been repressing had been taken from her, freeing her from her social cocoon. Cyril Crandall and Delmar became on-again, off-again companions, both having an interest in trains. Cyril's uncle had been a surveyor for the transcontinental railroad. Delmar's fascination was as an amateur historian. And Cyril, who had recently been invited to join the Oddfellow's lodge, had brought Delmar into their fold.

Even so, Naomi was surprised when the Crandalls invited all the boys in the neighborhood to a party for Joey's ninth birthday, even those from families they did not know. Richie complained about having to go, saying, at thirteen, he was too old for a kid's party, but Naomi told him he had better be a gentleman.

"Besides," she said, "we are all going, even your father."

"I still don't see why I have to get dressed up," Richie said. "It's just a party."

"That's right. It's a party, and you are hardly *dressed up*," Naomi said with the edge of anger in her voice. "Just your nice summer clothes, and I won't have Esther Crandall saying otherwise. Now wait here. I have to run up to the bathroom."

When Naomi was out of earshot, Eddie said, "If I talked back to Ma like that, Pop would give me a smack."

Richie shrugged. "I can complain if I want to, I guess."

A few minutes later, Delmar came in to the kitchen where the boys waited. "Where's your mother?"

"I'm right here," she said, back with her family. "Don't all my boys look nice."

"Do you have the gift, Edward?" Delmar asked. Eddie lifted it up the shoe box wrapped in tissue. "Let's be on our way then."

When they passed through the Crandall's back gate, Eddie was at the forefront with the present, a black cast iron dog. The man at the store called it a paper weight, but Eddie just though it was keen. He was the one who had chosen it, even though Richie thought it was a dumb idea. "What can he do with that?" Richie had said at the store. Naomi had come to Eddie's defense, saying she thought it was charming. "He can put it on a shelf, by his books," Eddie had said.

"Say, there's Charlie Alford," Delmar said, noticing their neighbor. "I need to go give him a few jabs about his New York Giants. The Cubs gave them a beating yesterday."

"Be nice," Delmar.

"Don't you worry about it. He'll know I am only teasing."

"All right, boys. Mrs. Crandall can probably use my help. So, you both be on your best behavior."

Just then Richie saw Billy Jensen at the back gate.

Naomi caught her son by the arm before he went to meet his friend. "I mean it, Richard," she said. "Best behavior."

Joey saw Eddie and ran over to him, grinning. "Hiya," he said joyfully. "Come and see the loot. He grabbed Eddie's hand and pulled him over to the gift table.

Eddie set their package down among the others, feeling a little jealous. Ma and Pop had never given him a party like this. Richie either. They just had a cake and Pop gave them one present on their birthday.

Joey picked up a cigar-sized box and shook it close to his ear. "Jacks, I bet," he said. He shook it near Eddie's ear.

"Yeah. Jacks, I bet," Eddie said. He was glad they hadn't chosen that gift, because only girls played jacks.

"Come on. Let's get a root beer," Joey said.

Soon a troop of boys were gathered around the snack table, drinking soft drinks and munching on crackers and pretzels.

"This has turned out so well, Esther," Naomi said. The two women had settled into folding chairs, away from the hubbub of boys, several of whom had begun playing badminton, while others, like Richie and his friend, were playing catch.

"It was all Cyril's idea, you know. I thought it was too much trouble."

"Joey is happy."

"He is. He has been ever since he started school."

"And how is that going for him?"

"That child adores school. I was always afraid for him to go, with his leg. And I was darn angry when that truant officer showed up at our door. How they knew about him, I can't imagine." Esther shook her head. "But school has been good for Joe, and he tells me the other children in his class do not make fun of his limp. Most of them anyway."

"How reassuring that must feel," Naomi said. She knew that not all children were kind. Her own sons were not always kind, but you can't keep a child swaddled at home forever. Sooner or later, they have to learn to make their own way in the world—not that she shared this opinion with Esther Crandall.

"I wish Eddie liked school as much as Joey."

"Joey idolizes Eddie. I just know they'll be lifelong friends."

Esther heard Cyril calling, so she rose and called back, "Coming." She smiled and shook her head, whispering to Naomi, "He can't get along without me, can he?"

Naomi laughed. The Crandalls could still be odd ducks, but she found herself enjoying their company more than she thought she would.

Naomi was about to wander over to the cake table, when Delmar arrived with a cup of punch for her.

"Thank you," she said. "Cyril's little gala has turned out fine, hasn't it? And little Joey is having such a good time, just like a normal kid."

"He will never truly be normal, though, will he?" Delmar said. "Not with those thick glasses and his limp."

"Oh Delmar," Naomi said. "Why say such a hurtful thing? I hope no one else heard you," she said, pushing the cup into his hands before leaving him alone.

When the call came that it was time to open presents, Naomi stood by Esther. Delmar and the other men stood behind the circle of boys, who pushed their way to be closer to Joey.

"Make your circle wider, boys," Cyril Crandall said, "then everyone will be able to see."

"Open mine first," said a boy.

"Mine next," said another.

Eddie did not urge Joey to open their gift because he had begun to think maybe Richie was right and it was a stupid present. Who would want a little statue of a dog? Eddie watched the gifts stack up: puzzles, jacks, a wooden truck, a bag of marbles, and two books. Joey chose the shoe box next, and Eddie held his breath as Joey tore off the tissue.

"Well, isn't that the sweetest thing," Esther said when Joey held up the little dog.

Eddie heard Richie snickering. It didn't matter. What mattered was that Joey had pulled the little dog to his chest and smiled.

"Only one left, Joe," Mrs. Crandall said.

"That's from me," called out a boy that Eddie did not know.

"Keen," Joey said. "Toy soldiers."

Eddie and the other boys looked upon those soldiers with envy. A couple of the boys picked them up to play with, aiming the small figures at each other making shooting sounds.

Then Mrs. Crandall said it was time for cake, so they left the soldiers on the tablecloth field of battle.

That night when Eddie was getting his pajamas on, Richie came into his room and set a small lead soldier on the chest of drawers.

"Look what I got," he said.

"Hey, that's one of Joey's. What'd you take that for?"

Richie laughed. "Don't get all twisted up over it. He'll never even know. There had to be thirty of them in that box."

"But you stole it!"

"And if you ever say a word about it," Richie said close to Eddie's face, "you'll be sorry."

While Eddie was tempted to swipe the little soldier away from Richie and give it back to Joey, Richie's warning had sounded so mean, he was afraid to cross him.

Then, on Saturday, a month later, Richie handed the soldier to Eddie. "Sneak it back to him, or he'll think *you* took it."

Eddie looked up at his brother in disbelief.

"Just shut up," was all Richie said.

Chapter 16

October 1912

Eddie was in seventh grade when a new girl came to his class about a week after the school year began. She sat in the first row by the windows in the desk next to him. Her clothes were too small and she smelled like wood smoke. None of the other girls would talk to her. She had chestnut brown hair and bright blue eyes. Her name was Belinda, and Eddie thought she was beautiful.

One afternoon, the teacher kept Eddie after school for being inattentive, and when he went outside, Belinda was there in the play yard, sitting on a swing, scuffing the toes of her shoes as she swung back and forth. When she saw Eddie, she smiled and waved.

A group of Richie's friends surrounded Eddie. They wanted to know where Richie was and why he'd missed school. Eddie told them he was home with the mumps. The tallest one said he had something he wanted Eddie to give to Richie, then he punched Eddie in the stomach. Hard enough that Eddie doubled over. He was embarrassed that Belinda had seen it.

She was off the swing now and walked over to where Eddie was. Richie's friends had left.

"They were mean," Belinda said.

"It's okay," Eddie said. "They're my brother's friends. They were just kidding around."

"No. They were being mean."

The way she said it made Eddie feel as if he should have told them to knock it off, but he had just stood there and taken it.

"Well, I'll see you, Eddie," Belinda said. Then she walked away.

Eddie wanted to follow her, but something held him back. "Tomorrow," he told himself, then he walked home.

The next day at recess, Eddie saw Belinda on the swings again, looking his way. Instead of going over to her, he stayed with a group of boys from his class.

"That new girl is a goop," Frankie said.

"Yeah, and did you ever get a whiff?" Archie said. "And I bet she's lousy too,"he said, scratching his head as if it were full of lice."

"You take that back," Eddie said.

"Or what? You sweet on that little hunkie girl?" Archie said. "Hunkie girl, hunkie girl."

Later, as Eddie sat in the principal's office waiting for his father to come, he couldn't remember anything but the rage he'd felt when he reeled back and let his fist fly into Archie's face.

That night, when Eddie was ready for bed, his mother came up as she always did to say goodnight. He did not want to hear any more about how childish it was to lose one's temper. The principal, the teacher who had pried him away from Archie, and his father had made that perfectly clear.

"Here," Naomi said, handing him chipped ice wrapped in a washcloth. "It'll help that bruise." She made a tsking sound, then sat on the edge of his bed. "What were you thinking? Fighting? I might expect it of Richie, but not you. You're my sweet boy."

"I'm not sweet," Eddie mumbled, pressing the ice to his cheek. He had wanted to kill Archie, and if the teachers had not pulled the two of them apart when they did, Eddie would have kept pounding away.

Naomi sighed. "You have no idea how sweet you are," she said. "But I do worry about your temper. Seems like sometimes you resent the whole world. No one's against you son. No one. We're in your corner."

Eddie felt a lump grow in his throat, but he wouldn't let himself cry. He got under the bed covers and turned to face the wall. Richie wasn't in his corner. Pop was always against him. She hadn't heard what Pop said to the principal. "We'll straighten him out, sir," he'd said, and then he agreed when the principal said he had his work cut out for him. Bet Archie's pop had not said anything like that.

"All right," Naomi said. She patted Eddie's shoulder. "You sleep. Thank goodness tomorrow's Saturday. You won't have to face that boy, though he's as much to blame as you are. Don't you even think about him, now."

After Ma closed his door, Eddie laid the ice pack on the floor, got out of bed, and quietly opened the door to the airing porch. He wasn't supposed to go out there because the railing was wobbly, but Eddie didn't care. It was a cool night and he wanted to feel the chill air. He stood in the dark, moonlight on his plaid pajamas, and thought about Belinda. He had been defending her honor, but when the fight ended, when he looked over for her approval, she was gone. Had she been disgusted with him for fighting? Was she disappointed in him too?

In that moment Eddie felt an urge to run. He thought if he could disappear into the night, no one would miss him. He had no idea where he would run to, but it didn't matter. Away. Anywhere but here. He imagined his shoes hitting the alley, then a street, then a farm field, then another. He'd run so fast that at times his feet would leave the ground and he would be striding on air. Even faster he'd be then. Even farther gone.

The screech of an owl drew him to the present. Eddie sucked in his breath. He was tired. When you were too old for crying, it was hard when all you wanted to do was cry.

In the morning, Eddie sat at the kitchen table and ate his toast. His father said nothing but patted him on the shoulder before going out the back door in his work clothes. Eddie took it as a sign that the previous day's contention was behind them.

"Richie is going to help your father paint the garage today," his mother said. "You want to help?"

Eddie shook his head. There was something else he had to do. "Going over to Johnny's," he said. "He and his dad are building a lean to, and they told me I could help." It was only half a lie. He had helped build that little clubhouse weeks ago.

"Your face looks better," Naomi said. "By Monday, you'll barely know there was a bruise."

He finished his milk and wiped his face with his sleeve. "Thanks, Ma," he said, then he grabbed his jacket and cap from the hook by the door and went back through the house and out the front door.

Unlike the night before, this morning he didn't feel like running. He was on his way to find Belinda's house, and he wanted to go deliberately so he could remember how he'd gotten there. It might be he'd want to go see her every Saturday. He wanted to explain, tell her he wasn't really a fighter. He'd only done it because of Archie, you see. Archie had said something mean. She would smile and take his hand and tell him thank you.

Eddie had only a vague idea of where she might live. Kids had talked cruelly about her living in a shack, but Belinda said they lived with her uncle in a house behind his bakery. She spoke once of a nearby park where she and her little brother would go. But there were little parks all over the city, and it was a big city, Eddie was finding out.

After six or seven blocks, houses turned to shops, and the streets became congested with motorcars, horse-drawn carts and wagons, and people milling about. He stepped into a street to cross, and a wagon driver yelled at him to watch where he was going. Eddie nodded gratefully, before sidestepping a fresh pile of manure. The noise and bluster of the city beyond his usual haunts had Eddie disoriented, and before long, he realized he was lost. Instead of stopping and going back, he kept trudging on, hoping to see familiar landmarks he may have seen from trips on the trolley with his parents.

Before long he was in a neighborhood not unlike his own. There were girls out on the sidewalk with their dolls and buggies and others skipping rope. He slowed as he walked among the dark-haired girls. Not one looked like Belinda.

When the houses turned again to shops. He kept his eyes open for a bakery. He saw a woman in an apron setting out apples in a bin outside a little grocery.

"Is there a bakery near here?" he asked her. "A bakery with a house out back?"

"What are you talking about boy? There are houses everywhere." She raised her fat arm and it jiggled as she pointed to the second story. "I live up there," she said. "Whose house do you want?"

"A bakery," he said again.

She looked at him as if he'd spoken gibberish.

"Are you lost, boy? Or is there something wrong with you? Stupid maybe? You have an odd look about you." She laughed. "Yes. Very odd. You'd better move on. I don't want you bothering my customers."

Eddie felt his cheeks burn. Past the next shop and the next, her laughter followed him. At the corner, Eddie felt a pull to turn right. There was no reason except for something he couldn't explain. Just a notion to turn. He was now on a treeless street. The sun was high and bright and felt good on his face. With renewed hope, Eddie began peering down each alley as he passed it. Most were narrow pathways, gates to backyards like his own. Before long, the smell of freshly baked bread hit his nose and his face brightened. He had found her at last. Across the street he saw the sign: Bakery. When he stepped inside, two women were waiting in line. He stood patiently. When it was Eddie's turn, a thin, balding man behind the counter barked, "What can I get you?"

Was this man her uncle? Eddie smiled. "Does Belinda live here?"

"What?" the man said, looking past Eddie out the open door. "Do you want to buy a loaf of bread, boy?"

"I—. Does a girl named Belinda live here?" The question felt thick in his throat.

The man shook his head. "No," he said, then motioned with his hand for Eddie to move on. "Now, Mrs. Milner," the baker said. "What can I get for you?"

Ashamed and defeated, Eddie left the bakery. If he'd had a nickel, he would have bought a bag of sugared donuts. All those pastries had made his mouth water with hunger. He was certain it was nearly lunch time. Except when he'd been sick, he had never missed lunch. Ma would be worried about him. Or maybe she wouldn't. Maybe Richie would say he probably got invited to stay for lunch at Johnny's house. Maybe Pop wouldn't say anything. Maybe Pop would be glad he wasn't there. Maybe Pop would think it was nice, just the three of them.

Many blocks past the bakery, the homes turned stately, and Eddie knew Belinda did not live in one of them. No one he knew lived in one of those grand mansions. A yellow motorcar drove toward him on the cobbled street. Eddie stared at it, admiring its shiny chrome, the sound of its puttering engine. Pop said the trolley was good enough for the Reeds, but he was envious of Uncle Stanley's automobile. Eddie had seen his father paging through magazines, stopping to stare at advertisements for fancy automobiles. Boy, Eddie thought, as he watched another car drive past him, this one black with a canopy, I sure am going to have one someday.

He sighed. He didn't have a car now. He didn't have trolley fare, and Eddie realized he was much farther from home than he wanted to be. He turned around and walked back towards more modest houses. Not far off a dog barked. The sound drew his attention to a white clapboard house. He stopped to watch for a moment. A man knelt before the porch steps with a paintbrush. A little girl sat nearby with a doll. Eddie thought of his father and Richie and their own paint job. He imagined Ma bringing them cookies. She'd stand approvingly and comment on what nice work they were doing. Would any of them give Eddie the briefest thought?

Eddie glanced up. In the distance, dark clouds hovered over rooftops. It was time to give up and go home. Maybe when he saw her in school, Eddie would ask Belinda if she wanted to him to walk her home. But then again, if the fellows had harassed him before, what would they make of that? Instead, he'd just talk with her for a while after school as usual. Having chosen the easier path, Eddie breathed easily and smiled. When he got closer to the little grocery, he decided he would not walk past the apple lady in case she felt like jabbing him with fresh insults, so kept straight for one more block south before heading east. But if he had gone past the apple cart, he could have nicked an apple, or two. Eddie's stomach grumbled loudly, as if scolding him for his lack of courage.

There were no such opportunities ahead. A barber shop, a milliner, and a fix-it shop only. Not even a candy store. He kept on going, and by now his feet felt tight inside his shoes. They had fit loose when he'd got them right before school started. Room to grow, the salesman had said. Maybe his mother was right. He was growing overnight. Another reason for Pop to be angry. "I'll need to get a second job," he had said, "to keep that boy in decent clothes." When Eddie scowled, Pop had ruffled Eddie's hair. "I am joking, boy," he said, in softer tones. "Can't have my son looking shabby."

Eddie brightened when he saw the steeple of the Lutheran church, for he was now on familiar terrain. He headed toward his school. Illogically, it occurred to him that Belinda might be right where he last saw her, sitting on the swing in the play yard. But when he got to the play yard, it was vacant. The only climbers on the jungle gym were crows. Still, he went through the gate and sat on Belinda's swing. No one was around to give him any trouble, no one around to call her names, so Eddie stayed a while and thought of her. If only he'd sat next to her yesterday instead of huddling with his friends. They would have taunted him about it later, but he wouldn't have cared. They could say anything they wanted about him, but not about her. Eddie could not fix what was already broken, but in school on Monday, he would tell her it didn't matter what people said.

Eddie took a piece of paper from his jacket pocket and unfolded it. He had drawn her a cat because she had once told him she liked cats. He had worked on it secretively in his room. His model was one of his mother's porcelain figurines, a yellow tabby curled in repose. He had rubbed out its face three times with his gum eraser before the likeness came out right. Right enough anyway. He liked to draw, but just like most things, he wasn't any good at it. Still, he thought now, it looked like a cat. No one would think otherwise.

A drop of water hit the paper, then another, splotching the shading he had so carefully done. Thunder cracked and sent the crows into a flutter.

Eddie glanced up at the stormy sky. What if he had found Belinda's house? She might have been on the stoop playing with a doll. Or at some work with her mother. What would she have said? He was just a boy from school. He was nothing to her. He probably wouldn't even have had the guts to show her his drawing. And now it was ruined. He crumbled the paper and threw it to the ground. The rain now as heavy as his mood, drenched him. It ran into his eyes and stung bitterly.

Belinda was not in school on Monday. Nor on Tuesday. By the end of the week, her absence had Eddie worried she might be sick with the measles or the mumps. After school on Friday, he asked his teacher about her. With an offhandedness that made Eddie angry, Miss Cameron said, "Her family has moved to Milwaukee. Or so I was told." She smiled weakly at Eddie, then shooed him away. She was marking spelling tests from that morning, and he did not want to be around when she came to his.

On the way home from school, Eddie felt once again like running, but instead he took up a long, sturdy stick and used it to hit at everything he passed—trees, fences, gates, a bicycle that he sent to the ground, almost a stray dog, though he thought better of that impulse after the dog barked at him before ambling away. By the time Eddie reached his alley, the stick was not much longer than a pencil. As if it had been the source of all his anguish, he broke it in two and threw it to the ground before grinding the bits under the sole of his shoe.

Chapter 17

December 24, 1914

It was Christmas Eve morning, the day after Richie's eighteenth birthday. He padded down the hall to Eddie's room and shook his brother awake. Richie felt bad because he'd been hard on the guy, especially the past few weeks. It wouldn't be a big deal if Eddie knew how to take a joke, but he never did. And anyway, Eddie blew his stack so fast, it was sort of fun to rile him up. At least Eddie no longer ran crying to Ma. He just sulked about until she asked him what was the matter. And that was almost as bad. They both had to lie to her then and say nothing was wrong.

Eddie rolled over. When he saw it was Richie he drew his arm up over his eyes. "Whaddya want?" he said. "I was asleep."

Richie smiled. I know that you dope, he thought. "Hey, wanna come up to the attic with me? I need to look for something."

"No," Eddie said, rolling back toward the wall.

"You're not still sore are you? About me teasing you about flunking your history test?"

Eddie pulled his pillow over his head.

Richie yanked it off. "Come on. I've got a secret."

Eddie sat up and glared. "What secret?"

"Nope. You gotta come up to the attic with me."

Their mother's voice startled them. She was in the hallway, using a hairpin to fasten a loose strand of hair.

"Oh, good. You're both awake," she said. "Get dressed and get your breakfast. Your father and I are going to the butcher shop to get the turkey."

She was gone as quickly as she had appeared, her long skirts swishing the hallway carpet.

Richie nodded to his brother. "Meet you downstairs. Then we'll go exploring."

The September issue of *Boys Adventure* magazine had started it. Richie had seen a picture of a California citrus farmer on horseback riding in the groves, pulling oranges bigger than baseballs off the trees. "Now that looks like a great life," Richie had said to himself, paging through the article.

Since then, those images of California lured him deeper and deeper into believing he could get himself away from the life his father had in store for him. A life he had no interest in. Each night as Richie lay awake plotting each detail of his escape, the improbable became real, and now it was as if there had never been anything but this. Richie could not imagine himself as anything but a rancher now.

The door to the attic stairs was at the end of the hallway adjacent to Eddie's room. Richie turned the skeleton key that was always left in the lock before turning the brass knob and opening the door. Just inside, he switched on the light. They climbed the six stairs that formed the angled ceiling of the closet in his own room. At a landing, the stairs turned right and led up to the open attic that spanned the length of the house. The front windows cast their own light over the attic floor. "Been a while since we've been up here," Richie said.

"Yeah."

"Remember? It was the day of that bad snowstorm a few years back. School was canceled, so we came up here to play." He and Eddie had taken their marbles up there. They'd drawn a chalk circle on the wood floor and had just begun to play when Ma ended the fun.

"You'll freeze up there," she'd said. How was Richie supposed to know there was no heat in the attic?

"I remember," Eddie said. "We weren't cold."

"Here it is," Richie said, pulling a leather handle out from under a plaid wool blanket. He yanked the blanket off and released a cloud of dust that caused Eddie to cough spasmodically. Reaching for the bag, Richie felt a twinge in his side, a pain sharp enough to cause a catch in his breath. He had not been feeling well for a couple of days, but he thought whatever was wrong would pass as it usually did. Then this morning, the pain in his side started.

"You okay?" Eddie asked, wiping his tear-filled eyes.

"Yeah. Just a side ache. What about you, you baby? Can't take a little bit of dust?" Richie examined the bag. "Remember this? Ma bought it for the trip down to Grandpa Fletcher's funeral."

"What do you want that for?" Eddie asked, picking up the blanket.

"You have to swear you won't tell. No one."

"Tell what?"

"Boy, Eddie, you're slow sometimes. My secret."

"Oh. Yeah." Eddie lifted his shoulders. "I won't. I swear."

“I’m taking off the day after graduation. Going to stuff a few things into this bag and head out for California. I’ve got money saved up, so I’m taking off for the territory, just like ole Huckleberry Finn.”

Eddie expressed confusion.

“Never mind,” Richie said. “I gotta get away, kid. I mean, can you picture me in a stiff collar, sitting at a desk, doing city planning, or some such thing? I tell you, every time Pop talks about *my future* I get a sick feeling in my stomach.” Richie lifted himself up on his toes, then contorted his face into a serious expression. “While my job as postmaster,” Richie said, mimicking his father’s voice, “is a respectable profession, I want something better for you boys.”

Eddie laughed. “You sounded just like the old man.”

Richie shrugged. “So, you gotta keep quiet, right? If he knew what I was up to, he’d put a stop to it.”

Eddie mimed locking his mouth and throwing away the key. “Hey what’s wrong,” he said. “You okay?”

Richie sucked in his breath. “I told you. Just a little side ache. Probably indigestion.” When the stab in his abdomen subsided, he managed a smile, which seemed to put Eddie at ease.

Eddie held up the blanket. “This would make a good fort. We could sew up this hole—”

“You’re too old for forts, aren’t you?”

Eddie twisted his face in embarrassment then tossed the blanket aside.

“Yeah. This should be perfect,” Richie said, undoing the clasp of the bag. “Just big enough— Aw, hell,” Richie cried, dropping the bag to the floor. “Why’d she do that?”

“Do what?”

“It’s full of baby stuff. Pink stuff she knitted.”

“Why?”

“You know why. Don’t act like you don’t.”

“It’s okay. You can just take all that out.”

“No, siree! That thing is haunted,” Richie said, stepping back from where the bag lay. “Let’s get out of here. I shouldn’t have come up here in the first place.”

Eddie followed Richie down the stairs. “It’s okay. After Christmas, you and me can look for one in a secondhand store,” Eddie suggested. “You’ll find something just as—”

“Naw. Just forget it.” Richie said, padding down the hall to his room, closing the door behind him. Sometimes it felt as if the whole world was against him. Pop's plans for him. Even Ma, who talked about her son, the college man, even though he had said again and again that he didn't want to go to college. They never listened. There were times he wished he could switch places with Eddie. Ma and Pop never included Eddie in such talk. Eddie wasn't cut out for college. Even Richie knew that. Eddie could come home again and again, bruised from this or that fight at school, but not him. Not that he got into fights. He didn't. Not anymore. Expectations were greater for him. He was the smart one, the one who made them proud. Richie pulled his blanket up. "Poor Eddie," Richie said out loud quietly. It could not be a good feeling to have your Pop think so little of you. Maybe it was even worse than having him think too much of you. Still, right now Richie would trade places with his brother in a heartbeat. Eddie had it made, even if he didn't know it.

Later that afternoon, Richie was not feeling much better, but he could not see a way out of helping his parents trim the Christmas tree. It was an annual expectation for both him and Eddie, a family tradition. If he complained about the pain or how he had been feeling sick to his stomach since mid-morning, his mother would probably make a big fuss over him. Richie did not want to make trouble. His mother loved the Christmas holidays. She had been busy for days in the kitchen baking sweets and preparing for their big Christmas Day dinner. Eddie was already in the living room when Richie joined the family, and Pop was putting their Christmas record on the Victrola.

His father pulled a chair from the kitchen and stepped onto it so he could place the angel on the top of the tree.

"Oh, you fool," Naomi said. "You'll fall. Let Richie do it. He's taller than you."

"I'm not an old man yet," Delmar said, climbing off the chair. "Guess you're the man of the house now, Richard," he said with a wink.

Richie took the gauzy golden angel from his father, stepped up on the chair, and stretched to reach the top. Immediately the pain in his side returned, this time so sharp that he audibly gasped. He dropped the angel to grab his abdomen.

Naomi saw her son's face go from rosy to white. "Help him down, Delmar. Eddie, clear that garland from the sofa." They settled Richie and brought him water. He refused it, saying he didn't think he could keep it down.

"I'll call the doctor," Delmar said.

Naomi came back from the kitchen with a cool cloth for her son's head. "You're burning up." She could not imagine what was wrong.

Delmar hung up the phone. "He says we need to get him to the hospital right away."

"Oh, my boy," Naomi cried. "What is wrong with you?"

Richie began to shake from the pain. Wrapped in a blanket, they helped him out to the street where Delmar stood by their new Model T. Naomi sat with Richie in the back. Eddie was in the front seat with his father. On the way to the hospital, Naomi urged Delmar to drive faster.

"I'm going as fast as I can."

Minutes later, she said, "Oh, Delmar, he's just vomited."

Richie moaned and Naomi covered the mess with the end of the blanket. "Are we almost there?" she asked anxiously.

"Nearly," Delmar said. "Hang on, son. We'll get you there."

At the hospital, Naomi stayed with the boys while Delmar ran inside to get help. Moments later, two orderlies whisked Richie away on a stretcher.

After Delmar parked the car, he went inside, where Naomi and Eddie were with a nurse. After questioning the family about Richie's symptoms, she led them upstairs to a waiting room.

"There are toilets down the hall," the nurse said.

"Thank you," Naomi said. "Do you know how long it will be?"

"It could be a while. The doctor will know for certain, but from what you've told me, it sounds like appendicitis, so they may have to operate."

Naomi's hand flew to her mouth.

"Try not to worry," the nurse said. "I will return with news as soon as I can." Then she walked swiftly away, her white form ghost-like at the end of the dimly lit hallway.

Naomi sat, her head resting in her hands.

"Did Richie say anything to you, Eddie" Delmar asked.

"This morning he said he had a side ache. But he—"

"This morning? Why didn't you tell us?" Delmar said.

"He told me not to. He said it wasn't serious."

"It is obviously something serious, Edward."

"It's all right, son," Naomi said. "There's nothing you could have done."

"He could have told us when he saw his brother struggling. He should have come to me immediately."

"Whatever is wrong with Richie is not Eddie's fault," Naomi said.

Time passed interminably for the Reeds. Delmar tapped his foot and paged mindlessly through a copy of *National Geographic*. Eddie sat stiffly, watching the clock on the wall. Naomi sighed and got up and paced the hallway. She went to the restroom and splashed water on her face. In the mirror she looked haggard and old. The ceiling light cast a greenish tinge over her.

Back in the waiting room, she filled a paper cup at the water cooler and drank it. Then she filled one for Eddie, who gulped it down without thinking. She handed one to Delmar and he waved it away. When she insisted, he took the cup. But instead of drinking the water, he walked to a trash can and tossed it away before disappearing down the hallway.

"How long do we gotta wait," Eddie asked.

She brushed a lock of hair from his forehead. "Things like this take time."

"I should've told you," Eddie said.

"Shhh. Don't worry about that. Once Richie is back on his feet, we'll forget all about this. Let's just try to stay calm."

Ninety minutes later, the nurse returned, a doctor at her side. Naomi and Delmar rose to greet them.

"How is he?" Delmar asked, smiling hopefully.

"Yes," Naomi said. "Can we see him?"

"Mr. Reed. Mrs. Reed," the doctor said. "The news is not good, I'm afraid. We did everything—"

"What are you saying?" Delmar asked, his voice caught in his throat.

"Your son did not make it."

"No!" Naomi cried.

Delmar felt his wife begin to crumble beside him, and he wrapped his arms around her. "There must be something else you can do," he said.

Eddie stood off alone, hiding his own tears.

The doctor shook his head. "You see, his appendix had ruptured, likely had done so before you arrived, and—"

Delmar nodded. "I'm sure you did everything you could."

The doctor waited a moment, then spoke softly. "I am truly sorry for your loss." A moment later he added, "Nurse Gray will help you take care of the necessary papers. Again, I am very sorry."

Then the doctor walked away.

Delmar, Naomi, and Eddie Reed ate their Christmas dinner in silence. None of them felt like eating, but the dinner was made and Delmar said it wouldn't help any of them to starve. The table that should have been set for four was a desolate tableau.

Because they felt ashamed to do otherwise, they waited until the first of January to open their presents. The task was perfunctory, and now the family sat like mannequins in an artfully arranged department store window. "Christmas Morning" it might have been called. Everything around them looking like a joyful scene, but the figures themselves were hollow inside.

Naomi began gathering tissue, but Delmar told her to leave it until later. She sat back down in the chair and looked blankly at the tree.

"He wanted to go to California," Eddie blurted out, as if the words had been rising in his chest for days.

Delmar's eyes narrowed. "What's that you say?"

"After graduation. Richie said he was going to hop a freight and go to California and be an orange farmer."

"Don't talk nonsense."

"I'm not. That's what he told—" Eddie shifted in his chair. "We were up in the attic," he said, "looking for a traveling bag."

"Traveling bag?" Naomi said in alarm.

"We couldn't find one, though" Eddie said quickly when he saw the pain in his mother's face.

Delmar paced towards Eddie. "Whatever he told you," he said, pointing his finger at Eddie, "your brother was pulling your leg. He was going to college to study city planning, or even architecture. We had everything arranged."

Eddie bolted to his feet. "You never listen. He didn't want to be a city planner or go to college. That was what you wanted. And the more you pushed him, the more he—"

"The more he what?"

"The more he hated you."

Eddie felt the slap burn and his own words ring in his ears, but he didn't cower. He stood tall and did not look away. The longer he held his father's gaze, the more his father seemed to weaken, until Delmar's shoulders dropped and he walked away.

"Delmar! Don't. We can't leave things like this."

Naomi was behind Eddie now, her hand on his back. He could feel her suppressed sobs. "Surely Richie never said such a thing, Eddie. He couldn't have meant it," she said.

Eddie stared at the floor and spoke softly. "He never wanted any of it."

Chapter 18

March 1916

When Eddie got home from school, he let the back door slam behind him. Instead of scolding him about it, Naomi told him to sit at the table and she'd cut him a slice of pie.

"Not hungry," he mumbled and passed through the kitchen and took the stairs to his room two at a time.

Naomi didn't doubt Eddie was feeling low. She had a call from his history teacher that afternoon, telling her that Eddie had failed another exam and that they may want to arrange a special tutor for him. Naomi dreaded passing the news on to Delmar, but she didn't see any way of keeping it from him. However, it would wait until after supper. If she said anything before hand, no one would eat a thing. Instead of calling Eddie back down, Naomi let him be. Anything she said right now would probably make him feel worse.

Waiting was a miscalculation on her part, for apparently the teacher had also phoned Delmar, so that when he got home, he started in on Eddie almost immediately.

"Where's Edward," he said, hanging up his coat and hat.

"Why," she said slyly.

"He's failing history. Did he tell you that?"

"Now Delmar, it was just one exam, and the teacher said—"

"He called you? You already knew?"

The look on Delmar's face made Naomi feel a sickness in the pit of her stomach. "Yes, but, Delmar, he thinks that if we—"

"We? This is on the boy. He does not begin to try," Delmar said before climbing the stairs.

Naomi followed him.

Delmar flung Eddie's door open.

"Stand up and look at me when I'm speaking to you," Delmar said before he had even begun his screed.

"I didn't do anything," Eddie said, not moving an inch.

"That's right. You didn't do anything. You didn't crack a book, you didn't take a note. You probably didn't listen to a single word of the teacher's lectures."

"I listen," Eddie said.

"In one ear and out the other, like it has been your whole life."

Eddie leapt off the bed and leaned in, face to face with his father. In the past year he had grown even with the man. "You just wish it was me who died instead of Richie," Eddie said.

"How dare you," shouted Delmar, grabbing Eddie by the arms.

"Let. Me. Go!" Eddie said, struggling to free himself.

Delmar pushed against his son until Eddie lost his footing and fell, the edge of his mattress softening his thud to the ground.

"Delmar!" Naomi shouted. "Stop torturing him."

Delmar stepped back and Eddie got to his feet. Eddie's eyes were filled with fury, his hands balled into fists. With his right, he pulled back, ready to let a punch fly.

"No! Eddie," Naomi pleaded, her heart pounding loudly in her ears.

Eddie's eyes met hers and he dropped his fist before pushing past her and down the stairs and out the front door.

Delmar turned and faced Naomi, his face wet with perspiration, his breath heavy. He said nothing.

She expressed her wordless disgust and left him in Eddie's doorway.

"Are you happy with yourself?" Naomi said a few minutes later when Delmar came into the kitchen. "Who knows where he's off to."

Delmar did not answer. Instead he got a beer from the ice box and took it outside, where he guzzled it before tossing the bottle on the ground and walking out the back gate.

"Coward," she screamed out the screen door, hoping her voice would carry to his ears. Delmar and Eddie had fought before, but this time felt different. This time she was not sure there would be a way to the other side. This time she had no idea what she could do to fix it.

Eddie wished he had eaten that slice of pie his mother had offered him earlier. His stomach churned and pushed the taste of bile into this throat. The farther he walked, the angrier he got. Pop was really out of control this time. It would serve him right if I just kept going and never came back, Eddie thought.

Hadn't his grandmother gone away? Maybe he was just like her—wrong in the head, disturbed. Things like that get passed down in families, he had heard. Maybe he was just like his grandmother Fletcher. Maybe that's why school was so hard. Or maybe he really was dumb.

Just ahead, a woman was in the alley emptying a dirt pan from a sweeper. "Hey boy," she said. "You look strong. How about you come inside and carry out a box of old books for me. "I'll give you a nickel."

Eddie had a nickel. "I'll do it for a sandwich," he said.

She nodded and motioned for him to follow her. He was unhappy to learn the box was in her cellar. "I'll make your sandwich while you go down and fetch it."

When he was back in the woman's kitchen straining under the weight of the box, she held the door and he stepped carefully down the porch steps and back to the alley. She followed him with a sandwich in a paper bag.

"Go ahead and set it right there by barrel," she said.

"Why are you throwing out books," Eddie asked, taking the bag from her. Everyone in his world revered books like they were holy.

"They got soaked in that last rain we had. Water backed up. All ruined." She waved her hand. "Okay. Off with you now."

In his world, people said thank you when someone did something nice for you. He bit into the sandwich and tasted rancid butter. The meat tasted okay, so he ate that and threw the buttered bread to the ground. Some mangy dog would get it soon enough, he thought.

Before long, Eddie was far from his neighborhood in a grimy section of town populated by taverns and pawn shops. Eddie had passed through there three years earlier when he had tried to find Belinda. The little grocery where the woman had mocked him was now vacant, a "To Let" sign in its front window.

From a breezeway nearby came voices, and Eddie recognized the sound of a marble game. Eddie's mood lifted. Richie had taught him how to play, even though their father had warned them that boys who played gambling games grew up to be criminals. Eddie laughed. Richie was no criminal and never would have been. Eddie walked cautiously to the edge of the game. Three boys, younger than Eddie by the looks of them, stood near a chalk circle raggedly drawn on the pavement. Within the circle were a dozen marbles, ready for a new game.

"What do you want?" a wiry redhead asked Eddie.

"Get in the game?" Eddie asked tentatively, his nickel in his outstretched palm. Maybe Richie was up there somewhere looking down and would send Eddie a bit of luck.

"Where's your shooter?"

"Don't have one," Eddie said, flicking his fingers against the coin, now back in his pocket.

The redhead, who warmed his big cat's eye in his hands laughed. "Gotta have your own tonk to get in this game, so get lost." Then the redhead's chest thrust forward, his feet stumbling, as if someone had pushed him from behind. "Hey!" he said, looking around, then seeing no one, he shook it off.

"What's got you, Matty? A charley horse? Or just the spazzes," said another boy, who then doffed his cap and spoke more kindly to Eddie. "Sure kid. We're happy to take your money."

"But Frankie," Matty sputtered. "He ain't got a shooter."

"Then give him yours."

Matty sneered but held the marble in his outstretched hand.

"*Go ahead, take it*," came a voice. Eddie jerked his head around to see who had spoken, but there was no one there besides him and this group of boys. Then the voice spoke again. "*What have you got to lose*?" And that time Eddie felt the hair stand up on the back of his neck.

"Take it," Matty said.

So Eddie, who felt trapped in an eerie situation, accepted the shooter and made his play. He quickly lost, but instead of accepting his defeat, he convinced himself another try would bring him a better outcome. Unfortunately, his second bet wasn't backed by another coin, so he soon found out there was more than one way to repay a debt.

"What do you mean you ain't good for it?" Matty said. "What kind of lowlife are you?"

"You are the low—" A punch to Eddie's gut landed before he could get the last word out. Stunned, Eddie reeled back on his heels. When he reclaimed his balance, he advanced on Matty and hit him hard on the jaw.

Frankie and the other kid, as if fights with Matty were a common occurrence, kept their distance as Eddie and Matty threw punch after punch. Eddie landed the last one, and it sent Matty finally to the ground.

"I give," Matty said, wiping bloody snot from his nose. "But I better never see you around here again. Next time I won't go so easy on you."

Eddie brushed his hands off and stepped backwards until he was out on the street, where he turned and walked quickly away. That voice—"*What have you got to lose*" echoed in his throbbing head. This time, the sound was followed by a disparaging laugh.

Two blocks away, Eddie stopped to regain his composure. He wiped at his mouth, and grunted when he saw fresh blood on the back of his hand. Touching his lip, he could feel its puffiness. He saw now there was also blood on his shirt. He leaned against a limestone building until he saw a beat cop appear at the corner across the street. Eddie pushed off the wall and slunk away, out of sight.

It would be dark soon, and going home didn't seem like a good idea, but Eddie was feeling bad all over. That old lady's hunk of meat had started to churn in his stomach, and he wished he hadn't eaten it. Somebody ought to report her for doling out lousy food, he thought. His fingers fumbled in his pockets. Having no money made a fellow feel desperate. Walking endlessly solved nothing, and now a cold, sleet-filled rain had begun.

"Damn it!" Eddie muttered under his breath. He was stuck. There was no where to go but home. No matter how angry his father was, Eddie figured he wouldn't want his son to be out in the cold, alone on the city streets. Or maybe he wouldn't care. Eddie didn't know what to think.

A few blocks later Eddie brightened with a thought. Maybe by the time he got home, Pop would be up in bed. If so, it would be easy enough to sneak upstairs to his room. He had done it before. And if he couldn't get upstairs, he would slink down to the cellar. At least it would be warm and dry. Instead, Eddie found his parents in the kitchen, waiting. He was told to sit and not say a word.

"Disgraceful," Delmar said, as Naomi wiped the dirt and blood from Eddie's face.

She touched her finger to his lip, and he winced. "I don't think this will heal right," she said with a sigh. "You will have a scar." She dabbed iodine on the boy's split lower lip with tender caution.

"Doesn't it bother you, Edward, to see how distraught you've made your mother? The school matter was one thing, but going out and getting into a street fight? Have you no regard for this family? You were not raised to be a hooligan—"

Eddie jerked his head at the word and glared at his father. But he would not speak. He would not speak to his father ever again.

Upstairs, Naomi stopped at Eddie's door and nudged it ajar. His light was out, but she knew he was not yet asleep. She wanted so much to say something comforting to her son. Delmar had treated him unfairly, and yet, school was important. This chasm between them had to end.

"Things will be better in the morning," she said, feeling it was just a vain hope. Then she closed his door.

When she entered their bedroom, Delmar was already in his nightshirt. He moved toward her and tried to comfort her, but she pushed him away.

"Now, now, Naomi. I know I was hard on him, but he has to learn."

"Learn what? That his father has no patience? You berate him for fighting, but your own behavior was hardly acceptable."

Delmar's chin dropped. He shook his head. "I don't know what came over me. I was angry. And I think— It's just that since Richie died—"

"We all miss him, Delmar. We *all* do. You are not the only one who's hurting. You might try to remember that," Naomi said.

Delmar got into bed and turned off the lamp. He reached in the dark for his wife, but she turned her shoulder away from him. When she heard his breathing quiet into sleep, she pulled the quilt over her head and cried silently into her pillow.

At his mother's insistence, Eddie agreed to work with a tutor. A senior boy named Clinton met with Eddie two days a week after school. Right away Eddie felt better. Somehow when Clinton explained the causes of the Civil War, it made sense. He told it like a story, not a list of facts. Clinton even tried to help Eddie with English, but that effort was less successful.

"I can't read the book for you, can I?" Clinton said.

Eddie was hoping for something exactly like that. He thought if he could hear the words, he would understand them. Over the next few weeks, with Clinton's help, Eddie made some progress, though having a tutor didn't mean he was suddenly an A student.

After school one day, Naomi told Eddie there was no shame in having a tutor. "Everyone needs help one way or another," she said.

"Richie didn't," Eddie said, before gulping down a glass of milk. He had been craving milk for weeks. It felt good on his stomach which had begun to pain him daily.

Naomi thrust her finger at Eddie's face. "Just stop it," she said. "Stop using your brother as an excuse. You are not him. You never were, and no one expects you to be." The lie echoed in her ears. Delmar had expected it, and in many ways, he still did.

The anger with which his mother had spoken to him left Eddie feeling even more ragged, but he learned that if he kept his head down and his mouth shut, he could avoid aggravating both of his parents, so he let the matter drop.

For a time, things in the Reed home reached a peaceful equilibrium. The routines of life carried each one through the day. But the sometimes jovial times of the past when the family would share the events of their day and laugh about this thing or that were gone. Now it was all about doing one's duty. Earning a living. Keeping the home. Making the grade. Eddie felt like a robot at times—each day an exact replica of the one before. But if this new routine tamped down his pent-up frustration, Eddie knew he and his father could avoid an all-out war.

Chapter 19
May 1916

More than anything, Eddie wanted Pop to be proud of him, even a little bit. Then one day in May, everything Eddie had striven for unraveled, though if he had known the consequences of breaking his father's frayed trust, Eddie would have gritted his teeth a little harder and let Archie O'Connor's insult go. But it was Archie, whom Eddie had hated since kindergarten. He was an idiot then. He was an idiot now. And in hindsight, Eddie thought even Pop might not have turned his cheek.

That morning, after a game of basketball in gym class, the boys were headed to the locker room when Archie purposefully tripped Eddie, sending him to the floor.

"Hey, Reed. Maybe you need a tutor to teach you how to walk," Archie said, laughing.

"You shut up," Eddie said, on his feet now, face to face with Archie.

Archie continue laughing and raised his fists as if he were ready to box.

"Come on, Eddie. Forget him," another boy said.

But Eddie felt only black-out rage.

Archie never saw the punch that knocked him out. When the gym teacher cleared away the gawkers, he was starting to come to.

"Get yourself to the principal's office," the teacher shouted at Eddie.

Looking back, Eddie should have obeyed, but he didn't think anyone would understand that he had only been defending himself. While everyone knew Archie O'Connor was a bully, Eddie had a reputation too, and it wasn't a good one. So, still wearing his gym clothes, he walked to the main doors and left school, knowing he would never go back.

This time, instead of trying to run, Eddie went home and waited for the hammer to fall. When the phone call came to say that Eddie had been expelled, only his mother was surprised.

The hammer came in a strange form, but Eddie was in no place to complain about anything, not if he still wanted a room in his father's house and meals at his mother's table. Two days after his expulsion, Eddie did not grumble when his father woke him early and told him to get dressed. They drove south and by 8:00 a.m., they arrived at Union Stockyards, which Eddie thought they could have found by their noses alone. An acrid stench permeated the air, even blocks away.

"Pee ew," Eddie said.

"Better get used to it," Delmar said unsympathetically, as if the smell did not bother him.

They approached the main gate, a strong limestone edifice. A carved head of a steer crowned the arch of the main entry. In the early days, they drove herds of cattle right though here, Delmar explained. On each side were two smaller arched gates for pedestrians.

Delmar lifted his arms and gestured broadly. "Daniel Burnham designed this gate. Isn't it marvelous?"

"Who?"

Delmar glared at his son. "Burnham. One of the fellows who designed the Colombian Exposition."

Eddie thought the spires on each side of the main arch looked a little ridiculous, like ice cream cone capped rockets. But what did he know. "Oh him," he said.

"Yes, him. I've told you more than once about the time I attended the World's Fair, where I saw the white city he and others created out of—out of nothing, really."

Eddie nodded politely. Of course he knew. It was his father's favorite ongoing tale, about how most of the buildings had been constructed of plaster and cement, meant only to survive a short time. It was like an ancient city sprung again to life. When Eddie and Richie were boys, Pop had taken the family to see the Palace of Fine Arts and The Wooded Island, relics of the World's Fair. But Eddie had been very young, so his memories of that experience were hazy. It was the retelling of that outing and Pop's visit to the World's Fair as a young man that had turned Burnham and Olmstead and others into god-like men. And it was why he had wanted Richie to be an architect.

"Over there. That's the building we want," Delmar said after they were through the gate.

Minutes later, they stood in line in the hiring office. Ahead of them were seven or eight men. No one in line spoke, but all waited for their turn as if they were livestock themselves.

Eddie's stomach grumbled audibly, though the cause was nerves, not hunger. His father glared at him as if he ought to be able to control his stomach. When the slender man who'd been in line before them went through the office door, Delmar said, "You will be next. Make a good impression, Edward. It's this or you're out on your own. Do you understand?"

Eddie felt his knees threaten to buckle, but he would not show weakness. His father did not deserve it. Eddie would comply but he would do it without feeling. Without any emotion at all. Eddie would not give his father a chance to gloat.

The Reeds stood before Mr. Overton, who had grunted and waved them in. When prompted, Eddie handed the man the employment form he had filled out at the secretary's desk.

"I see you've not worked before," Overton said.

"He's helped me in—" Delmar offered.

"Just the young man, please," Overton said. "In fact, you can wait outside." Overton raised his hand and waved Delmar out to the waiting room. Then he read the boy's details again. "Not yet seventeen."

"In October," Eddie said.

"No diploma either? Well," he laughed, "this isn't a law firm." Overton placed the paper in a tray on his desk. "You outsize many of our men, and you look strong."

Eddie remembered the man in line ahead of them, his ashy complexion and how he had fumbled with the pen at the secretary's desk. In comparison, Eddie must appear like an Olympic athlete.

"We need you in the slaughterhouse. You think you could stomach that?"

Eddie shrugged.

"Say, do you want a job or not? Plenty of able bodies if you don't."

"Yes, sir. I can stomach that."

A gruff foreman Eddie did not see again for weeks, led him from the office and handed him over to Jimmy Nolan, a stocky middle-aged man, who showed Eddie his spot on the line.

"All right," Nolan said, his eye on a hog arriving on a conveyor hook. "Slit right down. Like this."

Eddie watched as slick, white globs fell from the pig.

"You look a little green," Jimmy said. "You'll get use to all this blood sooner than you can imagine. And don't forget, it's the likes of us who put pork chops on the nice folks' tables."

"Where does that go?" Eddie asked. "The guts."

"Ever eat bologna or a hot dog?" Nolan laughed.

"You're pulling my leg."

Jimmy Nolan made the sign of the cross. "God's truth, it is. You won't believe what they make out of some of this stuff."

When Nolan slit open the next animal, Eddie felt his stomach lurch. This is what he would be doing for days on end, ten hours or more each day. He watched Jimmy gut three more.

"Next one is yours, kid. Gotta work fast. No hesitation. That knife is sharp enough. Don't you worry about that."

In one long slash, Eddie replicated the move Jimmy had shown him, and the guts of his first hog spilled out into a tray on the conveyor belt.

"You see. Let the knife do the work."

Through the course of the day, Eddie met the men working around him.

"Good guys mostly," Jimmy said. "A lot of them don't speak English though. We got Irish like me, some Polish, Lithuanian, Austrian, and Czech. This is Samuel," Nolan said. "He's our squeegee man."

"Pleased to meet you," Samuel said.

Eddie nodded and said hello. "What is a squeegee man?"

"I push blood into drain."

"Then where?"

"I don't ask no questions. But there is a creek where I live, Back of the Yards, worse than a toilet that smells. All this gotta go somewhere, and it ain't going to Mr. Armour's neighborhood."

Jimmy and Samuel laughed.

One man down the line from Eddie was Otto Fuchs, an Austrian.

"Jew," Jimmy Nolan whispered to Eddie when Otto stretched out his hand to greet his new co-worker.

"I'm Eddie Reed," Eddie said, shaking the man's hand.

"Willkommen," Fuchs said.

Eddie had never met a Jew before, but it seemed to him that it didn't matter at all what religion a person was. Eddie was no religion at all. Delmar Reed believed church was a waste of a good Sunday. Otto seemed like a nice fellow, and even though his English wasn't good, it was Otto who warned Eddie about what can happen if he were careless. Otto's left hand was missing his last two fingers.

The men on the line kept their heads down and did their work. Samuel was the only one who sometimes hummed a tune while he used his squeegee to push the puddles of blood into the floor gutter, over and over and over. By the end of the shift, Samuel's arms and shirtsleeves would be splattered with blood. But they would all be splattered with blood to one degree or another. Eddie imagined how horrified his mother would be when she saw his clothes. Did not think of that, did you Pop? Eddie thought.

That afternoon, Samuel smiled at Otto as he worked behind him. Otto looked at the floor and shook his head. Then he pointed his long index finger and wagged it at Eddie. „Du hast einen guten Job. Du bist glücklich!" Otto said.

Eddie looked at the man in confusion.

„Du håst a goot Job. Du bis lucky!" Otto said, this time in something that sounded more like English.

"He said you are lucky," Samuel said. "You got a good job." Samuel shrugged. "I guess he don't like what the squeegee man do."

Eddie could not see that gutting pigs had any advantage. They all had backbreaking, bloody work. They all would go home stinking of the same shit.

The morning of Eddie's second day, he rose and ate the plate of food his mother had made. "You don't have to get up for me, Ma," he said. "This is not your punishment."

"I'll do as I like, thank you."

"Thank you for the oatmeal." Eddie poured cream over the steaming porridge. "And I'm sorry about my clothes. I don't know how—"

"Tonight, when you get home, go down into the cellar and strip. I'll have the wash tub full of water. Stick your things in there. Some of that—"

"Blood, Ma."

"Might never get some of it out, but you'll have clean clothes each morning. And I got you a terry robe to wear up to the bath.

Eddie bit his lips. "I'm sorry you have to do all of this."

Naomi sipped her tea. "How will you get there today?"

Eddie laughed and pulled a slip of paper from his shirt pocket. "Pop drew me a map." He traced his finger over it. "I'll take the trolley as far as

I can. Then walk."

"I will insist he drive you in winter," Naomi said.

Eddie smiled but didn't say that he did not plan to be working there that long. He ate his breakfast, then donned his cap. "I have to go, Ma. Jimmy says that if I am even a minute late, they'll dock me a whole hour."

"Jaysus, the lad is back. I'm glad of it," Jimmy said, greeting Eddie with a broad smile. "Though I owe Fuchs a dime. I bet him you'd quit after one day. He said you'd be back."

Otto's faith in Eddie made him feel good, and he waved to the Austrian as he took out his knife and got ready to work.

Chapter 20

April 1917

It was nearly 7:00 p.m. when Eddie arrived home. Though the sun had set, he saw his father sitting on the front porch steps, waiting for him. A tingle of apprehension rose in his head. His steps slowed, until he saw his father raise a dark bottle.

"What are you up to out here?" Eddie asked, facing his father.

Delmar handed Eddie a beer. "Mother's not up to making dinner tonight, so I thought the two of us could go to a diner."

Eddie took the church key and snapped off the cap. The beer was cold, and Eddie guzzled over half the bottle.

"What's wrong with Ma?"

Delmar took a sip from his beer. "There's no easy way to tell you this,Edward, but—"

"Just say it. She's sick again." Eddie remembered the times his mother had been in the hospital when he was a boy. But that was related to pregnancies, and that couldn't be the problem now.

"No. It's your Uncle Stanley."

Eddie's expression went flat.

"He was killed this morning in a motorcar accident. A collision with another car."

An expletive came to Eddie's lips, but with his father there, he did not express it. "I can't believe it," he said instead.

"It was a shock to your mother. And to me of course."

Eddie finished the beer but the last sip tasted bitter in his mouth. "Poor Ma," Eddie said. "I should go—"

"Later. She's in bed. When we get back, if she's awake, I'm sure she'll want to see you. This is going to be very hard for her." Delmar stood and held his hand out for Eddie's bottle. "Let's go get something to eat. You can tell me how the job's going."

"That's the last thing I want to talk about," Eddie said.

"Then we can talk about Stanley. Or not talk at all."

When they got to the corner, waiting for traffic to clear, Delmar asked, "You okay?"

"No. I'm not. Jesus Christ, Pop. Uncle Stanley—."

Chapter 21
May 1917

Eddie was on the trolley, in the back with a few other grimy workers. They had run out of hogs early today and been sent home. It was one of those rare evenings he would have dinner with his parents instead of alone with the plate his mother kept warm for him. Men with newspapers read about the war in Europe. The United States had officially declared war on Germany the month before and posters urging young men to do their duty could be found all over the city. Some of the men on the trolley were talking about enlisting.

"Gotta be better than fixing sewing machines all day," one man said.

"If I join the Navy, I'll be out on the ocean blue," another said. "Seeing the world."

"And when you get back, all dapper in your uniform, you'll be swatting off the dames."

Eddie smiled. All of that sounded swell. A hell of a lot better than gutting hogs.

At dinner Eddie reported what he'd heard. "I want to go. Do my part."

"Absolutely not," Naomi said. "I cannot lose you too. Besides, you're not old enough."

"I nearly am, and if you sign, I can—"

Naomi slammed her fist on the table. "I said no!" Then she thrust her chair back from the table and fled upstairs. Eddie could hear her sobbing.

"Guess you were born lucky," Delmar said. "Just young enough to keep yourself out of a bloody war. Unfortunately not lucky enough to know how to keep from upsetting your mother."

"But you get it, right Pop?" Eddie said hopefully. "You'll sign for me?"

Delmar expressed a sigh of exasperation. "Honestly, Edward. I wonder if anything will ever get through that thick skull of yours. No. She won't sign. I won't sign. You are stuck where you are. Get used to it."

Eddie got up from the table and slammed the back door on his way out.

For weeks afterwards, Eddie obsessed about ways to circumvent his parents, until one day at work, Jimmy Nolan overheard Eddie talking about his latest scheme.

"You listen to me boy," Jimmy said. "Them posters the government has up, the ones with Uncle Sam pointing his finger at you, are nothing but propaganda. You hear. You know what that is? It's a lie they tell you. They make it seem like fighting the Germans is going to be glorious. I'm telling you, it is no such thing." Jimmy's knife, now only inches from Eddie's face, dripped with blood. "You listen good," Jimmy said. "Those boys over there are getting massacred. You want to be one more tossed onto a heap of bodies? Nothing more than a hog carcass?"

Eddie felt his heart clutch in his throat. All he could do was shake his head no. The rest of the day, as Eddie worked, Jimmy kept a close watch. Finally, near quitting time, Eddie faced Jimmy and shouted, "Okay. I get it. You don't have to hound me."

"That's me good lad," Jimmy said, then he pulled Eddie to his blood spattered apron and gave him a fierce hug. "War is no kind thing, son," he spoke into Eddie's ear. "Don't you ever forget it."

Chapter 22

September 1917

By September, casualty reports began to include Chicago boys. The numbers of dead and wounded were too many for Eddie to ignore, and he no longer thought about enlisting. Instead Eddie found himself in the grips of another dilemma. His thoughts of the army, going to Europe, had been so real that he had convinced himself that he had finally found a way out of the slaughterhouse. But just because that door had slammed shut, his mind would not let go.

One afternoon, Eddie considered for a moment that he could go back to school, not high school, but one of those night classes where you could earn your diploma. That had been his mother's idea. But whenever Eddie thought about wedging himself back into a desk, he broke into a sweat of anxiety. Plus, how could he go from work to school? When would he sleep? No. There had to be some other way.

He could learn to fix engines, maybe? A couple of weeks ago when the overhead conveyor had chugged to a halt, one of the men on his line, a Pole, had tinkered with it and got it going, just as the shift mechanic saw him and asked "what do you think you're doing?" The Pole froze, holding the rod he'd used to dislodge a hoof. "Your job," someone shouted anonymously from down the line, eliciting a chorus of laughter. But because of his quick thinking, that Pole was now training to keep the line clear, and while he was still ankle deep in the slop, he no longer had to wield a knife.

I could learn a trade like that, Eddie thought. Or build? Carpenter, maybe. He could draw out plans? He had no training, but he was not bad at drawing, and hadn't Johnny's pop told him he was good with a hammer that time he had helped build the lean to? And the summer after that, they'd built a pigeon coop. And he'd been just a kid. He'd be even better now.

Eddie had begun to look at the help wanted ads in the paper. He had even ditched work today so he could check out a job at a west side carriage garage. The owner, after hearing Eddie had no experience, sent him on his way. Eddie had barely reached the sidewalk when he overheard the man say, "What a dumb kid."

Eddie felt more dejected than ever. There seemed to be no way to extricate himself from the stockyards, not without his father's help anyway. And that would mean admitting defeat.

Mid-afternoon, Eddie stood as the trolley neared his stop. He'd be home early, with clean clothes, but he had a story for that. Livestock stuck on a train in Iowa. They'd been let out early for situations like that before. He felt certain no one was going to call up his boss to verify his story.

Eddie hopped out onto the street and eyed the Jewish deli Ma liked. A knish would hit the spot right now. Unlike the area further beyond, where he had lost that marble game, this edge of his neighborhood was coming alive. New or rebuilt brick buildings held apartments above and shops below. Shops he had been in on his own or with his mother. Once with his father, who needed his watch repaired. Shops that never had "help wanted" signs in their windows.

A cry drew Eddie's errant attention.

"Thief!" shouted a man outside the jewelry shop, pointing to a young man who ran in Eddie's direction.

Eddie quickly intercepted the perpetrator. "Not so fast," he said, both arms tight around the struggling youth.

"You got him," said a breathless man in suit, who was now at Eddie's side.

By then the shopkeeper was there too, trying to reach into the boy's pockets.

"I got him, Gilberto," the man in the suit said. "You can go back inside. We'll settle up later."

Gilberto shook his head. "But he stole—"

"Yes. Now go on back before you end up getting hurt. You're just lucky I was in the vicinity."

Mr. Gilberto backed away, but when he got back to his jewelry shop, he remained outside under his storefront awning.

"I can go get the police," Eddie offered.

"No need," the man said. He shoved the youth to the ground and told him to stay there if he had any idea of keeping all his fingers. The boy snarled a look at the man but didn't make a move.

"Name's Nelson," the man said, extending his hand to Eddie.

Eddie returned the greeting.

"Around here, Ed, I am, or at least I—" Nelson coughed, "represent the law, and the watchmaker over there, well, I'm here to protect his business.

And he graciously pays me for my service." Nelson bowed as if he'd been thanked for his service. "This dummy— Hey you," he said, kicking the boy in his shins, "you must be from outta town."

"Whaddya think, Ed? Should I let this miscreant go or should I finish him off right here?" Nelson rubbed his hand over the lapel of his jacket, intimating the presence of a pistol.

Finish him off? Eddie thought with a wave of unease. Was he serious? The kid looked no more than thirteen or fourteen. "Seems like he's not going to cause more trouble," Eddie said. "That is, he's probably learned his lesson?" Eddie wished that instead of inserting himself into this situation he had minded his own business.

Nelson nodded, then pulled the kid to his feet. "Hand over the goods."

The boy laid a watch and a gold chain in Nelson's outstretched palm.

"If me or my friend ever see your mug around here again," Nelson said with his face close to the boy's, "it'll be the last time anyone sees you anywhere." He pushed the boy away, and the kid ran off.

"Well, I should—" Eddie said, taking a step toward home when Nelson grabbed him by the arm.

"That was fast thinking on your part," Nelson said. "And you got muscle."

Eddie felt the man squeeze his bicep. "Thank you," Eddie said, almost as a question. Nelson made him nervous. He seemed like one of those guys you didn't want to be on the wrong side of.

"Say," Nelson said as if he'd just struck upon a brilliant idea. "You in need of employment by any chance, Edward? I think the boss would like to meet you."

Eddie gulped. "The boss?"

"Yeah, I work for Mick Sheridan. You heard a him?"

Eddie had heard of him. Jimmy Nolan, who served as a sort of counselor to the new men, especially those who had very little English, had spoken about Sheridan at work one day. He said that guys who crossed Mick Sheridan sometimes disappeared. At the time, Eddie thought Jimmy was just telling tales as he often did. Now here he was, unwittingly pulled into Sheridan's orbit, all because he had done a good deed.

"Yeah, Mick's a good guy to work for. I help him keep the peace in these parts. Remind people, like that old watchmaker, that it's in their best interest to let us help them."

"I have a job right now," Eddie said. A job. He had a life sentence.

"Suit yourself kid. But a guy like you—tall, strong—I could really use what you got, as I ain't as young as I used to be."

For half a second, Eddie wanted to shoot his hand out to Nelson and shake on a new business partnership. The way Nelson dressed, his fine suit. Clean hands. But he couldn't work for a guy like Sheridan. How would he explain that to his parents?

Nelson leaned in confidently. "You think about it, why dontcha. I'm sure I'll be seeing you around one a these days." Nelson tipped his hat and walked toward the watch shop, jingling the jewelry in his hand.

Chapter 23

Saturday, October 13, 1917

Eddie had been working at the stockyards for one year and seven months. His body had somewhat adjusted to the work, but his mind was more unsettled than ever. While many of the men Eddie worked with were grateful for the work, Eddie still wanted out.

Today had been particularly hard. Mid-morning Otto Fuchs collapsed. Jimmy held Otto and gave him sips of water while they waited for the ambulance drivers. Eddie and the others spoke words of encouragement to their friend, but when Otto was carried out on a stretcher, they watched in silence.

"Back to work," the foreman barked.

Afterwards, an unspoken sentiment passed from face to face. *Otto would not be coming back.* Along with Jimmy Nolan, Otto Fuchs had been Eddie's savior in his early days. They more than showed him the ropes. They kept him from stepping on his own feet. It would not be the same without good old Otto.

As he did most Saturday nights to mark the end of a long work week, Eddie met Jimmy and a few others at a tavern for a beer. Tonight's gathering was somber, with no word yet on Otto's condition. They lifted their mugs to the man anyway.

It was nearly 9:30 p.m. when Eddie got home. After stripping off his clothes, he washed in the basement. Long ago Ma had set things up for him. A bar of soap, a fresh towel, pajamas, and clean clothes for the morning. She had even nailed a shaving mirror to the wall and put up a shelf, where he kept his comb and razor. When he was finished scrubbing off the day, his soiled clothes went into the wash tub, which he would cover with water. In the morning, she'd go down and wash things, just like she did every day, including Sunday.

When Eddie emerged from the cellar, he saw his father sitting at the kitchen table and a surge of bitterness rose in his throat. All he wanted to do was eat and go to bed.

"I thought you'd turned in for the night," Eddie said without concealing his disappointment. He took a bottle of milk from the ice box and poured himself a glass. Then he took his plate from the oven and set it on the table.

"It was a hard day, I take it?" Delmar said.

Still tired and sad, Eddie only muttered, "Yeah." He would not tell his father about Otto. He would not tell the man that there were others he cared about. Stories of work life were his alone, and he did not share them with his parents. He sat down and began to eat.

"You might not believe it, but I admire that you have stuck it out. I didn't think you would last a week."

"Is that what you think?"

"I think most men do what they have to do to put food on their tables."

"Your job seems pretty soft, though, doesn't it? Postmaster. I mean, what do you do all day besides make sure everyone else is doing their job? You probably never even break a sweat."

Delmar said nothing. Eddie watched his father, somewhat amazed that he had not taken the bait. He just sat there. Eddie felt self-conscious about every bite now. Why was his father so calm? What was on his mind?

"My father, your grandfather, for whom you are named—William Edward Reed—arrived in this country in 1849 at the age of eight. His father, Aidan Reed had been a miner in Ireland but the great famine drove him and my grandmother away."

"I've heard all this," Eddie said, thinking to stop the tale at the start.

"It's a good story," Delmar said. "About hard work. About doing what one must do, don't you think?"

Eddie could tell that he was going to hear it all again, whether he wanted to or not, so after finishing his last bite, he slunk down in his chair and stared at the ceiling.

"Mining was all my grandfather knew, so when he heard there was mining work in America, he scraped together passage. And where would I be if he hadn't come? Where would you be?"

"In Ireland?"

Delmar ignored him and continued. "My grandparents settled in Pennsylvania in a small community of immigrants, mainly Irish, but some Welsh, some German. He took a job in a coal mine. That autumn, a section of the mine collapsed, killing twelve men. Afterwards, there were some who set off for the Midwest, to farm country. But your great-grandfather stayed, because he had a family to support and he thought the journey would be too great a hardship.

"My father was younger than you when he started mining coal. It was the Civil War that got him back on the land for a time.

"I wish I could have known him," Delmar said. He was at the ice box now, taking out two bottles of Grolsch. He opened them both and handed one to Eddie, before continuing his story. Eddie took the beer gratefully and sat now with a bit more tolerance for the ancestral tale.

"In 1862, my dad, young Will, was conscripted into the army. He was only nineteen. My grandmother did not want him to go. No mother ever wants her son to go to war, but he had no choice."

"So was he killed in the war?" Eddie asked.

Delmar furrowed his brow. "Well if he had been, I'd never have been born. You know he wasn't. Miraculously he came home without a scratch. My grandmother always said her son was blessed. My father went back to the mines, met my mother a few years later, got married, and when my brother Richard was a baby, Will told his parents that he'd had enough of the mines and was moving his family to the Midwest to try farming.

Delmar sighed. "I know people can be unforgiving, Edward, but my grandmother never spoke to my father after that."

"Never?"

"Never. She said the war didn't spare him just so he could abandon his mother. My dad used to tell how he and my mom went back to Pennsylvania for my grandfather's funeral, and the whole time they were there my grandmother didn't speak one word to him. I know people can hold on to things, but that woman was like granite. She was eighty-two when she died and she never relented."

"She was probably lonely."

"I think she was too hard-hearted to be lonely, but if she was, she had no one to blame but herself. All my father wanted was to get out of the coal mine and see what kind of life he could make on his own."

Eddie did not express the thought in his mind. All he wanted was to get out of the slaughterhouse. Maybe he had more in common with his grandfather than just a name.

"In 1870, my parents and my brother moved to Illinois. They settled in Peoria and became tenant farmers, working for a childless widower named Joshua Roberts. By the time I was born, my dad found out that the old coal dust had gotten in his lungs after all. I was nine when he died. My brother Richard was thirteen.

"Mr. Roberts let us stay on the farm. Richard took over some of what my father had done. He loved that work, you see. And he was built for it. My mother took in sewing and even I helped by feeding chickens and gathering eggs. We managed as best as we could. Then a peculiar thing happened. You know this story too. My mother married Joshua Roberts, and we moved from the tenant house to his big house in town."

"And your brother was mad about that, right?"

Delmar nodded. "He thought my mother had betrayed our father. Plus, once we moved to town, Richard and I were done with work on the farm. We were told to put our efforts to our studies. Mr. Roberts was a big believer in education. I suppose I got my feelings about that from him.

"He was a kind man. I never had any problems with him, but your uncle did, and over time Richard's anger grew. My brother sometimes made things hard on our mother. She was caught between trying to please her husband and trying to do right by her son.

"If my brother had not been so hot-tempered, he would have realized what a great gift we'd been given. Instead, he quit school at fifteen and took a job with a farmer in the next county."

Eddie remembered the next part of the story. Richard had only worked on the farm for a month when a plow horse bolted and trampled him.

"I suppose you could say it was Rich's inexperience that killed him. I think it was his rashness. Had he stayed in Peoria, he might still be alive."

"Life is not fair," Eddie said.

"No. It is not. Life gives and takes. You know that as well as I do. It has been a long time since my brother died, and I am sad to say, I barely remember him. I barely remember my father. I don't think that is fair. And it wasn't fair that my mother got cancer and died when she was only fifty-four." Delmar let a moment of silence pass, as if what he wanted to say next would be hard. Looking directly at Eddie, he said, "I hope you will never forget your brother, Edward. Your mother and I think about him every day."

"I think about him too," Eddie said. Then he yawned, not out of boredom or disrespect, but simply from fatigue.

Delmar took pity on Eddie and came to his conclusion. "My point is, fortune is fickle. As a schoolboy, I did not know what kind of life I wanted. Mr. Roberts told me many times that I could take over the farm when I was older, so for a time, I thought I was destined to be a farmer whether I wanted it or not. Then my world changed course. I met your mother. She was so pretty, I knew from the moment she first smiled at me that I would marry her. I also knew I didn't want her to endure the life of a farmer's wife, so I started delivering mail. Not long after we were married, we moved to

Chicago, where I worked my way to postmaster."

"I didn't know that. About Ma, I mean."

"She was my angel. And we have made a good life here. Yes, my job is soft in comparison to the work my father and grandfather did. Soft compared with yours. But we never know what we are capable of until we're called to do hard things. Farm work is good work for some, but farming keeps your feet in one place, and I wanted to go places."

"But you never did."

Delmar smiled. "I had you." He sighed then pulled out a small box and slid it over to Eddie.

"What's this?"

"You won't know until you open it."

Eddie lifted the lid of the velvet case. "A watch?"

"A gift for you, from Mother and me. You will be eighteen tomorrow, or have you forgotten?"

Eddie had forgotten. He opened the case and saw his initials were inscribed. "EWR"

"Thank you."

Delmar nodded. "I know you work hard, son. But I hope it is work that has taught you something about what you are made of."

Eddie did not know what to say. He rubbed the gold case with his fingers. It was a nice watch. He wondered if it had come from Gilberto's shop. That same old man who'd come running out into the street a month ago, chasing the boy Eddie had taken down.

Chapter 24

October 14, 1917

It was past 10:00 a.m. when Eddie finally opened his eyes. A dream had startled him awake. He stretched and tried to remember, but only the vaguest sense of it remained. He was with that guy, Nelson, the one who'd asked him if he needed a job. Eddie shook his head. What was he—? Then a flash of the dream came to him. He and Nelson were running from the cops. They had a bag full of jewels they had stolen. They were the crooks, not that kid on the ground.

Eddie kicked off his covers and got up to get dressed. I should be in the movie business, he thought, with the wild dreams I have.

In the kitchen, Naomi was spreading white icing on a chocolate cake.

"What's the occasion," Eddie asked, opening the ice box door for a bottle of milk. The consequence of sleeping late was that he missed whatever big breakfast his father had enjoyed. A bowl of shredded wheat would have to suffice.

"Oh, stop pulling my leg," Naomi said.

Eddie dumped the wheat biscuit into his bowl. "Oh. My birthday," he said, remembering.

His mother laughed and handed him a rag for the milk he had splashed. "I sometimes forget how old I am," she said, "if that makes you feel better."

A few minutes later, a knock at the back door drew their attention. Naomi answered it. "Hello, Joe," she said. "Come in. Can I make you something to eat?"

"No. Thank you, Mrs. Reed."

"All right. I'll leave you two alone," she said.

"Hey. It's been a while," Eddie said, cereal still in his mouth.

Joe Crandall sat down. "Had to come wish you a happy birthday," he said. "Got you something."

"You're kidding. You didn't have to do that." Eddie pushed his bowl to the side and took the package Joe handed him.

"I did not actually buy it. It's a book off my shelf. Odd, I know, since you don't do a lot of reading."

"You can say that again."

"But I thought you'd like this one. It is illustrated."

Eddie tore the brown paper off a copy of *The Adventures of Huckleberry Finn*, then paged through the book. "Hey, this is neat. There's Huck. And Jim." In chapter seven Eddie saw a picture titled *Shooting The Pig*. "I know this story. It was Richie's favorite. This is when he uses pig blood to fake his own death, right, so he can escape his father?"

"Yes," Joe said. "That's one of my favorite parts too."

"Awfully thoughtful of you, Joe. I really appreciate it." Eddie laid the book on the table. "You sure you don't want something to eat?"

"Nah. I better go. My parents will be home from church soon, and I should be there. I got out of going by saying I didn't feel well, because just telling them I don't want to go doesn't work. Anyway, if I'm not home, it won't look too good for me will it?"

Eddie shook his head. "No, it won't."

"We should get together soon, though."

"You bet. Throw the ball around, like the old days," Eddie said. "Jesus, I make it sound like we're old men."

"Luckily we've got our whole lives ahead of us," Joe said. "Modern twentieth century men is what we are."

Eddie laughed. "That's right. I can see us now—tycoons. You'll be the new Rockefeller and I'll be the new Carnegie."

"Too bad you don't read, Eddie. With your imagination I think you'd really like it." Joe tipped his imaginary top hat, then bowed to Eddie. "Good day, sir."

"Good day to you, sir."

They both laughed and Eddie's heart felt lighter than it had in days. He watched Joe cross the yard then leave through the alley gate, and for the briefest moment, Eddie wanted to call Joe back. Instead he let the tether to simpler times fall from his hands.

After closing the door, Eddie opened the book cover and saw something he had missed earlier. On the flyleaf was written, "To my friend Eddie, Happy Birthday and Best Wishes on all your adventures. J. Crandall."

Damn Joe, Eddie thought. What a fine fellow you've turned out to be.

Chapter 25

November 1917

Sunday evening, just after supper, Eddie excused himself and said he was going out. "Don't wait up."

"Do we ever?" Delmar said in a dismissive tone.

"Stay out of trouble," his mother said, as if he were still fourteen.

Eddie left out the front door and closed it gently behind him. At the end of the block was Nelson, leaning against his car.

"You ain't had your supper yet, have you kid?"

Eddie said he had not, but the fried pork chop he'd eaten to keep up appearances sat heavily in his stomach.

"After you," Nelson said, opening the car door, pretending like Eddie was a big wig and Nelson his chauffeur.

Curiosity more than anything made Eddie go along with the charade. He wanted a glimpse of the life Nelson was offering. For about an hour, Nelson drove around, showing Eddie some of the businesses they protected. "They're all pretty swell fellas. No one grumbles too much. They just pay up, and we all get along fine."

Entering Sheridan's night club, Eddie felt immediately that he did not belong. A cocktail waitress met them at the door and handed them a drink in a fancy glass. "Compliments of Mr. Sheridan," she said.

Eddie stared at the drink in his hand, then watched the most alluring woman he had ever seen disappear into a host of tables filled with glittering people dressed in fine clothes. Beyond the sea of tables, rose a stage, where a ragtime band tuned its instruments.

"Martini," Nelson said. "Drink up. There'll be more at the table. I guarantee it."

A waiter appeared and said, "Hello, Mr. Nelson. Mr. Sheridan is expecting you," the he said, then he led the way.

Mr. Nelson. Eddie had just assumed Nelson was the man's first name, not his last. He had also made assumptions about what Mick Sheridan would look like, envisioning him as a giant of a man with movie star looks. The kind of man people remarked on and admired. So when the real Sheridan stood to shake Eddie's hand, Eddie worked to conceal his disappointment. Sheridan was five inches shorter than Eddie, at least.

And what he lacked in height he made up for in girth. Not that he was a fat man, just stocky, like a wrestler. Sheridan looked like he could pick up a man twice his size and easily toss him aside. Though his mud brown hair no longer covered the top of his head, it grew in an abundant mustache, which he twisted into a handlebar shape at each end. It was Sheridan's icy blue eyes that unnerved Eddie, though at the time, the man was nothing but congenial.

"Pleasure to meet you, Edward. Please," Sheridan said, gesturing to the big corner booth where he had been sitting, "Join me."

"Nelson," Sheridan said.

"Sir," Nelson answered.

"I hear you've been at the stockyards," Sheridan said. "We had a guy from there once. A boxer on the side. You ever box?"

"No," Eddie said, like a teenager whose voice was breaking. "No, sir."

"Boss was a middleweight champ," Nelson said as if crowing about his own accomplishments.

Sheridan waved off the remark. "Those days are long gone."

Ten minutes later, the waiter returned with their dinner—thick Porterhouse steaks with peas and mashed potatoes topped with pools of butter. "I ordered this earlier. Figured you wouldn't turn down our house specialty." He said it in a way that meant he expected everyone to be grateful.

"Looks great, as usual, Boss," Nelson said.

Was Eddie expected to be this—he didn't know the word for it, but *agreeable* came close. It was as if Nelson was afraid of making the wrong move, afraid to say or do anything to contradict Sheridan. He'd been a tough guy on the street, but now Nelson seemed almost timid. It was only a role, Eddie concluded, part of the game. He gave Nelson a smile, and Nelson nodded, as if an understanding had been reached.

As Eddie stared at the huge steak, he also knew he would be expected to finish the meal before him. One bite at a time, he thought. At least it looked delicious.

"Your Mr. Armour makes some fine beef," Sheridan said.

Mr. Armour didn't make anything but money, Eddie thought.

"Another round, sir?" the waiter asked.

Sheridan lifted his empty glass and nodded. "Now, let's eat. We can talk business later."

When Nelson dropped Eddie off at home just after midnight, Eddie was more inebriated than he'd ever been, enough that he barely remembered the ride across town. Martinis were a lot stronger than tavern ale. Something else he'd have to get used to, he concluded.

"It's going to be great working with you, kid," Nelson said. "Now go get a good night's sleep. Tomorrow, you can say goodbye to the stockyards for good. Then sleep in on Tuesday. I'll pick you up about two-ish and we'll start easy with a few collections."

"What'll I tell Ma and Pop?"

Nelson shrugged. "As little as possible."

"I'm serious."

"Tell 'em you are the new doorman at the club. That'll explain your strange hours. You can tell 'em you met me at the tavern, and when I saw how big and strong you are, I offered you the job. Believe me, when you start bringing home the kind of dough I make, your folks'll be so happy they won't care what you're up to. And if not, I'd say it's time to move out on your own. You aren't a kid, you know."

For now, nightclub doorman was a plausible story, even though Eddie was certain his parents would eventually see through the lie. If it came to it, he would have to find his own place. But that was down the road. One step at a time.

The next step was leaving the slaughterhouse without too much commotion. Jimmy Nolan had warned the crew about Sheridan, and Eddie didn't want to hear that he was making a big mistake. Besides, now that Eddie had actually met the man, he thought Jimmy's tales about the club owner were exaggerations. Nevertheless, it was better to not say a word, and that way he wouldn't have to explain, or lie, which he wasn't very good at. The thought of leaving the men Eddie he had grown close to made him sad, but it couldn't be helped. Besides, they'd soon forget all about him.

There was just one thing Eddie wanted from the slaughterhouse before he vanished, and that was his knife. After each shift, as they walked off the line, those who used knives cleaned them then laid them in a drawer, where they remained until the next day. Once a week, all the knives were sharpened.

To the boss, one knife was the same as the next, but each man's knife had conformed to his use, though to make it easier to find each morning, some of the men had marked theirs, generally with just their initials. Jimmy had carved a small cross in the hilt of his knife. Eddie's knife had a distinctive streak in the bone handle, and he thought that was good enough. If a man picked up a knife that was not his, he knew it, just from how it felt in his hands.

Today had been a long day, twelve hours. Eddie had counted on the men being in good spirits as they usually were on their way out for the night, but they looked so dragged out, he wasn't sure his plan to nick his knife would work. He had to try anyway.

Eddie began his diversion by telling a dirty limerick, hoping others would take up the game. It was something they often did at the tavern. The man whose joke caused the greatest groan, would be treated to a pint.

"Ah, Edward, it's not the time for shenanigans," Jimmy said.

But Eddie wasn't ready to give up. "You didn't like that one, eh." He told another, which elicited guffaws.

Then one of the men near the back voiced his joke, and afterwards another man chimed in too. Eventually Jimmy jumped in with his own offering, and everyone's eyes were on him. Jimmy's Irish stories were the crown jewels. It's what Eddie had counted on.

With Jimmy rising to the punch line, no one saw Eddie pull a rag from his shirt and wrap it around the blade, before slipping the knife up his sleeve. Just before it was Eddie's turn to lay his knife in the drawer, he shouted loudly, "Jaysus, Jimmy, you're a nasty one." Everyone laughed even harder at Eddie's imitation that no one paid any attention to the fact that Eddie had not placed his knife in with the rest.

By that time the shift foreman had had enough, and he shouted for the men to hurry it up.

Outside, a few of the men were still snickering over the jokes.

"See you tomorrow," Jimmy shouted. "Me missus is waiting under the covers for me."

Eddie wanted to clasp Jimmy's hand, or thrust his arms about the man and squeeze hard with an embrace that would say what he could not say. Instead he said, "Not if the milkman got there first."

Jimmy laughed. "See you, kid," he said, then he sauntered off on his way to where he lived, Back of the Yards.

At home in the basement, after he washed, and dressed in his clean pajamas, Eddie unwrapped the knife and scrubbed it clean. Then he rubbed his towel over the blade and bone handle until it shone. The knife was a fine thing. Sharp. Gleaming. And he was glad he had not marred it with a carving. But it wasn't a souvenir. Eddie wanted the knife to remind him that he'd done a hard thing—and he had not failed.

Eddie was little more than Nelson's shadow the first few weeks on the job. He was there to learn the ropes. Now and then, Eddie held a guy's arms behind his back while Nelson relayed his message, inches from the goon's face. "Goon. Punk. Skunk. Stool Pigeon." There was a lot of new lingo to learn. Being a tough guy did not come naturally to Eddie. He'd pounded Archie, but that had come on suddenly, out of rage. He hadn't planned out in advance how he would take Archie down. But that's often what he and Nelson did. They talked about their strategy before hand.

Eddie was generally the one who held a guy down, while Nelson said how it was going to be. Sometimes, when Eddie let a guy go, he would look at Eddie as if he would live to regret it. Such looks always unnerved him, and he told Nelson about it one night.

"Looks don't kill, son," Nelson said, "but you being afraid might. Anything that takes your mind off the job is dangerous."

"I guess that's right," Eddie said. "Even so, I need a pistol."

"Need to learn how to use it first, so you don't end up shooting me," Nelson said, "but sure, I'll get you one."

When he got home that night, Eddie lifted the loose floorboard under his bed and retrieved his knife. This morning, he had bought a leather sheath for it, and now he used an old belt to fashion a sort of holster. The contraption felt awkward, but until he got his gun, it would have to do.

A few days later, Eddie and Nelson listened as Gilberto described the guys who'd shaken him down that morning for a hundred bucks. The old man was so frightened he had paid.

"You are supposed to protect me," Gilberto said, scowling at Nelson.

"You are supposed to be smart," Nelson said. Then he shrugged his shoulders. "All right Gilberto. Here's your dough." Nelson slipped his money clip off and gave the old man the man two fifty dollar bills.

Gilberto gave a short, satisfied bow, then he retreated to his shop.

"It's the Weasel," Nelson said. He's done this before. Thinks he can just take over my territory.

"Weasel in," Eddie said.

"Ha. I never put that together," Nelson said. "Guess so. But he's sneaky too. And he'll bite."

Eddie expressed confusion.

"He shoots first and thinks second."

"So, what's his angle going after our people?"

"I like how you say that, Edward, 'our people.' He wants my job, is what I'm thinking. Wants to get in with Sheridan. I guess it's time to show him what's what."

A few nights later, Nelson and Eddie found Weasel at a diner on Central, sitting in the front window as if he owned the place.

"Looks like he's got himself a new punk," Nelson said moving out of the Weasel's line of sight. "We'll wait in the car, then follow them."

As Nelson lit up a smoke, Eddie felt for his knife. Secure and ready, but no match for a gun. He felt deep waves of anxiety for the first time on the job with Nelson. Not that it'd come to a stand-off. Nelson would probably just have a conversation, impress upon the man how dangerous it was to be "weaseling in." At least Eddie hoped that would be all. He slunk down in the seat, anxious every time someone walked by.

Twenty minutes later, Weasel and his sidekick emerged from the diner. They crossed the street and got in their car. Seconds later, Eddie and Nelson were on their tail. It had begun to spit rain and Nelson's wipers smeared damp dust over the windshield. Eddie perched forward in his seat and kept a keen eye.

"Left," he said, and Nelson made a sharp turn.

Several blocks ahead, Eddie spotted Weasel's car slowing down to pull under a trestle for the L. Nelson killed the headlights then drove slowly under the tracks, and Eddie felt his stomach lurch. They parked alongside a concrete pier, close enough to observe Weasel. He and his kid were out of their car now, smoking.

"Look," Nelson said. "He's got a bottle of hooch. We ought give it time to kick in, dontcha think?"

"Evening," Nelson said, at Weasel's side now.

"Saw you come in, boys," Weasel said. "Saw you all the way from the diner. You come for the libations, Nelson?"

"Came to ask what you were doing with a certain old watchmaker."

Nelson's question had been simple enough, but it must have put fear into the kid, for he took off running.

"Take care of him," Nelson shouted to Eddie, after pulling out his gun and aiming it at an inebriated Weasel.

Eddie took off after the kid and found him about a hundred yards away on the cindered-ground, breathing hard and rubbing his ankle. As Eddie stood over the kid, he knew exactly what "take care of" meant. It had been drilled into his head. He knew that an order from Nelson was an order, and as light-hearted as Nelson could be, Eddie was certain that not following his orders would be unwise, at the very least. Eddie felt sweat overtake his entire body. He had never "taken care of" anyone before, and as he gulped his fear down, Eddie realized he didn't want to do it now.

"Leave me alone, you thug," the boy said with a growl.

Overhead a train shook the iron trestle and steam hissed from the engine. The rumble of a train drew Eddie's attention momentarily upward, and in that split second, the boy was up, pointing a pistol at Eddie.

"You don't want to do that," Eddie said, but his words were erased by the sound of the gun ringing in his ear. Eddie stood motionless for a moment, not understanding what had happened. Then he saw the tear in his jacket and felt the sting in his forearm. Eddie's fear gone, he retrieved his knife and sneered at the boy.

"Keep away or I won't miss the next time," the boy said.

Eddie watched the boy fumbling with his gun. A round in the chamber had jammed, and Eddie heard the empty click of the trigger. Without hesitation, Eddie plunged forward, and with the knife that had gutted pigs, he made no mistake about where his blade needed to go. The sound of the train obscured the boy's cry, and no one saw him fall, or saw Eddie as he stabbed again.

The rain came down hard now, and Eddie left the bloodied boy where he lay, his eyes open in their dead stare. It was a look he would never forget.

When he returned to where he'd left Nelson, Eddie stared at Weasel on the ground, blood seeping into the white front of his shirt.

"Forget him," Nelson said. "We gotta get out of here.

As they squealed away, Eddie's heart pounded with adrenaline.

"You hurt bad?" Nelson asked.

Eddie shook his head. "I don't think so," he said. "Messed up my coat though."

Then after Nelson's jalopy careened around the corner, Eddie said, "I need that gun. And it better be a good one."

"Sure thing, kid. And I know a tailor who can make that tear look invisible."

Eddie exhaled a deep breath.

"How's it feel? Getting the first one out of the way."

Eddie shrugged. He was not about to tell Nelson that he had never felt more alive.

Chapter 26

September 1918

In early September, an article appeared in the newspaper about sailors at the Great Lakes Naval Training Station becoming ill with a new virulent strain of influenza.

At breakfast, Naomi read the details to her husband.

"I shouldn't worry too much, dear," Delmar said. The training station is way up in Waukegan. And you say they've got those sailors isolated."

"Nevertheless, it does sound alarming," she said.

Delmar took the paper from her and skimmed the article himself. "See here," he tapped the paper. "This doctor says common sense and good hygiene are called for."

By September 30, there were at least 260 cases of influenza in the city, and everyone was worried.

"Some are dying now," Naomi said that night at dinner.

Delmar agreed that the situation did seem to be getting worse. Then he told his wife what he had learned at worked that day. The greatest number of cases were in the overcrowded, poorer areas of the city.

"That's awful," she said.

Delmar set down his fork. "I agree, but I say it only to reassure you that if we take precautions, we should be just fine."

Chapter 27

Monday, October 7, 1918

By early October, the influenza that had hit the naval training base so hard was rampaging its way through Chicago. And Delmar's conviction that it would affect only the poor and indigent had been proven false.

"They're talking about quarantines," Delmar had said. "It'll be hard on business if they do that."

Naomi had wanted to say that people dying would be hard on business too, but she did not want to aggravate her husband. This morning, he had gone off to work with no trace of concern.

And Eddie, Lord only knew what she was going to do about him. At 3:00 a.m. she had heard his bedroom door close. Not long after, she got up to use the bathroom and lingered a while at his door. Wrinkling her nose at the odor of cigars and whiskey, she shook her head. What could she do? He was a man now.

This morning Naomi had done everything she could think of to quietly busy herself while Eddie slept. When the doorbell rang at eleven, Eddie had still not come down, but she was not going to tip toe around any longer. It was nearly noon for goodness sake.

Cyril Crandall was at the door, wearing a white muslin face mask and carrying a basket.

"Good morning, Naomi."

"Same to you, Cyril." Naomi looked behind him for Esther, who was nowhere to be seen.

"I come bearing gifts," he said, lifting the basket slightly. "Face masks for the Reed household. You may have heard that health officials are advising everyone to wear them now, even those of us who are healthy." Cyril handed Naomi a paper sack. "There are a half dozen in there. If you need more, let me know."

"Thank you," she said, accepting the bag. Naomi was well aware of the mask campaign. Delmar had ranted about it when he learned of the plan. "They can't make us wear those ridiculous things. How would I do my job?"

"A mask might be the only thing that saves us," Cyril said. "Have you seen today's paper? Over 300 dead yesterday. And it isn't just older folks.

People our age and younger are dying now too."

"It certainly is distressing news," Naomi said.

Then, even though she had not asked, Cyril explained why he was the one at her door. He had volunteered to distribute the masks to their part of the city. "Esther was dead set against it. She won't leave the house. She's even afraid to open the door for the newspaper."

"You were good to volunteer, Cyril," Naomi said before wishing him the best of luck.

"Thank you. I appreciate you saying so."

As Cyril bounded down her porch steps, Naomi was hesitant to shut the door. The autumn air smelled so good. If Delmar had not already taken the screen door down to the cellar for the winter, she would have left it open.

Naomi opened the paper sack and peered inside. "I hoped you little masks are not too late to keep us safe." Naomi pictured Delmar wearing one at work, trying to greet customers, trying to be charming, and she almost laughed out loud. Then she put the sack on the shelf of the coat rack before returning to her feather duster.

Monday mornings were busy at the post office, so at 9:00 a.m., when Delmar's head sorter, Jakub, had still not shown up for work, Delmar got worried and decided to call the Dvorak home. A young girl answered the telephone. The phone in their apartment was something Delmar had made happen the year before. He had told Jakub he wanted them to have the phone in case he needed to get in touch with Jakub for some sort of work emergency. The real reason was that Delmar Reed did not want any of his employees to be without life's necessities. What if the Dvoraks needed a doctor in the middle of the night? What if one of their children came down with appendicitis?

"Are you Maren?" Delmar asked the small voice on the line. Maren was the youngest of Jakub's three children. Little Maren had just turned five and was not yet in school. Delmar knew the entire family, by name and age anyway. The eldest son, Arno, had finished his schooling and was now a masonry apprentice. The middle child, Natálie, was in grade school.

"Ano," she said. "Yes."

"Is your Papa home? Can you tell him I am on the line?"

"Tati is sick. Mami too. They got a cough."

"Is Arno there? Let me speak with him."

"He is working. Natálie is at school."

Delmar felt the hair on his neck rise. "Stay away from Mami and Tati," Delmar said with urgency. "Do you understand?" He could hear only the child breathing on the other end. "Did you hear me, child?

Maren's voice trembled. "Ano."

"Do not worry. I will call the doctor," he told the girl. "Hang up the phone, now."

Delmar stuck his head through the assistant postmaster's door. "I have to leave for a while, Karl. I need you to take over out there."

One of Delmar's best workers, Jakub Dvorak, a sturdy Bohemian fellow, had a jovial personality and was well liked. This past Friday morning, as he did every Friday, Jakub had arrived with a box of poppy seed kolaches. "From Hana for the boys," he said. The week before they had been made with raspberry preserves. Everyone at Delmar's branch looked forward to Fridays and Hana's pastries. Somehow, they all worked faster on Fridays. Delmar tried to remember the other details of that day. Had Jakub seemed off? Less good-humored? Tired? No. Nothing in how Jakub behaved that day gave Delmar any idea the man wasn't feeling well, so this news that both he and Hana were ill came as a shock.

The Dvoraks lived on the third floor of a four story building in a Czech neighborhood, flanked by several buildings exactly like theirs. Delmar held his handkerchief over his face as he opened the main entrance and began the climb. At each new story, a variation of odors emanated, some sweet and cinnamon-y, some savory like meat and onions, some like sour sickness.

He knocked on their door, number 301, and immediately a curly-headed blonde with big brown eyes answered. When she saw Delmar, she began to sob. "Mami," she cried. "My mami."

Delmar took the child's hand and squeezed it, then settled her on the sofa in the living room, a small but clean and comfortable room. He went to the windows and slid open the sashes. The Dvorak apartment overlooked the street, and Delmar searched the sidewalk below for any sign of a doctor.

A horse's clip clop got his attention, and seconds later a wagon appeared, a hearse with one pine coffin on its bed. Such wagons were everywhere, but this one appearing now was a bad omen, Delmar thought.

"You stay here, Maren. I will talk to Tati."

Delmar called out "Jakub" as he walked toward the bedroom. "It's Mr. Reed."

Jakub came out wearing a crumpled nightshirt. His pale, unshaven face contorted in anguish. "No, no, boss," Jakub said, holding out his palms to obstruct Delmar's movement. "Not good."

Delmar nodded, then he stepped back and went to the open window. Jakub stumbled into the living room and sank into a chair. Maren flew off the sofa and thrust herself into his arms. Jakub squeezed his daughter, then said. "You go back, now. Sit."

The girl obeyed without a word, and Delmar looked upon her with heartache. How awful this influenza was, not just for the sick, but for their families too.

"What I am going to do without my Hana?" Jakub said.

"Are you certain, Jakub? That she's—gone?" The unspoken answer was clear. Delmar stood speechless as he looked into the man's tear-filled eyes.

Jakub held his head in his hands. Then a spasm took him, and he covered his coughs with a handkerchief. When he regained his breath, he said, "You go now. I don't want you get sick."

"No." Delmar said defiantly. "Not until the doctor arrives."

Minutes later, Maren went to the kitchen and returned with a glass of water, which she held out to Delmar. "Thank you," he said. Instead of taking a drink, he set the glass on the window sill.

A knock at the door brought Jakub to his feet.

"You sit. I will get it," Delmar said.

It took only minutes for the doctor to verify Hana's death, Jakub's infection, and the threat to Maren and Delmar. "This paper—" the doctor held out a pamphlet. Then he considered Jakub. "Can you read English?"

"Ano. But Arno better. My boy."

"Show him. It says you must wash your hands. Clean with disinfectant. And wear these." Out of his bag, the doctor took two masks, handing one to Jakub, tying one on Maren. He also insisted Delmar take one. More for the rest of the family, he set on the table.

"Probably too late to do any good," the doctor said in Delmar's direction, "but it's all I can do for them."

Delmar had hoped for better news. "I understand."

"You should go now," the doctor said. "I will wait for the hearse."

Before he left, Delmar turned to Jakub. "When Arno comes home, tell him to call me. I will do whatever I can to help." Delmar pitied the man before him, far too young to be a widower. It wasn't right. "You must get well, Jakub. Your children need you more than ever now."

Chapter 28

October 10, 1918

The shrill whistle of the teakettle roused Eddie from sleep. He had been at his father's bedside all afternoon and had nodded off. The rain, relentless, had run in rivers upon the windowpane all day. It was now near dark, and his father's breath had slowed to an almost imperceptible wheeze. Eddie rose from the chair near the window and looked down onto the street. Strewn with wet leaves, it was amber colored under the streetlight.

"Tea is ready," Naomi called from the foot of the stairs.

"Be right there."

In the bathroom, he splashed water on his whiskered face. The light over the mirror made his face look sallow, deepening the dark circles under his eyes. He would turn twenty in only a few days. Drying his face, he thought, I look so much older. Before going down, Eddie ran a comb through his thick black hair, heavy with pomade. He thought of Nelson's balding head and laughed. "I guess it could be worse."

In the kitchen Eddie sat across from his mother.

"Is he any better?" Naomi asked, pouring her son's tea.

Eddie poured a small splash of milk into his cup. "His breathing sounds worse, ragged."

"Shouldn't we call the doctor?" Naomi asked.

Eddie dipped a cookie into his cup and let the brown liquid wick into it. "He's already been here. He's done all he can do." It sounded callous.

"I know. And you're right." She pushed a platter of leftover roast beef and carrots towards her son. "You should eat more than cookies."

He took the serving fork and transferred a small amount of both to his plate, then pushed the platter back to her. If anyone needed to fortify herself, it was his mother. She had grown so thin. Her house dress hung loosely from her shoulders. Uncle Stanley's death had been the start of it. She didn't eat for days after she got that news. The pendant light over the table lit silver strands in her dark brown hair. Despite a few indicators that she was aging, his mother had always seemed so young, especially compared with his father, who had turned white in his mid-thirties.

Eddie's parents had sometimes joked about Naomi marrying such an old man. It was funny, Eddie learned, because his mother was the older of the two by seven months. His parents' ages had meant nothing to Eddie as he was growing up. They were just his parents and he had not been curious about them as children. But they were his age once and not so long ago.

Naomi lifted her cup and sipped. "I wish there was more we could do."

Eddie nodded and chewed his food. He thought of Mrs. O'Brien who lived down the street and believed burning incense would kill the disease. At night when her lights were on, it looked like her house was on fire with all the smoke from the potions she burned.

Steam curled from the spout of the teapot as delicately as the hand-painted flowers encircling its ivory bowl. Eddie lifted it and held one finger on the lid to keep it in place as he filled his mother's cup before taking the remainder for himself. She had eaten the rest of the carrots but left a slice of beef for him. He offered her the plate of cookies, but she shook her head no. Eddie set the plate down, then rolled the crick out of his neck. He wished he could make things easier for his mother. Goodness knows he had been the source of her heartache over the years, though this disease had nothing to do with him. People who said it was a curse on the wicked were wicked themselves.

"He loves you, you know," Naomi said, breaking the silence that had settled between them.

"He loved Richie. I was always a disappointment."

"That's not true."

"You don't have to try to make me feel better about him, Mother. His dying doesn't change the fact that he never thought much of me." Eddie winced and cocked his head. "I used to care. Used to crave his approval. But—"

"I wish you wouldn't say these things. He's your father and—"

"He is who he is. I am who I am. We both should have stopped expecting anything else a long time ago."

Naomi rose and went to her son. She put her hands on his shoulders, then leaned in to kiss the top of his head. "He might not always have understood you, but he never stopped loving you."

Eddie put his hand on hers. I know, he wanted to say, but he couldn't.

"I should go up," Naomi said. After setting the dishes in the sink, she pulled her mask from her pocket and tied it on. "Better put yours on too."

Eddie adjusted his mask, just as she had asked.

"Delmar," Naomi called quietly when she entered the bedroom. Her husband did not answer, and for a moment she wondered if he was already gone, but when she touched his forehead, he called her with a low moan from deep within. She swished a clean cotton rag in an enamelware basin before wringing the water out.

"There, there," she said as she wiped Delmar's face and neck, "Doesn't that feel better?"

His fever had not lessened as she had hoped. The cruel irony of such a terrible sickness. His skin so hot, and yet he visibly shivered. Naomi knew that paradox herself—burning up and freezing all at once. She took a blanket from the armoire and Eddie helped her cover him. She leaned in and kissed his forehead through her gauzy mask.

"Don't you leave me," she whispered. "Don't you dare leave me. I'm not ready to be alone."

"Come on, Ma. I don't think you should be so close. I'll stay with him." Eddie pulled her wrist, but she resisted.

"Just a little longer," she said. "What if—"

Eddie realized he would not persuade her. "All right, but just for a little while. I'll be back soon, and then you need to sleep."

Naomi nodded. She sat on the edge of the bed and drew her husband's hand from under the blanket. As she kneaded his fingers, he moaned in recognition, from pain or from her tenderness she could not know. Even this tiny kindness was pitiable, she thought. What lasting benefit? There was none. Naomi had never felt so helpless.

Naomi sat on the bed in Richie's old room, almost too weary to lie down. She had been sleeping in there since Delmar got sick. But the room was more than isolating, it was heavy with memory too. When they'd first bought the house, her two boys shared this room, first in their cribs, then later in twin beds with matching quilts and hand-stuffed feather pillows. Her boys. They'd been inseparable until suddenly they were adversaries. How quickly babies grew into irascible teenagers. How quickly their innocence turned to guile.

After changing into her nightgown, Naomi turned down the bed covers, then she looked out the window at the house next door. She hadn't spoken to Esther in over two weeks, but she had seen Cyril come and go as he usually did, so she assumed the Crandalls had escaped this awful influenza. Cyril had led the mask brigade, after all. Tomorrow she would telephone them. Or the next day.

Lying awake in the dark, Naomi stared at shadows on the ceiling. In the hallway, she heard the toilet flush, then Eddie's steps to his room. Her body hummed with fatigue, and no way she turned brought her comfort. She said prayers, but they felt hollow, desperate. She had not been to church since Delmar had resolutely refused to go, saying he no longer cared to be told what a sinner he was. His declaration one Sunday when the boys were still very young had shocked her. Church was the obligation of every good person, wasn't it? But he had argued that if ministers felt so confident that we were all born evil, what was the point of living at all. And once Delmar had made a decision, he rarely changed his mind.

She had admired his confidence when she first met him. How sure he was of the world, at a time when life often frightened her. She had been on a loose footing since her mother disappeared when Naomi was only thirteen, and Delmar gave her a sense of balance. If she disagreed with him now and then, she remembered how often he was right.

She thought now of how Delmar looked when they had first married. His dark hair parted down the center, a small wisp of a mustache, and the way he smiled whenever he looked at her. No hint of the paunch he'd soon carry around his middle. She had been twenty-two and completely unprepared for married life. But she felt safe in his arms.

When they first moved to Chicago, they lived in a tiny apartment with a shared bathroom, a place with barely a kitchen and walls so thin they could hear the neighbors—their snores and tussles and worst of all, their crying babies. But she had liked that little third-floor apartment. It was hers and she could easily arrange it and decorate it however she wanted.

In 1899, Delmar was promoted to postmaster, giving them the means to buy their own house. When Delmar had first shown her this one, she thought four bedrooms, a living room, and a parlor was too much of a house for their small family, but as Richie toddled across the polished oak floors, Delmar patted her growing belly and said, "it won't be small for long." Twenty years it had been since that day. Naomi lay on her side, listening through the darkness for her husband's breath until she could no longer keep her eyes open. "All I ask is twenty more," she prayed.

Chapter 29

October 11, 1918

Naomi woke and looked at the clock. Past nine! She stretched and yawned, embarrassed to have slept so late. Was it Friday? The milkman would have delivered. If Eddie had forgotten, the milk and cream would still be out in the box. The rain had stopped, but everything outside was still drenched. As she tied her robe, she saw a bold, black crow perched on the bare limb of the linden tree outside the window. The stillness of the house became suddenly unmistakable, and she knew why Eddie had let her sleep so long. There was no reason to wake her.

Eddie had known for hours, and had only waited for morning to call the authorities. Afterwards, he had sat in silence at his father's desk, letting his mother sleep. She would need strength. His second call had been to Nelson, who told Eddie to take as much time as he needed. "Don't you get sick, kid. I need you," Nelson had said. After he hung up the phone, Eddie smiled. He wondered if anyone but him knew Nelson had a soft side.

Eddie heard his mother's footsteps and he raced up the stairs to stop her, but she was already with Delmar, her head on his chest, sobbing. Just as there had been no words when Richie died, there were no words now. Eddie stood at her side and laid his hand on her shoulder and let her weep.

Later he made her tea, and they waited in the kitchen for the knock at the door.

Even though the undertaker's presence was expected, it was a shock to Naomi and Eddie both how swiftly Delmar's body was conveyed away. But when Naomi learned Delmar would be buried immediately with the dozens of others who had been collected that morning, she nearly collapsed. Eddie grabbed her and steadied her against his chest as she wept.

"This is just the way it has to be," he said.

They followed the men out onto the porch and watched them lift the stretcher into the medical truck. Moments later, it was gone.

Inside, Naomi refused to rest, insisting they had work to do. The coroner's men had left them a leaflet describing how they must air out the house, boil the bed clothes where Delmar had slept, or burn them, as well as his personal clothing, then scrub the room with disinfectant. Wordlessly mother and son went about each task.

After the room was clean, Naomi left the mattress bare. "I could never sleep in here again," she said, and she closed the door.

That afternoon, Eddie heard her cry out. "What's wrong," he said, rushing down the stairs.

She held the phone receiver in her hand, then pushed it toward him.

"I cannot do it. You need to call the post office."

Afterwards, Eddie called the Crandall house, then Charlie Alford. Charlie said he would pass the word to their other neighbors. "Just let me know what you need, Eddie."

At dinner, Naomi and Eddie ate a small portion of a noodle casserole Cyril Crandall had delivered. They didn't speak. When they finished eating, they both cleared their plates and Naomi washed and Eddie dried the dishes.

"Nice of Esther," Naomi said when they were done.

"Yes."

They went in the living room and silence engulfed them.

"How about a sip of brandy. It will calm your nerves."

"No." She had not meant to speak so abruptly. She smiled at Eddie. "Thank you, though."

Later, when Naomi's chin began to bob against her breast, Eddie went to her and took her hand.

"You need to sleep, Ma," he said.

"Yes."

"Let's go up early, then?"

"Yes."

In bed, Naomi thought about how sad it was that there was no one to notify of Delmar's death. As young as he was, he had outlived his entire family. Naomi had no one left either. Eventually a notice of Delmar's death would be listed in the newspaper, but it would be one of hundreds of other notices from the week. The cruelest thing of all, Naomi thought, was how easily a life could slip into oblivion.

Chapter 30

October 14, 1918

The dreariness of the past few days was finally swept away on Monday morning, and by afternoon it was sunny and warm. Eddie opened the living room windows to let in the fresh air.

"We could sit on the porch," he said, but Naomi told him she was satisfied where she was on the sofa.

"Play the Victrola for me," she said.

He pulled her favorite record out of the cardboard sleeve and put it on the machine, setting the long needle gently into a groove.

Naomi smiled at the first notes of "Il mio Tesoro" by the Irish tenor John McCormack. The aria from Mozart's opera, *Don Giovanni*, was a tonic compared with all the eager songs of war and patriotism that were popular right now. Naomi laid her head back and hummed the tune. She did not understand the Italian words, but there was no need to. "That's lovely," she said. Her hand moved in time with the singer's voice.

"You want to dance, Ma?" Eddie said, reaching his hand down to hers.

She laughed. "You don't dance. Remember when I tried to teach you and Richie the waltz? One, two, three, one, two, three. Richie was a natural, but you just couldn't make your feet work."

Eddie noticed a familiar black car on the street, but by the time he pulled back the lace curtain to get a closer look, it was out of sight.

"I was just a kid, Ma."

"You're still just a kid."

A kid would not have done the things Eddie had done. No, he had not been a kid for a long time. The car returned and the driver dipped his head enough for Eddie to recognize Nelson behind the wheel. Eddie lifted his hand in recognition, then the car drove off. Before his father got sick, Eddie and Nelson had been tailing a two-bit private eye who had been nosing in where he shouldn't have been, and it was only a matter of time before they'd have to take care of him.

When Nelson's car came by the third time, Eddie went out to meet him.

"Time to get back at it, Cowboy," Nelson said.

"I can't right now. Ma' still needs me."

Nelson grunted. "Yeah. I see." Then he shrugged. "I was mostly hoping we could find some way to pass the time. With the club shut down and all, I've been gettin' fidgety. Besides, it's your birthday and I figured we could at least find a bottle of hooch."

Eddie's eyes widened. "My birthday? Whaddya know. Guess I forgot all about that."

"With all that's happened, it's an easy thing to overlook," Nelson said. "Take care of yourself, and your Ma." Nelson pressed his foot against the gas pedal, revving up his engine.

"Take care of that jalopy before you burn out the motor," Eddie said laughing. "I'll see you. Soon as she gets well."

Back inside, Eddie went to the kitchen and made more tea. His mother wasn't eating and she needed something. He handed her the cup and she looked up at him.

"You are taking good care of me," she said, "but I don't —"

"A few sips, Ma. For me."

She smiled and obediently held the cup to her lips.

"Want me to turn the record over?" he asked. When she didn't answer, he did it anyway. The first song hit a skip, so he lifted the needle and placed it down to play the second number. "You like this one?"

"Mmm?" she said, as if from somewhere much farther away.

Eddie went to his mother's side and noticed her soft, powdered face was flushed red with perspiration. He took the cup from her.

"You don't look so good, Ma. You feeling okay?"

Naomi lifted her chin and squeezed her watery eyes. "I think it's got me, too," she whispered.

The first thing Eddie did was telephone their doctor, who was out seeing patients, the nurse said. Then she told Eddie about what he expected to hear. The same thing they had heard when they had called for Pop. Eddie didn't know what he had expected. Maybe some new medicine? A miracle cure discovered in the past week?

"Keep her warm," the nurse said, "and comfortable."

It was a useless litany.

Eddie helped his mother upstairs, waited for her outside the bathroom, then guided her back to Richie's old room. When she fumbled with the buttons on her dress, he gently pushed her hand away and did it for her, helping her slip out of her dress.

"Where's your nightgown, Ma?"

"Just—" she said, her voice triggering a cough. "I will just stay in my knickers and chemise."

"Slip in and I'll cover you." He placed a second pillow under her head, but she said it hurt her neck and to take it away.

"You sleep. I'll bring up something to eat later."

Chapter 31

October 17, 1918

By morning, Naomi's fever had diminished, though her cough had grown more coarse. She insisted her throat hurt too much to eat, but resigned herself to sips of water.

Hoping to help her take her mind off her discomfort, Eddie brought the Victrola upstairs and played John McCormack's record so often he had the tunes memorized. Even when the record ended, Eddie hummed them as he cooled his mother's face and hands with a washcloth. He did his best to read to her from *The Saturday Evening Post*, but he was grateful when she told him to put it away.

"Tell me about your work," she said, lying on her side facing him where he sat in a chair near the doorway.

He had already told her what truths he could. The doorman job had evolved into a bodyguard for Mr. Sheridan. Eddie had explained it this way. The more successful a person is, the more some people want to take it all away from you. He was there in case someone tried to take a grievance too far.

Today Eddie told his mother about some of the famous people he had met. Ballplayers like Joe Jackson and Lefty Williams were regulars at Sheridan's private club, a room off the main area by invitation only. Other bigwigs like the governor stopped in now and then.

"They treat you well?" Naomi asked. "These people you work with."

"Sure, Ma," Eddie said. "They are a swell bunch."

Naomi coughed, but unlike the strong spasms that had wracked her body earlier, this cough was weak, as if she had no energy left at all.

"I am proud of you, son."

Eddie felt a jolt of guilt when he saw his mother's eyes gleam with tears. He squeezed her hand. The choke in his throat prevented him from saying a word.

"When I am gone, I want you to sell the house, sell all my useless trinkets and have the life you deserve."

"Don't say that, Ma. You're going to come out of this," Eddie said. "You're strong. I know you are."

In the middle of the night, Eddie bolted upright. He thought he had heard his mother's voice, crying out for him. Pounding down the hall, he went to her.

"What is it Mother? What can I get you?"

Only stillness answered. He turned the switch on the lamp by her bedside and saw the blue tinge of her skin, which he knew before he touched her, would be cold.

Chapter 32

November 11, 1918

Today was Armistice Day. The war to end all wars was finally over. The evening paper spoke of a joyful city, but for Eddie, there was little to celebrate. He chose not to join the others as they flooded the streets, waving flags, cracking open kegs of beer. Only the most superstitious still feared the pandemic. The worst of that was behind them now, too, and citizens were no longer restricted to their homes.

Eddie was surprised at how easily he lost sense of time after his mother died. In the first days, he had become ill himself, and though he expected to die, he did not. His cough lingered for a week, and then one morning, he rose feeling well. Feeling as if he had never been sick at all.

On his own Eddie did the tasks he had done with his mother after Pop died. Beyond her bedroom and belongings, he cleaned it all. Wiped down tables, shelves, the mantle, doors and doorknobs. He had watched his mother often enough in her work to know how to operate the ringer washer and move a hot iron over his shirts. His attempts at cooking were mediocre, but he could make bacon and scrambled eggs. The milkman kept coming, as did the ice man, and the mailman, with magazines and newspapers, and household bills, still addressed to Delmar Reed.

The one thing Eddie did not feel up to doing was returning to work, but that was something he could not avoid forever.

The next afternoon, as he was walking home from the Jewish deli with a sack of rye bread, pastrami, and mustard, he saw Joe Crandall out on his front porch. Eddie calculated he had not spoken to Joe since— Over a year, he realized. It might be nice to just sit down and catch up.

"Hello, Joe," he said. Eddie held up the sack. "I went to the deli. Want to come over for a bite?"

Joe smiled. "Yeah. That would be nice."

Joe's unbalanced steps worked slowly down the porch stairs, then his ever-shifting gait approached Eddie. When they were kids, Richie and some of the fellas had made fun of Joe, but Eddie never did. He just thought that was how Joe walked. Everybody didn't have to be the same.

"Come on in. There's beer, too. Or maybe you'd like—"

"I'll have root beer, if you have it."

In the kitchen, Eddie told Joe to have a seat, then he set the bag on the table and got plates and napkins and the butter dish. "You need a glass?"

"Bottle's fine," Joe said.

Eddie got the drinks from the ice box and a jar of pickles before he sat down. "They sliced it for me," Eddie said, referring to the bread. He unfolded the paper bag, and offered it to Joe first. Then he transferred the shaved pastrami onto a plate.

The young men assembled their sandwiches. Eddie saw that Joe had laid only one small slice of beef on his buttered bread. "You're going to want more than that.

"I've never tried pastrami."

"No? This is the good stuff. From Borowsky's."

Joe tore a bit from the edge of he meat and stuck it in his mouth. "Umm," he said. "Good." Then without reservation, he piled more meat on his sandwich.

"And a slather of mustard tops it just right," Eddie suggested.

They ate without talking. Eddie finished his beer and got up to get another one. He didn't know what to say. "Glad you came through this awful thing."

"You, too," Joe said. "Real sorry about your mother and father."

Eddie nodded. "Guess I was the only lucky one in the family," he said, even though he did not feel lucky. "And you're all okay?"

Joe nodded. "It was touch and go with my dad," he said. "His heart's weak. But doctors think he'll be fine. My mother, as you might suspect, is too ornery to die."

Eddie laughed. "She means well."

"What kind of work do you do now?" Joe asked. "You must be glad to be out of that stockyard job."

Eddie took a sip, wondering what Joe knew. Had Pop said something to Mr. Crandall? Or had Ma? He hoped the fact that his parents were both a bit ashamed that their son worked for a guy with a sometimes dubious reputation had kept their details brief. "I'm security for Mick Sheridan. Doorman at his club, other places when he needs me."

Joe's eyebrows shot up. "Sheridan? You're the big cheese."

"Hardly," Eddie laughed. "It's mostly just a lot of standing around, looking for—. Let's just say that now and then some unsavory types show up looking for favors. I'm there to make sure they don't do anything crazy."

"Sounds—" Joe paused, as if searching for the right word. "Interesting."

Eddie shrugged. "Enough about my dull job, what about you? You are done with school at least."

"Nope. This is my last year though. We just went back this week. Before then, our teachers made up packets of work for us to do at home."

"No break, not even for an epidemic?"

"Ha. No."

"Then what?"

"After graduation? Go to college I guess."

"Hoo boy," Eddie said with a wide grin. "Now who's the big cheese?"

Joe smiled. "You ever think things would come to this? It's gotta be tough, all on your own. My mother thinks you are going to let this house fall down around you."

"I'll get on. There's some who got a worse deal."

"Yeah, that's so," Joe said. "My mother ought to mind her own business."

"Naw, she's okay. I would think the same thing if I were her. I'm not exactly the domestic type, am I?"

Joe smiled as if he did not know how to respond.

They spoke about what a good thing it was that the war was over. Then their talk shifted to the mundane details of day to day life.

"I'd should go," Joe said.

Like a good host, Eddie walked outside with his friend. Outside snow had begun to fall. They walked down the front walk, their shoes leaving prints. "Could get really cold tonight," Eddie said, staring up into the deepening dusk.

Joe tapped Eddie's shoulder to get his attention. Then Joe lifted his face to the sky and stuck out his tongue to catch a flake, like they had done so often when they were kids. Eddie followed Joe's lead, but only for a moment. Not because he worried someone would see him. He didn't give a damn what anyone thought. It was sadness that made him stop and give Joe a shrug.

"Kid stuff," Joe said.

Eddie gave his old friend a slap on the shoulder. "Yeah. Kid stuff," he laughed, but there was a sting of regret in his words. He and Joe had been their best selves as kids. At least Eddie had. If he could rewind time and do it all over again, he knew he'd make better choices. If he could start over, he would not make the same mistakes.

"Well, I'll see ya, Eddie," Joe said, then shivering, he ambled home.

Eddie remained outside a while longer, the cold biting his face, and watched as front room lamps came on in the Crandall house and here and there up and down the block. Across the street, Charlie Alford had just come home.

Eddie waved and Charlie waved back.

"Going to get a few inches tonight," Charlie called over.

"Looks like it," Eddie said, sounding, he realized, just like his father, talking about the weather with the neighbors. "Well, good night."

"Same to you," Charlie said, then he went inside. Moments later, the yellow glow from Charlie's living room lit the white square of lawn outside his house just like all the others on the block.

Charlie Alford was a genial man, a widower. It occurred to Eddie just then that he and Joe and Charlie were all men alone. The three of them ought to have found companionship in their common situation, but that kind of life did not belong to Eddie. Neighborly banter. Nelson had warned Eddie to keep his distance. Safer, he'd said. "For them."

Lately, Eddie had even given serious thought to selling the house. He imagined a swanky apartment in the city, where he could come and go without prying eyes. A well-tipped chummy doorman wouldn't care about his late hours or a smudge of blood on his hand now and then.

Living here meant all of his neighbors kept an eye on him. He knew that. His parents had done the same. Watched out the window, commented on how a lawn grew scraggly, pointed out a light on upstairs for too long, wondering where a person was off to at such a late hour.

Inside, Eddie stamped his feet on the rug and flipped on a living room lamp. The stack of mail he had let pile up under the mail slot caught his eye.

"Better get on that," he said. In the kitchen, he laid the mail on the table and cleared away the remains of the dinner he had shared with Joe. From the ice box, he took the last beer and sat at the table before the stack of envelopes. One by one he opened them. Some were past due bills, and he set those aside to take care of the next day. Some were advertisements. One was a notice from city health officials about proceeding safely in the waning days of the pandemic. It would have been nice, he thought, if the doctors and the mayor had done a better job of telling people how to stay safe when the disease first hit those guys at the naval base. They should have handed out those damn masks on the first day, whether people wanted them or not. Maybe his parents would still be alive if they had.

Eddie held up the last envelope. It was addressed to his mother in an uneven hand. He slid the letter out and read:

October 16, 1918

Dear Mrs. Reed,

I write to express my sorrow at the passing of your husband.

You may know that I was new to this country when Mr. Reed hired me. I worked hard, and in time he made me head sorter. Because of my better salary, I could afford a nicer place for my family to live. Mr. Reed gave us Christmas bonuses too. He was a generous man. Always thinking of others.

I will never forget the day my Hana died. Mr. Reed came to our house. He called the doctor and comforted our little girl while we waited. I was very sick too, but he gave me strength. He told me to hang on because my family needed me.

My family and I grieve his loss. Delmar Reed was a great man.

With sympathy, Jakub Dvorak

(Written by Jakub's son Arno, because my father's English is not so good).

"Christmas bonuses." "Generous man." "We all grieve his loss." Eddie's mind swirled in confusion. How could this portrait of his father as a "great man" be true? This was not the hard-headed, opinionated Delmar Reed he had known his entire life. Could it be that Pop had lived two lives? Was he a different man in the world? Did Ma know? Had she known this family? Were there other families like this? Eddie re-read the letter. The sentiments were so honest. The Dvoraks had loved Delmar Reed. His father, Eddie realized, was someone he hadn't known at all.

Chapter 33

January 1920

On January 17, 1920 The Volstead Act went into effect, changing everything for Nelson and Eddie. The first thing to change was their partnership when Sheridan hired Luther Cantwell. "You boys are moving up and you are going to need extra muscle," Sheridan had explained.

Luther was a tremendous man, built like Babe Ruth, only taller.

"They call me Bear," Luther said, meeting the boys for the first time.

Nelson's eyes widened with amusement. "I can see why." Nelson shook Luther's hand, and after massaging the blood back into his fingers, Nelson said, "This is Eddie."

"You look like that cowboy actor," Bear said.

Nelson looked at Eddie as if seeing him for the first time. "Damn," he said. "Bear is right. You look just like him."

From then on, Eddie was Cowboy and Bear was Bear. Eddie had slipped up once and called him Luther. Never again.

In addition to keeping their coppers in line and making sure they weren't getting shorted on their "dues," Eddie, Nelson, and Bear began to oversee shipments of bootleg whiskey. As always, rival gangs were trouble, but now the posse, as Nelson had named them, faced a new threat. G-Men, the FBI's goons.

"You'd think they'd play by the rules," Nelson said, "but they don't. They got their own ways, and they ain't always on the up and up."

Eddie thought Nelson was right about that, but he laughed at the idea that anything they were doing was on the "up and up." More and more it had become necessary for them to solve their problems with a gun. Sheridan didn't play by the rules either. Despite warnings from rivals, he continued to expand his Midwest territory, even if it infringed on rigid gang borders.

Chapter 34

February 14, 1921

Eddie, Nelson, and Bear sat at the bar, watching a jazz show. Tonight was the grand opening of Sheridan's new speakeasy. The boss had told them to enjoy themselves, but no drinking. "I need you sober in case someone tries to ruin my party."

A negro band played, and Eddie tapped his foot.

Bear jabbed him in the shoulder. "Wanna dance, sweetheart?"

Eddie just shook his head. Bear could be hilarious at times.

"Hoo boy," Nelson said when a singer in a slinky gown stepped onto the stage. "I bet that canary's got a voice on her," Nelson said, using his hands to make an hourglass shape in the air. Then he put his fingers to his mouth and whistled.

Eddie glowered at Nelson. "We're supposed to keep a low profile, remember?"

Nelson shrugged. "How is tonight different from any other night? There are always eyes on us. We're one foot in the grave all the time now, aren't we? Not like in the old days before Prohibition when all we did was shake down little watchmakers and bakers."

Bear put his finger to his lips.

"Yeah, yeah," Nelson said. "I'll zip it."

After another number, the singer bowed and Sheridan took the stage.

"Thank you for coming tonight folks. Isn't Trixie something? Let's give her our appreciation one more time." The crowd applauded, and a few stood and whistled. After a moment, Sheridan motioned for them to be seated. "I want to just say—" Sheridan cleared his throat.

"Boss is snookered," Nelson whispered.

"I know there are many fine establishments you could have taken your sweethearts to on this fine Valentines Day, like those associated with Mr. Capone, who is, we have to admit, king of Chicago. But if you'll allow me, I'd be honored to be your prince."

Eddie shook his head. "What is he on about?"

Bear squeezed Eddie's arm, a signal to keep his mouth shut. Nelson didn't get the signal. "Boss has a lot of nerve," he said. "Gets me more than a little agitated."

"Enough from me, though," Sheridan said. "You came here to have a good time. So enjoy yourselves."

At that moment, waiters appeared with bottles of champagne, and the place erupted in cheers.

Nelson dropped Eddie off at home just after 3:00 a.m. Eddie had never followed through with his plans to sell the old house. It wasn't that he didn't want to. At times he still did, but whenever he thought about what that would mean—selling their things. Things that still reminded him of his mother and brother, and even his father. It felt like he would be erasing more than his memories if evidence of their lives on earth was gone. So he stayed, despite his neighbors' prying eyes.

Eddie padded up the stairs to bed. Keeping quiet was an old habit. There was no longer anyone to wake. His jacket stank like cigar and cigarette smoke, so he stepped out onto the airing porch and hung it on a valet stand he kept out there for this purpose. The winter air would freshen it in no time. In the bathroom, Eddie turned on the faucet to his new shower. He'd had it installed recently. He remembered almost losing his temper when the plumber asked to be paid up front.

"Never done a tony job in this neighborhood," the plumber had said.

Eddie had wanted to punch the guy's smug face, but he wanted that new brass plumbing even more, so he kept his composure and paid the man.

Tonight, as Eddie let the spray rinse away the nightclub, he thought about what Nelson had said. *Gets me a little agitated.* Eddie understood. Sheridan's willingness to play loose made Eddie nervous too.

Chapter 35

June 1921

A knock at the front door woke Eddie from a disturbing dream. He looked at his watch. Nearly five. He had been asleep on the living room sofa since 2:00 p.m.

When the knocker banged again, Eddie shouted, "I'm coming. Hold your horses."

Eddie opened the door. Instead of some annoying door-to-door salesman who would be easily sent on his way, it was Joe Crandall.

"Oh, hey, Joe. Come on in." Once Joe was inside, Eddie saw the living room through his old friend's eyes. Eddie's dinner jacket lay crumpled on a chair, empty beer bottles sat upon newspapers strewn across the coffee table, and a plate with a half-eaten sausage link covered in ketchup lay on the side table.

"It's a disaster in here," Eddie laughed. "Maybe I need a maid." When Eddie went to remove his jacket from the chair to make a place for Joe to sit, he realized his holster and gun lay under it. "Let's go in the kitchen," he said. "Want a beer?"

"Beer?" Joe said. "Isn't that illegal?"

Eddie shrugged. "Perks of the job."

The kitchen was also a mess, but at least it was free of incriminating details. "What brings you by Joe?" Eddie grabbed two bottles from the ice box.

"Been a while," Joe said. "I thought we might grab a steak or something. Some time. It doesn't have to be tonight."

Eddie snapped the bottle caps off with a church key and handed a beer to Joe. "Yeah. I'm pretty busy at work these days."

"Even now that Prohibition has closed all the clubs down?"

Eddie wanted to smile at his friend's innocence, but did not dare. "I'm more of a bodyguard now. I—" Eddie really wished Joe had not come. Keeping certain facts away from the kid was not easy. "Hey, wasn't it your birthday recently. How old are you now? Seventeen?"

"Always a kidder, aren't you? I will be twenty next week."

"Twenty. Catching up to me almost," Eddie said with a laugh. But it bothered him that he had not known how old Joe was. Ten-year-old Eddie knew exactly how old his friend was. On the other hand, ten-year-old Eddie wasn't preoccupied with who lurked in alleyways or who drove a new Packard that had tailed him two nights in a row. Twenty-one-year-old Eddie no longer had the luxury of keeping life's mundane details in mind.

"So what've you been doing to keep yourself busy?" Eddie asked.

"University of Chicago."

"No kidding? Don't tell me you are studying architecture."

Joe narrowed his eyes. "No. Why would you guess that?"

"Family joke," Eddie said, tipping his beer to finish it. "What are you studying, then?"

"Sociology."

"What the heck is that?"

"Basically helping people," Joe said. He explained the kind of work he hoped to do when he graduated. Chicago was full of people who needed a helping hand, he said.

"Good for you. That is, you always did care a lot about people."

"So did you, at one time." Eddie steered the conversation to another topic. "Got a girlfriend? Some dame also taking classes in socialism?"

"Sociology. And no." Joe tapped his leg and pointed at his special shoe. "Still me, remember? The gimp?"

"Yeah. Richie shouldn't have said that." Eddie went to the ice box and got two more beers, then opened the door to the back porch. Joe followed.

They sat on the steps, the evening sun slanting across their legs. Eddie clinked his bottle against Joe's, then took a long drink. "That bother you much? What kids said about you? What Richie said?"

Joe didn't answer right away. He sipped his beer and looked down at the ground. His shoe scraped at the dirt near a pill bug. "There are people a lot worse off than me. So I guess that makes me feel lucky sometimes. You know, when you put your life up against a fellow who has nothing."

Eddie nodded. He understood. Though in his case, he had sometimes felt cheated when he compared his life with Mick Sheridan and guys like him. It didn't seem fair that they had it all, when it was Eddie, Nelson, and Bear who did the dirty work. Still, compared to many, Eddie had to admit he had nothing to complain about. *Quit your grousing*, Pop would have said, and he'd have been right.

"You're a good egg, Joe."

Joe laughed. "You are as well."

A cat the color of coal ash appeared in the yard. "That one of Mrs. O'Brien's?" Eddie asked.

"Could be." Joe called out, "Here kitty, kitty," but the cat strode toward the side yard without giving the men any notice.

"Ma always said cats in the neighborhood made for good gardens. Never knew what she meant by that, though."

"Cats eat the rabbits, so the rabbits don't eat your lettuce?" Joe suggested.

"Yeah. That's gotta be it." The talk of gardens and his mother made Eddie take notice of her old flower beds. Eddie felt ashamed he had let them go to weeds. Even so, a few plants defied his neglect. A clump of deep pink peonies were in full bloom. Maybe he could start to work on them, like he used to with his mother when he was a boy. Even though Eddie barely kept the grass cut, he remembered how to pull a weed.

"You still a bookworm?" Eddie asked, trying to get his mind off of the fact that he had done a poor job keeping his mother's house.

"Still. Yes. I like this new writer, Fitzgerald. He's good."

Eddie was not the least bit interested in books or writers, but he listened attentively to Joe, who grew animated as he spoke, his words little more than sound to Eddie. "Say," he blurted out, "I read a few chapters in the book you gave me years back." It was a lie. He hadn't even opened the book. He'd stuck it in the bookcase in Richie's old room.

Joe looked askance at Eddie. "A few?"

"Yeah." He cleared his throat. "Still hard to make those words mean something."

An awkward silence lay between them, and Eddie stared at the porch floor, until a moment later when Joe made things easy again.

"I should go," Joe said. "Since Dad died—. Just can't leave my mom alone much, you know? But it was good to see you."

"Oh that's right. I did read that. I'm real sorry Joe. I guess I dropped the ball. How are you doing, you and your mother?"

"Fine. I mean she's just going through the motions some days. But Charlie Alford has been a good friend to her. He knows what it's like to be alone."

"And she has you."

"She has me."

Eddie shook his head. "I'm a blockhead, Joe. I really am. I hope you can forgive me for that."

Joe appeared to agree without saying so. Then with a serious expression, he said, "We can't let our friendship die, Eddie."

Eddie could be dense at times, but even he could not mistake the sense of loneliness in Joe's voice. "No. We can't," Eddie said.

At the gate Joe waved. "See you soon," he said.

"Yeah. See you soon," Eddie said, knowing he did not mean it.

Chapter 36

November 1926

"Get in," Nelson said to Eddie, who nodded to Bear in the back seat. "You look like shit, kid."

"You would too if you'd only got four hours of sleep." Eddie didn't add that he was also hungover.

"Someone's hijacked our hootch," Bear said. "We're going up to Kenosha to snoop around. Sheridan thinks it's a guy running an operation from his engine factory."

"Everybody's gotta get in on the action nowadays," Nelson said, almost failing to see the light turn red.

"Jesus, Morrie. Keep your eyes on the road," Bear said.

Eddie turned his head to the window and grinned. Ever since Bear had found out Nelson's first name was Morris, he'd been calling him "Morrie." Now and then, Nelson replied back with "Luther." Eddie decided it was wise to stay out of that little game.

"Kenosha's not that far away," Eddie said. "Why so early?"

"Bear knows a place just across the state line that makes pancakes the size of your plate. So we're going to get pancakes first."

"Jesus Christ," Eddie muttered, then he pulled his hat over his eyes and tried to sleep.

At breakfast, they went over the plan. By arriving mid-morning, the engine operation would be going, business as usual. Since bootleg shipments usually came in under cover of night, they weren't looking to catch them in the act, per se, just see if there were crates of Canadian Club that hadn't had time to gather dust. Nelson said he and Eddie would pose as businessmen looking for an opportunity, while Bear poked around back.

"I don't like day jobs," Eddie said.

"We aren't going to *do* the job this morning. We're just reconnoitering. Might not even get a whiff of what we're looking for."

"Don't think we'd be going if you weren't kinda sure," Eddie said, forcing another bite into his mouth.

Nelson shrugged. "Could be we hit the jackpot. Save us another trip. All I'm wondering is whether or not you'll be ready no matter what."

"Christ." Eddie said, rubbing his temples. "Yes."

After a wrong turn and a long drive down a gravel road that brought them close to the Lake Michigan shoreline, they finally found the place. They had driven right past it the first time, but now, among a copse of pines and thick shrubbery, they saw the sign at the mouth of the driveway—Pitzen Machine Company. A quarter mile back from the road sat a newish looking two-story cream brick building. Nelson pulled in and parked near the rear edge of the gravel lot. Along the front of the building was a line of old Model T's and a few Runabouts. It was eerily quiet, no voices or sounds of machinery.

"Gotta say, it's the perfect location," Nelson said. "Maybe we take 'em all out and go into the engine business for ourselves."

Bear grunted a half laugh. "Engine business."

As planned, Bear slipped his Tommy gun under his coat and headed around back to snoop, while Nelson and Eddie secured their machine pistols and casually sauntered into the office.

"Good day, sir," Nelson said to a young man at a desk littered with ledger books and papers. A chest-high counter separated the office from the small lobby furnished with two chairs and one potted plant.

"Are you here for the Meyer contract?" he said, squinting at Nelson and Eddie through thick glasses.

Nelson coughed. "We are the Morris brothers, looking to engage your company in a new manufacturing concern."

"Never heard of you," he said.

"We're a small firm up near Appleton."

"Why didn't you go to VanWert's then?" The secretary rose and took several steps towards the door at the rear of the office, as if he were not sure what to do.

Despite his foggy head, Eddie caught on faster than Nelson. "A matter of a family dispute," he said. "Let's just say that we felt it was better to—"

Eddie's explanation was interrupted by machine gun fire. Immediately he and Nelson drew their guns, but not before the secretary, who had seemed mild mannered, drew his first and fired, missing Eddie by inches but blasting out the front window.

Nelson fired back, killing the secretary. "Go find Bear," Nelson shouted as he darted down the hall to another door. Flinging it open, Nelson disappeared inside.

Eddie hoisted himself up and over the counter and plastered himself against the back wall of the office until another round of staccato pops died down. Hoping it was still Bear at the trigger, Eddie pushed through the door.

"Get down, Cowboy!" Bear called out.

A single pistol shot rang out and hit the wall behind Eddie. He crouched down and tried to get his bearings. He saw Nelson come in through the big barn doors behind Bear and take a bullet to the gut. From the floor of the machine shop, Nelson raised his gun and fired. Eddie heard the thud of a body hitting the floor. In the moments that followed, Nelson's heavy breathing was all he could hear, but Eddie knew silence could be deceptive.

Bear pivoted and paced toward the side of the shop where rows of stacked shelving held parts. The deep aisles were dimly lit.

"Behind you," Eddie shouted, now on his feet. He fired at two men in the doorway. Bear swerved and released a spray of bullets. Then, a shot hit Bear in the shoulder, sending him to the floor not too far from Nelson. The shooter who emerged from the stacks zeroed in on Bear. When he saw Nelson, he laughed. "Two birds with one stone," he said right before Eddie got him between the eyes.

This time the silence held. Bear got to his feet. "Bring the car around, Cowboy. Nelson's hurt bad."

Eddie counted five dead, including the secretary in the office. When Eddie got to the parking lot, it was empty, except for one Runabout. If one of those guys in a Model T had seen their faces—. Or maybe they'd be too afraid to say they'd been at work that day. Either way, this skirmish meant an escalation.

Nelson lay in the back, unconscious. Bear had taken off his shirt and was pressing it against Nelson's wound. Eddie pealed out of the gravel driveway, leaving dust in the air. At county road intersections, Eddie ignored stop signs whenever possible. On the main road, he pushed the accelerator and was grateful for very little traffic.

"How's he doing," Eddie shouted.

"Just drive."

"Maybe a hospital this time?"

"No," Bear said emphatically. "Get to Doc's as fast as you can."

Eddie pulled up to a big white farmhouse south of Gurnee and honked the horn. Doc and Mrs. Doc were out the door in seconds.

"We've got him," Doc said to Bear. "You just go in and sit down before you pass out."

They took Nelson to a back bedroom set up as Doc's surgery, and laid him on the exam table. "Bear's going to have to wait," Doc told Eddie. "You go on out there with him."

Eddie found Bear in the kitchen. "Didn't want to bleed on the nice rug in the living room," Bear said.

Eddie examined Bear's wound. "Bleeding's stopped," he said. "But you took a bullet for sure."

"Mrs. Doc is good at getting them out. I'm not worried. For me anyway. Different story for Nelson. He's in bad shape."

"I'd pray if I prayed," Eddie said.

Bear laughed and repeated what Eddie had said. "You got a way with words sometimes, Cowboy."

Eddie went to the cupboard and found a couple of glasses, then filled them with water. Bear gulped his and held it out for another one.

"Why do you call her Mrs. Doc?" Eddie said, turning on the faucet.

Bear shrugged, taking his glass from Eddie. "Don't know her real name. All I know was that she was a nurse during the war. I've known her—" Bear shrugged. "Long time." Bear sat quietly, almost meditatively, as if he were willing his pain to diminish.

An hour later, Mrs. Doc entered with a medical bag. "All right if I tend to you right here, Luther?"

"Fine," he said.

"Eddie, right? Help me get his undershirt off, will you?"

Bear winced when they lifted his arm. Eddie could see the entry wound clearly now. Mrs. Doc got a basin of water and cleaned the area.

"I don't think it's in there too deep," she said. "Guess that you're tough like a bear, too, aren't you?"

Bear's laugh was weak.

"Don't you worry," she said, as she injected him with morphine. "In a minute, you won't feel much."

Eddie sat to the opposite side so he wouldn't be able to see the procedure. Not that he couldn't handle blood, but when they started digging around inside with those big tweezer things, he could get a bit queasy.

".45 caliber, I would say," Mrs. Doc said, holding up the bullet she pulled out of Bear's shoulder. "No bone damage. You are lucky." After she finished her last stitch, she bandaged Bear's wound.

"You are going to be sore for a while," she said. "But you know that." She dressed him in a spare shirt. "Sorry it's a little tight." Then she positioned his arm in a sling.

"Thank you," he said.

"Eddie, help me get Luther to the living room. He's too woozy to go alone. And from the looks of it, you could use a few winks yourself."

They settled Bear on the sofa, and Eddie took the chair and ottoman. Moments later Mrs. Doc returned with two blankets. After she had them covered, she closed the drapes and told them not to worry about a thing.

It did not take long for either one to fall asleep.

It was early evening when Eddie woke. Bear was still snoring, so he found his way to the lavatory. When he came out, he heard noises coming from the kitchen.

Mrs. Doc smiled when she saw him. "I'll bet you are starving," she said.

"A little," Eddie said. He wondered how this woman could take in three fugitives, ask no questions, then treat them like sons home for a holiday. "Smells good," he said.

"Baked ham and potato casserole."

Just then Doc appeared. He nodded to Eddie.

"How is he?" Eddie was almost afraid to ask, in case the answer would not be the one he wanted to hear.

"He'll pull through," Doc said. "If an infection doesn't set in."

"That's great news," Eddie said, visibly relieved.

"Go check on Bear," Mrs. Doc said. "Dinner will be ready soon."

Bear was awake when Eddie returned to the living room, so he turned on a lamp. "How are you feeling?" Eddie asked.

"Didn't know where I was for a minute," Bear said. Then he tried to push himself up and yelped. "Oh, right. Gunfight at the O.K. Corral."

Eddie helped Bear to his feet, then to the bathroom, and then, because Doc said it was fine for a few minutes, they went in to see Nelson.

"Normal for him to be asleep right now," Doc said.

"He looks awfully pale," Bear said.

"He lost a lot of blood, but we're going to keep an eye on him. All we can really do is wait, and rely on his body to do its work."

"How long until he wakes up?" Eddie asked.

"Can't really say," Doc said. "I expect by morning. But—"

An anxious silence fell between the men. Eddie's eyes met Doc's and somehow he understood.

"Bear and I should be on the road after dinner."

Doc did not argue. "I'd like to keep you, but sounds like that was bad business up there. Better if your car isn't around, not that I expect any trouble, but just in case. Saturday, at the earliest, you can come for Nelson. I'd hate for him to be moved before then. He almost didn't make it."

It was late the next morning when Eddie found Bear in the kitchen drinking coffee and reading the paper. He had freed his arm from the sling and appeared almost as if he had not been shot at all.

Eddie poured himself a cup and asked if there was anything to eat.

"Just bread and butter," Bear said, pointing to the loaf on the table. "Sorry. I wasn't expecting guests. You sleep okay on the davenport?"

"I was so tired I probably could have slept on the floor." Eddie sat at the table and took two slices of bread from the waxed paper bag. "How are you feeling?"

"Not going to throw a runner out at second, but okay."

"Did you call Doc's?"

"Yeah. Morrie's awake, doing better. No fever. Sore as hell. Doc says one more night there though."

Bear slid the paper over to Eddie. "Take a look. Page three."

Mass Murder in Kenosha

Five men were found dead in an apparent gangland slaying at the Pitzen Machine Company in rural Kenosha, Wisconsin, Thursday, Nov. 18.

Local police, who found evidence of liquor trafficking in a storeroom on the premises, said they will turn the case over to federal law enforcement.

Oscar Pitzen, owner of the manufacturing company, stated he was not in the office at the time of the shootings. "I am devastated by this tragedy," Pitzen said. "I cannot imagine how something like this could have happened," he said.

Pitzen disavowed any knowledge of a bootlegging operation. "I run a clean shop," he said. Pitzen could not explain an empty crate and several smashed whiskey bottles in his storeroom, saying only, "You think you've hired good men. You can never really know what goes on behind your back."

Mick Sheridan, Chicago real estate developer and suspected bootlegger, denied any involvement with the shootings.

"Instead of harassing legitimate businessmen, why don't you ask Bugs (George) Moran what he's up to?" Sheridan asked reporters, alluding to Moran's alleged attempt on Alphonse Capone's life on Sept. 20 of this year.

At this time, no witnesses to the Kenosha slaying have come forward.

"Sheridan's tricky, eh? Pointing the finger at Moran. Makes a lot of sense." Eddie sipped his coffee. "This means we're in the clear, right?"

Bear shook his head. "Not if any of those stooges that took off after the shooting started recognized us. Or if the feds connect those broken bottles to our operation."

"We should call the boss."

"Already did."

"And?"

"Soon as Nelson's able to travel, he wants us in Miami for a few months."

"Miami?"

"Guess he's got a hotel down there, and we're supposed to go check on it. See if that big hurricane did as much damage as they say it did." Bear got up to put his dishes in the sink. "And Eddie?"

"Yeah?"

"He's not happy about the hooch."

"But there was nothing there, right? You checked?"

"Didn't have a chance. They started in on me right away, almost like they knew who I was."

"You do have a memorable presence," Eddie said.

Bear shrugged. "Based on what the paper says, I think Sheridan's whiskey got cleaned out after we left. Then they called the coppers. Don't tell me Pitzen wasn't in on that little show."

Chapter 37

November 1926, Florida

It took Eddie, Bear, and Nelson four days to get to La Paz, Sheridan's place in Miami Beach. Damage from the Great Miami Hurricane in September was still evident everywhere, but amidst piles of rubble, construction and restoration were in the works across the area. Eddie parked across the street from the hotel. A new-looking sign featured a painting of a white stucco, Art Deco hotel flanked by tall palm trees. Script lettering promised patrons "*un experiencia elegante.*" At the moment, the entrance to the soon-to-be four-story structure was enclosed in scaffolding, and there wasn't a palm tree in sight.

"I'll go in and see if there's a foreman I can speak to," Eddie said, swinging open the car door. On the street, he lifted his shoulders and breathed deeply. There was just something about the air in Miami. Eddie didn't know what it was, but it felt good here.

"I'm staying put," Nelson said, when Bear got out to stretch his legs.

"This isn't bad, is it?" Bear said. He squinted up to a cloudless sky. "Not this warm in Chicago. Not by a long shot."

Bear and Nelson waited for Eddie and watched the construction crew in action. "Going to be a swanky place when it's done," Nelson said. "La Paz. Is that French or something?"

Bear shook his head. "Sounds like Español to me."

Nelson grunted. "Since when do you speak Spanish?"

"I don't, but I think it might be a good idea to pick up a few words. While we're here." Bear pulled a cigarette out of his case and lit it. He peered at the matchbook cover. "Hey, would you look at that." Bear held the matchbook out for Nelson to see. "El Tropicana."

"That's in Havana. When were you in Cuba, Luther?"

"Just this week. Don't you remember? That's where I got this shoulder divot."

Nelson laughed, then held his belly. "Stop joking. It hurts." Nelson grimaced and leaned back in the seat.

Eddie was back now. "No accommodations yet," he said. "But believe it or not, they figure to be open for guests in six weeks."

"I don't believe it," Nelson said, "but the sooner the better."

"There was damage to the main floor," Eddie continued. "They had to shovel out sand. Wrecked the lobby carpet. But otherwise the first two floors came through pretty good. Guy I talked to said Sheridan had wanted six floors, but the storm changed all that. Now the boss just wants it done."

"What's our job then?" Nelson said. "He expecting us to pound nails?" Nelson's normally genial demeanor had devolved into outright orneriness. They all had slept poorly on the road, in spurts of time at first, thinking to push ahead and get to Miami as soon as they could, but then Nelson begged for a night in a bed, so they found lodging. His wounds had only begun to heal and being jostled in the car didn't help matters. And today, all they'd had to eat was a greasy breakfast at a roadside shack south of Jacksonville.

"I guess we will find all that out later. Until then, the foreman told me about a place north of here where we might find rooms."

Forty minutes later, Eddie, Nelson, and Bear checked in at the Palmetto Motor Court, which had emerged mostly unscathed by the storm, except for the last cabin on the left. It had been crushed by a palm tree, which still lay across the roof like a scaly log. The office and remaining nine cabins sat on the edge of a stretch of beach. The ocean beyond the caramel sand was calm and sparkled in the sun. White ibises patrolled the shore. Eddie was sure La Paz would be a swanky place, but as he surveyed the Palmetto, he thought it might be an even better place to spend a few weeks in paradise. One thing was sure, it was quiet here. None of the city's bustling and pounding. Now and then a car engine sputtered by, but otherwise, all you could hear was the rustling of the breeze through the palms and the gentle lap of wave upon the shore, punctuated only now and then by the squawk of seagulls.

Leaving their jackets in their rooms, they walked down the road to The Pelican Perch diner that boasted about having "Florida's Best Red Snapper Sandwiches." Several cars were parked out front. Half of the diner's metal roof looked new, but one of front windows was still boarded up. Out back, a pile of rubble gave evidence of a former shed or garage. Remnants of a small piney woods lay beyond. Its trees, snapped mid-trunk, emitted faint echoes of their sharp, resinous scent.

The dining room smelled bleach-clean. Eight square tables lined the side walls. Diners who ate quietly or waited for their food were seated at three of the tables. Eddie, Nelson, and Bear were told to sit where they liked. Moments later, an overly thin, sun-tanned waitress named Rose handed them the menus she'd carried tucked under her arm. "Welcome, gentlemen," she said, setting a pitcher of ice water on the red-checkered tablecloth. "Special is fried grouper and skillet potatoes. We make those with onions and pimento."

Bear nodded. "Sounds just fine for me," he said, handing his menu back to her.

"Yeah. Make it simple," Nelson agreed. "The special for me."

"I'm going for the red snapper sandwich," Eddie said.

Rose pursed her lips. "Just out of snapper," she said.

After Eddie poured water into his glass, he handed the pitcher to Bear. "Then the grouper, unless these guys got the last of that?"

Rose laughed. "Just about."

"I don't expect you have a beer back there?" Eddie asked.

Rose shook her head. "You from Mars? Must be if you never heard of prohibition." Rose winked. "It's not on the menu, but we have a *Caribbean* lemonade I think you will like."

Eddie nodded, understanding her coded language. "Yes. I think we'd all like that."

After their meal and two Caribbean lemonades each, Sheridan's boys went back to their rooms.

With his door ajar, Nelson said he was going to wash up and go straight to bed. "That lemonade has done me in."

"Sleep till noon, or all day if you need to," Bear said.

Nelson exhaled a deep breath. "I might just do that." He stepped inside, then a thought brought him back. "You going to call Sheridan?"

"Yeah. Tomorrow," Eddie said. "But first, I think Bear and I should go back to Miami in the morning to get a better sense of things."

Nelson nodded. "Thanks fellas. If I don't wake up till Tuesday, don't you worry about it."

Eddie and Bear returned to the Palmetto late afternoon, bearing gifts—suits of lightweight linen, short sleeved shirts, and slip-on boat shoes that needed no socks, according to the salesman. Despite Nelson's intentions of sleeping for days, Eddie and Bear found him in a patio chair under the shade of his cabin's veranda. He looked to be sipping a familiar glass of lemonade.

"Carry out service," Nelson said, lifting his glass in a mock toast. "Rose saved us all some snapper for dinner, too. I think she's got the eye for you, Cowboy."

Eddie snorted, then handed Nelson a flat-brimmed straw boater. "Promises to keep the sun out of your eyes," he said.

"Main reason is to blend in," Bear said. "The new clothes, I mean."

"But also cooler," Nelson added. "No small thing. Thank you gents."

Eddie grinned. "Look at these!" He held a pair of short trousers against his waist. "Boat wear."

"Who needs boat wear?" Nelson asked.

"I guess we do," Eddie said brightly. "Sheridan's setting up a meeting tomorrow with a guy. We're supposed to meet him at his boat down in Key Largo. Looks like we're getting into the rum business."

"Jesus Christ," Nelson said. "I don't like the sound of that."

As much as Nelson grew to revile Florida, Eddie loved it. He donned sunglasses and grew a pencil mustache. When they were out on the water, Eddie wore short sleeves and swimwear that showed off his ever-darkening skin. Boating became a passion. Trips to the Caribbean made Bear seasick and Nelson's pale skin blister, but Eddie decided this Florida lifestyle suited him fine, and he didn't care if they ever went back to Chicago.

In early January, they moved into La Paz, taking rooms on the first floor while work on the rest of the hotel continued. Eddie had hated saying goodbye to the Palmetto and The Pelican Perch and Rose. Their time up the sea shore had felt like home, and Eddie would miss it. Most of all, he would miss the solitude of that beach, where he would often go after long days in the city or a weekend of business in Nassau or Havana. It was the only place he could truly think. And some nights, long after Bear and Nelson went to bed, Eddie would walk along the water's edge in the moonlight.

But there was no sense complaining. Hotel life was nice in its own ways. The restaurant was up and running, and the chef Sheridan had stolen from a posh hotel in San Francisco was trying out new dishes with "Creole" flavors. Eddie hadn't known what that meant, but he liked what he tasted. He also liked having crisp, clean sheets on his bed each night as well.

Sheridan arrived a week later, not one bit happy at the state of his hotel.

"You boys don't mind dilly dallying, I guess," Sheridan said to them at dinner that night.

"Things move at a different pace down here," Nelson began, but Sheridan shut him down.

And we've been moving your rum, Eddie thought.

"I don't need excuses," Sheridan barked. "What's the actual status? How close are we?"

"Eighty rooms are finished," Eddie said. "And the parquet floor in the ballroom is set to go down this week. It's only a few suites—"

"Then I want an ad in the papers tomorrow," Sheridan said, interrupting Eddie. He sliced a hunk off his steak and thrust it in his mouth. "Fancy lettering and all. La Paz is open for business."

"Sure Boss," Nelson said.

"At least you got one thing right, Morrie. Opening the restaurant ahead of schedule was a smart move. But Jesus H that scaffolding has to go. You can't even see my big beautiful doors. By the end of the week, you hear?"

Sheridan held the grand opening in early March, just in time for tourist season. By seven, the lobby was filled with men and women, dressed in their finest, mingling and sipping rum punch. Since Eddie had paid the requisite bribes, drinks at La Paz flowed freely. Sheridan, decked out in a white tuxedo, made his way through the crowd, attempting to welcome everyone personally. Now and then, he shepherded small groups over to see his cherished goddesses. Cast in brass, the ten-foot winged sculptures adorned each side of the grand marble staircase that led to the second floor ballroom.

"He thinks he's the king now," Bear said, nodding to Sheridan.

"You got that right," Nelson said.

At eight, everyone was ushered into the dining room, where they took a seat at one of fifty round tables, each one set with gleaming china, polished silver, and sparkling crystal, including champagne flutes. The edges of each white tablecloth draped nearly to the floor. A cadre of waiters appeared with champagne, which they poured for each guest.

Before taking his seat at "his table," a large round booth near the door to the kitchen, Sheridan clinked a spoon against his glass to get everyone's attention. "Friends, I am grateful for your presence tonight. Please raise your glass with me to christen this marvelous place. To La Paz."

Later, while Sheridan and his guests enjoyed one of La Paz's three specialty dishes—charcoal grilled sirloin steak, swordfish au gratin, or braised Spanish mackerel—Eddie, Nelson, and Bear kept watch over the entire hotel.

"Never thought I'd be a security guard again," Nelson grumbled as they reconvened in the lobby. "We gotta hire our own goons for this."

It did not take long for La Paz to become the new fashionable destination for rich tourists. There was the novelty of its newness, its renowned chef, and its covert Cuba Libres. But the hotel also had a reputation for pampering its guests, and this was due to Nelson. Not that he cared one whit about taking care of hotel guests. His decision to double the hotel's staff was purely pragmatic. It was a way to conceal their ever intensifying stream of rum money.

Capone had funneled his extra dough through laundromats in Chicago, so why not cook the hotel's books, Nelson figured. All the extra bellhops, maids, and waiters made it seem, at times, like guests had their own personal attendants. The upside was that Sheridan's Miami Beach La Paz became the place to be. It was a good life.

Then in early August, when their Key Largo captain and two of his guys were found dead aboard "The Sea Nymph" adrift half way between Cuba and the Keys, each man more full of holes than a peg board, Sheridan decided rum running was too hot. So nine months after they'd arrived in Miami, tired and haggard, Eddie, Nelson, and Bear were on the road again, back to Chicago. This time, they drove in Nelson's brand new car, with a satchel of cash stowed in a hidden lock box under the back seat.

Chapter 38

August 1927, Chicago

The three men had been back in Chicago only two weeks when news of Mick Sheridan's murder hit the papers. Now they were at Nelson's sister's house waiting for a good time to make their getaway.

As they finished the fried chicken and mashed potato dinner Edna had made, they recounted their plans. Nelson would be off to Mexico, and Bear was headed to Northern Wisconsin. The only place Eddie could think of at the moment was California. It's where his brother Richie had dreamed of going.

"Thank you, Edna," Eddie said, taking a dish of peach pie from her.

"You ever wish we'd stayed in Miami?" Nelson asked.

"Every day," Eddie said. "But as nice as that idea is, I don't think we would be any safer down there. Besides, who could have seen this coming?"

"You mean the boss getting whacked? I figured it woulda happened before now. And," Nelson said, "you know how it is. Doesn't take a genius to figure out that we're probably up next in the firing squad."

Bear got up and looked out the kitchen window. "Dark enough to get going. I'm getting nervous just sitting here."

"Finish your pie, at least," Nelson said. "Who knows when you'll next have a cook as good as my sister."

Eddie excused himself to go to the bathroom. Before stepping out into the hallway, he pulled out his money clip and counted out three hundred dollars. Then, opening the door quietly, he listened to make sure everyone was still in the kitchen before sneaking into Edna' bedroom, where he tucked the money under her pillow. He was almost back to the kitchen when Nelson came around the corner.

"Thank God," he said. "I gotta go something fierce."

When the three departed fifteen minutes later, they embraced as if they would never see one another again.

"It's been a riot, hasn't it?" Nelson said, his voice on the verge of breaking.

When Eddie saw Nelson's eyes puddle with tears, he about called him an old softie, but thought better of it. No man wanted to hear something like that. Instead Eddie said, "Best of luck in Mexico. When things cool down, I woudn't mind a trip down there myself."

Bear coughed, then pushed his hand out to shake Eddie's. "All right, kid," he said. "Get going. I don't know how, but they seem to be two steps ahead of us, so stay low and move fast."

Eddie nodded, then he stepped out into the night.

PART FOUR

Chapter 39

August 24, 1927 5:30 a.m.
Chicago

Eddie's first inkling that something was off was when he tried to lift himself off the floor. It was no use. He had no strength at all. He couldn't move his head and could see only a wedge of the wallpaper in the dark corner at the bottom of the stairs. He must have fallen. Knocked himself out? Then Eddie remembered he had been all set to flee. He remembered Moose had been there. Or was this all a dream?

"Hello, Edward," a quiet voice said.

Eddie felt a cold sensation pulse through him. "Who's there?" he said, or thought he said. He had not heard his own words uttered aloud.

"Edward, hello," the voice said again, calm and muted, as if coming from far away.

Now Eddie knew he was dreaming, and everything would be all right when he woke up. But then the voice, which had sounded distant, was now sharp and clear.

"Let's get you upright," it said.

Eddie felt himself being stretched and pulled and conveyed across the room.

"There," the voice said, settling Eddie into a chair. "You are as floppy as Raggedy Andy, but this is an improvement over the floor."

Eddie saw the voice now, a man, or at least he saw his shoes. Why couldn't he lift his head?

The man bent down to look up into Eddie's bewildered eyes. "How are you feeling—that is, do you notice anything unusual, apart from me?"

"Still kinda woozy and can't move my head," Eddie said as if the situation he found himself in were perfectly normal, until it came to him that it was not. Not even close. His eyes widened in alarm. "Say what is this? Did you drug me? Is that what this is? What do you want? Money? Who do you work for? You're not one of Moose's guys."

"That is a lot of questions," Adi said with a chuckle. "My name is Adi Fattoré. I did not drug you. I have no need for money, and, as you will soon understand, I am here to help you."

Eddie's consciousness struggled to concede he needed help. He was still convinced this nightmare would end soon. Then an agonizing cry swelled within him, reverberating at the edges of his being. "What is this?"

"Edward," the voice said softly. "You are in no harm. My name is Adi and I was sent here to help you. Will you let me help you?"

From deep within came Eddie's reply. "Yes."

"All right, Edward," Adi said, "I want you to try something. If you are successful, you will feel better, I promise you."

Eddie could see that he was between a rock and a hard place. He didn't trust this fellow one bit, but he could see no other way to get himself out of this situation. "What do you want me to do?"

"It is quite simple. Just think to yourself, *I want to lift my head.*"

Eddie snorted. "What?"

"Please. Do as I say. Or would you rather be a rag doll all day?"

Eddie grunted. He was in no position to call the shots. "Lift up my head," he said, as if he were intoning a magic spell.

"Try again, with less sarcasm this time. And do not use your voice. Just concentrate on thinking that you want your head and neck to work just as they should."

Eddie felt a prickle of apprehension, as if he were a child about to fail a simple task. But instead of allowing himself to feel defeated before he even gave it a good try, Eddie closed his eyes and did as he had been told. It took several minutes and repeated attempts for Eddie to convince his head to stay upright, but finally when he opened his eyes, Eddie realized that not only could he see straight ahead but he could also move his head to see things all around him. A sense of relief flooded through him.

"Bravo," Adi said.

Morning light fell across the room. A pile of newspapers lay on the sofa, and on the table next to his chair were two empty beer bottles and a half-eaten sandwich on a plate. A black house fly nibbled on a crumb. When Eddie was feeling better, he would have to tidy up. In the background, the grandfather clock chimed six times. And that brought him back to the present. "Adi? That's your name?"

"Yes, of course."

"How'd you get in here? I keep that door locked tight."

Adi moved to the door. With the tip of his index finger, he pulled the door slightly open. "Do you mean this door?"

"I don't understand," Eddie said. "I—"

"Your adversaries—what is the phrase? Jimmied the lock."

"My adversaries?"

"Moose? You made an earlier reference to *Moose's guys*."

"Nah. If they'd got in, I'd be dead."

Adi went to the living room windows and looked out. The pink of the eastern sky was beginning to brighten. It would be a sunny day. A man across the street was already outside watering his flowers. A paper boy sped down the street on his bicycle, tossing newspapers onto porches.

"This is a nice neighborhood, Edward."

Eddie could see his captor clearly now. A thin man dressed in a gray chambray shirt and dark wool trousers. He had a long face, a hawk-like nose, and high cheekbones. His dark hair, parted to the side, brushed his shoulders, and he wore it tucked behind his ears. His short gray beard gave the fellow a serious look, Eddie thought, like a statesman from the past century. Still, when I get my strength back, I can take him.

Adi laughed and Eddie had the oddest feeling that Adi was laughing at him. "What's so funny?" Eddie demanded.

But before Adi had a moment to explain, Esther Crandall pushed open the front door and screamed. And at the very same time, Eddie saw a body lying at the foot of the stairs.

"Oh, Charlie," Esther said, turning away from Eddie's body. "He used to be such a nice boy."

Who was she talking about? Eddie wondered.

"Come now," Charlie said, clutching his neighbor's arm. "There's nothing we can do here. We'll go to your house and telephone the police."

She nodded and Charlie led her away.

Eddie listened to their footsteps fade, then he faced Adi and said in a panic, "We gotta get out of here. If the police find me—"

"Calm yourself, Edward. No one can see you. At least not this you," Adi said gesturing to the slumping Edward. "That you," Adi pointed to the contorted body, "they can see, naturally."

Eddie looked back at the body at the bottom of the stairs. In a flash of memory, he saw himself slip and tumble. "I was trying to get away. I fell."

"Yes," Adi said.

"And I am—. Dead," Eddie said. "That's me over there."

"Yes."

Because Eddie insisted, he and Adi watched as the police tore over the scene. Even after the coroner had given the go ahead for Eddie's body to be removed, they searched. Desk drawers in the parlor, book shelves and knick knack niches. They even lifted the sofa cushions, coming so close to Eddie that he gasped, forgetting for a moment that he was invisible to them. One officer bounded upstairs. Two others went to the kitchen, from where Eddie heard the sounds of cupboards opening, dishes clattering to the floor. Footsteps on the cellar steps. Then, when he heard the screen door to the back porch slam, Eddie had the urge to jump up and go after them. His knapsack wouldn't be hard to find. Then Eddie laughed.

"Something humorous?" Adi asked.

"Just thinking about something my father used to say. '*We bring nothing into this world, and it is certain we can carry nothing out.*' He wanted Richie and me to understand that we have just one life, and we'd better make the most of it, because you can't take your money with you."

"That is wise advice," Adi said.

"Sure. But—."

"But what?"

"He never expected me to make the most of anything."

Just then the cop from upstairs was back in the living room. The two who had been outside were back now, empty handed. How could that be? He knew coppers could be on the dim side, but blind?

"Find anything upstairs?" one asked.

"No. You?"

"No. Too clean if you ask me."

"Yeah. Something don't smell right."

Eddie smirked. For now he felt like breathing a sigh of relief. When he had a chance, he'd go get his knapsack and be on his way after all.

After the police left and the house quieted, Adi moved a chair over to sit and face his new soul. "Now then, Edward. They say repentant souls have eternity to figure out what went wrong in their lives, but that is not quite true for you and me. That is, I have a job to do, two jobs actually, though one is of no concern to you. Nevertheless, now that all the excitement regarding your demise has calmed down, I would like to get started."

"Started?" It was then that Eddie remembered. He was no longer alive and this guy Adi was calling the shots. "What are you anyway. An angel?" Eddie let a moment pass before he added, "A demon?"

Adi suppressed a derisive laugh. "An angel, of a sort," he said. "However, as you can see, not one with wings. More precisely I am a spirit."

"You're a ghost?" Eddie shouted triumphantly. "And now I am too."

"Spirits. We are spiritual beings. Ghost is such a common term."

"Have it your way."

"Now, as I was saying, it is time to begin, so let me formally introduce myself. My name is Adi Fattoré, and I have been sent to help you atone for a life that was, well, less than it could have been. Much less according to most accounts."

"What? Atone—?"

"Let me explain. A benevolent being interceded on your behalf, granting you the opportunity to atone for your unfulfilled life. If you accept this gift, you will be granted the ability to see things anew."

"Mumbo jumbo," Eddie said. "Can't you just get this over with? Send me wherever I'm supposed to be?"

"You *are* where you are supposed to be, Edward," Adi said with a sigh. He stood and went to the window. A few neighbors were gathered on the sidewalk looking up at the house, no doubt gossiping about the morning's events. Edward Reed would forever be remembered by those folks, and not in a good way.

"Sorry to be so much trouble," Eddie said, facetiously.

Adi did not reply. Instead he watched the neighbors until a short-haired dog loped across the street and sat by one man who reached down to scratch its ears.

"All right," Eddie said in exasperation. "You say you are here to help me, but how am I going to do anything sitting here like a blob."

Adi turned and clapped his hands before pulling them in a praying gesture to his lips. "I hear willingness on your part. Is that what I hear? If so, I can remedy your "blob" situation immediately. At least in good time relative to eternity."

Adi moved the chair he had been using back to its place near the front window. Then he stood before Eddie and appeared to be thinking of what to say next.

"Any time there, Boss."

"Boss," Adi snorted. "I quite like that."

Eddie's eyes expressed amusement.

"Do you remember, Edward, how earlier you learned to control your head? By thinking? You simply have to learn to do that with the rest of your body and in time you will be able to move about as effortlessly as I do."

"I'm going to need a refresher."

"I am not sure you will understand this now, but in time you will. When you died, you transformed from a solid body to a gas, and your entropy increased, which means you are now a freer being."

"You call this free?"

"You need to be patient. You are in a new relationship with gravity. In time you will see that moving, touching, doing anything requires a different approach, for you no longer have a physical body. Instead, your new entity—your gaseous form—will take its cues from a thought, an idea. Mind over matter, so to speak, though in this case, literally all in the mind."

Eddie emitted frustrated sigh. "I feel like I'm in school. Can't you just wave your arm and poof?"

"This is serious, Edward. I want you to understand what is happening. It is not magic. It is physics."

"Like I said, school."

Adi ignored him. "You need to learn that you can no longer do things as before. Actual physical actions—basic things like walking—are no longer possible like they were when you were alive. It is all ideas now. First allow your mind to think of the intended action. Then you, your mind that is, will form it and execute it in its confines. You will then feel it as if it actually happened. You will not sense any difference. I know this does not seem easy now, but in time it will be."

Adi knelt on the floor before Eddie. "Try something for me. Concentrate. Imagine your hand rising to touch my shoulder. For now, close your eyes and think only of this one action."

Eddie closed his eyes. Quieting the distraction within his mind was difficult. *Imagine your hand rising*, Adi had said. Imagine—. The words themselves were a distraction. Memory of Adi's voice was a distraction.

The tick-tock of the clock was a distraction. The more he tried to think, the more Eddie heard only noise in his head.

As if he were present with Eddie in his mind, Adi said, "Instead of saying the words, try to picture the action. See it happening."

Eddie quieted his thoughts and tried to conjure the image, as if in a day dream. This too came with distractions. In the room as he imagined it was the memory of those damn coppers ransacking his things. Con-cen-trate. See it. Minutes later, his arm rose just as he was picturing it.

"Ha ha! Did you see that?" Eddie exclaimed triumphantly, his hand resting on Adi's shoulder. "I did it!"

"Yes. Well done. Now, in the same way, lower that arm and raise the other."

As he completed this next task, Eddie's confidence grew. Then, without Adi telling him to do so, Eddie closed his eyes and imagined himself standing. Moments later when he faced Adi eye to eye, Eddie felt the burden of uncertainty begin to lighten. "I thought standing would be harder than just lifting an arm, but it was easy."

"As walking will be. But you will find that instead of standing and walking we spirits tend to hover and glide."

Eddie nodded and pictured himself walking, gliding, and just as easily as lifting his arm, he moved from the living room to the parlor to the kitchen, where he saw the floor littered with shards of broken dishes. His heart sank to see his mother's favorite tea cup, the one he liked to use, on the floor broken in half. Animals, he thought. They didn't have to destroy things looking for my loot.

"Gotta check something," Eddie said abruptly. "But it's out there. How do I open the door?"

"Learning to manipulate things, like the door, with your hands and fingers will take longer," Adi said, "but eventually you will learn to pick up or move objects. Shall I open the door for you?"

"Nah. It's not important."

"It seemed important."

"Well, it's not." He wasn't about to tell Adi about the rucksack. If the cops hadn't found it, that meant Moose did. What did he think he was going to do with money anyway? A dead guy can't spend money.

He stood for a moment, looking out at the yard. The grass was so green it was almost hard to look at. Hard to look at for another reason too. He had not mowed in many weeks. Wherever Pop was, Eddie was sure he was fit to be tied. Delmar Reed's neat lawns, front and back, were a source of pride, which he never neglected, though when Richie and Eddie were old enough, it was their job to push the mower and Pop's job to supervise. And that he did to the most minute detail. Eddie turned his gaze away from the door and went back into the living room where, with effort, he thought himself back onto the sofa.

"Now, Edward—" Adi said.

"Could you not call me that?"

"Edward?"

"Yes. Call me Eddie or Ed or nothing at all."

"Cowboy?"

"How do you know about that?"

"I know everything about you. I know what was under the porch. I know that you are ashamed that you let the grass get long. I know—"

"All right! You don't have to torment me. Or did you lie about being a demon. Are you here to make my life a living hell, only showing me how to walk so you can play me like a puppet?" Eddie could almost have sworn he felt his heart pounding. "Hey wait a minute. You know about my rucksack? Maybe the cops didn't find it because you took it."

"You have a vivid imagination," Adi said. Then he pulled the chair back over and sat across from Eddie. "So imagine this. Now that you can move about reasonably well, tell *me* what comes next."

"What do you mean?"

"I am wondering whether or not you will accept the gift offered to you as transmuted by me to be executed by you. Your atonement."

"If you could use words I understand, I think you would get your point across better."

Adi let out an exasperated sigh. "Are you willing to do what is needed to make up for what an *idiot* you have been?"

"Hey. No need to be rude. I get it. I'm supposed to say I'm sorry and—"

"Expressing contriti— Saying you are sorry is only the beginning. But yes. Why not start with that? Tell me, Edward. Eddie. How many would you say you ended up *taking care of*? What is the technical term? Bump off?"

Eddie laughed. It sounded funny to hear such lingo coming from Adi's mouth. "As I understand it, you already know that," Eddie said.

"I do, but as part of this arrangement you must—"

"Sing?"

"I suppose you could say that."

"Why's that? Seeing as how you already know?"

"Because, in order for you to begin to atone, you must concede there is something you need to atone for."

"And if I don't?"

"If you do not—." Adi stood. He appeared larger, no longer the slender, meek being Eddie had first taken him to be. Eddie sensed the spirit's impatience. "If you do not, you will become one of billions before you who failed to live up to their potential, the greatest sin some would argue. And because of that, but also because you destroyed instead of created, because you took instead of gave, because you—"

"I get it. I get it. You don't have to be so dramatic."

Adi sighed. "Come with me," he said, rising and moving up the stairs. Near the end of the hall, adjacent from Eddie's bedroom, was the door to the attic. With Eddie beside him now, Adi opened the attic door and glided up the stairs, where he waited for Eddie to follow him. The attic space spanned the length and width of the house, and even without the ceiling bulb turned on, it was a bright space, lit by double sashed windows on all sides. The glass had begun to accumulate the film of neglect, but that could easily be remedied with a rag. Were this his own place, Adi would attend to that without much delay. And he would sweep the floor, although it looked as though it was once swept regularly. Only a few cobwebs had begun to form where the ceiling sloped on the gable ends. Unlike some attics Adi had seen, this one was not cluttered with the forgotten detritus of life. Only one short stack of boxes rose at the foot end of a small iron bed. On it, a patchwork quilt lay neatly folded.

Eddie sat down on the bed, moving his fingers over the quilt. "I used to come up here after Richie died, to be alone. They didn't think to look for me up here. One time I stayed up here for two days, only sneaking down for food and to use the toilet when I knew they were out of the house. When I finally appeared in the kitchen one morning, they acted as if I had never been gone. Ma made me breakfast and Pop told me to not be late for school."

Adi remembered it had been Christmas Eve when fifteen-year-old Eddie had come up to the attic with his brother to look for a traveling bag of their mother's. A bag filled with sorrow. That day would be Richard Reed's last and the start of Eddie's lifelong grief.

"One thing I hope you will eventually learn," Adi said, "is that humans are deeply imperfect. Things you thought to blame your parents for are not good to dwell on now. Instead, let us consider this attic. It would, I think, be a good place for you to stay while you sort through everything. It is, what is the term, *cozy*, is it not?"

"Stay up here?" Eddie asked surprised. "You mean live here?"

"You cannot remain in the house among the new tenants."

"New tenants?"

"Certainly they will sell your house soon."

"No family to give it to," Eddie said. "I was the last of the Reeds."

"Yes, you were, I am afraid. Now as I was saying, it would be best if you established yourself up here. Not that you cannot be among the living. To accomplish your atonement, you absolutely must go among the living. But for now, it will be best if you and they do not occupy the same space. Up here, you will be far enough removed from their daily life."

"If it's going to be a problem, why don't I go somewhere else, then? How about a suite in the Palmer House?"

"Droll. Trés Droll."

"I could be serious. Couldn't I make amends from a swanky hotel?"

"You need proximity to the errors and regrets of your life for them to be instructive. So no, you could not make amends from a swanky hotel. Though that is not a bad idea for me when I come to visit from time to time."

"Visit? Where are you going?"

"Nowhere. Come. Let us go down." Adi rose and motioned for Eddie to join him. As Eddie approached, Adi could see he was already gliding and had given up trying to swing one foot out in front of the other. That kind of intuitive thinking would serve Eddie well, Adi thought.

They were in the kitchen now, and Adi began to pick up the broken dishes. "Is there a broom?"

Eddie pointed to the cellar door, and Adi retrieved the broom from the hanger on the back of the door and started sweeping.

"I never figured an angel would do housework," Eddie said, amused. "Like to keep things tidy, do you?"

"From the state of the living room, I assume you do not."

"Yeah. That's fair. If you show me how, I'll pick up the mess in there later." Then changing the subject to the thought he had carried down with him from the attic, Eddie asked, "How long will I be here? I mean how long does this atonement thing take?"

"That all depends on you. Twenty years. Fifty—"

"Fifty years?" Eddie gasped.

"That is no time at all relative to the future. Again, it depends on you."

Eddie bent down and tried to pick up the handle of the tea cup, but succeeded only in moving it a quarter of an inch. Adi paused sweeping to pick it up for him and set it on the table.

"I don't know, Boss. No matter what you say, fifty years seems like forever. Wouldn't it just be easier to send me to hell for my sins. I am sure there are plenty of guys like me down there already, so I would fit in fine."

Adi ignored the disingenuous suggestion and emptied the dustpan into the trash. "You know Eddie, you have never asked me about your benefactor. Are you not curious?"

"All right. Sure," Eddie said, lowering himself into a chair. "Who is it?"

Adi stood near the sink, the broom in his hand, looking more like a janitor than an angel. "When you died," he began softly, "your mother cried for you. Then, without knowing if her plea would be heard, she asked for mercy from those who would judge you. She blamed herself for not doing more to set you straight when she saw your path veering into trouble. She knew you felt guilty about Richie, and she regretted she did not tell you enough that his death was not your fault."

Eddie sighed and nagged the cup handle until he was successful in moving it, then turned it around and around in a plaintive circle. "At least she never knew the worst of it. About me, I mean."

"She knew more than you think. Not details, but she knew you were connected to criminals. It broke her heart, but she never stopped loving you."

"Ahhh," Eddie groaned in pain. "Why did you have to tell me that? It makes everything worse."

"How? To know how much your mother loved you?"

"Yes. Because it means I'm an even worse person than I thought I was. She knew I was lying to her, and she just kept on pretending."

"Self-knowledge is one of the greatest tools you will have moving forward."

"Can't you get it through that head of yours. I am not worth saving."

Adi kept silent for a time, knowing that Eddie was, for the first time, experiencing true pain. For spiritual beings, emotional and intellectual pain were far worse than the physical pain of mortal beings. "I want you to know that it was not your mother's plea alone that convinced my superiors to send me to you. Something you did revealed your worthiness."

"That I did?"

"When your parents were dying, you took care of them. You stayed by your father's side, a man you were at odds with most of your life, and you cared for him. When he died, you cried with your mother in her grief, and when she died, you shed tears for her."

"And that makes me a good person?"

"That makes you a good person in many ways. But—"

"But it's not quite enough to erase the bad."

"No. However, it is a point from which you can begin to see the person Edward Reed could have been if only he had made different choices."

"I did the best I could, you know. I got dealt a bad hand."

"Not a few people are dealt bad hands and they do not end up wielding Tommy guns."

Eddie forced a wry smile onto his face. "You got a certain way with words, when you're not trying to be professor Adi."

"Be that as it may, you need to concentrate on what I am saying. You have been given a gift here, time to atone for your sins and, I hope, along the way learn what Edward Reed's life could have been if you had chosen to live differently. However, if you refuse this gift, which is your right, your spiritual energy will be thrust back in time and you will have to start all over. I mean all over."

"Where's Ma now? Are Pop and Richie there too?"

"They are in a place of peace. And if you trust me, you will be there one day too. But if you do not, you will be yanked away, and I will be given some other hapless soul to lead, because that is what I do. When you have decided, find me and let me know."

Then Adi opened the kitchen door and went out onto the back porch.

Eddie's chin fell to his chest, and he let it rest there. It was nearly an hour before he moved again. When Eddie opened his eyes, he knew what he wanted to do. He got up, pushed against the screen door, and joined Adi where he was seated on the back porch.

This day had been one for the books, Eddie thought. He smiled to think how much Joe Crandall would enjoy hearing about it. Joe couldn't resist a good story, and Eddie had a feeling that Joe would not be bothered one bit by the otherworldly facts of this tale or its narrator. But Joe would already know about how his mother had found Eddie's body. And about the police bounding into the Reed house. Maybe Joe had known about him all along, like Ma had known. Eddie felt a sickness rise within him. Maybe he hadn't fooled anyone after all.

"Going to rain?" Adi asked.

Dark clouds had formed in the west. The air was still and thick.

"Looks like it might," Eddie said, amused that they were talking about the weather.

From somewhere down the alley came the sounds of boys playing baseball. Eddie smiled and looked back at the sky. He knew that even when the first fat drop of rain fell, those kids would stay out until their game was done. Because that's what you did. You played the whole game.

"All right then, Adi Fattoré, tell me what to do."

Chapter 40
August 24

"Are there a few things you want, Edward, up in the attic with you, at least for now? Things from your life tie you to memories. Memories will be your most important possessions. So if there is something—"

In Richie's old room, Eddie let his hand trail over the top of the little bookcase Uncle Stanley had made. "I'll take this," he said.

Adi made no sarcastic comments about how Eddie did not read. Instead the spirit moved it all up to the attic and set it against the wall at the top of the stairs. Then he settled the books back on the shelves, in alphabetical order by author Eddie would discover later.

"How did you do that? You looked like a cloud gathering the bookcase, swirling all the books into your arms."

"I simply increased my volume. I can show you how to do it yourself, but perhaps after you have managed other things first."

Eddie touched the top of the bookcase, feeling closer to his brother than he had in years. His chest swelled with love and regret. Then Eddie turned and looked over the rest of the attic. "When did all this—" he said, surprised.

"Just a bit of decorating," Adi said. "I found it all in the cellar. I did not think you would mind." Adi had placed the old kitchen table in the front gable just under the windows and tucked two chairs under it. On top was a deck of playing cards. Near the bed an upturned peach crate held a little lamp, which glowed over the yellow pine floorboards. "Quite homey, if I do say so myself. As for the lamp, I would not worry. The trees will diffuse the light. In my experience, humans rarely look up or notice things beyond their own two feet. You do not need the lamp, but it is nice, is it not? As for the new tenants coming up here, they may, to store things, boxes of Christmas baubles and the like, but I doubt they will want to remain for long. You cannot feel it, but it is stifling up here right now. It will be cold in winter. I do not think your new tenants are going to turn the attic into a playroom or the like. But, if it would ever happen that someone wanted to clear all of this away, your ability to do your work would not be affected. Just like the lamp, you need none of these things."

Eddie not even considered the effect of the lamp, on or off. Nor of people bringing their own things up. At the moment, he was so mesmerized by it all, that he was not thinking clearly. He was still not used to being dead. He ran his hand over the old kitchen table. "I haven't seen this in years." He stooped to peer underneath where he found his and Richie's names carved into the soft wood. They had used their father's pocket knife, which Richie had secretly taken from Pop's dresser tray the day before. While their parents were away all morning, the boys had gouged their names. Eddie remembered now, he had nicked his finger and had rubbed the blood into his hands.

It was at this table that his mother had taught him the alphabet, never once losing her patience when he'd make some letters backwards. What a dope he used to be. Eddie wondered now if his mother had ever seen their vandalism. Richie had returned the knife, and neither boy thought Pop was any wiser. Was this one of those *put-back* things? Get some wood putty and fill in the carvings? Even he knew that wasn't what Adi meant when he said, "fill a spiritual void by replacing what you took away."

The memories of his mother and himself as a four-year-old were as sharp as if they were just now happening. He saw her in his mind, young and beautiful, as if time had stopped in 1904 and she had not aged one moment beyond then. The sensation of her presence was so strong that it reordered Eddie's consciousness in an unsettling way. A feeling like nausea hit him, and he placed his hand, or tried to place his hand, on the table to steady himself.

"Are you unwell?" Adi asked.

Eddie was too embarrassed to tell the truth, even a truth that Adi most likely already knew. Eddie laughed. It was all so absurd.

"Something is funny?"

Eddie closed his eyes and sighed deeply. "I could not have imagined it would be so tiring to be dead," he said.

Adi understood. "Tomorrow," Edward. "Tomorrow is soon enough. Or the next day. We do not have to do a thing right now. How about not thinking about anything but lying on that little bed? I think you have done enough for one day."

Then Adi vanished. It was something else Eddie would get used to, Adi appearing out of nowhere and leaving just as quickly. At the moment, he was not sorry to see the man go. He had no energy to listen to one more sermon. However, Eddie did think it was a good idea to rest, so he situated himself upon the bed. The mattress was the same one that they had taken out to the porch for Ma that summer she lost the baby. Lying there now, Eddie's mind refused to calm. Adi had explained that Eddie would not sleep, but instead would find peace within his mind. It took Eddie more than an hour to quiet his thoughts, there were so many, but once he did, he was amazed at the deep sense of relief he felt.

At 9:00 a.m. the next morning, a different team of police officers came to the house. This time, instead of ransacking, their search was methodical. By noon they had found nothing other than evidence that a family had lived in the house for many years. Nevertheless, Eddie told Adi he thought he could feel his heart beating from fear.

"You do not have a functioning heart, obviously," Adi said, "but your psyche can still experience anxiety. In fact, emotional and intellectual experiences will be highly instructive throughout your atonement process."

"All right, boys," the detective said. "We've scoured this place. There's nothing here."

After the officers left the house, Adi suggested they go out onto the back porch again. "I like it out there, and it will be a good place for a lesson."

"If I'd known I'd be in school so much, I never would have died," Eddie said.

Adi snickered. "You do make me laugh, Edward."

"Hey," Eddie said, "who mowed the grass?"

Adi took a bow.

"How the hell?"

"During the night. You were resting."

"But how?"

Adi narrowed his brows. "The way you would. I pushed the mower over the grass. The blades snipped the grass."

"I know how a mower works. How did you—"

"As you have seen, I am able to move objects, quite easily, and before you ask, no one saw the mower criss-crossing the yard on its own. Your neighbors were fast asleep, I assure you."

They settled on the porch, and Eddie admitted that if Adi could cut the grass again next week, he might be useful to have around.

A cardinal tweeted and drew Eddie's gaze up into the branches of the sycamore tree. Ma had loved that sound. On a day like today, she'd have had the wash on the line early. It would be too hot to turn on the oven, so she would make cold roast sandwiches for dinner. If there were still beans in the garden, she would pickle them for dinner too.

"You know something else, Adi? A beer would hit the spot, right now," Eddie said. "Don't you miss stuff like that. A cold beer. A juicy steak?"

"You can still have all of that."

"Ha," Eddie snorted. "Sure."

"I am not joking. You want a beer? Conjure it in your mind. Serve it up right now in a big frosted mug."

"Mind tricks."

"You keep saying it is tricks. I am simply conveying a truth about the way spiritual beings operate." Adi held out his hand, as if taking a mug from a tavern keeper, then he lifted it to his lips and drank. "Ahh. Nothing better on a hot day."

Eddie stared incredulously.

"I cannot conjure one for you. You have to do it yourself."

Eddie closed his eyes and remained in concentration for several minutes. When he could not produce the effect he longed for, he gave up. "I quit."

"You will get there. Just be patient. And next time, if you get an actual bottle of beer from the ice box, it will help you visualize it. Now obviously drinking the physical beer does nothing for you, but you can imagine drinking it and smell it and taste it."

"Tell me more about that," Eddie said, "how you operate. As a spirit."

"Very well," said Adi, who stood and faced Eddie as if he were about to make a great proclamation. "I cannot be everywhere at once. However, I can get from one place to another in a moment of thought. I do not need to eat or sleep, though, as I have demonstrated, I am able to appreciate those human pleasures. And my mind and soul do get weary. You have already experienced that yourself. We spirits also need rest.

"I cannot start or stop an act of nature, which is a tragedy, for earth's sudden disasters—not acts of God—are swift and ruthless killers.

"And to make this very clear, I cannot will a certain roll of a die or place a royal flush into your hand, at least not without the cards flying all over the place. I do like to play cards though. I find it to be a good diversion. Which is why I set that deck over on the table."

"What about people. They can't see you or me, right? But you say I will have to 'go among the living.' I'm wondering how that works. Do you just bump into people?" Eddie asked.

"Not in the way you imagine, for I am as insubstantial as you are. But I can concentrate myself, lower my entropy, and push into them. When our beings collide, they feel me like a hiccup. It is enough of a bump to wake them up, so to speak, alert them to the present moment. In the same way, I can momentarily envelop a person within me, which I would *only* do to save someone from harm. Doing so takes tremendous concentration, so it will be some time before you learn to do that."

"And they can't hear us either, right?"

"This is the odd part, Edward. They can hear us better than you might think. Humans are constantly searching for connections to the spiritual world, so they are predisposed to believe we exist. Ever hear of a Ouija Board? Mediums? Psychics? Fortune tellers? Humans crave messages from us. But can they hear me with their ears. No. For we have no real voices do we? It is through the mind we hear each other. And the same is true for when we speak to humans. But that does not mean you should not speak to them. Go ahead. You never know what someone may hear."

"I think I get it. It seems like talking isn't going to be as effective as knocking into them. Like if you—" Eddie searched his mind for an example. "Say you bumped into Richie right as he was about to steal Joe's toy soldier and you caused him to drop it. He probably wouldn't have taken it then, right?"

"It is possible. All actions create reactions. But in our case, the reaction to any action we take depends on how a person perceives the action."

"You are making my head hurt."

"How can I help it hurt less?"

"Maybe a bit less, you know, teacher stuff, and just tell me what you want me to do?"

"Think of it this way. Doing a good deed. Whispering a kind word. Nurturing goodness in others. Those are ways you can atone for your sins. All well and good. I happen to be even more interested in seeing how you discover what your life could have been."

"I suppose you couldn't just show me?"

"Even your parents did not guide every step. You learned many things on your own, from the mistakes you made, from your successes too."

"Or as my pop used to say, 'you've made your bed, now you have to lie in it.'"

"And another thing," Adi continued, "A good deed must arise from a pure and compassionate intention. It must happen in a spontaneous moment as response to human need. But do not despair. It will happen because you will find within yourself—when the time requires it—that same sense of love for another as you felt for your mother in her last days."

"All right. So I do a good deed and the world gets better?"

Adi could not begrudge Eddie's simplistic conclusion. "If that were true, we would live in a perfect world, because there are a lot of people, spirits too, who are doing nothing but good. And while the world in this house might get better, or the world in this neighborhood and in your city, please do not think I am asking you to fix the world. What a tremendous burden that would be."

"Why bother with good deeds then?"

"Because through them you are mending *your* soul, Edward. You do it to heal yourself." Adi shrugged. And if you happen to make things around you a little bit nicer for a while, all the better. Who knows, one kind gesture from you might spark a chain of kindness. A kind word to one person might generate an act of kindness towards another, so it may be that your kindness becomes a catalyst for something truly remarkable. Think of it like ripples on a pond when it rains. Each drop of rain creates its own set of ripples, but together, the effect is—"

"A lot of ripples?"

Adi laid a hand on Eddie's shoulder. "I am not worried about you finding ways to put goodness into the world in the years ahead. Nor am I worried that you will find the embers of the flame that once existed in you, before you began to blow it out. The most difficult thing for you will be to reorient your sense of time. Before long, an hour, a day, a year will mean nothing to you, except as they have meaning to the people you encounter."

"And you'll be here with me, so that'll make it easier."

"I can be here, when I feel you need me, but as in your human life, this afterlife requires you to learn through experience. So once I am confident you are well on your way, I will leave you to your task. That does not mean I will stop watching over you, but I cannot hold your hand through your entire atonement."

A forlorn sigh emanated from Eddie.

"Do not worry, Edward. For now I will be by your side. And I have faith that this will go better than you think. Just watch. And listen. Listen with your heart. You will figure it out."

Chapter 41
August 25

Eddie and Adi spent the morning on the front porch watching the neighborhood. Adi wanted to know about everyone they saw, so Eddie did his best to tell their stories, but when a woman he did not recognize came out onto the porch of the house next to Charlie Alford's and when another woman from down the street walked up to visit with her, Eddie realized there were people on the block that he had never met.

His mother would have found that to be a foreign concept. She knew everyone up and down the street, and when a new family arrived, she baked something to take over to welcome them. People on this block knew that when a need arose, whatever it was, they could count on each other. That's just how it was in this neighborhood, or how it had been when Naomi Reed was still alive. So when Esther Crandall had walked across the street this morning to converse with Charlie Alford, Eddie did not care that they were probably talking about him. It was good, he thought, that a widow and a widower had each other.

At half past eleven, a mailman Eddie did not recognize, a young fellow, probably new to the job, sprinted up the steps and shoved a handful of letters through the mail slot, oblivious to the fact that the former occupant was deceased. When he zig-zagged across to Charlie's house, Esther Crandall's animated body language indicated she was letting the mailman know what everyone else already knew. Then the three of them stared at the Reed house for a moment before the mailman tipped his cap to Esther and Charlie and trotted to the next house, then the next. Afterwards, Eddie and Adi went inside.

"Who's going to pay the electric bill now?" Eddie said, trying but failing to pick up an envelope from the growing pile of mail on the floor.

"Not your concern obviously," Adi said. He watched Eddie fumble with the envelopes. "I know your instinct is to move all of that over to the desk, but if you had been successful, someone soon will wonder how it got there. No one can see you, but the effects of what you do can be seen. Good to remember that always."

They made their way up to the attic where Adi suggested they play cards. "Excellent learning opportunity," he said.

Adi, who manipulated the cards as if he were a speakeasy card shark, was attempting to teach Eddie how to hold his cards, trying not to laugh each time they spluttered out of his hands back onto the table. After a while, Adi gathered the deck, and after tapping it back into shape, he laid it aside and said, "It is time to try something else. Hold your hands out. Yes. Like that. Now, with your left hand—you were left handed correct?"

Eddie nodded, but a sharp memory of his first grade teacher taping his left hand to his desk to force him to use his right brought back the same sickness he had felt before. Would every bad memory make him feel ill?

"With your left hand hovering, push just your index finger down and tap the table."

Eddie closed his eyes and tried to see the action. It took him less than a minute for the action to materialize.

"Excellent," Adi said. "Now try to repeat that with your right hand." Adi waited. "Good. I think you can see where this is going. Tap each finger on its own in sequence, like pressing piano keys, in a way. Did you ever learn to play?"

Eddie shook his head. "Stop distracting me," he said.

Adi watched as Eddie tapped, increasingly with more confidence and speed. "If this were a piano and not a table, you would be playing some kind of tune. Not a good one, but you would be playing. Well done."

"I don't suppose I will ever be able to manipulate things with my hands without having to close my eyes."

"As with any new skill, the intensity of concentration needed to learn will diminish over time. So, yes, before long you will be able to do things with your eyes open. You will learn to integrate your imagination and actions so fluidly that one day soon, you will not even have to think. And good thing for you, because if you always have to tune out your sense of sight to play a hand of cards, I will win every time."

"Speaking of cards," Eddie said, "Let me try again."

Adi dealt ten cards each. Minutes later, Eddie had them all in his hand, though they looked less like a nice fan and more like a twisted pinwheel.

"It's progress, isn't it?" Eddie said, laughing.

By mid-afternoon, Eddie's skills had improved enough that they had played several solid hands of Gin Rummy.

"I win again, Edward."

"Or did I let you win?" Eddie no longer cared that Adi called him by his formal name. Adi was somewhat of a formal guy and besides, when he said it, he never meant anything bad. It wasn't like Pop's stern "EDWARD!" whenever Eddie had done something wrong.

"One more round before we call it a day?"

"Why not?" Eddie said, grateful he was getting the hang of things. "Let me deal?"

Adi peered over his nose. "You can try."

A half hour later, they were each holding their ten cards, although Adi had counted twice to be sure.

"I have a question," Eddie said, placing a card on the discard pile. "How are people supposed to reach their potential when they're always messing up? You said earlier that people are mostly good. But I think humans do bad things all the time."

"The age old quandary. Are people innately good or bad," Adi said. "I certainly do not have the answer, but I have seen enough of life to have a theory. I think we are all born with the potential to be good, but we can only reach that end through education. Someone has to teach us the difference between right and wrong. We are not born knowing that. Those who are not shown the right path might end up like—"

"Like me."

"But you *were* shown the right path."

"So why did I take up with Nelson? How do you explain that?"

"You must have thought about that more than once. Why do you think?"

Eddie knew the answer. He had known almost from the start that he had agreed to work with Nelson because it was something his father couldn't control. It wasn't just because being one of Sheridan's guys got him out of the stockyards, it was because he could stick it to his father for once. "I think it was the suits and the dames," Eddie said sarcastically, knowing that Adi had heard his every thought.

"So a child raised right can still choose a wrong action. You were still a child when Nelson found you. Some would say he exploited your innocence."

"Nelson never treated me bad," Eddie said defiantly.

"I understand you and your other fellow, the Bear—"

"Just Bear."

"I understand they were like brothers to you, I might even argue like fathers, replacing the role Delmar should have had. You and your father both held your grief so close that it clouded your view of the other. You were both hurting over Richard's death, but neither one of you could talk to the other about it. You both let the pain turn to anger."

"Yeah, well, I never told him it was his fault Richie died."

"I agree that was not a wise thing for Delmar to do, but do you not think over the years he felt sorry for what he said?"

"I don't know, Adi. I really don't. Even before Richie died, Pop didn't think much of me. He cared more about the people he worked with than me. I guess in the end, I proved him right."

"And through the years you thought, what is the use. I may as well live up to my father's expectations of me?"

"Who are you? Dr. Freud? You trying to psychoanalyze me?"

Adi just shook his head, then rose and went to the little bookcase. He searched for a copy of what he hoped was there. Stevenson, Tennyson, Tolstoy—. Hmm, he muttered to himself before he found what he was looking for in the C's. He laughed a bit at his own expense. Samuel Clemens, not Mark Twain. Adi could sometimes be a bit too fastidious.

When Adi handed the book to Eddie, he just laid it on the table.

"Why does everyone want me to read that damn thing?"

"I am not sure about others, but for me, because it is a book about fathers and sons. About a son whose father abuses him but finds his own light nevertheless and in the process finds a man who becomes a true father, despite what society allows. It is about a boy who would rather go to hell than betray the only person who ever truly loved him."

Eddie opened the cover and peered at inscription on the flyleaf. *To my friend Eddie, Happy Birthday and Best Wishes on all your adventures. J. Crandall.*

"I agree with Joe," Adi said. "Maybe one day you will give that book a second chance. You might find that you and Huck have a lot in common."

The rest of the day Eddie spent on his own, Adi having disappeared for a meeting in Celestia, wherever that was. Adi could be secretive when it suited him. Before he left, Adi suggested Eddie practice moving things about, such as pushing chairs in and out, unfolding and refolding his quilt—turning the pages of a book? The latter Eddie refused to do on principle. Just because he was dead it didn't meant he had no rights.

When the sun set, Eddie went out onto the back porch. Over the fence the Crandall house was lit up like a jack o' lantern. He imagined Esther inside, her feet up on a stool, listening to a radio program. For a brief moment, Eddie thought about asking Adi to get him a radio for the attic, but obviously he'd say no. "If I don't start thinking things through," he said, "I'm going to embarrass myself one of these days."

Eddie thought about what Adi had said about him living up to Pop's low expectations. Could that be true? What would his life have been like if he'd not taken up with Nelson, Eddie wondered. Would he still be at the stockyards with Jimmy Nolan and the other men? Going further back, if he had not been in a constant battle with his father, would he have tried harder in school, graduated, found a job? Maybe in a print shop or somewhere he could make signs or advertisements. He had never even tried to see what he could do with his ability to draw.

He remembered that girl then, the one with the dark hair. Belinda. That was her name. He had made her a drawing of a cat. But that was a foolish errand and thinking she might like him for it had made him feel even more foolish. He had put away his pencils after that, and only began making sketches again when Nelson needed to "see" their plans. The first time Eddie had drawn a map of a getaway route, Nelson smiled broadly and called him Rembrandt. Eddie didn't explain to Nelson that he was anything but.

And now, who was he? He was nothing. He was a dead guy who had been given a chance to change. But even if he did, he would still be dead. That's the part that Adi always failed to tack on to the whole grand scheme. I might learn what I could have been, Eddie thought, but so what? How will that make me feel any better about my life. It can only make me feel worse.

When the lights went out next door, Eddie rose and went up to the attic. He stared out the window at the vacant street for a while, thinking of lost chances and futility. And when he turned around *The Adventures of Huckleberry Finn* was staring at him.

"Just shut up," he shouted, as if the book were a thing that could hear him. Then Eddie stretched out on his little bed and let the night pass, because what else was there to do? People slept at night and old habits were hard to break.

PART FIVE

THE MASONS

Chapter 42
October 1927

After the state of Illinois determined that Edward Reed had no family to inherit, an estate company was contracted to ready the Reed house for sale. As soon as the sign was planted in the yard, a truck arrived with three men, who made swift work of clearing the house of all its furnishings. Eddie watched them drive away that afternoon, still astonished that they had not cleared out the attic. Eddie learned later that Adi had momentarily drawn everything into himself so that the movers saw only an empty space. That feat was something of a trick, Adi admitted, one that would be difficult for Eddie to master.

Two days later, a fair-haired young man dressed in a gray suit arrived with the estate manager. After scrutinizing every room of the house, the young man handed the manager a list of improvements he wanted made.

"If you can guarantee it will all be completed by an October 15 move-in date," the man said, "we can go back to your office and sign the papers."

"Won't be a problem, sir."

Eddie thought the reassuring smile on the estate manager's face looked a bit greedy. Eddie knew how things worked and was sure that guy was going to skim his share off the top of this whole deal. But the man in the gray suit looked like a good fellow.

As promised, by mid-October, the house had been repainted and a leak in the porch roof fixed. Out back, the dying sycamore had been taken down and a young sugar maple was planted in its place, its vigorous leaves bright red. Eddie felt somewhat reassured knowing it would take a long time for those branches to be sturdy enough for climbing.

Inside, the biggest change happened in the kitchen. New plumbing, new cupboards, and a new stove. An electric ice box too. What a fine thing that was, Eddie thought. Ma would have loved it. As it always did, memories of his mother made him sad. She would have been fifty-six in November, far too young to be gone. Life was not fair, but it did move on. The hubbub of activity in the house these past weeks had made that very clear to Eddie.

At 7:30 a.m. on October 15, the man in the gray suit returned. He was Frederick Mason, a twenty-eight-year-old physician. Along with him was his wife Anne and their five-year-old twin daughters Mathilde and Genevieve.

"It's charming," Anne said just inside the front door. "I am sure we will be very happy here. What do you think girls? Did Daddy choose a good house for us?"

The two little girls giggled and spun in circles in the empty living room.

"All right, you silly things," their mother said. "Settle down. Nana and Papa will be arriving soon, and it will not do for you to look all worn out."

Eddie smiled when the twins complained in tandem and took one another's hands and spun an even wider circle.

The truck with the family's furniture arrived at eight, and Eddie watched with interest as this piece was placed here, that piece there, Anne directing it all as if she had done it many times before. Eddie was delighted to see a grandfather clock arrive, one that looked nearly identical to the one his family had. Even more astonishing was that Anne had it placed in the exact spot where theirs had been, on the wall separating the parlor from the living room, just at the edge of the hallway that led to the dining room and the kitchen, as if that space could accommodate only a grandfather clock.

All morning, amid the Mason family's swirling energy, Eddie swirled about as well. In the past month he had reached the outcome Adi had told him to expect, the fluid integration of mind and movement. Unlike the weight of gravity that in life had held his feet to the ground, movement that on certain days, especially after he'd imbibed too much gin, had felt like an elephant's weight instead of his own, he now moved with such effortlessness that he thought at times it was nice to be dead. Moving from one place to the next was just as effortless. Just as Adi had promised, all Eddie had to do was think himself to another part of the house and almost instantly he was there. However, despite this fluid mobility, Eddie took care to watch the Masons from a distance. They could not see him, but he knew if he brushed too closely, they would be able sense him, if they were not too pre-occupied to notice.

Anne had shown the movers where to put the girls' beds, and was coming down to find the box with their bedding, when she heard a knock, then a "yoo hoo" at the front door. "Mother," she muttered under her breath, not ready for the intrusion, but turning to put on a smile nevertheless.

"Anne, dear," Sybil Henry said, leaning in to kiss her daughter on the cheek. "Can you believe it? Your father insisted on driving all the way from St. Louis. I must look a fright."

Anne craned her neck to see the car out on the street. Frederick was outside now, greeting her father who waited on the sidewalk.

"It's a Pierce Arrow. Quite something, he assures me."

"Hello, Nana," the girls said dutifully.

Sybil smiled and patted them both on the head before turning her attention back to her daughter. "So this will be your home *and* Frederick's practice?" She shook her head. "Such a quaint neighborhood, but I suppose if anyone can make it work, you can."

Tobias Henry pulled his son-in-law by the elbow over to where the car was parked in front of the Crandall house, a safe distance from the moving truck. "How's that for a motorcar?" he said, beaming with pride.

Frederick peered inside. "It is beautiful."

"I thought we could go for a ride later."

"I am sure the girls would enjoy that very much," Frederick said.

"There is room for us all, son," Tobias said, as if Frederick had not understood the invitation.

Frederick smiled. In Tobias Henry's world, others did life's menial tasks, and Frederick was certain it had not occurred to the man that he and Anne had far too much to do today to be driving around Chicago. "Perhaps after we are settled. I'd like to get my office and patient room set up. My advertisements have me open for business at 10:00 a.m. on Monday."

Tobias dropped his chin, then nodded. "Quite right. I forget that some of us still hold office hours."

Frederick knew his father-in-law did not mean to be condescending, but a man who had made his fortune and had nothing to do but enjoy it often forgot what it took to get there. "I ought to go in—"

"Of course. Right behind you Freddie."

It was a nickname Frederick hated, but he put up with it because it wasn't worth his aggravation. At least Tobias tried. Anne's mother never addressed him personally. She only ever spoke to him through her daughter or granddaughters, saying "your father," or "Doctor Mason." However, as uncomfortable as these visits were, Anne's parents rarely made the trip up from St. Louis, so he put up with them.

Then when he and Anne went to Missouri to visit Tobias and Sybil, the exhausting action of society life and attentive servants left no time for frustration. Anne shared his feelings. She found her parents to be as difficult as he sometimes did. Not that they couldn't be generous. Not that they couldn't be kind. But they lived in a different world, one that they never quite forgave Anne for marrying out of.

"Frederick will use the parlor to see patients," Anne was explaining to her mother, showing her the pocket doors that closed off the space, "and he will convert the dining room into his office."

"Suitable for the present," Mrs. Henry said. "Of course once Frederick's practice is better established, you will be able to move to more a more prestigious neighborhood."

Anne held her tongue. She would not engage in an argument in front of the movers, who stood on the porch with the dining table. "I've got to direct the movers, Mother," Anne said. "That goes in the kitchen," she told the men.

"Certainly," Mrs. Henry said. "The girls and I will stay out of your way."

"You don't have to sound put out, Mother. I told you when you called and said you and Father were coming here today that we would be busy unpacking."

"So put me to work. What do you want me to do?"

Anne, who had no intention of "putting her mother to work" led her up the stairs with Mathilde, Genevieve and Eddie close behind.

"There's so much light in this sweet room," Sybil said. It was Richie's old room, and the light, though filtered through the linden tree, was bright. "Is this where the girls will sleep?"

"Frederick and I will be in here," Anne said.

"Watch out, Mama," Genevieve said. "Your bed is coming up the stairs."

Naomi maneuvered her mother toward the front rooms. "The girls will be in here," Anne said, showing her mother the bedroom Naomi had once set up as a nursery, which later became the guest bedroom. "And this room," Anne said, pointing to Delmar and Naomi's bedroom, the largest of the four bedrooms, "will be their playroom."

Sybil leaned down to the girls and spoke sarcastically, "Seems you two are the ladies of the house."

Again Anne ignored her mother's tone, leading Sybil instead to the bathroom, where she clicked on the light. "Isn't this marvelous? A shower. In a house of this age. I cannot wait to use it," Anne said. Even Sybil Henry did not have a shower in her grand house.

"If you care for that sort of thing," Sybil said, turning her attention to where her daughter stood at the door of the back bedroom. Eddie looked on with pride as Anne presented the room that had been his. A full bed, a highboy, and an antique sink stand had already been moved in.

"And this is where I thought you and Father could stay. Close to the bathroom—convenient for you both."

Sybil looked over the room, then said "Your father has arranged the Charles Hotel for us, dear."

"Hmmph," Eddie grunted. Sybil Henry had no intention of *making do* in his old room. Just as well, Eddie thought. He didn't much care for Anne's mother.

"Whatever suits you," Anne said. As much as she knew her mother would refuse the offer, it had to be made. All pretense. All propriety. It was an exhausting game.

Just then, Tobias Henry appeared. "Freddie's going to be ready for patients before you can cook a meal in that disaster of a kitchen, Anne. Surely there is someone we could employ to organize it for you."

"We don't have that many things, Dad, and it doesn't all have to be done today."

"Quite right. And your dear husband has agreed to let me take you all to a restaurant for dinner tonight."

Anne smiled gratefully. "That is kind of you, Dad."

"Happy to help," Tobias said.

Anne gave her father a wry smile. "Girls, take your papa to the play room. He is going to help you unpack your dolls and toys." Anne knew her father would take the "order" to work as it was intended, as an opportunity to be with the girls, his Mattie and Gigi. He adored them. Thank goodness one of her parents had a heart, Anne thought.

Tobias nodded and let himself be dragged off to "play."

"What's this door," Sybil asked, turning the knob to the attic. Inside she flipped the light switch. "Oh my," she said, climbing the stairs. "Would you look at that. I wonder if this was a child's bedroom at one time, or maybe they stuck their old grandma up here," she said with a little laugh. "You'd never think of putting me in such a place in my old age, would you?"

"Oh, Mother, don't be silly. Besides," she said with a wink, "you know you'd fight me tooth and nail."

"Will you just leave all of this up here?" Sybil wondered, looking over the furnishings.

"It won't bother me. I don't plan on coming up here often, or ever."

"You're not still afraid of ghosts are you?"

"Of course not." But even as she spoke, Anne recalled a night from her childhood when she had stayed overnight at her aunt and uncle's house and how her cousin Clara had lured her up to the attic and told her how it was haunted and then how her horrid cousin Cedric had jumped out from where he had been hiding and had frightened her so bad she wet her nightie. Of course she was not afraid of ghosts, but attics still gave her pause. Though as attics went, this one was quite nice, and Anne could not help thinking it did look like someone's bedroom.

"It is odd, though, that all of this is still here," Sybil said.

"Frederick says the estate company's movers probably left it because they didn't want the added work."

Sybil fingered Naomi's antique tea pot that Eddie had placed on top the bookcase. It was the one she never used but kept in a curio cabinet in the parlor. It was one of only a few things she had left from her childhood and her mother, and thankfully it had not been destroyed in the police search. "Isn't this charming," Sybil said.

Anne agreed. "Maybe I should take it downstairs and use it."

"I wouldn't dear. Your own is far nicer. This one is a little too common. I suppose the girls could play with it."

"Let's go down mother," Anne said anxiously, the teapot in her hands.

At six, Frederick declared it was time to quit for the day. Anne agreed. The bedrooms were all set and clean towels were in the linen closet, and she had unpacked enough of the kitchen for the family to have breakfast in the morning. Besides, Anne was looking forward to sitting down for a nice dinner and having someone else worry about the dirty dishes.

"It really is a lovely car, Dad," Anne said to her father as he helped her into the back seat. Mattie and Gigi sat between their parents, too excited to sit still. No one was prouder than Tobias Henry when he imagined all the envious eyes on them as they drove away.

Eddie watched over the Masons as they padded indoors, put the twins to bed, then turned out their own light and sank into bed. He was filled with a great satisfaction that his house had a family. A very nice family.

"What do you think of them?" asked Adi, who had suddenly appeared.

"Ma would like those two little girls in her old room, playing with their dolls. She always wanted a little girl of her own."

"Might be nice having children around."

"Not sure what I'm supposed to do with them. I'm mean I'm not the kind of ghost I used to imagine when I was a kid. I'd never spook them."

Adi frowned. "We do not use that word, remember? But of course, you will want to take care that you do not do anything to startle them or otherwise make them aware of your presence."

"It's nice he's a doctor. He'll help people."

"It feels good, does it not?"

"What does?"

"Just the sense of life's potential, youth, the hope of what could be."

Eddie shook his head. "Everything with you is a lesson, isn't it?"

"No need to feel peeved, Edward. You and I are not here as casual observers. There is a job to do, and if I take advantage of a moment to teach you, you ought to be grateful, not annoyed."

"Sorry," Eddie grunted.

"Then I will continue, if you do not mind."

Eddie waved his arm as if to say, be my guest.

"Everyone has an opportunity to make something of life. When we start out as young adults, even in our adolescent years we don't think, 'Why bother. I will be dead before I know it.' No. We dream of a long life, do we not? We imagine a family. Or if one is not inclined to marry, one at least imagines doing something worthwhile."

"I don't know if everyone looks at it like that."

"No?"

"What I mean is, sometimes it takes all you've got just to get through the day. Those guys I worked with at the slaughterhouse were never going to get out of there. They were going to work at it until it killed them." He was thinking of Otto Fuchs, in particular.

Adi conceded that not everyone started on the same fair footing. "But in the main, people strive for better. And those fellows who spoke little English came to America hoping for something more."

Eddie nodded. "So, what is your point, Adi? Are you saying I have to help the Masons get ahead? They seem to have their future well in hand. Or are you saying that I need to strive for my own future, such as it is?"

"Both, I think," said Adi. "This endearing family is your responsibility now. Helping them in any way you can will be a good first step in your atonement. Find ways to do good, to bring good, to inspire good."

"I have a feeling none of this is going to be easy," Eddie said.

"I would not be too disheartened, Edward. You do not have to accomplish anything overnight. You have many years to become a virtuous soul."

Eddie sighed and remembered what Adi had said about years—twenty, thirty, fifty. He would be dead more years than he had been alive. It was a sobering thought.

Chapter 43
November 1927

During the Mason family's first month in his house, Eddie tried to be of service to them as much as he could without getting in their way. He had replaced an important letter that had been knocked off Dr. Mason's desk. He had watched Anne on the tips of her toes go woozy with a porcelain vase in hand as she tried to place it on the top shelf of the china cabinet. In a blink, he was behind her, enveloping her in his arms, and his presence was enough to help her regain her equilibrium just in time. She had turned with a look of confusion on her face, and Eddie realized he had come too close.

A week later, Eddie had been in the kitchen as Dr. Mason was preparing breakfast for the girls, and Eddie smelled sour milk. He saw his chance when the doctor, who had tucked the milk bottle under his arm, picked up two plates of eggs. It took a concentrated effort, but Eddie was able to push the bottle to the floor. The only ill effect of this bold move, besides a mess to clean up, was how mercilessly the twins had teased their father for being clumsy. But it brought them all to laughter, so even that was good.

Such acts seemed minor to Eddie, but maybe they were enough? Maybe their laughter had started a ripple? He had no illusions that keeping Anne from breaking an ankle or a vase would atone for a life he'd taken, but Adi had explained there was no one deed that would vindicate him for a death. And Adi had also said a good deed could not be planned. It had to occur spontaneously out of human need. So Eddie realized he would have to be in the right place at the right time, which meant he couldn't spend his eternity in an attic. And sooner or later he was going to have to venture out of the house.

But for the time being, Eddie stayed close to home and made himself useful as he was needed, keeping watch over Doc as he saw to patients, sitting at the kitchen table with Anne and the twins each afternoon after the girls got up from their naps, watching with satisfaction as Mattie and Gigi practiced their alphabets, not once making a backwards letter. Increasingly, when they did well, he understood what a father might feel.

He marveled at Anne and how easily she managed the house, having to navigate between home and being a busy doctor's wife. She had found time to talk with neighbors, and in the old tradition, a few had brought the Masons a pie or cake as a welcome gift. Esther Crandall came by with a pound cake and Anne sat with her in the kitchen. Eddie was surprised but grateful that Mrs. Crandall had not recounted the morning that she and Charlie Alford had found his body. Maybe even Esther Crandall, who was known to gossip, thought that bit of news would give the family a bad impression of the neighborhood as a whole. But perhaps the Masons already knew? The estate agent might have related the whole tale. If so, they bought the house despite its associations. Eddie never once heard them mention Edward Reed, the man who had once lived there, and it was somewhat disappointing that he hadn't. He thought at least he would live on in infamy.

At the end of the month, the Masons made their annual obligatory train trip to St. Louis for Thanksgiving. They were gone an entire week, and Eddie found he missed them. Eddie also missed the energy of club life, he soon realized. The music, the dancing, all those dames in their glittery gowns, the way some of them used to slink up to him and tell him how handsome he was, how they'd playfully pout and get him to buy them a drink. Now that he was dead, that life was over.

Nevertheless, one evening Eddie went to McGinty's to see what was happening there. McGinty had been smart. If a copper walked in the front door, he'd see only a tavern turned diner, a neighborhood place serving simple food. Regulars knew the way to get a splash of something in their orange juice or soda. On weekends, the speakeasy downstairs was active with a different crowd. Not that McGinty was worried about the local police. They were on the protection payroll and knew to look the other way. The pretense was in place for the feds, or for the new eager types who actually believed in prohibition. The Declan McGinty Eddie knew would do anything to keep from losing his business.

It was after 9:00 p.m. when Eddie followed a man through front door of the tavern. Tonight was Wednesday, a quiet night, and there were only a few late night diners. There were three people at the bar, and one, Eddie was happy to see was Old Ned. Way back when he and Nelson had been regulars, Old Ned was one of McGinty's more lively characters. Ned's humorous tales were second only to Jimmy Nolan's.

But not all of Ned's stories made them laugh. After Ned had had a few, he would tell about Vicksburg, about the time a troop of rebels had found Ned and the remaining men from their regiment near a copse of loblolly pines, where they had taken shelter and a moment to eat a bit of hardtack and reload. It's where Ned lost three of the best men he knew. "Then the rain came down hard," Ned would say, "and Johnny Reb lost his footing on the muddy hill, giving us time to pull our wounded deeper into the woods and eventually get away. We helped save the Union that day," Ned would say with teary-eyed pride. "Some gave everything for it, but all I had to sacrifice was these three fingers," which he lifted in evidence every time. "But hell, I can still hold a whiskey glass."

"War is hell," McGinty always said when Ned ended that story. "One more on the house for you, Ned."

Which was how, over the years, Ned came to need the bottle more than the time and place to tell his stories. Eddie sat on the stool next to the old man. Unshaven and bleary-eyed, Ned stared at the empty glass before him.

"Jus another small one, Mac," he said.

McGinty took Ned's glass, but was interrupted when the door chime sounded. Then he laid his hand over the old man's. "Gracie's here to take you home, Ned," McGinty said gently.

Grace was Ned's daughter, and she had been caring for him since her mother died in the great influenza epidemic. One more reason to drink, Eddie thought. There wasn't much you could do to fix what ailed the old man, but Eddie wanted to do something for Ned anyway. So when Grace and Ned left the bar, Eddie followed them and helped buoy the old man, who was so thin, Eddie thought a gust of wind might topple him. Eddie stayed with them, and steadied Grace's hold on her father, down the block and around the corner, and down the steps to the garden level apartment in the brownstone where Ned and Grace lived, and Eddie waited until Grace had her father in bed, and he stood by her until she saw her father's chest rise and fall in a snoring sleep, and he stayed with her too, until she fell asleep, and when Eddie left, he vowed to come back every night to do the same. If one night he would be needed for more, he would be there.

And he was. In June of 1932, a few months after Ned had stopped going for his nightcap at McGinty's because he just didn't have the energy to make the trip, his heart gave out and he died in bed. "He was a good man," Eddie said, hoping to console Grace. "A hell of a character though." Eddie laughed. Then he saw a brief smile form on Grace's face, as if she'd heard him. At times like that, Adi had said, the living imagine a thought is their own, not realizing that it originated with someone else, so Eddie repeated his words. "He was a good man."

The only mourners on the night Ned died were Grace and Eddie. But at the old man's funeral the following Saturday, the church was filled with those who had known and loved the old soldier. A bugler, a fellow Ned had served with, played "Taps." It was Ned's last "lights out."

Eddie kept tabs on Grace for a while after that. She was a good woman, and Eddie was sorry she had never married, for a family would have been a comfort to her. Grace took in a boarder, a single woman Grace's age with similar principles, industrious and community minded. They aided immigrant families, helping them find suitable housing and steady work. Later, when the stock market crash left people without, they opened a soup kitchen. And the two women worked to repeal prohibition, which they both agreed, the ill effects of liquor aside, had caused more harm than good.

Eddie was at the front windows early one morning, watching Joe Crandall's uneven gait as he made his way on the snow-covered sidewalk toward the trolley stop.

"He doing all right?" Adi said, startling Eddie from his thoughts.

Eddie turned from the window and looked at his mentor. "I figured you forgot all about me. I haven't seen you in over a month."

"You have done well? Yes? Making progress?"

Eddie shrugged. "Little things. Mostly, I feel like I'm in the way."

"Sometimes it is about what you learn instead of what you do."

Eddie's forehead furrowed. "I can't think of anything I've learned."

"No?"

Eddie did not want to invite one of Adi's lectures by commenting further.

Adi turned the conversation back to Joe Crandall. "Have you visited your old friend? Gone over to see him, see what he might need?"

"Not yet."

"But soon?"

"Why are you so anxious about Joe? Is something wrong? Is he sick?"

"Not that I am aware of," Adi said. "You know, Edward, there were some who mourned your death, despite you having been a criminal."

Eddie looked surprised. "Joe?"

A cry from downstairs drew the spirits' attention and they moved quickly towards it. They found Anne walking calmly but quickly to where the twins were making bird tracks in the snow under the tree. Near the fence, an emaciated black dog staggered as if he were drunk.

"Inside. Now," Anne said, one eye on the dog, her arms around her daughters, ushering them toward the porch and inside the kitchen. Then she went to the hallway to telephone the police.

At the same time Eddie went to the dog and with sympathy for the poor thing, he knelt and stroked its back. "It's going to be okay, boy," Eddie said, holding the dog steady.

Back in the kitchen Anne watched out the window, not quite believing what she was seeing. The dog had grown calm, and almost as if it had been sedated, it lay on the snow, its head resting on its front paws. She had seen its glassy eyes, foaming mouth. The signs of rabies were clear. So how was the dog now so peaceful?

"Can't we put him out of his misery?" Eddie asked.

Adi shook his head. "We do not kill. Ever."

The animal control officers arrived ten minutes later. Anne was grateful they leashed and led the dog out of her yard and into the alley. She did not want to see what she knew would happen next, what had to happen.

"Try to keep him still, Edward," Adi said. "It will be easier for the dog and for officers."

Eddie spoke comfortingly to the dog. "It'll be over soon."

From the house Anne heard the gunshot and wrapped her arms around herself. "That poor thing," she said.

"What happened, Mommy?" Gigi asked. "Where is that doggie?"

"It was sick, darling. Some men came to—take care of him." For weeks afterwards, Anne Mason double checked the latch on the alley gate before she allowed the girls outside to play. Surely there would not be another such dog wandering into their yard, but she was taking no chances.

The next day, after Esther Crandall left the house with her market bag, Eddie finally went next door, entering through the back door as he always had as a kid. The place hadn't changed much, except there were unwashed dishes in the sink and a vase of dead flowers on the table. The Mrs. Crandall he knew would never have let the dishes go.

Eddie was in the living room now, and it was no tidier. Newspapers and magazines were strewn about. Mrs. Crandall's shawl laid in a clump on the sofa, a bed pillow at one end, as if she'd been recently napping there.

Everything had the look and feel of exhaustion. Eddie did wonder about that, but it really wasn't Mrs. Crandall he was curious about. It was Joe.

Eddie had not seen Joe since he had come over to invite Eddie out for a meal. That was— Six years, Eddie calculated with shame. But Nelson had said it was smart to break old ties. "You wouldn't want some wise guy to use a good friend against you," he had said. Keeping his distance seemed like the right thing. Eddie would have felt horrible if anything bad had happened to Joe. He was safe from all that now, though, thank goodness. Eddie's shoulder's rose to meet a thought. "Hmmph," Eddie vocalized. He is safe because I'm dead.

Joe's room looked much the same as Eddie remembered. On his desk was a green blotter, a stamp collecting book, and the small cast iron dog he and Richie had given him on his ninth birthday. There was a stack of pamphlets for Oak Valley Community Center under the dog. Eddie looked through one of them and saw Joe's name listed with other staff. Director of Community Outreach he was. So that's what you do with a sociology degree, Eddie said.

Eddie picked up a sympathy card and opened it. Inside it read, "From all of us at Oak Valley, our condolences on the loss of your grandfather." Then he remembered the flowers. The disarray. Poor Joe. Mrs. Crandall's father, maybe? Eddie laid the card back on the desk and thought about expressing his regrets. Then he laughed. How absurd that would be, the dead consoling the living over a death.

Joe still had a lot of books. Even more than when he was a kid. Eddie had never seen this many books in a person's house before. One hundred and twenty-three books to be exact. Eddie clapped his hand to his head. "How'd I know that?" To be certain he wasn't just inventing that number, Eddie counted the books one by one, and sure enough, 123. He'd have to mention this to Adi. Not as flashy as shuffling cards, but you had to admit, it was a good trick.

Like they were bars on a xylophone, Eddie ran his fingers over the different colored spines. When he came to *The Adventures of Tom Sawyer* he stopped. It was the book that had finally broken him. Eddie was in fifth grade when the teacher passed a copy to everyone in his class, and then, one by one they were called on to read aloud. When it was Eddie's turn, he had done so poorly, he was humiliated. The words were all a muddle in his head. He'd never forgotten how awful it felt. He pulled the worn blue copy from the shelf. Joe must have liked this one, Eddie thought. A few of the pages were dog-eared. He opened to the beginning.

Eddie hadn't intended to read. He couldn't read. Not a book like this anyway. He read news articles, short ones, and that was about it. He had convinced himself long ago that books were beyond him. But now as he turned the pages, the words made sense.

"It makes sense," Eddie said in bewilderment. The words in this book no longer danced around as they once had. Then in almost no time at all, Eddie had read the entire book. But how had he been able to read so easily? Hesitantly, he took another book from the shelf, *David Copperfield*. He sat on Joe's bed and turned to page one, almost afraid that none of this had been real.

But this story came alive just as easily. Even more so, for it wasn't long before Eddie realized that the story was almost reading itself. It was like how he had known, almost without counting, how many books were on the shelves. Even turning the pages was miraculous, as he didn't drag each page aside with his fingertips. All he had to do was wave his hand over each page to make it move. And the speed with which he turned the pages was astonishing. Boy, if teachers could make this trick happen, every kid would love to read.

After reading three more books, Eddie heard a door open and close downstairs and realized Esther Crandall must be home. Back in his attic, Eddie faced the little bookcase he had brought up for sentimental reasons, and counted the books there. Only forty-two, but all there at a moment's beckoning. And yes, there was Tom Sawyer, but also *Oliver Twist*, *The Last of the Mohicans*, and *Tarzan*, among others. He would read them all, in time. He didn't want the experience to end too quickly. Most of these were Richie's favorite books, and he wanted to savor every word. He would read Huck Finn now, of course he would. But he would begin with *The Blue Fairy Book* because it was the one his mother liked reading to him and Richie when they were very young.

Chapter 44
May 1928

In the week after he discovered he could read, Eddie couldn't get enough. He had read every book in the attic, then the family's books, even the children's books in the playroom. When the Masons were asleep, he scanned the books Doc had in his office, but those were mostly medical and anatomy textbooks. They were interesting though. One evening Eddie learned about cell mitosis and cancer.

"I'd do so much better in school now," he thought, then he laughed at the implausible and ridiculous notion.

But it was adventure stories Eddie liked best, and he had run out of his own, so this morning, even though Mrs. Crandall was still in the house, Eddie went back to Joe's room. All he planned to do was read, and if he were careful, Esther Crandall would never know he was there.

The first book he took from the shelf was *Great Expectations*, a book he was to have read in tenth grade. About a boy named Pip, he recalled now. He hadn't read a single sentence in school, but now he was curious about a boy named Pip, such an unusual name. Eddie opened the book and a newspaper clipping fell to the floor. Setting the book aside, he picked up the paper, unfolded it and was surprised to see his name in bold print: "Edward W. Reed, Notorious Chicago Gangster Found Dead." The rest of the story had almost everything else about him wrong. Though to his shame, his parents' names were spelled correctly. He hated to think people would only remember them as the parents of a criminal. And Joe. Did Joe remember him only as a criminal? Why had he saved the article?

Eddie no longer cared about Pip. He slid the newspaper story back into the book and re-shelved it before leaving. He no longer felt like reading. His own adventure had taken an unpleasant turn.

Back in the attic, Eddie plopped on his bed, a knot of remorse within him. He wondered how long Joe had known about him. Was he ashamed? All those years when Eddie had tried to pass himself off as a quiet bachelor, had his other neighbors suspected something too? Yes, he'd kept odd hours. Sometimes left the milk out on the porch. Neglected the yard. But none of that made him a criminal, just irresponsible. Now he wondered, all those years working with Nelson and Bear, had he fooled anyone?

It was dark when Eddie realized he had passed the entire day on his bed. Moping. Yes. That's exactly what he had been doing. Feeling sorry for himself. But why? That article got it all right after all.

Eddie rose and went outside. He peeked in the living room windows of his neighbors' homes. Some were reading. Some were knitting. Some had gone to bed. Normal. Boring. Oblivious to the fact that the criminal from the block was still around.

Near the watchmaker's shop, Eddie discovered a pack of kids in an alley shooting marbles. He hovered over them and shouted, "Go home! Get to bed!" Where were their mothers? How could they allow their children out like this, no more cared for than feral cats. When the boys did not move, Eddie kicked up a patch of cinders, sending them raining onto the game. That ought to scare you home, Eddie said. The boys did scatter then, one of them crying out, "What the hell was that?"

Satisfied that he had done a good thing, Eddie went home.

Still not able to relieve his humiliation, Eddie spent the next week in bed. He kept imagining Joe seeing that article for the first time, imagining his shock. Or had he not been shocked at all? Which was worse? Mostly Eddie wondered how he could have been so naïve. Did he really think he could die without public notice? Adi had lifted him from that life into this existence with little effort. And yes, Adi had forced him to reckon with his faults, but never had Adi made him consider his neighbors. He did not think interacting with the living meant discovering how his life had impacted them.

Eddie awoke in a fury one morning. "I'm dead, damn it!" he said. Then, calmer, "What does it matter?" He turned to the wall and made himself small. "What can I do about anything now?"

"Joe must have had a reason for keeping that article," Adi said, "hiding it in a book that way."

Startled, Eddie sat up to face his mentor. "I think you need to start knocking. At least a hello before you launch into a conversation."

Adi bowed. "I will try to remember. But back the article. Why do you think he did that?

"I can only think he was ashamed of me."

"And now you feel that shame?"

"I am sorry people will always think what a shame it was that Naomi and Delmar Reed's kid turned out so bad."

Adi said nothing and did not attempt to diminish Eddie's negative feelings. Instead he changed the subject. "I see you have been reading," he said. "How have you found that experience?"

"Easy. You knew it would be. Why didn't you tell me it would be easy?"

"And spoil your joy in discovering that for yourself? By the way, since you are a reader now, you really ought to read *The Jungle* by Upton Sinclair. The fat cats did not like him much for writing it because he exposed your meat industry for what it is.

"My—what?"

"Have you gone back? Visited to see how your old pals are doing?"

Eddie had not had a chance to respond when he felt himself being sucked up in a vortex of cool vapor. Then just as quickly he was in the slaughterhouse with Adi, hovering near the ceiling looking down at the exact spot where Eddie used to gut hogs. Instantly the acrid smell hit Eddie like an assault. How had he ever grown accustomed to that vile odor? Maybe he hadn't. Maybe he had only resigned himself to its reality.

Very little had changed. There was Jimmy Nolan, the lines around his eyes deepened by time, his beard now the color of salt. Around his left hand a bandage seeping with yellow on the ridge of his knuckles. That was no work wound. A wound like that, Eddie thought, came from a fist fight. With his right hand, Jimmy wielded his knife and made quick work of the next hog on the line. A man next to Jimmy did the same, and the next man, and on down the line. Eddie had forgotten how much blood there was.

When the break whistle blew, Jimmy and the other men laid down their knives and wiped their hands on their aprons.

"Nolan's knife looks a lot like one you used to work with," Adi said. "Bone-handled like yours."

Eddie looked suspiciously at Adi. "Why are we here?"

Adi did not answer.

"Some lesson to discover on my own?"

Adi remained silent.

"Let me see," Eddie said, his frustration rising to anger. But he didn't see. "I'll tell you this. I am glad I got out of this hell-hole when I did."

And then in no time, Adi and Eddie were back in the attic.

"That was some stunt, Adi."

"Provoking memories sometimes requires such *stunts.*"

"You sound amused. I am not amused."

Adi settled in his chair at the table and began shuffling the deck of cards. Eddie paced the floorboards. Being back at the slaughterhouse had triggered memories. All of them. How could he not remember everything from the first humiliating day when his father had taken him to stand in line with all of those unfortunate men who would do anything to make a dollar to the first slice of his knife, releasing a gush of blood and entrails that had made his stomach lurch, but he'd had to swallow that too so he would not be humiliated even more. To be seen as weak by Jimmy Nolan would be worse somehow than being seen as weak by his father. Then the months and months and months of that grueling work, how tired he had been at first, then how numb to it, as if he had become an automaton. He remembered it all so vividly that he looked down at his hands for blood. But the blood he saw was not the blood he expected to see.

"You have remembered."

"What have I remembered?"

"That boy. The boy you killed under the L."

"Aah!" Eddie cried.

Adi did not respond.

Eddie grunted then disappeared out on to the back porch. Anne Mason was in the yard, raking the patch of ground that had been his mother's garden. On the ground near her were seed packets. Beans and squash. The twins were on a blanket near the base of the maple tree with their dolls. Compared with the peaceful tranquility before him, Eddie's turmoil raged even louder within him. Adi had to have known the story. So why the theatrics?

"You stole that young man's life from him. Such a thing requires—"

"Atonement." Eddie rolled his eyes. "Jesus, Mary, and Joseph. I get it." He rose and fled to the front porch, where he sat on the new swing Frederick had installed. But the respite from his guide lasted only seconds. Evading Adi was impossible.

"There is no need to take your frustration out on me," Adi said, plopping down beside Eddie. "I am only doing my job. And just to clarify, I do know how you feel."

Eddie scoffed. "I thought you were perfect. An angel."

"I told you, I am no angel." Adi paused as if he was not sure what to say next. "Believe it or not, I was once like you, and someone interceded. I was given a chance to atone. Then, inexplicably, someone in Celestia decided to turn me into the crazy spirit guide you have grown to love."

Somehow that made Eddie laugh. "You're crazy all right. But were you notorious?'"

"Perhaps not, but a lot of people died because of what I did."

Eddie squinted and shook his head. "I don't believe for one—"

"Oh, be quiet and let me tell you."

"I was twenty-nine when I died in 1347. Yes. The same age as you. It was an unpleasant end. When you can, if you are interested, get yourself over to the library and research bubonic plague."

"The library!" Eddie said, as if a revelation had just struck him.

Adi emitted a cold stare.

"Sorry to interrupt."

"The year before, my father, and our family's livelihood, died at sea. Two men who had clung for days to the wooden shards of their ship reported a swell had risen up like a great whale breaching over the main mast before it crashed down upon them. My father sank with the ship and all his goods.

"One morning not long after, my mother and I sought out the guild for help. With Father gone, the other merchants' businesses would benefit. My mother thought it only fair they offer her some recompense. They would not dare not refuse a poor widow, she reasoned. But that is exactly what happened. 'Who can make good on an act of God,' the merchants told us, bowing their heads in agitation, or was it victory, as we left.

"I offered to start again. I thought if I could go to sea, learn the trade, I could earn back our fortune. She only scoffed at me. She said we would starve before that plan bore fruit and told me we would manage with the wheat. I strove with her again, confident I could become successful at sea, but my mother did not have faith in my abilities.

Our farm, or rightly my grandfather's farm, was an ample tract of land on the Eastern coast of Italy, just west of Rimini. It did, in favorable weather, and by the labor of our serfs, produce enough grapes to make the household's wine and a fine hard wheat that was milled into flour. And while our flour was prized, I worried we would not be able to earn enough to secure our home in the city. The wheat alone would certainly not keep Mother in silk. She had grown accustomed to fine things and was terrified of losing everything. Eventually we had to leave our villa in town and move to the farm permanently. Mother was never quite the same after that. She grew bitter and blamed our situation on God.

Along with my grandfather, I oversaw the work and we managed. Then we got news of a terrible plague ravaging Asia, and Mother's fear became unreasonable. 'What if you and Father sicken and leave me alone?' she cried. I assured her we were safe, but she would not see reason. She became distraught and increasingly angry. She lashed out at our servants, the field serfs, even me. I had never seen her like she was then, so distrustful and blind. However, that summer the wheat flourished, and she found a short respite from her madness.

"Then the end began. That harvest season, with the plague still far from our shores, a great storm threatened us. With black clouds churning in the sky, Mother forced me to take up a whip alongside her and use it to make our serfs work faster. Above all, she feared becoming one of them if we lost our crop. So, we beat them.

"Striving furiously to stay ahead of the storm, I whipped a man who had fallen to his knees. If I had been a more observant person, I would have seen he was an old man. It is likely he had collapsed from malnourishment and fatigue, and that was surely my fault as well. But did I see it? All I saw was indolence, so I continued screaming at him to get up. Then others came to him, to offer the poor wretch what little they had in their waterskins. It was too late.

"When they realized the man had died, they backed away. I raised my whip. 'Get back to work,' I barked, believing they would do anything to avoid the same fate. But instead, a young woman raised her fist at me. 'We will no longer serve you,' she said. I had never seen anyone more defiant, and her fierceness shook me. Dumbly I watched as the others stood tall and dropped their scythes. When I told mother of the mutiny, she spat her disgust on the ground. 'Let them go, the rats,' she said.

"The only grain we had in store was what we had gathered to that point. The storm wiped out the rest. But there was still flour to mill, and now we had no help. I was sent to the wharf to entreat others into service. What pay I offered was barely enough to subsist on, but I was able to enlist a few seamen with the additional promise of a bottle of wine each day. I had no way of knowing those three seamen would bring us our end, for when their ship had been in port in the south they brought more than wine and olives aboard. They had also taken on one new crewman who brought with him The Black Death. By the time that man's illness was discovered, our three were already at work in our mill.

"On the morning of the third day, one of our fellows was dead.

Immediately the other two fled. Had they stayed and died with us, I would not carry such guilt. If they had stayed, perhaps the disease would have died on our land with us, but that was not to be. My mother was the next to go. She perished quickly, and Grandfather and I followed soon after. In the end, ours were unremarkable deaths among millions of others. And all that un-milled grain we had brutalized our workers for was left in the store to rot.

"So, you see Edward, I, too, was far from perfect."

"I don't see how it was your fault. I mean whipping people isn't good. But in those days—"

"I could have acted otherwise. I could have entreated our workers with kindness. Paying them more would have been effective. But I was not kind. Fear of failure drove me to cruelty. And then I met death at the wharf and brought him home."

"The plague wasn't your fault. As for the rest, wasn't it kind of self-defense?"

"How so?"

"Either your servants worked, or you'd lose everything."

"What about you then? Was not the young man under the L a matter of self-defense as well?"

"He shot me, so in that way, yes. I stabbed him to defend myself."

"What is the problem then? He deserved to die."

"That is probably what he thought about me. I think that kid and I were both doing our jobs. Like soldiers in a war. You can try to make me feel better about it, but I could have let him live. My first wound didn't kill him. No. I chose to keep on him. Worse—"

"Worse?"

"Worse is I felt no remorse. I felt more than lucky to be alive. Besting him made me feel—powerful, I guess. You did what you did on account of lousy circumstances."

"Well, Edward, you know, I have never thought about it like that before, believe it or not. Though lousy circumstances, as you put it, are no excuse, not then, not now. I told you my story as a parable, I suppose. You may believe you are on this sojourn alone. But we are two among many. So many. My father granted me grace, just as your mother granted yours. As I have told you, it is a great gift."

"I understand that. But you have also said I have plenty of time. Is there something I should be doing that I'm not?"

“You saw your old friend Jimmy Nolan today? What are things like for him at home? How about the others? You have neighbors and acquaintances that you could see to.”

“I’ll bet what Jimmy needs is cold hard cash. And while I did have some of that on hand, it has mysteriously vanished.” Eddie had Adi cornered now. Who else knew where it was? Who else had easy access? “Just admit you took my rucksack.”

“Why on earth would I take your money, Edward? I have no use for it. As for just giving people money, would that really help?”

“You said it yourself, Adi. You did what you did because you were afraid of poverty. So yes, I do think money would help.”

“Be that as it may, transferring physical objects to the living is, at the very least, problematic. The psychic disturbance they would feel to see money floating their way—”

“I’m not an idiot. I think I could figure out a better way than just handing it over. Like sneaking it into their wallets or pocketbooks.”

Adi shrugged. “I suppose that could work. I doubt too many would look very far down the mouth of that gift horse. But Edward, it is really best if you focus on kindness, the way you did with that old man and his daughter. An lot of good will came out of that.”

“Good will won’t put food on the table, though, will it Adi?”

Chapter 45

October 1929

Even before stories of Black Monday and the severity of the stock market crash hit the Chicago papers, Anne Mason telephoned her father, who reported his own losses as "significant." Tobias Henry told his daughter that at least they had been sensible enough to keep cash reserves and other assets at home in their safe.

"We are not quite destitute, my dear," he said. "Your mother is far more worried about you and Freddie."

Anne imagined her mother was far more worried about having to "make do," as she had done as a very young wife before Father became successful.

"Frederick tells me it won't be easy," Anne said, "especially if our bank fails. But we do not have a mortgage, so we are not in danger of losing the house. We fear Frederick's patients will not be as fortunate. He is more concerned about them than about us." Anne paused, then she spoke tentatively. "Those who are able might see to it to help the less fortunate. Don't you agree?" It was an oblique suggestion that perhaps her parents could do something for those in need in their own community. While Anne knew her mother's social obligations did not generally extend to charity work, maybe these dire circumstances would soften her heart and loosen her purse.

Tobias did not respond to his daughter's suggestion. "You must give Mattie and Gigi a kiss from their Papa. I don't know when we will be up again to see you."

"Of course. Give my love to Mother."

Eddie snorted derisively. *Sybil Henry give money to the needy? I have a better chance of getting into heaven.* Then he laughed. *I guess that is what I am working for though, isn't it?*

That night after the Masons were in bed, Eddie went into Doc's office and read the papers. He wanted the full story. "Speculation." "Unchecked credit." "Panic selling." That last one was the dagger in the national economy, one writer explained. "The waves of this crash will be felt worldwide," the reporter wrote. Eddie did not understand economics, but he knew the difference between having money and not having money. He knew that each led to its own kind of spiral. The rich got richer. The poor got poorer. It was almost like someone, somewhere was pulling the strings to make that happen.

The next day, Eddie ventured out and did his duty among the people, raising up the dejected, saying in their ears, "better times are on the horizon." A long line of men waited for bread, then in minutes the bread was gone. The last lucky man tore his loaf and gave half to the fellow behind him. "Bless you," the recipient said. "Bless us all," the giver said.

If I could bake bread, Eddie mused, I'd get into that kitchen tonight and conjure up a lot more for tomorrow. That got him thinking of what he could do that would make a difference. A few days later, after witnessing longer and longer lines, Eddie started to notice that some of the people in bread lines were visibly hungrier than others, their faces thinner and grayer, as if they had been destitute long before the crash. Not to say that everyone who was looking for a handout didn't need it, but some needed it more than others.

He singled one fellow out and followed him home. Four kids the man had. And his wife was expecting another from the looks of it. She took the bread and sliced it, then spread a thin layer of lard on each piece. Each child also got a bowl of broth, with meager bits of carrot and onion. The man sat with his children and told them a cheery story of how he had seen a basket of kittens that afternoon. As he described each kitten, "one gray, another black and white, one with blue eyes like yours, Eleanor," the children's faces opened in wide smiles.

"Now before you go begging your dad for a kitten," the mother said, "remember we haven't even a pint of milk for you." She poured hot water over a used tea bag in her husband's cup, then sat beside him. He covered her hand with his.

"I'll find work soon," he said. "If not tomorrow, then the next day."

After days of the same story playing out again and again, Eddie came up with one way he could begin to help. Tonight as he played cards with Adi, Eddie explained his plan. "Bakers start very early, I have learned. So each morning, while the bread is cooling, I will take a few loaves from their shelves and while the folks most in need are still asleep, I'll put the bread on their tables."

Adi took the last trick, then shuffled the deck and dealt the next hand. "An admirable idea, Edward. Have you considered the ripple effect?"

It was always ripples with Adi. "Like what?" Eddie fanned out his cards and frowned. He would never accuse Adi of cheating, but somehow Eddie always got a crummy hand.

"Like the baker who could swear there were twenty loaves to sell, not eighteen. Or the woman already prone to superstition who cannot explain a magical loaf of bread. I can even picture her saying "ptu, ptu, ptu" to ward off the evil eye. What if she then throws the bread out into the alley for the dogs? Your good deed is wasted."

Eddie grunted. "What is your suggestion then? More kindness? You know how ridiculous I feel telling people to take heart when their bank accounts have vanished or they've lost their jobs?"

"You cannot fix the world Edward. Not even your small part of it. You can only fix yourself."

"But you said I have to do good things."

Adi laid his cards aside. "Yes. And you do. And over time the good you put into the world will matter, to some, a little or a lot. It will not make a difference to others, who will still endure hardship, or will wonder why they must bear the weight of the world on their shoulders. You cannot fix that. I cannot fix that. I suppose if a government would rule against the injustice of inequality—"

"Hmmph," Eddie said. "Fat chance."

Adi slid one of Eddie's bankrolls across the table. "I have been thinking that the idea of tucking a dollar in a fellow's pocket or dropping one in a woman's cookie jar is now warranted. At least it is not magic bread."

"I knew you had it!" Eddie said, sliding the rubber band off and freeing the bills. "Where's the rest?"

"Why not see how this goes first? You would not want to bet everything on one roll, would you?"

"I guess not," Eddie said.

Then Adi placed something else on the table, something that made Eddie smile. It was the little tin soldier that had also been in his rucksack.

"Sometimes a thing like that can be a reminder."

"Reminder of what?"

"Of whatever you need it to be."

After Adi disappeared for the night, Eddie reclined on his bed thinking of how he would distribute twenty C-notes. A hundred bucks was a lot of money. If a guy ended up with a hundred, maybe his wife would accuse him of stealing. A hundred bucks would be very hard to explain. But if

Eddie could break these hundreds down to smaller bills. Yes. That was the way he'd start. If the banks had any cash left. He had no idea, but he was going to find out.

The next morning, Eddie entered the nearest bank and waited for his opportunity. It took no time at all to count out a stack of ones, fives, and tens and replace them with a hundred. Eventually, some brainy banker would notice the lower stacks of smaller bills, but when he counted again, the tally would be accurate. He would be at a loss to explain what had happened, but he would not say anything, fearing he'd be accused of losing his mind.

Eddie did not care a whit about that predicament. He had not robbed a bank. He had merely rearranged one, and a few days later, he would rearrange another bank, and so on for as long as was necessary. For years, he would take great pleasure in the fact that he had confounded bankers all across northern Illinois. But today he would begin his role as a kind of Saint Nickolas.

Eddie went first to the bakery and instead of making off with bread, he placed ten dollars in the cash register. That would buy a lot of flour and feed a lot people. Next he went to Grace's soup kitchen and put a ten dollar bill into the cigar box in her office where she kept her cash. Feeding the multitudes. And then the few. There was no shortage of opportunities.

He accomplished these feats using speed, laying a bill in place in a split second. Even the most fastidious did not keep a constant eye on their money tray. Eddie counted on the fact that most people were not keenly observant. It was more difficult to tuck a bill into a fellow's pocket.

Eddie's first attempt caused a ruckus when the recipient in the job line turned to accuse the man behind him of shoving him. A third man intervened and reminded them that they were all in the same boat and fighting each other didn't solve a thing. After that, Eddie carried coins, which dropped unseen into all sorts of slots—pockets, shopping bags, and handbags.

It was late when Eddie went back to the tenement flat where the first family he had visited were sound asleep. He crumpled a five-dollar bill and dropped it onto the floor next to where the man's slippers were tucked under his bed. Eddie hoped the fortuitous gift would be grasped gratefully by the man, who perhaps would not tell his wife of the miracle, but would instead bring home a slab of salt pork, potatoes and turnips, and maybe even a bit of real butter. He might explain, and it could happen, that he'd been given a job at the grocers, unpacking a shipment of apples. Anything was possible. A man who could conjure kittens would know what to do.

The next morning Eddie followed Joe Crandall to work. Outside the office was a line of people that stretched down the block and around the corner.

"Going to be another busy day, Aaron," Joe said to one of his co-workers. "Is Martha here yet?" Joe asked as he hung up his coat and hat on the rack at the rear of the office.

"I'm here," called a woman appearing from the back room. "I have made coffee, and we're going to need it."

"What we need is an influx of cash," Aaron muttered.

"Which I can do," Eddie said, gleefully. "When the time is right."

Aaron went to the door and spoke loudly but gently. "I'm sorry folks, but you won't all fit inside. We are going to take care of you all, I promise, so please be patient." Aaron craned his neck looking down the line. "Help us out. Is there anyone among you in a dire situation? Be charitable now. Let them in first."

It took a moment, but then a frail old woman emerged. Eddie thought she might barely have the fortitude to walk the short way to the door, so he held her by the arm and with Aaron, he guided her toward Martha, who was just inside ready to help the old woman. "Marina dear," Martha said. "Where is Anton?" Martha helped the woman into the chair near her desk.

"He sick."

"You poor thing. Any food at home?"

"Only one bread now. Our money gone from bank." The old woman spat on the floor. "Devil take banker," she said.

Martha reached across the desk and placed her hand over the old woman's. "I think there are many saying that." Martha gave the old woman a fifty-cent piece. "Now, can I call your son? Where is he?"

"No work. He stand in line all day. But no jobs."

Martha went out the door and peered over the people standing in line until she found the man she was looking for. "You. Walter Krejčí. Come here." A neatly shaven middle-aged man appeared as summoned. "I know you will help Marina home. And you will stay there until the doctor arrives for Anton." She placed two coins in his hand. "For this, and for your family." The man nodded then followed Martha inside where he helped Marina to her feet, then guided her slowly out the door. Afterwards

Martha phoned the doctor.

Eddie went with Walter and Marina, and they got her home safely. Eddie was dismayed to find Marina lived on the top floor. How did she manage? What kept such people going? The one-bedroom flat was sparsely furnished, but clean. In bed with a cough was Anton.

"I got money, Anton," Marina called into the bedroom, before removing her coat and scarf. Then she looked at Walter and said, "I make tea."

"You sit here," Walter said, leading her by the elbow to a little settee near the front window. "I will make the tea."

An hour later a doctor arrived. After examining Anton, he explained what was wrong. Pneumonia. "Keep him warm. Give him water and tea with honey. Do you have honey?"

Marina shook her head.

"Then tea," the doctor said. He gave the old woman's hand a sympathetic squeeze. The doctor had spoken hopefully, but Eddie did not think the old man would live much longer. He was too frail and undernourished. And if Marina's son could not find work, then who would care for this old woman? Eddie mentally added Marina to his list of folks to provide for. And Walter to those who deserved a reward, for he stayed with the old couple until their son came home. Only then did Eddie go.

When Eddie returned to the community center, he stood behind Joe as he worked. Had he eaten today, Eddie wondered? Had he had a break?

A young woman with a baby on her lap was seated on the chair next to Joe's desk. The baby was fussy, but Joe did not seem annoyed. Instead he reached out and took the baby's fingers in his, and spoke soothingly to him. When the baby quieted somewhat, Joe returned to his mother. The coin he pushed across the table had come from his own pocket, Eddie noticed.

"Bless you mister," the young mother said.

"You always were a better man than me, Joe," Eddie said.

Then he left the office and went home to figure out how best to provide the Oak Valley Community Center with an "influx of cash."

Chapter 46

November 1929

It was not until mid-November that Eddie finally ventured down to Back of the Yards, where Jimmy Nolan, Samuel, and many of the other slaughterhouse workers lived. He had not wanted to face the reality that he could have done something for all of those fellows while he was alive. Hadn't Jimmy done everything for Eddie when he first started at the stockyards? How had he repaid the man? He hadn't done a thing. After a few years under Sheridan, Eddie had plenty of dough and opportunities to meet his old gang in a bar and treat them to a few drinks, stick a hundred in their hands, and brag that it was nothing. But he had done none of that, and now Eddie was afraid to see how the crash had affected his old friends.

Back of the Yards had changed very little since 1917, his first and only visit to Jimmy Nolan's home. How was it possible that in one city some lived so lavishly and others lived like this, Eddie thought? Crowded, filthy, and maybe worst of all, rivers of sewage. When it rained, those rivers ran into other rivers, and that made things bad for everyone. Doing things for the poorest would benefit everyone, Eddie thought now, though he hadn't even considered such a thing when he'd been alive.

Jimmy Nolan's daughter Erin was no longer a freckle-faced child. With her own child on her lap, Erin sat with her father at the kitchen table. Before them was the remains of a shepherds pie, made with meat Jimmy bought at the company store. But there was no bread today. And the tea in Erin's cup looked weak, as if she had used the leaves too many times. The tea in Jimmy's cup looked like whiskey.

Erin's child, a two-year-old girl with curly hair and bright blue eyes, was tucked in to her mother by Erin's shawl. She was sick with a fever. Poor thing, Eddie thought.

"A touch of whiskey would help," Jimmy said.

"A doctor more like, Da," Erin said.

Jimmy nodded. "Sure and I will take her, if she worsens. Don't you fret daughter."

Erin tightened her arms around her daughter. "When Finn comes home, he and I will take her."

"If that man of yours was worth something, you would not be living here with me."

Eddie saw the fire flare in Erin's eyes. "Finn didn't make the market crash, Da. But did he speculate? Yes, like everyone else. Who could have foreseen we'd lose everything we had? I blame the bankers, not my man. And now he's out there every day, standing in lines. Lines for work. Lines for bread."

Jimmy let his chin drop. "Forgive me."

"And you drinking all day helps no one, does it?"

When had Jimmy become so weak? Eddie wondered. This was not the powerful man he had known. The man who had everything under control. This damn crash was taking a toll on everyone. The child coughed and Erin rocked her until she quieted. Eddie fought the urge to grab the child and take her to the doctor himself.

It's the husband who needs my charity, Eddie thought, so he waited until Finn O'Neill came home, looking utterly defeated. Ten dollars would buy that child a doctor and more.

Chapter 47

January 18, 1930

The thermometer reached sixteen below zero on January 18, but men and women dependent on handouts were still lined up on the streets. Grace's soup kitchen, the beneficiary of mysterious donations of cash, vegetables, and meat, was able to hire workers and feed several dozens each day. Neither she nor her partner believed in Providence, but it was hard not to believe. They did not know who their unnamed benefactor was, for somehow they could never catch him in the act, but when they found him out, they would make sure he was honored for the saint he was.

When Eddie realized Grace assumed some anonymous person had left provisions, he figured others would think the same thing, so he went forward with less trepidation. He never did feel the slightest bit of guilt when he took Mr. Armor's meat to feed the poor. A pork loin or a sirloin of beef here and there would not make that man a beggar, but it sure would save some poor soul from a worse fate.

"You are Robin Hood," Adi said one morning. When Eddie had responded with a puzzled look, Adi said, "A folk hero from an eponymous adventure book."

"Epon—?"

"Means named after. I am somewhat surprised Richie did not have a copy of that book. Regardless, Robin Hood stole from the rich and gave to the poor."

"I guess I am a thief now," Eddie said with a laugh. "If it sends me to hell, so be it."

"Under the circumstances, Edward, I doubt anyone would even think of sending you "to hell."

Eddie took the comment as a blessing, so over the years ahead, he continued to provide what aid he could, and by the time the new president, Roosevelt, stabilized the banks and started his work programs, Eddie had kept hundreds from outright destitution.

Chapter 48

October 1935

By October of 1935, the nation was slowly creeping back from economic ruin, and Eddie no longer smuggled meat from the packing plant. Ordinary people still didn't have much, but most weren't on the brink of starvation. He would continue to help Grace's soup kitchen, but as time went by, fewer and fewer people relied on her generosity. And McGinty, in the two years since the repeal of prohibition, was doing well. He had closed down the speakeasy but had kept his food service, so now his regular customers came for meatloaf and mashed potatoes as well as a cold pint of beer. Eddie enjoyed being there, among the people. It was the best place to hear the area's gossip and know who might need a bit of help.

One evening, Eddie went to the post office where his father had worked and followed Jakub Dvorak home. He remembered Jakub's description of Delmar Reed as a kind and generous man and the clash of confusion it had caused him.

Jakub climbed laboriously up to the third floor, unlocked his door, then inside he flicked a switch, illuminating a time-worn living room. As Jakub hung up his coat and hat, Eddie noticed a row of framed photographs on a table near the bedroom hallway. A man in his thirties with his wife and two young boys. A woman and a man with a baby. A younger woman's graduation photograph. Framed in brass was an old tintype of a man and a woman in their wedding clothes. Eddie peered closely and recognized the younger face of the man who stood in the kitchen, ready to peel potatoes.

Not long afterwards, the door opened and a short, curly-haired young woman entered, the one in the graduation photo, Eddie noticed.

"Hello, Tati," she said. "How was your day?" She draped her coat over a hook before going to the kitchen to give her father a kiss.

"Same as yesterday. Same as the day before."

"Arno called me at work. He wondered if we could watch the boys Saturday night so he and Evelyn can go to dance."

Jakub nodded. "Those boys are old enough to stay home alone now, aren't they, Maren?"

"I think that might be what he's worried about." She took the paring knife from her father. "You go sit and read the paper. I'll finish dinner."

Eddie stayed a while longer. At first he had been ashamed he had forgotten about the Dvoraks. But tonight he saw that Jakub's family had come through the hard times well. He could not think of what he could do for them, but because they were tied to him through his father, Eddie promised himself he would not forget about this family again.

The next morning, Doctor Mason was just opening up for the day, and the living room was filling with patients waiting to see him. Eddie noticed a hard-on-his-luck man with dirty reddish-blond hair and told him there would be better days ahead. The man's shoulders rose in a sigh, and he smiled at a young mother with a baby who sat across from him.

"Pretty baby," he said.

"Only four months old and she already has the croup."

The man smiled in sympathy. "Nothing worse than a sick child," he said, knowing there was something worse. The rest of the story darkened his memory. A boy of six, his body covered in deep red spots, his mother distraught at his bedside, a doctor with no cure, a small coffin.

Eddie felt nothing but pity. No one should lose a child.

"Mr. Garish," the doctor said at the door.

"Take the baby," the man said. "My stomach troubles can wait."

The woman thanked him then took her child into the exam room.

"God rewards the good in us," another woman said.

"Don't know about that," said the man. God had not rewarded him. He had lost his son and four years later the influenza took his wife. He had tried to forge ahead despite his grief. No one could say he hadn't tried. Then the little he had in savings was wiped out in the crash. *I was a good man, and God left me with nothing.*

The front door opened and Eddie was surprised to see Joe Crandall guiding his mother into the living room. Esther Crandall did not look well. Not well at all. Joe led her to the end of sofa opposite from where the red-haired man sat, then he stood to the side by the built-in shelves where Anne kept a few potted plants and knickknacks that she hoped would cheer their patients.

Eddie had not been to the Crandall house since the first days of the crash. He told himself he had not wanted to bother them, but that was not true. He had just assumed they were doing well. Now he saw what a mistake that had been. How had Esther aged so drastically? Her silvery hair so thin on top it barely covered her scalp, and her once plump form was now little more than a skeleton in a dress.

When it was time for Esther to see the doctor, Eddie went with her and Joe. It was something he almost never did out of regard for a patient's privacy. This was different though. The Crandalls were nearly family and Eddie wanted to hear what the doctor had to say.

"How are you feeling this morning, Esther?" Doc asked.

"About the same," she said in a tired voice.

He took her wrist, felt for her pulse, then listened to her lungs with his stethoscope. Afterwards he pressed the base of her neck with his fingers.

"You've not been eating, Esther," he said.

"Oh, pooh," she said. "I have so."

Joe shook his head.

"If you don't eat, you can't keep your strength up."

She lifted her arm then let it flop to her lap. "I don't think I could lift a feather," she said. "And besides, sometimes I am too sick to eat. If I don't eat, it can't come back up."

Joe rubbed her shoulders. "I do try, Doc. Broth. Tea. Now and then she'll eat some rice pudding."

"I've had your rice pudding, Esther. It's so delicious I could eat a whole big bowl of it."

She laughed. "I'll do better. I promise."

"Her pain is worse, too," Joe said. "Aspirin does not begin to dull it."

Doctor Mason nodded, then went to a cabinet and withdrew a green glass bottle, which he labeled before handing it to Joe. "This is laudanum. It will ease the pain and help you sleep, Esther, but it is very strong, so follow my directions. Taking more than I've prescribed could make it hard for Joe to care for you."

She nodded.

He patted her shoulder, then faced both Crandalls as he spoke. "The cancer is worse and it's only a matter of time now. I wish I had better news. I wish—"

"I'm grateful to you, Doctor," Esther said. You've done your best for me.

At times like this, Eddie felt helpless. All he could do Esther was spend time with her and whisper kind words. He could do nothing for her withering body, but he could try to ease her mind and assure her that when she was ready, letting go would be easier than she could imagine.

Esther Crandall lived only four more months. At her funeral, Eddie stood by Joe. He understood his friend's grief. Losing a mother is one of the hardest things one can endure in life.

"She was a good woman. She was a good mother. She was a good neighbor in the end," Eddie said to Joe, who despite not being able to hear him as loudly as Esther had in those moments before her death, did hear, and the words, which Joe counted as his own thoughts, gave him peace.

Chapter 49
April 1936

Ever since "Scarface" Al Capone was sent to Alcatraz in '34, Eddie had paid special attention to the crime stories in the paper. Once in a while there was a story about someone getting nabbed or whacked. Others had come out of Prohibition without a scratch. If only I could say the same about me, he thought.

Eddie was infuriated to learn that Moose Loughlin had made it big in Miami running a gambling operation. It wasn't just that Loughlin was raking in the dough, it was that he was down there enjoying the sun and beaches and all the rest of what Eddie had loved about Florida. It wasn't right.

"We should go see Capone," Adi said one morning, and Eddie, incredulous, agreed. Just the word "Alcatraz" got Eddie's imagination churning. He'd read all about it—an island in the San Francisco Bay, waves crashing against the rocks. It was a modern-day castle with an epic moat that made the idea of escape seem impossible.

A short while later, Eddie and Adi stood outside Capone's nine by five-foot cell, where he was stretched out on his cot, a book in his hands.

"I hear he reads a lot now," Adi said with a wink in Eddie's direction.

Eddie ignored him. "He looks—small somehow."

"He was always a small man," Adi said. "I don't mean in stature. I mean in capacity. Made large through cruelty and fear. You cannot be surprised. You operated the same way. You and he were both in love with your own power."

Eddie hated to admit Adi was right. He had been no Capone, but if you boiled it down, they weren't that different.

"I saw him once," Eddie said. "In '26. When we were down in Miami. He was just walking down the street, broad daylight. I remember thinking, that guy has it all."

"What do you think now?"

Adi was always pushing him to see things from a new perspective. "That he was not as lucky as I thought he was."

"On the way home," Adi said "there is something you should see."

Minutes later they were in the Mojave desert looking at the recently completed Boulder Dam, which stood with one foot in Arizona and the other in Nevada. They touched down near the entrance plaza.

"Hey, would you look at that," Eddie said, pointing to two thirty-foot bronze statues, who sat as if on thrones, their winged arms reaching toward the sky. "They kind of look like the ones Sheridan had made for La Paz. Though his were dames and not as nice as these."

"I can tell you their story."

"Yeah, sure." Eddie said.

"They are called The Winged Figures of the Republic, and they were designed by a Norwegian immigrant named Oskar J.W. Hansen. It is said that he wanted to honor the aspirations of a democratic people. But this is the part that I find quite interesting. Hansen said his figures were a 'connecting link between the spiritual and the material world, shadows cast by the realities of the soul.'"

Eddie's eyes widened, then he lifted himself up to peer into the face of one of the figures, its eyes closed to the sun. "Are you like me, then? A shadow of a soul?" The figure made no reply.

They now sat 700 feet above the surface of the water on the arced parapet of concrete and gazed over the glittering surface of the lake created by the massive dam.

"Think on this, Edward," Adi said, "when you imagine people are too down and out to accomplish anything. They built this at a time when the country was at its lowest. I know the world is often a bleak place, but this thing is an inspiration."

"I agree," Eddie said, "but nearly a hundred people died, building it."

"Where is that fact coming from?"

"Capone's not the only one who reads."

"So he is not, Edward. So he is not, and this is a lesson to me as well."

"What do you mean?"

"I can no longer assume you are ignorant of the world, the way you once were."

"I wouldn't say I was ignorant."

"Perhaps only incurious. And now you want to know."

"And that's a good thing, I suppose?"

"You cannot learn a thing if you do not wonder."

Chapter 50

September 1938

The notion of looking at paintings came to Eddie one afternoon when he was out with Anne Mason. She had taken a box of lemon cookies to one of their regular patients, Mrs. Adamson, who had recently returned from a trip to Rome, and had, she said, "been punished for it with a fall down the stairs."

Generous as always, Anne told her the broken wrist most certainly was not punishment, though Eddie thought the old crone might have had it coming. Beverly Adamson was not the most gracious of Frederick's patients, and that was putting it mildly. Eddie also thought Anne's visit was going beyond what was neighborly, but it was what she did. So, Eddie sat there in the woman's parlor with Anne and listened to the tales of her trip. Despite himself, he was drawn in completely by her description of the Sistine Chapel. He had seen pictures in a biography of Michelangelo, so he did not doubt Mrs. Adamson when she said the sight had taken her breath away.

"Well, you and Doctor Mason simply must go," she said.

Eddie saw Anne's indifferent smile. "One day, perhaps," she said.

Anne wouldn't have said so, but a trip to Europe was hardly something she and Frederick could afford. They were only now recovering from the effect of the crash, and the long economic depression was still not over. Women like Beverly Adamson had no idea what most people could or could not afford. She wasn't one of the hoity-toity up there on the Gold Coast by Lake Shore Drive, but her husband had died and left her more money than she would ever be able to spend.

But I could go, Eddie thought. This very moment. He wondered why he hadn't thought of it before. After Rome, The Louvre. He grinned as he rose up and thought himself to Rome. But when he alighted from his brief journey, he was disheartened to find himself on a barely paved road in a little village in Illinois called Rome. Barely a town. Surrounded by fields and barns. Not a person around. Was this another one of Adi's childish jokes? "I must be more specific," Eddie thought, so he said distinctly, "Rome. Italy!"

After his third futile attempt, Eddie made his way back to Chicago, ready to complain angrily to Adi the next time he appeared. While he waited for that pleasure, Eddie consoled himself with what could be instead. His mother had once taken him and Richie to the Art Institute when they were boys, but he had not thought of that time in years. There are paintings there, he thought, and probably Roman art. Maybe even Michelangelo.

The next morning, Eddie glided up the steps to the museum along with other visitors, including one group of school children. Before long, he moved among the smooth, white marble statuary and ancient artifacts of Rome, and he wondered why he had not thought to come here before now.

"Incurious," Adi had said of him. Well, I am curious now, Eddie thought, moving next to Renaissance art. Eddie admired each painting he saw. He knew none of the artists, but they had existed ages ago. Perhaps Adi had known some of them in his lifetime? He was extremely old, Eddie snorted.

Finally, the line of patrons Eddie had joined was winding its way towards works by Michelangelo. He could have gone on his own, but Eddie liked hearing what the docent had to say.

He peered at a display of small sketches, mostly drawings of muscular men. Looking closely, Eddie could see how detailed even the outlines of bones and tendons were, as if the artist could see beneath the skin. They were good drawings. Better than Eddie ever hoped to do, but they were not the Sistine Chapel. So he moved on.

Eddie meandered from one high-ceilinged room to the next. Dark, religious-themed paintings and ornate triptychs gave way to Dutch and English painters, hunting scenes, landscapes, seascapes. Soon Eddie found himself among the bright colors of Pierre-Auguste Renoir.

"Two Sisters (On the Terrace)" captured his attention in particular. The painting was a new acquisition, the docent said. Eddie was drawn to the deep blue the older sister wore, her vibrant red hat, and the way she and her little sister were presented boldly against a colorful, but subdued background.

And yet it was something else, something— Then he saw it, felt it, the expression on the older girl's face. It was as if she saw him too. He reached out and traced the ridges of paint with his fingers and felt he knew exactly, in that moment, how the painter had felt as he had drawn his brush across the canvas and brought those sisters to life. The feeling was like an electric charge. From the passive way the people around him reacted to the painting, he was certain they did not see what he saw. "Look closer," he said. "Look with your soul." Instead, they nodded at their docent's invitation to follow him to the next room.

From then on, especially when news of the world made him feel low, Eddie returned to find peace and beauty in the paintings of Renoir and others. Like he had with books, he now immersed himself in the worlds within paintings, letting himself be drawn into the stories they told.

Adi finally showed up one morning about six weeks later, and Eddie's greeting could not have been colder.

"What is nagging you?" Adi asked. "Although I am not sure I want to hear it. I have had enough of malcontents lately."

Eddie shook his head. If he did not urgently want to know why he could not travel past the borders of the United States, he would have asked about the malcontents. "You have me land-locked," Eddie said.

Adi nodded. "Ah, well. Yes. But this is only because we want you here. There are others abroad. And I know how it would be if you were free to go anywhere. You would choose Greece or Italy or Southern France. I would. Those are far more salubrious places than Chicago, especially in winter. But everyone cannot be in the same place."

"I only wanted to see the Sistine Chapel. I had not planned on relocating to Rome permanently."

"I see. Perhaps something can be arranged. Soon. I will see to it."

Eddie was afraid that "soon" in Adi's world meant something entirely different. But for now there was nothing more he could do, so he turned his focus back to Adi. "Tell me about your malcontent. Was it your friend, Viggo?"

Adi nodded. "He is not my friend, however," he said. "And, I am happy to report, he now is well ensconced where he should have been a long time ago." Adi brushed his hands against each other, as if ridding them of grit. "I did learn something interesting, though, from Viggo. Having to do with you."

"With me?"

"Do you remember that marble game, when you were fifteen or sixteen, after your brother died. Viggo tells me he was the one who pushed that boy Matty and made him let you into the game. He says you were just lurking about, not sure if you were going to risk your only nickel."

A flash of memory appeared as if Eddie were right back there among

Matty and those boys. "I remember that. I felt like someone had shoved me too. But there was no one there. Only a kind of echo in my head, saying, "Go on. What have you got to lose?" It was creepy. I supposed I should have taken it as a warning and backed out of that alley."

"But you did not."

"I did not. And not long after, I was working at the slaughterhouse. I see now it wasn't my fault after all, but your friend Viggo's that I ended up there. If I hadn't lost my nickel and my temper, I'd have never come home with a bloody lip."

"Again. Not my friend. And do not deceive yourself, Edward. You may have been nudged towards that chalk circle, but no one made you take the bet. You did that on your own."

"I guess. You happy to be rid of him?"

"I feel positively elated. Though he was not such a bad sort after all. Just an imp who twisted things up. He caused too much havoc. I prefer my spirits to be on the benevolent side, like you, Edward."

Eddie laughed. "Me? I'm the good guy? You have to admit, that's funny."

Adi rose and changed the subject. "Your people do not come up here?" he asked.

"Not since that first day. Why do you ask?"

"I see a new acquisition," Adi said, pointing to a typewriter.

"I bought that at a second-hand shop."

"You bought it?"

"You know, it is when you exchange money for goods." After his marathon years of doling out money back at the start of the Depression, Eddie had kept a small amount of cash in reserve. He thought it might be good to have a bit of cash handy.

Adi laughed. "I was only wondering how you accomplished the transaction."

"I took it one afternoon when the shopkeeper was in the store room, and in its place left five dollars and a note that said, *For the typewriter*. And before you ask how many people saw a typewriter soaring overhead on its own, I made sure I went well up beyond their sight."

"You can write notes?"

"It took me a while, and I'm lousy at it. Ever since I'm dead, my handwriting is barely legible, so I thought I'd try a typewriter."

"Edward, I never cease to be amazed at your ingenuity. So, can you type?"

"I can plunk out a note. Getting the paper into the damn thing is the tricky part. Takes me all morning sometimes."

"Tell me about what you write, once the paper is in."

"A few weeks ago, I wrote a letter to Doc from Aaron at the community center where Joe works, asking if he would be able to see a few hardship cases."

"What did Doctor Mason think when he found out Aaron did not recall sending such a letter?"

"I thought of that, so I put a typed note on Aaron's desk with the heading *List of doctors to contact for charity work.* The only name on the list was Frederick Mason's. I counted on him thinking he just forgot he sent a letter. They get so busy in that office, I figured it could work, and it did. Doc called and now he's got a few new patients."

"Clever."

"Also, I used Aaron's typewriter for that note, so he'd be even more convinced he wrote it. Did you know all typewriters are not the same?"

"You know Edward, when your time is up here, I would like you to meet my friend Soraya. I think she would find you useful. She admires those with initiative. A possible second career, before going into another life could be interesting."

"In heaven. Or what's it called? Celestial?"

"Celestia. Yes. There. But that is all for much, much later."

"Which reminds me. How much longer, do you think. It's been ten years now. And as you pointed out, I have been doing a lot of good, so—"

"True. True," Adi said. "But there is more for you to learn. And more for you to do."

"Figured you'd say that."

"Oh, Edward, do not sound so dejected. Are you not satisfied, overall, with what you are accomplishing here? I am."

Eddie shrugged. "I just feel like there's a lot I'm missing out on. My life—"

"Your afterlife."

"My afterlife."

"What about it?"

"Are you not even a little bit bored? The sameness of it all?"

"What would you prefer? This is the task you agreed to take on, if you recall, to keep you in a forward progression."

Eddie didn't answer.

"You have made it over these periods of ennui in the past. You will make it through this one as well. What you need is a new feeling of purpose. I guarantee one such opportunity will arise soon. That is the way life works."

"You couldn't just grab me out of here like you did with Viggo?"

"I do not have a mandate for that, Edward."

Eddie nodded. "Hey," he said, as if remembering a forgotten thought. "How'd you get him. After all this time, did he just agree to go with you?"

"Not quite."

"Then how?"

"A bit of ingenuity of my own, I am not a little proud to say. I pulled him back in time to moments before Lord Malach lost control of him in the first place. And this time, the lad went into the loop as he was meant to."

In amazement Eddie said, "You can do that? Go back in time?"

Adi instantly regretted his moment of indiscretion. He said nothing and went to the front window.

"Charming neighborhood," he said.

"Stop changing the subject. If you can go back in time, why don't you just stop people from doing bad things. Why don't you just stop all the world's suffering?"

"Because that is not what we do."

"No mandate?" Eddie said sarcastically.

"Think about it this way. Viggo's escape was an error on *our* part. I was merely correcting that error, something Malach should have done in the first place. Do not ask me to explain Malach's hesitancy. I think he enjoyed how entertaining Viggo was. Quite selfish, really. But the situation is now remedied, and I can move on."

"You didn't answer my question. If you can go back in time, you could stop—"

"No! I could not. I am, that is, we are not allowed to change the past. The consequences of human choice and action cannot be reversed."

"That's not true!"

"Do enlighten me."

"When I finagled things so Doc would start seeing the community center's patients, I—"

"You intervened in the present, prior to action. Prior to any decision. At other times, did you perhaps sway a decision one way or another? Yes. Of course. But what you did not do is reverse an action already recorded in history."

"Only gods can do that?"

"Not even gods."

"But you did take a guy who'd been here, how long, a hundred years, a guy who'd done things. He did something to me, changed my history, and you took him back. That sounds like changing the past to me."

Adi looked into Eddie's eyes. "You think I am being contradictory?"

"Don't you?"

"I can see how it appears that way to you, but Viggo is a special case."

"Enlighten me."

Adi gave Eddie a wry look. "Viggo was a spiritual being, here among the living in error. Were he a living human, I would have had no agency over him. I could swish Viggo back in time only because he was already a spirit."

"All right. I will drop it. Except—"

"Except what?"

"You took Viggo back in time, right? So that means he wouldn't have been here when I was a kid. He couldn't have pushed Matty or me. But I'm still here."

"What does that tell you?"

Eddie shook his head.

"Viggo may have goaded you into the game, but clearly you were going to join those boys, with or without him. It was not Viggo who determined the course of your life. It was you."

"But—"

"Just let it go, Edward. Sometimes you just have to trust me."

Chapter 51

December 25, 1938
Rome, Italy

On Christmas Day, Eddie lay on his back as if he floated in water and reached up to trace the story of creation painted on the ceiling of the Sistine Chapel. Creation of the earth itself as imagined through the brushstrokes of Michelangelo, then Adam's creation, then Eve's, their fall from Paradise, the Great Flood—all stories he had read about a few years earlier when he had been curious about the Bible, but none were ever so vividly told as this one, none so adorned with heavenly gold. Could any work of art in the world be greater than this? What a giant Michelangelo had been. God himself must have guided his hands. While outside the chapel, the Vatican bells rang and kept time, Eddie Reed wondered if heaven looked like this, if the colors in heaven would be this magnificent. When Eddie placed the tip of his finger in the space between God's and Adam's, he felt a jolt of ecstasy. Years later, Eddie would continue to believe that the spark had been a message from God, and not simply his own sublime pleasure.

Chapter 52

December 7, 1941

When the Japanese bombed the airbase at Pearl Harbor, Hawaii, Eddie had been dead for fourteen years, but he listened to President Roosevelt's declaration with the Masons as if Americans at war would have a direct impact on him.

With solemn acknowledgment, Frederick told the family they would be asked to make sacrifices. But their sacrifice would be limited, he said. Families with sons would pay the highest price.

Eddie remembered how he had once been eager to enlist in the first world war and how Jimmy Nolan had put that idea out of his head. Ma had been dead set against it, but he'd have found a way despite her objections. It was Jimmy who had set him straight. If he had gone, Eddie was sure he would have been killed. At least he would have died young for a noble cause.

"Noble? No." Quoting Soraya, Adi said, "War is senseless."

"We've got to fight the fascists though," Eddie said. "That sounds noble to me."

Adi sighed. He had no desire to argue with Eddie.

"No comment?"

"You are right, Edward. Fighting fascism is noble. I only wish so many did not have to die in the process."

This war meant Soraya was going to be busier than ever," Adi realized. And while he could once again be useful in Celestia, he doubted Malach would call him back, at least not until Edward Reed's atonement had been accomplished. Then an amusing thought occurred to Adi. Soraya had probably been saddled with some new scribe. He hoped the fellow would not be too much trouble. But maybe if he were a dunderhead, Soraya would be reminded that Adi Fattoré had not been so bad after all.

Chapter 53

February 12, 1943, Chicago

It was nearly 10:00 p.m. when a screaming fire truck rushed past Eddie's house. The Masons and other neighbors were out on the sidewalk in their pajamas and robes, craning their necks to see where the fire was. A man from down the block rushed past them on his way to get a closer look. "I see flames," he shouted.

"Jesus," said another man. "It's Mary O'Brien's house." Eddie followed him. The fire, they would learn later, started in the parlor where a faulty kerosene heater ignited a nearby stack of newspapers Mary had been saving for the war effort.

Anne Mason tugged at her husband's arm. "If they need you, they'll come. Let's go inside. It's freezing out here."

"You go," Frederick said. "I should stay."

Anne nodded. "I'll go in and get your coat."

Eddie never liked Mrs. O'Brien, he remembered, but she didn't deserve this. She used to point devil signs at him when he walked past her house on his way to school. When he was a boy, he thought she was a witch, a story magnified by other children in the neighborhood, who made up cruel rhymes about her. That was until Naomi overheard Eddie and Richie telling stories one night. She had flung open their bedroom door and told them how ashamed she was that her sons would talk so about a poor woman who'd lost her husband and probably felt lonely. For an entire summer, the Reed boys mowed Mary O'Brien's yard, and if they thought to do it with heavy hearts, they would be shoveling her snow all winter too. They didn't doubt their mother was serious about that.

"Dear God," a woman said to the gathering crowd of onlookers, "Look at the flames coming out the front door."

Just then Eddie saw Mary leaning out of an upstairs window. "All my things are lost!" she cried, then she disappeared back inside.

The fireman who had gone inside, rushed back out onto the porch engulfed in thick smoke.

"She's going to have to jump," he yelled.

By that time Eddie was in the bedroom with Mary, watching her stuff photograph frames and costume jewelry into an oversized handbag.

"Leave it!" he shouted, but she didn't hear him. Behind her, yellow smoke curled under the closed bedroom door, and the brass doorknob glowed red hot. Eddie wrapped his arms around her, but she slipped right through him and was down on her knees looking under the bed.

"Buttons," she called. "Come to Mama. Come now Buttons."

A damn cat, Eddie thought. Like smoke himself, Eddie went under the bed. Easily enough he grabbed the cat, who hadn't the sense to fight against his captor.

Mary O'Brien rubbed her smoke-filled eyes and thought she must be hallucinating, for Buttons had risen into the air before her.

Eddie used the cat to lure the woman to the window, where she heard the fireman calling her. She reached out and took her cat in her arms.

This time when Eddie grabbed onto her his grasp held, and he eased the woman and the cat out through the window and onto the porch roof, where a fireman who'd climbed a ladder was waiting to assist her. He looked up to see Mary O'Brien, her cat in her arms, moving towards him as if a gust of wind pushed her from behind, the hem of her robe swirling about her legs, a cumbersome handbag on her arm.

"It's okay lady," the fireman said, now at her side. "I've got you."

"She's going to have to jump," came a voice from below. "That porch is going to collapse fast."

"I can't," she quavered. "Take Buttons."

"Lady," the fireman said, "I can't help you and the cat. You gotta hold him. Hang on tight. I'm going to help you, but you're going to jump. If you don't, that cat won't make it."

Eddie embraced Mary O'Brien and he and the fireman led her to the edge where men on the ground waited with the wide life net. Holding her tightly Eddie said, "Just jump with me. I won't let go."

She hit the net with once bounce, and a terrified Buttons leapt off and ran back toward the house where the fire chief intercepted him. He held the cat to his coat and spoke to it as if he'd had to rescue more than one cat in his day.

With her feet on the ground, Mary O'Brien was led away to where the Masons waited to care for her. Anne wrapped a blanket around the woman's shoulders, and the fire chief delivered Buttons.

Moments later, the young fireman also landed safely in the net.

"Let me carry that bag," Anne said. "It looks heavy."

"Take her home Anne. I'll speak with the fire chief," Frederick said.

On the way, other neighbors promised food, clothing, even money to replace what she'd lost.

"You're all so good," Mary said, then she and Buttons went with Anne down the street and into the Mason's house, where Mary had never been before, because, as she was known to say to anyone who'd listen, "You can't trust doctors."

It took hours for the fire to be put out completely, and in the end, the house was a blackened shell. In time a new house would take its place, but for weeks afterwards, the smell of smoke pervaded the entire neighborhood.

Mary O'Brien stayed that night with the Masons, who went out of their way to make her and her cat comfortable. With Buttons in the house, Eddie kept well away. The Masons didn't need anything more from him that night. The next afternoon, Mary's son arrived to take her home to live with him.

"I never liked that old house anyway," he told Frederick. "It was always drafty and Mother was too cheap to fix the windows."

Mary O'Brien lived to be ninety-two, and she never tired of telling the story of her rescue, about how afraid she had been, and how her cat and a kind young fireman had saved her.

Chapter 54

1945-1952

When the war ended in 1945, the general view was the world would never be the same, and Eddie was beginning to understand. Underlying the joyful homecomings was a shared fear of the horrible new atomic bomb and who might unleash it next.

"Now you see what humanity is capable of," Eddie said. "What possible atonement can there be for something like that?"

For once, Adi was speechless.

As there was nothing Eddie could do about the peril of world in general, he could do what he was meant to do. He focused his efforts on helping GIs reintegrate into society. Joe Crandall expanded the community center's outreach by instituting a special program for returning soldiers. Some vets didn't know about the benefits they were owed, so Joe printed pamphlets explaining the GI program at the community center, specifically focusing on how they were able to help the veterans enroll in college or get a home loan. Eddie distributed dozens of those pamphlets, until Joe, Aaron, and Martha were so busy they could barely keep up.

Anne Mason shifted her USO duties to supporting military families, especially helping the children whose fathers did not come home. Soldiers who returned with all their limbs intact often took up with life where they had left it, though the patina of war's horror laid over everything in ways no one who hadn't fought would understand. To be stoic and move on took a fortitude that Eddie admired greatly. Doc Mason began studying psychiatric therapy, which allowed him to help with minor cases. Anyone beyond his means, he sent to specialists.

Eddie spent most of his time with the wounded veterans. He couldn't help them strengthen their muscles or learn to walk again or how to eat with a hook for a hand. That they had to do on their own. But he could help them win at cards by hinting what the other fellow had in his hand, or he could quiet their minds when recurring nightmares kept them from sleep. Eddie thought about how much easier it was when he could help by giving a fellow money. All the money in the world would not help some of these men.

The post war years saw other changes for the Masons. In their first and only year of college, Mathilde and Gertrude met their beaus, quite lovely men, Anne thought. The following June they were married in a double ceremony, funded by their grandparents. Frederick was certain that Fourth Presbyterian had never before been adorned with so many white roses. Less lovely was the fact that both daughters would be living on the west coast. Mattie in California, where her husband had work in the motion picture industry. Gigi would settle in Oregon, where her husband would eventually be made partner in his family's law firm.

Whenever Anne lamented over how far away the girls would be, Frederick said they would go visit. The girls promised they would come home often as well. Somehow Eddie envisioned those promises being broken again and again.

But in 1949, both Mattie and Gigi did come home, each with a toddler in tow. The house once again erupted in sound and Eddie chased the babies around, laughing and helping them to their feet when they fell. The Masons had barely begun to enjoy the grandchildren, when a sleek black car came to pick up the girls and the babies to take them uptown to great-grandmother's hotel for a few days. Anne felt a twinge of betrayal, not just from her mother but from her daughters as well. The girls, it seemed, were drawn to the socialite life Sybil Henry had dangled before them since they were toddlers.

"I'll put up a rope swing," Frederick said one afternoon out on the back porch. "For their next visit. They'll like that, won't they?"

Anne slipped her hand around her husband's waist. What a wonderful grandfather he was, or would be if he was given the time.

Two years later, Frederick pulled Anne into his arms. "Dr. Antoni can cover emergencies. I think it's time we went to California. How about for Christmas?" Then he swirled Anne about as if they were dancing.

"If the mountain won't come to Muhammad, then Muhammad must go to the mountain," she said.

So, in December of 1952, the Masons boarded a train for a two-week trip to Los Angeles. They would spend Christmas week at Mathilde's house, and by Christmas Eve, Genevieve would arrive with her family and their newborn baby boy.

With much anticipation, Anne had sewn little sailor suits for the granddaughters, who were almost five now. She planned to finish the layette she was knitting for the baby on the train. Whether it was the rocking motion of the train or all the sitting, she didn't know which, but whenever she tried to knit, she got so sleepy she had to lay her needles down and close her eyes.

Frederick promised the southern California sunshine would perk her up, but the effect was limited. One late afternoon walk on the beach was so tiring that Anne turned down the invitation to a cocktail party that evening on Mattie's friend's ocean-view veranda, telling Frederick to go without her. Instead, everyone stayed home with her, and they sat on the patio under an arbor full of bougainvillea blossoms and talked about old times. Anne had never been happier.

Anne's listlessness had the twins worried, and Mathilde insisted that she see a doctor that week. Anne was against making such a fuss, but Frederick agreed, so on a bright morning four days after Christmas, Mattie and Gigi sat in a waiting room while their mother and father met with the doctor.

When Anne emerged, she shook her head. "It's my heart, I'm afraid," Anne told the girls. "The doctor gave me the name of a specialist in Chicago."

"That's good, right?" Genevieve said, taking her mother by the arm. "A specialist. He'll make you well, Mother."

"Yes," Frederick said, but his smile was weak. He knew that in most cases of heart disease, there was no cure. Like cancer, once it took hold, it was only a matter of time.

Anne spent the last few days of their time in California being doted on by her daughters. The grandchildren were told to not tire Nana, but it made Anne sad to have them taken away from her. Matilde and Genevieve had never really understood that all a mother, or a grandmother, wanted was to be surrounded by her children, noisy or not.

The morning of their departure, Anne told her daughters it would be nice if they would come home that summer. They both promised her they would. Anne bent to kiss the children, told them that Nana loved them, told them to be good and not cause trouble. Then she embraced her own girls, and whispered, "above all, you must not forget about your father."

Time had different plans. Anne Mason died in her sleep that spring, the day her first tulip bloomed, and Eddie Reed felt as if he had lost his own mother all over again.

Chapter 55
May 1953

Eddie had not been able to do much of anything since Anne's death. Grief had immobilized him. He could not get over the unfairness of it all. A good woman. A young woman. So much left to give.

"Sometimes unfortunate things happen to good people," Adi said one morning.

It was the worst thing he could have said, and Eddie barked back that maybe God wasn't the benevolent being people made him out to be.

"It might be wise, considering your current position," Adi said calmly, "to avoid aggravating the celestial order."

You're the aggravating one, Eddie thought, but he did not say a word. Instead he made himself disappear and was now sitting on the end of an isolated fishing pier on Lake Michigan, north of the city. He'd been going there lately when he wanted to avoid people, especially his sometimes infuriating mentor.

He rested there a while and thought about how odd it was that he could still feel angry after death. He understood the dead don't feel anger in the same way as the living do, in their hearts and lungs. They feel it instead as a gap, a wider distance between where they are and where they want to be.

Adi had once admitted that sometimes he himself got a bit peeved, and he supposed a certain amount of frustration was unavoidable. "Which, Edward," he had said, "does not mean you should not try to control your emotions."

Easier said than done, Eddie thought. Easier said than done. Gliding out across the water, Eddie spied a steam tug pushing a long barge northward. If it wouldn't be such a slow escape, Eddie would go along, take a little trip up to the Soo Locks in Sault Ste. Marie or wherever it was going, mingle with the crew. But there was no escape from Adi. No escape from anything. Doc's sadness. His own.

Eddie had come to realize over the past weeks that he was feeling much more than grief over Anne Mason. The truth was, he was grieving his own life. He missed being alive. All the feelings, the good ones, even the jolt his heart got when he and Nelson and Bear found themselves in a tight spot. He missed being with those guys. He missed his mother too, the way she smiled, told him things no one else ever did. How she believed in him. Anne's death reminded Eddie just how young his mother had been when she died. It was not fair.

Eddie went back towards shore and lowered himself onto the pier. The sound of water thudding against its sides lulled Eddie deeper into his thoughts. How lucky his family had been to have died without this obligation to atone. A good death took one directly from one way of being to the next.

His was a bad death then, a bad life, and now—? Oh, not such a bad afterlife. But lonely. And long. Twenty-five years. Not wasted, he supposed. He had done a lot in that time. He had been a force for good. But it had been quite a long time since he had done anything equal to what he had accomplished during the Great Depression.

He was back to simple tasks like steering someone away from stepping in a puddle to saving a lady from her burning house. While those were good things, especially helping Mary O'Brien, Eddie didn't feel the deep satisfaction he had felt when he had been able to change a family's fortune, even if only for a short while. Then he considered that if he had not been there to help Mary O'Brien, the firemen had been and they would have rescued her all the same. Did it even matter that he had been there? Did any of his so-called good deeds matter?

These days most people no longer needed him in the way they had during the Depression, and he hated to admit he was slightly annoyed about that. It was a lot easier to slip a dollar bill into a man's pocket than it was to find him a job. He was thinking in particular of Jimmy Nolan's son-in-law Finn O'Neill.

Back in February of 1946, not long after the end of the war, Eddie had gone to check on Jimmy Nolan. Nolan was seventy-four then and had not worked at the slaughterhouse since 1940, when his body finally told him it was time to quit. All in all, he was doing well and Eddie was gratified to see it.

Erin and her husband Finn and their two youngest children still lived with Jimmy, but they were no longer in the slums called Back of the Yards. Jimmy had saved enough for the family to move to a three bedroom house in a new suburb south of the city. It was new, clean, and Jimmy would no longer have to worry about sending his grandchildren outside to play.

Eddie knew it was not only his few additions to the family's account that had improved their situation. Jimmy's frugality after the crash enabled him build his savings, which, no longer trusting in banks, he'd kept hidden in a pouch in his mattress. So now, along with his social security and Finn's on-again, off-again ability to earn a living, the family made ends meet. It was those times when Finn was out of work that were the hardest.

Eddie couldn't figure why Finn O'Neill couldn't keep a job. He was strong, able, and seemed like an amiable fellow, so why was he perpetually out of work? Eddie had his answer after shadowing Finn for a few days. He learned that the man could not keep himself out of arguments. He thinks he knows it all, Eddie realized. He's got to correct people, even if he's wrong. For a time, Eddie tried his best to keep Finn from stepping on his own feet, but it was an impossible task.

One night after a simple dinner of potato and bacon hash, Erin and Jimmy and the kids were in the living room, listening to the radio. Finn was not there. Jimmy was staring at the clock.

"He'll be home soon, Da. He had a meeting about a new job."

"You really think he will get this one?"

"It's carpentry. Building new houses."

"It is not a fish until it is on the bank," Jimmy said.

"You have to have faith in him," Erin said.

That night after Jimmy had nodded off in his chair, Eddie found Finn at a tavern, already beginning to slip off the bar stool, and Eddie knew that the fish on Finn's bank was once again just an old shoe.

It was hard to have faith in people who kept disappointing you or in those who broke trust again and again, as Eddie had done as a young man. How Ma had kept on believing in him, Eddie thought, was a mystery.

A few years later, Eddie learned that Jimmy Nolan had died. It was the fact that he hadn't been there with him in his last hours that bothered Eddie most. That man had meant so much to Eddie, and in the end Eddie had not been there to comfort him in his passing.

Regrets solved nothing. Sitting on a bar stool trying to drown your sorrows solved nothing. Sitting on a lake pier either. The only way to solve a problem was to do something about it. So Eddie shook off his gloom and stared up at the morning sky. A glimmer of sun strained to escape the clouds. Despite his sense that he was useless, Eddie would find someone who needed him today and do whatever it took to make things better.

JOE CRANDALL

Chapter 56

March 1954

The country seemed to be a harder place these days Eddie thought. Suspicion and distrust were not hard to find. Now there was a cold war with people called Communists. Eddie had wondered what that meant, so he looked it up in the encyclopedia in Doc's office. Distributing wealth among everyone equally sounded nice, but even a dummy like Eddie knew a system like that could never work. People with money were never going to share it. But it also seemed to Eddie that the word "Communist," had lost its true meaning. People threw it around to describe groups they didn't like or those whose views they didn't agree with.

The divisive nature of the McCarthy hearings only made things worse. One night Eddie joined Joe Crandall, who was watching coverage of the hearings on television. One statement from Senator McCarthy, the man in charge, made Joe so angry he pounded his fist on his TV tray and broke it. Luckily, Joe had finished his dinner moments before.

The hearings were all anyone could talk about where Joe worked. Martha, who had been made their office manager after the war, was especially vocal. She said more than once that she hoped McCarthy would rot in hell. Eddie had been amused by that. Martha, now plump and gray, looked like a sweet grandmother, not a political activist. But Eddie did not disagree. McCarthy seemed like a pretty bad guy.

That afternoon, Joe and Aaron reminded Martha that while they shared her views, not everyone did, and the office was full of ears.

"People have to speak up against injustice," she said emphatically.

"She's right," said a young woman named Rachel, who'd recently begun working at the Oak Valley Community Center. "If no one speaks up, they'll get away with murder."

Rachel was just out of college and was ready to save the world. She wore her auburn hair straight, cut in bangs that swept over the dark rims of her glasses. Joe and Aaron had gone out of their way to make things easy for her when she'd started the job.

Martha had to remind Aaron that he was a married man. "It's fine for Joe," she whispered, "though, goodness knows he's too old for her."

Eddie hadn't liked hearing that. Joe was younger than he was, by a couple of years. Then when he looked closer, Eddie saw not the young man of his memory, but an aging Joe, wrinkles at the corners of his eyes, lines in his face, gray, thinning hair. Time had made Joe a fifty-six-year-old man.

Rachel pulled a pamphlet out of her bag and laid it on Joe's desk. Eddie looked on as Joe skimmed the document. "The Communist Threat Is Real" it read. A huge demon-like being hovered threateningly over an innocent looking young girl. "Don't be shy. Report all Un-American Activity."

"Tell me all this isn't just a witch hunt," Rachel said. She pointed to the shadowy Star of David faintly superimposed on the demon's form.

"It's antisemitism in new clothes," Joe said, not meaning to openly express such a strong opinon. Rachel had a way of stirring him to boldness.

"My boyfriend and I are going to a meeting tomorrow night at my church. Why don't you come too?"

"What kind of meeting?" Joe asked, taking notice of Martha's *be careful* look.

"It's just going to be some speeches. One from the Young Socialists, but the others will be from people like me, you know. We all just want to stand up for what is right."

"Oh, I don't think I should. I—"

"Don't you want to do something, Joe?"

"I thought we were doing something. Helping people."

"I thought you cared?" she said, now sounding annoyed. "You said it was antisemitism."

"I do care. It is. At least in my opinion. But I think I can do the most good by helping ordinary people."

"Benji and I want to do more. I thought you did, too."

The next evening as Joe neared the church, his only thought was that he was getting into something he shouldn't be. But this meeting was being held in a church, so how perilous could it be? He had decided to come tonight for Rachel, in case something got out of hand. In case he might be able to— To what? Save her? From what? Speeches? A wave of absurdity came over him, and he thought for a moment he should turn around and go home. The only thing that stopped him was the possibility that Rachel would see him leaving.

The night was clear and cold, and Joe shoved his hands in his jacket pockets and shivered. From his point of view, March was still winter in Chicago. The church, a single-steepled stone edifice, was brightly lit, emitting color through its stain-glassed windows. A throng of people gathered near the entrance, looking as if they were a big family who hadn't seen each other for a long time. Only a few of those gathered had started going inside.

Where was Rachel? Instead of pushing into the group to try to find her, he stayed off to the side on his own. He knew none of these people, and he wasn't there to socialize.

A city bus slowed to a stop at the corner and several people emerged. Still no Rachel. When that group dispersed, he finally saw her. He was about to wave when a tall, good looking young man emerged from the crowd and threw his arms around her. That has to be her boyfriend, Benji, Joe thought.

Just then a whistle drew their attention to a red-haired girl in a plaid coat, who stood at the top of the church steps and motioned for Rachel and Benji to join her. The young couple bounded up the steps and disappeared. After that, most of the others followed. Joe checked his watch. Nearly seven. The program would start soon, so Joe made his way up the steps, and even though he climbed them one at a time, he was winded by the time he got to the arched doors. He was often out of breath these days, but it was just the price of aging, he concluded.

Inside, a young girl who looked like she was still in high school handed him a bulletin, and he thanked her. The pews were nearly filled but Joe found a seat in the back. He had lost sight of Rachel, and as he searched for her, he realized there were so many Rachels, and Benjis, there tonight. In fact, nearly everyone he saw was young. Only a few bald or gray heads were seated before him.

Just then the congregation quieted when the pastor approached the lectern. "Welcome," he said. "I am heartened to see so many new faces among us. Thank you all for joining us tonight in our mission to spread the good word."

Even the pastor was young, Joe thought. "What am I doing here? I don't even go to church."

"You may as well see what they have to say, Joe," Eddie said, settling down next to his friend.

Joe was thinking about how he could sneak away when another young couple pointed to the space on the pew next to him, so that he was forced to scoot down and make room for them.

Smiling, the young man whispered, "Thanks! It's so crowded, I didn't think we'd find a seat."

Joe returned the smile, then resigned himself to the fact that he was stuck right where he was.

The organist began to play "My Country, 'Tis of Thee," and when the congregation stood to sing, Joe joined in. It was a song he had learned in school and knew by heart. The young couple next to him needed to follow along in the hymnal. Joe couldn't help feeling somewhat self-satisfied. At least I'm old enough to know a few things, he thought.

Several speakers followed the pastor's short sermon on unity. One spoke about the future of the country, saying that McCarthy and people like him only wanted to take us back. One talked about how the phrase "Red Scare" was used to cement power for the *right* people. He pointed out how blacklists and purges of Hollywood Jews, especially, were evidence of witch hunts. None of which Joe disagreed with. In fact, he found his head nodding throughout that speech.

The only thing that made Joe nervous was when the final speaker urged everyone to join him in a solidarity march next Saturday morning. "The details are in your bulletin," he said. Having opinions was one thing, Joe thought, but to force them on others out in the streets was something else.

When the program ended, the organist played what sounded to Joe like a Mozart sonata, though he was no expert in music. Soon he was nearly consumed by the crowd, which jostled its way toward the doors.

As Joe searched once again for Rachel, a young woman behind him said, "Excuse me, sir. Do you mind if I pass by? I'm trying to catch my friend before she gets on the bus."

He let her squeeze past him. "Sir?" he thought, shaking his head. "I'm so old they call me sir."

When he was outside on the sidewalk, Joe finally saw Rachel. She and her boyfriend were near the corner with that red-haired girl again. Then another couple joined them. Joe watched their animated conversation from where he stood and somehow felt it would be a mistake to join them.

Eddie thought differently. "Go ahead, Joe," he said. When Joe didn't respond, Eddie gathered a bit of force and pushed Joe just a little bit forward. Instead of helping, his nudge had made Joe feel that he had lost his balance. It was the last thing Eddie had wanted.

"I should never have come here," Joe muttered to himself. Then he turned away from the church and walked towards home.

Chapter 57

December 24, 1956

On Christmas Eve, Joe stayed late at the community center to help Martha clean up the food and wrapping and ribbons from the party they'd given for those families who couldn't afford presents for their kids. The community party had been Joe's idea twenty years earlier. An idea that Eddie had eagerly seconded.

And very little in Eddie's afterlife brought him more joy than watching a child open a present. In a way, each time a boy or girl held up a toy proudly, it brought Eddie as much happiness as that time he'd given Joe the little cast iron dog.

Usually this annual party brought the same sort of feelings to Joe. On one night a year, a man without a family was like Santa to a roomful of gleeful children. But tonight, Eddie could see that Joe's heart was not really in it. Joe's gloomy mood confused Eddie.

Was it still that girl? Rachel? Not long after that meeting at the church, she had told them she was quitting. She and Benjamin were going to get married and move to Wheaton. Joe's initial reaction was disappointment, but when he considered things with a clear head, he understood that since that night at the church her presence had become oppressive somehow. So even though he hated to admit it, he was glad to see her go.

"I've got the last of this, Joe," Martha said, stuffing wrapping into the trash can. "You want to take those leftover date bars home with you?"

"You keep them Martha. But thank you."

Martha's eyebrows shot up. "You crave my date bars. What's going on with you Joe? You weren't yourself tonight."

"Do you think what we do really makes a difference, Martha?"

"Don't you? What's this about Joe?"

"We hand out a few gifts, but those families still go home to their problems. We can't really fix that."

Martha went to Joe and laid her hand on his arm. "Oh, you sweet man. I cannot think of a single person who has tried harder to fix it all. Of course we cannot fix everything. But no one expects us to. We fill gaps. We create bridges. We give a little hope. And tonight, look what we—what you—did. For a while, this evening meant everything to those kids."

Joe nodded. "Thanks, Martha. I guess you are right," he said, but without conviction.

"You guess I am right?" She squeezed his arm. "Go home, Joe. Everything will look brighter in the morning. Remember, you are coming tomorrow night for Christmas dinner with Harold and me. I'll make sure to save you at least one date bar."

Instead of taking the bus, Joe walked the fifteen blocks home. Eddie was by his side. Overhead the sky was clear and filled with stars, and a north wind brought a bitter chill. The first snowfall of the winter had yet to arrive in Chicago. One of Joe's clients had given him a hand-knit scarf, and as he wrapped it tightly around his neck he was grateful for the gift.

Joe was nearly done in by the time he reached his front door. The walk that he had thought would clear his head had only muddled it more. In the kitchen, Joe heated milk and added chocolate syrup. After he filled his mug, he went to the living room and looked out onto the street. That day's paper was still out on the porch, so he went out to retrieve it. He stayed a moment and studied the neighborhood. It had changed so much. All of the neighbors from his boyhood had either died or moved away. He was the only relic of his memories.

He looked up at the Reed house, Doc Mason's house now, and let out an uneasy sigh. He missed those days with the Reed boys, especially Eddie. Eddie, whom he had considered a close friend. With the thought came the pang of guilt that had clutched his consciousness from time to time for thirty years.

Back inside Joe went up to his room and removed his copy of *Great Expectations* from the bookcase. He opened to the chapter where Pip meets Abel Magwitch and removed the newspaper clipping, yellowed and brittle with age. He had not read it in a long while. Now, knowing what he would do, he set the clipping on his desk and sat down to write a letter.

Dear Eddie,

I never wanted to believe what the paper said about you. They said you were a killer, but that's not the Eddie I knew. People would say of those Reed boys, the young one was trouble. But I saw things differently. Richie wasn't always nice to me. But you were, and it didn't matter that I was a "gimp." We played catch, and checkers, and toy soldiers all the same.

If you're out there, I need to tell you something that happened right before you died. I was coming home from work and a guy stopped me on the street, asking if I knew a guy named Edward Reed. The question startled me and I am sure I stuttered. When I said no, he must have thought I was just being a wise guy. He kept yelling, "Where does Edward Reed live?" I was pretty scared then, but I kept pretending I didn't know what he was talking about. Then he grabbed my shoulders and pushed me down. He started kicking me and kept screaming where's the Cowboy live? Reed? Where does Edward Reed live? So, I showed him. I'm sorry. I'm so sorry, Eddie. I didn't mean to give you up.

Your old friend, Joe "Joey" Crandall

When he finished writing, Joe lit a match and burned the words, thinking that if Eddie were out there somewhere, they might find their way to him, not knowing that Eddie had been there the entire time and had read each word as it emerged on the page. Ashes fell into the brass ashtray on the desk. After Joe burned the letter, he burned the newspaper article too.

A chill hit his neck, so Joe went back downstairs to make sure he'd closed the front door, but it was pulled tight. He locked it then and went to the kitchen to rinse out his mug. Up in the bathroom, he stared at himself in the mirror as he washed for bed. "I'm sorry, Eddie," he mouthed. "I should have been a better friend."

He got into bed and lay there, restless for a time, and stared at the illuminated alarm clock on his bedside table until midnight. Tomorrow was Christmas. Joe laughed. Will I wake like Scrooge, my sins absolved, a new man?

The chill returned, and Joe saw a shadow cross his ceiling. He knew it was only the wind swaying the tree branches outside his window, but the shadow had looked so human, not spindly like a branch. Maybe it was Marly's ghost. Or someone like Marly. What was the message though? What was it he needed to know?

"Ahh!" he cried. "What an idiot I've been." He pulled his blankets tightly to his chin and closed his eyes.

Eddie stood at the foot of the bed and tried not to cause any further disturbance. He hated to see Joe feeling so low. He hadn't known before today about his old friend's secret.

"That's okay, Joe," Eddie said. "I'd have done the same thing. And they'd have found me sooner or later without your help. So, you just forget about it, okay? You just keep doing your great job helping people. You're one of the good ones, Joe. One of the really good ones."

Chapter 58

November 27, 1960

"Hello Joe," Frederick Mason said, answering the front door. "Come in." Joe stepped inside the old Reed house for the first time in years. The last time he'd gone inside was with his mother, for one of her last appointments before she died. As he looked around at the inviting space, he realized he had no memory of the house as it had looked when Eddie lived there.

"How are you doing, Doc?" Joe asked.

"I am well. You?"

Joe wasn't here to complain about his ever-increasing shortness of breath or to mention that he'd felt a jab of pain in his chest the other day. It had vanished without any ill effects. "Fine. Just fine."

"What can I do for you, Joe?"

"I won't stay long," Joe said, remaining near the door. "I've got an odd request." He laughed, then rubbed his hand over his forehead as if he were reluctant to say what was on his mind. "It's a very last minute thing, I know, but I've cooked a turkey, and I'd like you to come over to dinner, unless you have something of your own in the oven."

Frederick's faced opened in a broad smile. "Well, Joe, I think that would be very nice. Can I bring anything?"

Joe shook his head. "I've managed it all I think. You sure this isn't an imposition? Maybe you had other plans?"

"Ha, no. I was just going to heat up a deli dinner."

"Okay, good," Joe said. "I'll head home now, but it's ready when you are."

"Thanks, Joe. I'll take care of a few things here, then I will be over."

In the kitchen, Frederick rewrapped the spaghetti casserole he had been about to stick in the oven and placed it in the refrigerator. Then he looked in the basement for a bottle of wine. He did not know if Joe drank wine, but he did not want to go next door empty-handed.

Eddie waited on the Crandall porch with Frederick, who had knocked twice. He was about to go inside to see what the hold up was when Joe opened the door.

"Sorry," Joe said. "I was stirring the gravy. Come in."

Inside, Frederick handed the bottle to his host. "I thought this might be nice," he said tentatively.

"Yes. Thank you."

"If you need to get back to the stove—"

Joe nodded. "I should. Yes. You can just toss your coat on a chair. Then join me?"

Frederick nodded. Moments later he made his way to the kitchen. "It smells wonderful, Joe. Anything I can do to help?"

"You could open the wine." Joe fumbled in the utensil drawer for the corkscrew, then took two wine glasses from the cupboard. "Along with a bottle of wine last Christmas, these were a gift from my co-worker Aaron and his wife. They thought to make me a bit more cosmopolitan." Joe laughed. "I've not used them since, so I think their plan failed."

"Far more important things in life than sophistication, in my view," Frederick said. "Like being able to cook."

Joe nodded appreciatively, then took a clean dishtowel from the drawer and handed it to Frederick. "You'll probably want to wipe those out. I imagine they're a bit dusty." The timer dinged and drew Joe back to the stove. He turned the burner off under the gravy and took a pan of dinner rolls out of the oven. "This is the last. I've already carved the bird, so there's nothing left to do but eat."

Frederick poured the burgundy and handed a glass to Joe. "A toast to us? Happy Thanksgiving!"

Joe lifted his glass. "Happy Thanksgiving!"

"I thought we could just eat in the kitchen, if that's all right with you. It's not fancy, but since it's just the two of us."

And me, Eddie said. How he wished he could be there, really be there, with these two men he had such a fondness for.

"That is fine with me."

The meal was laid out on the counter and each man filled his plate before sitting down at the table.

"This is quite a feast, Joe."

"Yeah. I maybe went overboard. It's nostalgia, I think. Lately I've been thinking a lot about my parents and our holidays. Even though it was just the three of us, my mother made enough for a small army."

"My mother was the same way," Frederick said, buttering a dinner roll.

While the men ate, they spoke about the weather, which was rainy but predicted to snow, and sports, they were both Cubs fans, and the news in general, whether Kennedy would make a good president. Both thought he might be exactly what the country needed.

"That was delicious," Frederick said after finishing the last bite.

"Thanks. There's more if you—"

Frederick shook his head. "How did you learn to cook?"

"By watching my mom, starting with those years when she kept me out of school. Then when she got sick, I had to. Anyone can cook. It's a matter of following directions."

Frederick said that was true. He'd had to learn or starve. "Can't go to the diner every night."

"No, but that place over on Delafield, McGinty's, has the best meatloaf. I go there sometimes just for that."

"That's about the only thing I can make well," Frederick said. "Or toast. I make excellent toast."

Joe laughed. "I better put the leftovers in the refrigerator, but I think I'll just leave the cleaning up until tomorrow morning."

"Nonsense. I'll wash up while you take care of the food. Then it's done."

Joe shrugged. "If you insist. Then afterwards we can finish our wine in the living room."

"Tell me more about your mother keeping you out of school. Why was that?"

"I suppose it was because of my leg. She probably thought kids would torment me, though she never said so. My reading and arithmetic lessons in the kitchen seemed normal to me. I didn't know it wasn't."

"What changed?"

"We moved here when I was seven, and Eddie and I became friends. He was nice to me, so I guess Mom figured other kids would be nice too. All I remember is one day I started going to school."

Eddie was gleeful at the mention of his name. He was rarely the topic of conversation. That he knew of anyway.

"Were they? I mean were there some children who treated you poorly?"

"Some. Honestly I don't remember. That was so long ago."

"Polio wasn't it? That caused your limp?"

Joe nodded.

"Thank goodness there's a vaccine for that now," Frederick said before turning to the sink full of dishes.

"You take the gold chair with the ottoman," Joe said. "I'll sit on the sofa."

"You mentioned Eddie. Was he a neighbor?"

Joe smiled. "Don't be coy, Doc. You know who he is, or was. Edward Reed. You live in his house."

"Oh, that fellow."

"Yes, that fellow," Eddie said, anxious to hear what would come next.

"Is it true what the gossips say, that he was a ruthless gangster?"

Joe set his glass on the table. His own mother had been one of the worst gossips, he remembered. "I wouldn't say ruthless. But he was mixed up with some bootleggers. Not that he told me about those things. That's just what the papers said. It was always hard for me to see him as anyone other than my friend. But we did grow apart as we got older. It was harder and harder to find time to get together. I had work and he had, well, whatever it was he did. All I know is that when we were kids, he was a great guy."

"Anne and I heard the stories, of course, but we chose to ignore most of it. She was more concerned with the ghost in our house."

"What?"

Frederick laughed. "Yes. She was convinced our house was haunted. It became our little joke every time we heard some creak or crack in the house that we couldn't explain. She'd say, "Hello. Who are you?" Silly, I know, but even now, I sometimes call out to him. Or her. Like we used to do. It makes me miss Anne just a little less."

A respectful silence fell between the two men, and Eddie's chest heaved with emotion. "I miss her too, Doc" he said.

Frederick got up and poured the last of the wine."I have some news, Joe," he said, tentatively, then returned to his seat before he spoke further. "I have decided to retire, sell the house, and move to California to be with Mattie and the kids."

Joe's head dropped to his chest. Then he lifted his eyes and sighed. "It won't be the same around here without you, but I understand. It has to be hard to be so far away from your family."

"Mattie has been trying to convince me for years. It's time."

"I guess I'm the last of the old guard," Joe said. "When Charlie Alford died, it was just you and me, and now it will be just me."

"And me," Eddie said, knowing his words could offer no consolation.

"You still have your work, Joe, your co-workers, all the good you do in the community. I've always admired you in that regard."

Joe nodded. "Thank you. I appreciate that. So when? Not soon, I hope."

"Fairly soon. I've already listed the house with a real estate agent. I'm selling fully-furnished, and I don't have much to ship out to Mattie's, so

I can go any time. I thought it might be nice to be in Los Angeles for Christmas."

"With no snow? I suppose that could be nice."

"Letters to my few remaining patients will be in the mail this week. I wanted to tell you in person, though, so tonight was kismet, wasn't it?"

"To you, Doc," Joe said, raising his glass. "I'll be forever grateful for everything you did for us, for my mother especially."

Then men spoke of old times for a while, the Depression, the War, the fire at Mary O'Brien's. Always they came back to neighbors helping neighbors.

"Say," Frederick said before leaving for the night with a plate of leftovers. "Let's go to that place you like before I leave, get some meatloaf."

"Yes. I'd like that."

Eddie was torn, stay with Joe to console him or go home with Doc? He chose to go to McGinty's instead. Declan McGinty died in '52, but the new owner had kept the name, a decision all the regulars were happy about. Declan "Mac" McGinty was a legend, and stories about prohibition days were good for business. New patrons wanted to hear all about it. "Was there really a speakeasy downstairs?" many asked incredulously. "Is is true the owner was friendly with gangsters?"

Tonight the place was filled with a lively crowd, people with no family for the holidays, Eddie surmised. A long table towards the back was filled with platters and bowls of food. Eddie wound his way among the patrons, taking care not to bump into anyone, especially those with newly-filled pints of beer. He curled himself up near the ceiling behind the bar and listened to the chatter. Joe should do this, he thought, next Thanksgiving, or any old night. Just because you had no family, it didn't mean you had to be alone.

Eddie sighed, then he conjured himself a pint of bitter ale. "Cheers!" he shouted into the crowded bar before drinking the beer as if it were as cold and satisfying as he imagined it was.

Chapter 59

July 1961

After Frederick Mason moved to California, Joe began going to the movies every Friday night. Getting sucked into a story helped him forget how quickly life changed, how soon everything he had counted on to stay the same would end. He and Frederick Mason had not been friends, but they had their routines, brief conversations over the back yard fence as each mowed his yard, or the same in winter as they cleared their sidewalks, calls to each other now and then when a neighbor passed away.

Joe hadn't realized until Doc was gone just how much he had relied on such things. There were new neighbors next door now, an older couple. He'd gone over to say hello, but they gave the impression they were not much for socializing. Neither was he, but that's not what being neighborly meant.

If anyone knew how easy it was to rely on routines, it was Eddie. He had never sold the house for that reason. Years after his demise he finally understood how the stability of place helped people feel secure.

The first movie Eddie attended with Joe, back in January, had been eye-opening. Eddie hadn't been to the movies since 1926, when he'd gone to see a silent picture called *Tumbleweeds*. He'd gone because he wanted to see the star, William S. Hart, for himself. No one in the theater had stopped Eddie to ask for his autograph, which he took as proof that he did not look that much like the actor, no matter what Bear said.

He couldn't believe how much movies had changed, and not just that there was sound now. Today's movies were so lifelike. So vivid it was like you were up there in the action. When a bomb exploded, the whole theater reacted, jumping in their seats as if they had felt the blast. If Eddie had known how enjoyable movies were, he would have carved out time for them long before now.

He and Joe had seen a lot of good movies in the past six months. Westerns, war dramas, a few romances, though Joe seemed to squirm through those. Movies about gangsters sometimes hit too close to home for Eddie, but he liked comedies. Probably because it felt good to hear Joe laugh. The only thing that would have made it better would have been if Joe had a real friend to go along. There were always a lot of couples at the theater, and Eddie thought that if Joe could meet a nice gal, and if she would get to know him and look past his outer shell, she would see what a great guy he was and how lucky she was to have met him.

Eddie never got the chance to play matchmaker, for on the second Friday in July, right in the middle of *The Guns of Navarone* with Gregory Peck up on the screen, Joe Crandall's heart gave out.

No one in the theater heard Eddie when he cried out "No! Not Joe." One woman felt a sudden chill, but she attributed it to the air conditioning. If she could have known that it was instead the passing of a good soul, she might have cried too.

It almost killed him to do so, but Eddie stayed with Joe until they came to take his body away. And Eddie went to the funeral home, even though it tore him up inside to be there while they prepared Joe for his funeral.

And he was there the next day, when Martha and her husband Harold came to make the arrangements.

"He had no family," she told the funeral director, "except for us." She chose the flowers, yellow chrysanthemums because they were joyful, and she wrote the obituary. When the director asked about a pastoral sermon, Martha shook her head. "Joe wasn't religious," she said. "If it would be all right, I'd like to say a few words instead. I don't think there's anyone who's known Joe longer than me."

"I did," Eddie said. "I knew him longer than anyone."

The ceremony began at 10:00 a.m. on Saturday, and because Eddie had been with Joe's body the entire night, he was already there when Martha and Harold returned. Not long after, Aaron arrived with his family. He was the office manager now, following Martha's retirement the previous year. Other office workers Eddie had not taken the time to know joined them.

Soon the large room was bursting with mourners. Some very old folks on the arms of their sons or daughters. Young mothers and fathers with their children. A few veterans Eddie remembered, two in wheelchairs, their hats in their laps. There were people of all ethnicities and race. The room looked like the Chicago Joe had been proud of, a city for everyone.

Adi was among the last to arrive, and he took his place next to Eddie. Instead of offering some statement of sympathy, he said nothing.

Martha made her way to the lectern using a cane. Her body had aged, but her eyes were as firey as they had always been. And through her grief she told Joe's story, how he had arrived at the community center in 1922, a young man eager to help others.

"We were all young and idealistic in those days," she said, "but Joe had something special." She paused to find the right words. "No matter how dire a situation was, and believe me, we saw so much despair over the years, Joe refused let folks give up. Even those rare times when he was close to doing so himself.

"Somehow, when times were darkest, little miracles happened. Gifts and money and avenues of aid appeared, as if someone were watching over us and knew exactly what was needed. Of course, there's no such thing as divine providence, only divine people. He would never admit it, but I think it was Joe that made all that happen."

Martha looked out over the crowd, those seated, those standing elbow to elbow at the back of the room. "I know you all have your own stories of Joe's generosity. How he gave out of his own pocket at times. Visited you when you couldn't come in to the center. Got you the help you needed. I pray that your memories of Joe will be a blessing to you."

Then she bowed her head in a silent moment before taking her place beside her husband.

"Do you feel the swell of love in this room?" Adi said then. "Joe meant a lot to so many."

To me too, Eddie thought. And then with a pang of regret, he remembered the letter Joe had written and burned, how he had carried unnecessary guilt for years. "I did that to you, Joe. It was me who was a bad friend. Maybe if I'd followed your example, I would have turned out better and we'd both still be here. We might even be two old bachelors. I wouldn't even care about that because we could listen to ball games, cook out hot dogs in the summer. We'd have had each other."

THE GAGES

Chapter 60
Easter 1961

Rutherford and Margaret Gage arrived in early February of 1961. A fire had consumed their home, so finding a furnished situation had been a godsend. Unlike the clatter and confusion the day the Masons had moved in, the Gages appeared without a sound. Eddie barely heard the click in the lock of the front door on the afternoon the older couple, carrying only one suitcase with their new clothes, stepped inside.

Rutherford, Eddie learned, was a city engineer who rode the train to and from work. He read the morning paper on the way to work and reviewed papers from his briefcase on the way home. He was polite to ticket agents, but he did not get to know them as some regular commuters did. And he did not engage with people sitting near him. Rutherford, if he could manage it, sat near the exit door, and he was always relieved if no one needed the seat next to him. He was exactly the type of man Delmar Reed admired.

Margaret stayed home and kept the house spotless, cleaning constantly as if one mote of dust was an abomination. She was an avid needleworker, knitter, and crocheter. Even in the evenings when the television was on, she had to have something to keep her hands busy. Due to her industry, there were doilies everywhere in the house. Too many, according to her husband.

Margaret Gage was, above all else, a devout Catholic, and she went to mass each day. Rutherford went to church on Sundays because the ritual established in his youth was simply expected of him.

This morning Margaret wriggled into her new mint green linen suit and pushed her permed hair into place before calling to her husband to hurry. She didn't want to be late.

"We aren't even close to being late, Margaret," Rutherford said, coming out of the bathroom, a speck of bloody toilet paper on his chin.

"Oh, you've nicked yourself," she said, reaching up to his face.

Rutherford pushed her hand down. "I'm fine. Let's just get going. I've got work to do today."

"On Easter? You're joking."

He ignored her and headed down the stairs.

After the morning's service, Adi joined Eddie at home. The ham that had been in the oven while the Gages were at church filled the house with a sweet, smoky aroma.

Eddie closed his eyes and breathed in the old familiar smell. "I still get it," he said to Adi. "Cravings for food."

"So do I. We could raid the refrigerator later."

They both laughed. For a time they watched Rutherford and Margaret eat in silence.

"They seem quite sad," Adi said. "Do they ever talk to one another? Or are they automatons, just going through the motions. Eating that ham as if it were commanded—*Thou shalt eat ham on Easter*."

Eddie snickered. "They have their moments. She finds ways to keep herself cheerful, but I sometimes sense that Rutherford finds life tedious. They are only in their fifties, but sometimes they act like they're ancient."

He mused silently for a moment. They were younger than he would be, if he hadn't died. "You know, Adi, I can understand if Rutherford feels like an old man at times. Now and then, I feel like I'm a hundred."

"Why do you think that is?"

"No idea. None whatsoever."

Rutherford scooted his chair back and carried his plate to the sink. Back at the table he picked a chunk of ham off the platter and popped it in his mouth. "You should have bought a smaller ham, Margaret. This will spoil before we are able to eat it all."

"You say that every year, and we always finish it. And every year after you eat the last of it, you are sorry to see it gone."

He grunted and carried the platter to the counter and began wrapping it in aluminum foil. Margaret took the roll of foil from him and covered the bowl of leftover potatoes. "I could make bean soup this year, if you like," she said.

He nodded. "It was a good ham though. Not too salty. Just right."

"Go along now, dear. I can finish up in here on my own."

He leaned over and gave her a peck on the cheek, then went to the parlor where he'd moved the desk from the doctor's old office.

"Hmm," Adi said. "I did not expect that."

"Like I said. They have their moments. Once in a while that man's heart softens."

"What causes his gruffness, do you think? Does Margaret nag at him or make demands?"

"No. Not really. If anything she fusses over him too much. That tends to annoy him."

"No one likes being smothered."

"It isn't like that, though. I think she's lonely. As you saw, they don't talk much. Not like my parents. They would often talk about the world's events. They were interested in what was going on around them. They shared the moments of their days. That was how Anne and Doc Mason were too. But the Gages— I don't know, it just seems like they are both tired."

"Of what?"

"You might think I'm crazy, but I think they are tired of living, as if each day is a chore."

"Hmm," Adi mused. "Antithetical to most people's desire, is it not?"

"You think most people want to live forever?"

"I think most people want to live as long as they can."

Eddie shrugged. "I guess so."

"One of the preoccupations of science fiction, correct? Humans attaining immortality. We think if we can live forever, we will be able to experience all of life, see it all, have it all. In reality, the idea of immortality causes the most powerful existential angst."

Margaret Gage had just finished the dishes and Rutherford was in the parlor stretched out on the sofa with a newspaper. Guess he didn't have work after all, she thought. Not wanting to bother him, Margaret went to the living room, where she put her feet up on a footstool, and took up her latest needlepoint canvas. She was stitching a scene of Jesus among a flock of sheep. If the sound of the grandfather clock had its effect, she would soon nod off herself.

Adi and Eddie went out to the front porch, where they settled on the front steps, their feet in the midday sun.

"If you recall," Adi continued. "at the beginning of your afterlife, you felt the weight of eternity."

"I sometimes still do," Eddie said. "But now I see that I missed out on an awful lot by dying young. I'd give anything to go back. And you bet I wouldn't take it for granted."

"It is because you are dead that you feel that way. The living rarely do."

"Just like Emily said," Eddie interjected.

"Who is Emily?"

"The young woman in Thornton Wilder's play *Our Town*. She dies young and is allowed to come back to review her life. She realizes that human beings don't know what they have until it's too late."

"Not unlike you, then."

"Yes, but she's not a real dead person. She is a character in a play, so it was Thornton Wilder who was saying that. How do some people get it, while dopes like me don't have a clue?"

"How do poets know? Or artists? How do some people see everything while others see nothing?"

"Yeah. I mean we're all human." Eddie waved to a kid who rode past on his bike. He liked that kid. His family was new to the neighborhood, and despite not having any playmates around, the boy always had a happy look on his face. If Eddie were alive, he'd sit out here, just like this, and wave to that kid. And maybe the kid would wave back.

"Some people are more human than others."

"What does that even mean?"

"What you ought to be asking me is, what does it mean to be human? Surely it must mean more than taking in food and water and learning to speak and walk. By that standard, the Gages are human, but they are not really living."

"So then how is it some people do better? Are better."

"Honestly, I do not know. How is it true that a person with everything can be miserable? At the same time, a person with very little can feel contentment? I do have a theory."

"What is that?"

"John Donne wrote 'no man is an island.' To me that means that humans were not designed to thrive alone. We need each other. We do best when we love and are loved. We shrivel in isolation."

"It's a good theory. Like I said, I think Margaret is lonely. Maybe Rutherford is too, in his own way."

"Edward, did you know that trees talk to each other?"

Eddie eyed him suspiciously.

"It is true. And it is proof that Earth's beings are social creatures. I understand that life can be hard, but if you are lucky enough to find someone to share it with, you ought never to take that for granted." Adi rose and made his way to the attic.

Eddie could not swear to it, but he thought for a moment his mentor looked sad, as if his words had hit a tender spot in his own mind.

Up in the attic, the first thing Adi saw was the typewriter on the floor. Then he saw what was not there. "Where is your bookcase, Edward?"

"Rutherford took it downstairs. It's in the parlor."

"What? When did that happen?"

"Right after they moved in." The day had remained sharp in Eddie's mind. He had felt disconsolate as he watched Uncle Stanley's bookcase and all the books go back down to the house.

Adi extended his sympathy. "Show me the memory, Edward."

Rutherford clicked the skeleton key in the attic door lock and climbed the stairs. Margaret was right behind him.

"My," she said, "look at this. Could this have been someone's bedroom? Can't imagine an attic would be a comfortable place to sleep."

"Might have been used during the Depression. Or after the war. There was a great shortage of places to live back then. Remember when our neighbor knocked a hole in the front of his house to make a new door to an upstairs bedroom in order to rent it out?"

She shook her head at the memory. "That man," she said. "I remember what his wife said one day. 'He's squeezed us all in so tight I can barely breathe.' We were lucky we never had to do that, take in boarders, I mean."

"And then our entire house burned down, so were we lucky Margaret?"

She ignored him and went toward the front of the room. "Look here, Rutherford. A deck of cards. If I didn't know better, I'd say someone had been up here recently. There's not a speck of dust on this table. In fact, the whole place is oddly clean for an attic."

Rutherford did not comment on her observation. When she turned she found him near the stairway, kneeled down looking at a little pine bookcase that she had not noticed at first.

"I read many of these books when I was a boy," he said, perusing the titles. He opened a copy of *Tom Swift and His Air Glider* by Victor Appleton. "My goodness. This is a first edition. It could be quite valuable," he said. "I wonder how many others are the same?"

"And what about that quaint old typewriter," Margaret said. "They don't make them like that anymore."

Rutherford was on his feet now, examining the typewriter that sat atop the bookcase. "Definitely an antique."

"Should we clean all this out?" she said, gesturing to indicate everything in the attic.

Rutherford's head rocked in indecision. "I am not sure it's worth the trouble. We'd have to pay a junk man to haul it all away. Besides, once we close the door, it will all be out of mind. However," he said, pointing to the bookcase, "I would like to take this downstairs."

"What about the typewriter, dear?"

"I don't have any use for that. Do you?"

She shook her head. "I suppose not. Just one more thing to dust." But for a moment, Margaret had thought it would be fun to type her letters on the old machine.

Adi patted Eddie's shoulder. "I am sorry for your loss, Edward. Though I did tell you at the outset this was inevitable. I cannot quite believe it took this long. You ought to count it as a blessing that no one has bothered themselves with your "junk" before now.

"That wasn't nice to say."

"You are right. Not junk. Your worldy belongings are not junk, to you. In the eye of the beholder, right? I wonder, though, if you were in Margaret and Rutherford's shoes, would you see things differently?"

"I feel a lesson looming."

"Not at all. I merely want you to look at it from an objective perspective. None of this should mean a thing to you. You hold onto it for long-ago sentiment. You are not even the person you were when I first brought you up here. You are—"

"Older. Much older."

"I was going to say wiser. Which I see for myself."

Eddie's mouth twisted in a wry acknowledgment of Adi's words.

"You are not the same man."

"What has that to do with my things?"

"You used to put your worth in things. But the Edward I know now puts his worth in deeds."

"Deep. That's deep."

"Mock me all you want, Edward, but you know it is true."

Eddie picked up the typewriter and moved it over to the table. He had not typed a note in a while. He pushed the H key. Then he turned to Adi. "Let's go back outside. It's oppressive up here all of a sudden."

Chapter 61

December 7, 1966

It was nearly 7:00 p.m. when Margaret emerged from the narthex. She had been talking with Father Mayes about mending the Advent altar cloth. He had heard from another parishioner that Margaret was good with a needle and thread, and she had agreed to take on the project when they changed things out for Christmas. She felt honored to be asked.

When Margaret stepped outside, there was no one around, but why would there be? Service ended twenty minutes ago. She had hoped to run into Catherine Shelley, whom she had first met yesterday. The two had hit it off, and Margaret thought she would invite Catherine to join her for coffee or tea sometime. Oh, well. Catherine had a family to go home to.

It was pitch dark out now, but that was the exact reason Margaret liked going to evening mass in December. The entire church was lit in warm candlelight and it lifted her spirits. At least the afternoon rain had quit. Which was good, she thought, pulling her scarf around her. It was cold enough now for rain to turn to snow. As Margaret slipped her gloves on, she heard Father Mayes calling her name. He must have found more mending for me, she thought, smiling at how much she was needed. Margaret's smile faded when the priest appeared, a grave look on his face.

"What is it? Has something happened?" she asked.

"It's your husband. There has been an accident."

Margaret felt her heart drop from her chest. "Rutherford?"

"It was a train accident. Two cars derailed. I don't have many details, but the hospital called trying to find you." Reacting to Margaret's troubled expression he hurried to say Rutherford was alive. "Badly injured, though."

How on earth did the hospital think to call the church? she wondered. Then a moment later Margaret realized Rutherford had told them it was where she would likely be. It was true. If she was not at home, she would be here.

"You wait a few minutes. I'll change and drive you to the hospital."

Margaret stood there in state of shock. The priest took her elbow. "Come, let's go inside. Try not to worry. I'm sure he's in good hands."

Neither Margaret nor the priest knew that Eddie had also heard the news and was already at Rutherford's bedside.

"Oh, my darling," Margaret said quietly. Rutherford was asleep and did not hear her. Gently she touched her husband's bandaged hand. A nurse appeared with a chair and Margaret sat.

"He's sedated right now," the nurse said. "This has all been quite traumatic for him, although he is one of the luckier ones. His worst injury is the break to his forearm, but even that was a simple fracture, and it will heal well. Those lacerations on his face and neck look alarming, but they're superficial. The only thing that required sutures was the gash on his hand."

Margaret lifted her hand from Rutherford's, afraid she had hurt him. "Were there— Did some from the accident not survive?"

The nurse nodded somberly. "Two, is what we heard."

"What an awful thing," Margaret said. For a moment the two women remained silent.

"I need to go now, but I'll be back to check on your husband soon. Of course if he wakes and needs us before then, come let us know." The nurse turned to leave, then she paused at the door. "Do you need anything? Have you eaten?"

"I'm fine. Thank you for thinking of me."

After the nurse left, Father Mayes came in. Margaret spotted a chair by the empty second bed and said she would get it for him. The priest patted her shoulder and told her to stay where she was. Father Mayes set the second chair near Margaret.

"I know he looks a sight," he said, "but believe me, he will heal."

Margaret knew the man had seen worse. Father Mayes had been an army chaplain in Korea. Many of his sermons on gratitude stemmed from his experiences with wounded soldiers. "We sometimes forget to count our blessings," he often said, "not remembering there are many who are worse off than we are."

Margaret had taken those words to heart more than once. Whenever she had sad days, she would remind herself of her good fortune. Looking now upon her husband, she hoped that in the days to come, he would be able to say the same.

"Would you like me to say a prayer, Margaret?"

Margaret could only express a grateful nod, for she felt that if she tried to answer Father Mayes, she would break into tears.

An hour later, when Rutherford had still not woken, the nurse and the priest convinced Margaret it was time for her to go home.

“He will likely sleep all night,” the nurse said. “If something happens, we will call, but I can’t imagine it will. Right now, what he needs most is sleep.”

“That’s right,” Eddie said. “Go home. I’ll stay for a while. You take care of yourself.”

The next morning, Margaret walked to the bus stop, her tote bag loaded with goodies. She had risen early to bake a batch of Rutherford’s favorite molasses cookies. Along with the cookies was the morning paper she had remembered to retrieve from the porch. She had also brought along Rutherford’s slippers, a pair of pajamas, his robe, and her crochet cotton. If Rutherford nodded off, she would start a new doily.

As the bus pulled to the stop, Margaret worried that she had forgotten something. This whole situation had her as nervous as a cat. And she had slept terribly last night, at home alone, listening to the dreadful wind. Each time it whipped the branches of tree against the front of the house, she woke with her heart pounding.

Then, around 3:00 a.m., she’d gotten up to go to the bathroom, and—she made the sign of the cross just thinking about it—she thought she had seen someone walking down the hallway before her. If she hadn’t felt like she was going to wet her pants, she’d have gone right back to bed and pulled the covers over her head. Of course, she would tell Rutherford none of this, if he even asked how her night was. It was the first time she had slept alone in— Well, she couldn’t remember. If she said anything he would just tell her she was letting her imagination run away from her.

She found a seat near the front behind the bus driver. A man seated across the aisle smiled at her, a man about her age. She returned his smile, then turned to look out her window, supressing a laugh. What was wrong with her, she thought, that she appraised every good looking man she saw in terms of marriageablity. It was absurd. If she were ever to become a widow, what man in his right mind—

As the bus chugged ahead, Margaret watched carefully for the hospital. When she saw it, she stood and pulled the cable to signal she needed to get off.

“Watch your step, ma’am,” the bus driver said. Margaret smiled and thanked him and was about to tell him that she hoped he would have a good day, but she quickly realized there were people waiting behind her.

The hospital lobby was sunny and warm and Margaret had the momentary urge to sit there alone and watch the people come and go, but when she saw there was no line near the elevators, she hurried over and pushed the up button. Darn. I should have stopped at the gift shop and bought flowers, she thought as the elevator door closed. Oh, well. Maybe tomorrow, though she knew Rutherford would scold her for spending money on something so frivolous.

"Good morning," she said as she entered Rutherford's room, glad to see him awake. "Did they tell you I was here last night? Father Mayes drove me."

Rutherford nodded. "Quite a mess, aren't I?"

She leaned over and kissed him on the head. "Hurt a lot?" she asked, setting her bag on the floor by the chair before removing her gloves, hat, and coat, which she draped over the back of the chair.

"It is manageable. The arm hurts the worst, but I told them to save the morphine for those who really need it. I can survive on aspirin."

Margaret smiled. "I wonder if I would be so brave," she said. She took the newspaper from the bag and laid it on her husband's lap. "On the bus, I read about the accident. Just awful." Then she realized with his cast and bandaged hand, it would be difficult for him to manipulate a newspaper, so she held it up to show Rutherford the front page photos.

"Hmm," he said. "Looks like I suspected it would." He closed his eyes and expressed a despairing sigh.

"Maybe the paper was a bad idea. With your arm and so soon after." She refolded the paper and set it on the table next to his bed. "But perhaps a molasses cookie?" She took the package out of the bag and opened a bit of the foil, releasing the warm, spice-filled aroma. Smiling, she offered the package to him.

"A bit later," he said.

She folded the foil back over the cookies and set them with the paper on the table. She wanted to take his hand to comfort him, but she didn't want to hurt him. "Is there anything I can do for you, dear? A sip of water? I could get a cloth and cool your forehead."

"Nothing. Truly. They're doing everything."

"The nurses are kind. I'm glad to see it."

"Of course they're kind. What did you expect?"

Margaret gasped at Rutherford's harsh tone.

"Sorry. Didn't mean to snap."

With a nod she accepted his apology. Then she sat silently for what felt like an hour. In reality it was only ten minutes.

"I am glad to see you, dear," Rutherford said, "but I'm terrible company right now. Come again tomorrow. I will be in better spirits. I promise."

"But I just got here," she said, wishing instantly she could take her words back. Even she could hear how petulant she sounded. "You are right. You need to rest and who can do that with someone hovering over them?"

So Margaret gathered her things and left.

Three days later, it was time to bring Rutherford home. Margaret rarely drove the couple's car. Rutherford rarely drove it himself. But now and then they took it out of the garage and drove out to the western suburbs to a hamburger place he liked. Rutherford drove there and she drove home, "so we don't forget how," he reasoned. Nevertheless, it had been many months since Margaret had driven. As she turned the key and slowly backed out into the alley, she wondered if Rutherford would begin driving to work now instead of taking the train. She was sure she'd be off trains forever if such a thing had happened to her.

Getting to the hospital went without incident, and she parked carefully under the big canopy at the side entrance where she had been instructed to park. Before long, the nurse she had met the very first night arrived with Rutherford in a wheelchair, which she pushed close to the car.

"Take care, Mr. Gage," the nurse said once Rutherford was settled. "We don't want to see you back here any time soon."

Rutherford said thank you and after Margaret did the same, she turned the key. Their drive home was silent, and Margaret, who needed to concentrate, was grateful for that. Usually when she drove, Rutherford was constantly instructing her. It was more than she could take at times. His criticism made her more nervous, and she was sure it was not safe at all.

When they got home, Margaret pulled up out front, but Rutherford told her to go ahead and park in the garage. "It's just as easy to walk from there to the back door."

Inside he stomped the snow off his shoes. The kitchen was warm and it smelled like home. Margaret was inside now, removing her galoshes and putting them on a rug near the door.

She took off her coat and hung it on the hook above the rug. Then she helped Rutherford off with his.

"You hungry?" she asked. "I have turkey and noodles I can heat up."

Rutherford turned to her and put his one good arm around her. He laid his head on her shoulder. "It is good to be home," he said.

When he did not raise his head or move away, she slipped her arms around him and felt him pulling her toward him. The warmth of his body radiated into hers, and Margaret hoped he would not let go too soon. The next moment she felt his body tremble, and then he began to weep. She had never once heard him do such a thing. She was stunned and confused. Was there something she should say? All she could think to do was to hold him tighter, so they stood there like that until his sobs subsided.

"People died," he said, raising up, stepping just slightly back. "I could have died."

Margaret's own eyes glistened as she said, "But you didn't. You're going to live a long time Mr. Gage."

From that day forward, she called him Mr. Gage. And she was Mrs. Gage in return. Neither one could say why, but the little quirk they shared made them feel closer. It was also an unstated reminder of the worst event in Rutherford's life, a reminder of how fragile it all was.

Chapter 62

December 25

After Christmas mass, which Rutherford attended without complaint, primarily to extend his thanks to Father Mayes, Mr. and Mrs. Gage came home to a Christmas turkey with sweet potatoes and cranberry sauce.

"What about a sip of wine after dinner," Rutherford said. "Would you enjoy that? And I can build a fire while you wash up."

"With one arm?"

"I'll manage, unless you'd rather I not."

"I think a fire would be lovely, dear," Margaret said, feeling almost as if she could not contain the swell of emotion within her at that moment.

When the dishes were done, she went to the parlor, where the fire had begun to crackle. They sat together on the sofa and sipped their wine, which looked to Margaret like liquid rubies against the golden fire light.

"We should do this more often," he said.

Margaret said she would enjoy that.

He laughed suddenly. "Did you see old Arnie Martin at church? That tie of his, with Santa and the reindeer."

"He's a character all right," Margaret said.

"Father Mayes's sermon hit close to home," Rutherford said, getting up to lay another log on the fire. "I felt him looking at me when he talked about the derailment. I know he wasn't. There were others in our midst who were also on that train, though thankfully they weren't injured."

"I wondered how you felt about that," Margaret said. "You haven't really said much about the accident."

Rutherford was seated next to his wife again. He sighed and finished his wine. Then, as if a switch had opened his mind, he began to relive that horrible day. Margaret and Eddie listened as the story spilled out of him. Rutherford recounted the terrifying sounds those rear cars made as they fell, his memory of being tossed against the hard wall of the train car, the cries of others in agony far worse than his own, and when he was finished, he never spoke of it again. Instead, Rutherford vowed to be kinder to everyone he met, because he thought, you never knew what a person had been through in their life.

Sometimes, Eddie thought, it wasn't such a bad thing to face death.

Chapter 63
March 1977

It was just before dawn when Margaret Gage's brain went silent. When the alarm went off, she did not rise as she always did, first up to the bathroom, first downstairs to put the coffee on. Her eyes opened with Rutherford's touch, but he could get no other response. He followed the ambulance in his car, certain she would be dead when he arrived at the hospital.

"A massive stroke," the emergency doctor told Rutherford when he was allowed in to see Margaret. "X-ray showed severe brain hemorrhage."

"How has she survived it?" Rutherford asked. "I thought—"

The doctor shook his head. "This is only an interlude. Her body has not quite got the message yet, but it won't be long now. So sit with her."

"Can she hear me?"

"There is so much we don't know about how the brain works, but I believe that as long as her heart is beating, there is someone in there who understands us."

Eddie wanted to tell the doctor that he was exactly right. But he also knew Margaret was only grasping onto life by a thread. Part of her had already left her body. Adi was with her, and the two of them hovered over the bed.

Rutherford took Margaret's hand. It was warm, alive, but her fingers did not respond as he squeezed them. He laid his head on her chest and felt it rise as he listened to her heart.

"How can I leave him?" Margaret asked Adi. "How will he manage on his own?"

"Edward will watch over him."

She gave a hollow laugh. "Can Edward cook?"

"Life goes on. Life always goes on. Rutherford will find a way."

"Look at him," she said. "He won't be able to cope."

Adi squeezed her hand. "He will. Slowly, but he will. You stay a moment longer. Let him tell you what he needs to say."

A second later, Margaret's body gasped and Rutherford sat upright. "Is that you, Margaret? Can you hear me?" He stroked her forehead, then looked around to see if he was alone. His confession was for Margaret only. "I was not a good husband, was I? Not for the longest time. I should have done better. I should have." In his heart he asked her to forgive him.

Then moments later he spoke softly in her ear, "Go along, Mrs. Gage, whenever you are ready."

"You are a good man, Mr. Gage," Margaret said. Then she let go of Adi's hand and disappeared.

Not long after Margaret died, Rutherford Gage sold the house and rented a one bedroom apartment in a building not far away. Except for Margaret's clothing, which he donated, Rutherford took with him only what he needed for the apartment. Everything else that had been in the house when they moved in was sold. The Realtor assured him that no one would buy a house full of old furniture. Rutherford was in no position to argue with the man, but he and Margaret had been lucky to do just that.

There was only one thing Rutherford wanted to protect. He told the estate sale company the little pine bookcase was a family heirloom, so it was to be marked as "not for sale." Then before Rutherford left the house for good, he moved it back up to the attic where he had first found it, setting it against the wall at the top of the stairs. The bookcase was the only thing up there now. The odd little bedroom he and Margaret had discovered was gone. The space had been swept and the windows cleaned and Rutherford thought of what Margaret had said, that even though it was in an attic, it would be a nice place for a child.

One by one, Rutherford set each of the books in place, in meticulous alphabetical order, except for one. *Tom Swift and His Air Glider* he kept. Not to sell, he would never do that, but he took it to remind him that boys grow up. If a boy could know what life had in store, he would hold onto his time more fiercely. I would be a better man, he thought, as he climbed down the attic stairs that day, if somehow I could start all over.

After he retired, Rutherford became a kind of grandfather to the seven-year-old twin boys who moved in across the hall, sometimes watching them after school until their single mother came home from her job. He helped them with their homework and sometimes they played catch in the back yard. He read them *Tom Swift*, endlessly, for each time he finished the book, the boys made him promise he would read it again. They were enchanted with the boy who invented things. And Rutherford told them that they could invent things too. They could be engineers one day, maybe even work at NASA and help send rockets into space.

Rutherford wondered if Margaret could see him with the boys from wherever she was. What would she think? Might she even forgive him for never giving her children of their own? That sadness had draped their entire lives. It had been the unspoken bitterness that divided them.

If he could start all over again—. But Rutherford had no power over the past. He could only control today. So it was that one morning, and each morning until the day he died at age eighty-two, Mr. Gage went to mass and lit a candle for Mrs. Gage.

THE BENNETTS

Chapter 64
July 1977

Galen Bennett came home from Vietnam in 1971 and went to college on the GI Bill. His years at the University of Wisconsin were a blur at times, but he'd met Amanda there. She was a bright young woman, who'd been so against the war that their first date ended in an argument. He was certain she'd never want to see him again. But life continued to push them together. It was the concession from each that the entire situation was a colossal screw up that brought them into accord. They were married six months later.

When Galen earned his doctorate in 1977, Amanda had been teaching high school biology for three years, and it was her salary that kept them afloat. Galen searched for positions at prestigious universities, but he found himself behind other candidates his age who had more experience, those who had taken college deferments and had already done their time at the community college level, which he now realized was where he would have to start.

He sent his resume to small colleges in Wisconsin, Illinois, and Iowa. Both Galen and Amanda had grown up in Wisconsin and they hoped to be able to stay as close as possible to family, primarily because Amanda had recently discovered she was pregnant. They hoped Galen could find a good position so she could stay home and raise their child. Now it was nearly the beginning of the fall term, and Galen had almost given up hope. Then he got a call from the dean of Sawyer College, a small liberal arts college in Chicago.

As soon as he was off the phone, Amanda threw her arms around him.

"Don't get too excited," Galen said.

She held her finger to her lips and shook her head. "You should stop being so negative."

This morning, while Galen met with Dean Ryerson, Amanda sat outdoors under a vine-covered arbor near the administration building. Less than an hour later, Galen was outside, beckoning for her to follow him.

"Let's get coffee," he said. "The student union is just over there."

"How did it go?" Amanda asked impatiently.

Galen shrugged.

"Oh, you are just being evasive. You have to know if they liked you."

Inside the little cafeteria, they found a table near the front windows.

"It is a pretty little campus, isn't it?" Galen said. When the waitress came to take their order, Galen asked her if she was a Sawyer student.

"Junior year," she said eagerly.

"How do you like it here?"

"Profs are great. I like the one-on-one I get here, like when I need a little extra help." The young woman tapped the side of her head. "This thing doesn't always get it the first time."

Amanda smiled and handed her menu to the girl. "Coffee and a cruller for me."

"Same here," Galen said.

When the waitress left, Amanda leaned in. "So—"

"So, the dean says they have been looking for someone with a focus in medieval literature. Apparently there is a glut of American literature profs. Dime a dozen, in her words."

"Her?"

"Dean Ryerson is a woman."

"I like her already," Amanda said. "Progressive, don't you think?"

Galen agreed. Women administrators were not common.

"You met her requirements, and she had to like you. Where did the two of you leave things?"

The waitress returned with their pastries and a carafe of coffee. After she filled their mugs, she pointed to the cream and sugar on the table. Galen thanked her, then waited until she was at another table offering refills.

As if it were a state secret, Galen leaned over and said quietly, "Ryerson offered me the job, full load, starting immediately, if I want it."

Amanda's eyes widened in surprise. "Well, do you?"

"I'd be teaching World Lit I and II, Comp I, and an honors course that shifts from time to time. Last year the focus was medieval sonnets but this spring, it will be all Dante Alighieri."

"Galen!" Amanda said. "If this job isn't tailor made for you, I don't know what would be."

Galen had done his master's thesis on Dante's *Comedy* and his dissertation on the influence of Petrarch on Shakespeare and other subsequent poets.

He grinned. "It seems so. And you heard our waitress. The profs are great. I could go back to see the dean before we leave and let her know. I just wanted to talk with you first. It's Illinois, not Wisconsin."

"That's right. It is Illinois, not New York, Princeton, or Berkeley. I think it's perfect."

Galen squeezed his wife's hand. "I hope so." He was always anxious whenever things seemed to good to be true.

Galen and Amanda had been looking at possible homes all morning. One was a maybe and the other three were definite nos. Amanda was starting to feel worried they would ever find anything.

"I'm the worrier, darling," Galen reminded her as they drove up to the last property for the day and parked across the street to wait for the agent.

"This is a nice neighborhood," Amanda said. "Older, like that last one, but these houses are kept up nicely. Let's just go take a look."

Eddie had noticed the couple right away, and he watched intently as they made their way to the house and up the porch steps.

"I like these old Victorians, don't you?" Galen said. "What do you figure? Late 19th century?"

"Something like that," she said.

"Looks a lot like my old house in Sheboygan, and that was built around then."

"It will need some updating," she said, looking through the living room windows. "But that woodwork. It's just gorgeous."

"And look in here," Galen said, peering in the parlor window. "There's a fireplace. I think that's marble around it."

Amanda sat on the porch swing and patted the space next to her. Galen sat beside her. "I could see sitting out here on summer nights, couldn't you?"

"It is a peaceful spot," Eddie said proudly. "Nice in the back, too, as you will soon see, though the old garden is in sad shape. Are you a gardener," he asked the woman. She seemed like someone who would be.

"Where is that Realtor?" Galen asked impatiently.

"He'll find us. Let's go around back." On their way to the side gate, Amanda pointed out the Queen Anne's lace growing alongside the house. "So old-fashioned," she said. "They look like little clouds." Then her eyes were drawn upward by the sound of a chirping bird. "How do you feel about having to paint, Galen? Looks pretty bad up there."

"We can hire that out," he said. "I'll be too busy and you are in no condition to be climbing ladders." He smiled before opening the gate and letting her through first. "Big yard," Galen said. Then they walked up on the back porch and looked in at the kitchen.

"I just got the weirdest feeling," Amanda said. "Like I've been here before." She ran her hand over the painted porch railing. "Somehow this all seems really familiar."

"Spooky," Galen said with a laugh.

Very odd, thought Eddie. He wondered what it meant.

"Yeah," she said. "Spooky." But her sensation had been as real as the sun on her bare arms. She couldn't explain it, but she had felt as if a warm surge of light had moved through her. And far from being frightened, the experience had only convinced her that this was the right house for them.

A week later, after all the papers had been signed, Galen and Amanda Bennett turned the lock on the front door of the home they hoped to live in for a long, long time, and Eddie Reed, who had felt an instant affinity for the young couple, was happy again.

"We are going to need more furniture," Galen said after the last of their things had been unloaded from the moving truck. "It echoes in here." He cupped his hands around his mouth and called, "hello-oh-oh-oh."

"Oh, stop it," Amanda said, laughing. "I think it's just fine for now. We have all the time in the world to make this place home. And we won't start down here, anyway. We'll have to get the nursery things soon."

Galen patted her abdomen. "Yes. Top priority."

Just then, one of the moving men appeared at the front door with a clipboard. He cleared his throat so as to not intrude on the moment.

"Oh, sorry," Galen said. Then he signed the paperwork and handed the man the check he had written out earlier. Galen waited for the truck to pull away before shutting the door.

"Ours, all ours," he said in a manic, mad scientist's voice. Then he swept Amanda off her feet and carried her in his arms to the stairs, where, winded, he set her down. "Not the man I thought I was," he said.

"You fool. Come with me. I want to show you something."

They ran up the stairs like two kids at summer camp.

"In the bedroom? Is that where you are taking me? What do you want to show me?"

She ignored him and went to the attic door and turned the skeleton key in the lock. "We never even looked up here with the Realtor," she said, then she clicked the light switch and climbed the stairs.

"Look," she said, pointing to the bookcase. "Isn't it bizarre? There's not another thing up here except for this."

Galen's eyes widened in amazement. He ran his hand over the top of the bookcase. "Someone made this. You can tell." He bent down to study the titles. "These are old books. Really old."

"Why is it up here, though, is what I am wondering," Amanda said. "So odd." She left Galen with the books and went to the front windows and looked out onto the street. They would get to know the neighbors soon. But for now, she wanted nothing more than to settle in. Galen was right. They would need more furniture. They had lived like hermits in their apartment, having to pinch every penny while Galen finished his PhD, and they weren't rich now, but they could afford a few splurges. This house was an empty slate at the moment, and Amanda was dying to make it hers.

"What?" she said. Galen had said something but she was so deep in her thoughts that she hadn't heard.

"I said I am going to take these books downstairs."

"For your study? Did you decide yet to turn the parlor into your office?"

"If you are okay with that."

Amanda nodded.

"But I was thinking this bookcase should go in the nursery."

"Really?"

"These are children's books. Most of them, anyway." He held out a worn blue volume. "*The Blue Fairy Book.* We had this at home when I was a kid.

Can you imagine us sitting with our little boy—"

"Or girl."

"Or girl, and reading her stories?"

Amanda went to her husband and rose on her toes to kiss him on the cheek. "I love you, do you know that?" She took the book, looked inside, then set it on top the bookcase. "Come with me. I want to show you something in the bedroom."

Chapter 65

September 1977

Amanda lay in bed, unable to lift her head from the pillow. She had only forced herself down the hall to the bathroom when it became too urgent to ignore. At first Eddie gave her the time she needed, but now, it had been three days, and he was worried. He filled the space beside her and sighed his sympathy into her. He understood her grief. He had been there with his mother when she lost her last baby and had seen how her sorrow lingered.

For Galen, the situation simply required patience. The next time it would go well, he told Amanda. He had read up on the causes of miscarriage and said that her situation was not uncommon. That was when she told him to get out in the most hateful tone he'd ever heard.

As Eddie lay there now, he came to discover that what Amanda was feeling was not sorrow, though she was sad. What she mostly felt was fear. She was deep in her memory, thinking back to when she was in college, a year before she met Galen, when she found out she was pregnant. There was no question at that time that she'd get an abortion. After all, she wasn't even quite sure who the father was.

It was a time in her life she wasn't proud of, but she had decided then that it was silly to feel ashamed. Young men were forever free to sleep around. It was not fair that young women were held to a different standard. But now she wondered if that was the cause. What if her body had been injured? Or was she somehow being punished?

"You are not being punished," Eddie said forcefully. "This is not your fault." Then he repeated himself, again and again and again, until Amanda fell into a deep, unperturbed sleep.

She appeared at Galen's office door the next morning, showered and dressed. It was Saturday and he was busy as usual with student work. She told him she was going to the store. She needed chocolate chips and eggs. She was going to bake. Cookies cure everything, her mother had once told her. And as ridiculous as it seemed, somehow a cookie fresh from the oven did make things better.

A while later, the house filled with the aroma of chocolate and baked sugar. She laid two cookies on a plate and filled a glass with cold milk.

She was going to take them to Galen and tell him everything would be all right. But just then he was in the kitchen behind her. He took her in his arms and rested his face in her hair at the back of her neck.

"I'm so sorry," he said.

She turned in his embrace to face him, her eyes welled with tears. She let them fall. She had earned each one. She nodded and laid her head on his chest.

Eddie watched them. They stood motionless together for a long time, not speaking, not needing to speak, for Galen had done the exact right thing at the exact right time. And sometimes there were just no words.

Chapter 66

January 1978

Eddie began attending Galen's literature classes for the spring term. He was ecstatic at the thought of being a college student, only slightly acknowledging the irony. It didn't matter. People can change, he thought.

The assigned texts were easily found in the library, and he would go there at closing time and when he was alone, he would read. He even attempted the composition assignments, typing them out on the library's machines, but they were electric models now, and he had the hardest time controlling them. One tap sent a line of letters across the page. He eventually gave up, not only because the typewriters were difficult to manage, but because he found reading was far easier than writing. There were just too many ideas in his head, so his attempts were often jumbled nonsense. It was not like Galen was going to call Eddie to his office and question his failure to turn in a single paper.

Eddie was just grateful that he had thought to join the class in the first place. His true frustration came from Galen's real students who were reluctant to engage. "He asks good questions," Eddie told Adi one day, and some of them just sit there. "I can hear the ideas forming in their heads, but they muzzle themselves for no reason, or worse, just shout out the first thing that pops into their head."

"They are young, Edward, very young. And keep in mind, they have not read all that you have. More important, they have not lived much of life. They, thank goodness, do not have the gift of insight that comes only after death. So, it is probably time to ease up on them and let Galen do his job."

But that morning had been particularly frustrating. They were discussing Remarque's *All Quiet on the Western Front*, and Galen asked them to focus on two scenes: the one where Kat secures the chicken and the one in the trench with the dying French soldier. "What can we make of each scene on its own," Galen had asked, "and what themes are suggested if we compare the two?"

Without a thought, a still-pimpled young man shouted out "The brutality of war. How unfair war is."

"Yeah," echoed another. "Like Paul is face to face in that trench with death. It's so gruesome," she said.

After the girl's response, the class sat quietly for several moments. Galen never filled such silences with his own explanations. It was important for students to wrestle with ideas. But Eddie was not as patient.

"This is—," Eddie grumbled. "You're missing it," he shouted. "Neither Paul nor the French soldier Duval should be there in the first place. They're young men. They both have families. This war has robbed them of everything. And Kat, he's a father figure, isn't he? He provides for the men, and when they eat that chicken, their bellies full, they feel a sense of home and family again. It's almost cruel, the juxtaposition of the two. Life and death, hope and despair. But the whole book— War is cruel, and people can be cruel. But there are times when they can be generous and kind. And when Paul kills Duval, he's not being cruel. He's acting out of love by putting a dying man out of his misery. The war has already killed Duval, just as the war has already killed Paul. He just doesn't know it yet."

"Definitely the brutality of war," a third student said.

After class, Eddie wandered around campus and hovered over groups of students, spouting phrases like "be curious," "try harder," and "read the damn book for a change." He went home thinking he was glad he had never wanted to be a teacher.

That afternoon, Adi arrived, begging a card game. They still played in the attic, but now they sat on the floor, cross-legged. After Eddie misplayed a couple of hands, Adi wondered what was going on.

"Your mind is elsewhere, Edward. Is there something you want to tell me?"

Eddie shrugged. "Nothing I can do about it though. I can't make people want to learn. Some of those kids don't even half try."

"Well, you—. That is, no I suppose not."

Adi wondered if Eddie had put the pieces together. Did he hear his father's voice saying the exact same things to him as a young man? Adi decided not to point it out. "On the other hand, *you* are getting quite the education, are you not? To think how you used to hate school."

Eddie laid down his discard and drew the queen of hearts. "It is a funny turn, isn't it? Me hungry to learn."

"I can understand the lure, being there in the hallowed halls of learning, even if it is just little Sawyer College, not Harvard, not Oxford. But you realize you are going to have to move on soon."

"Move on?" Eddie said, sounding panicked. "You want me to learn. I'm learning."

"Yes, though Western literature is not what I had in mind. Not that there is no value in what you are doing. That book by Remarque is quite good, and there are many lessons there. One of the great things about books is that people can read them and take truth from them. And if they apply those truths to their own lives, it can be an edifying thing."

"You are saying what exactly?"

"Your real education is what you are learning about yourself. Through the years and your interactions with the living, you are gaining a deeper understanding of who you were and who you could have been."

"Haven't I done that?" Eddie said, sounding exasperated. "A hundred times over? I know who I should have been. Someone like Joe Crandall, always thinking of others first. Generous like Old Ned's daughter Grace. Compassionate like Doc Mason. Or Anne. Forgiving like Margaret Gage." He stopped his list and tossed his entire hand on the discard pile. "How much longer do I have to learn the same lessons? What more is there to learn?"

"I wish I could tell you."

"But you can't, right? That's not how it works. I'm Dorothy and you're the wizard and you haven't anything for me. But you know Adi, there's no Glinda the Good Witch of the North to point at my ruby slippers and tell me I had the power to go home all along."

"Listen to me, Edward," Adi said with compassion, "I would show you that path this instant if it were the right thing to do. But everything of value we learn in this world we learn on our own, through trial and error, success or failure. If your truths are to mean something, you have to discover them by yourself."

Chapter 67

December 9, 1980

Amanda turned on the television as she always did after clearing the breakfast dishes to get the news from CNN. Galen was in his office stuffing papers in his bag, nearly ready to head to work, when she cried out, "Oh my God. He's dead."

Galen, in the living room now, saw the headline across the bottom of the screen. John Lennon, former Beatle, shot dead at age 40. "What?" he gasped.

"Someone shot him last night. Outside his home. I can't believe it," she said, her voice now quavering with tears. "Oh, Galen."

He pulled her to him, and they sat quietly and watched for further details. The killer's motives were unknown, the reporter said. Apparently the suspect, who had remained at the scene, was found reading the novel *The Catcher in the Rye* after firing five shots at Lennon.

In Eddie's mind, that odd fact was a defilement of good literature. It wasn't the book that had propelled the man, but some abnormality in his mind. From the hallway Eddie watched the television. "Senseless, senseless," he muttered to himself.

He had heard of The Beatles, but he had never paid much attention to them or to any popular musicians. Eddie's favorite tune was still that aria by John McCormack that he had played on the Victrola for his mother when she was so ill. Clearly this man Lennon was beloved. Galen and Amanda were as heartbroken as if he'd been a brother.

Eddie remembered when President Kennedy had been assassinated, how Margaret Gage and Joe and everyone at the community center and everyone in the neighborhood had stopped what they were doing to watch the news on television, shocked and horrified that such a thing could happen. Even Cronkite, the newsman, was brought to tears.

Today, Eddie sensed a similar feeling of grief throughout the city. House after house, the sound was the same—CNN's continuous broadcast of the news. Eddie thought the new network's twenty-four-hour news format, which had begun that summer, was already having a detrimental effect. People couldn't get away from it. It was as if they were addicted to the non-stop onslaught of bad news. The way Eddie figured it, that could only make people feel worse.

Before long, notes of Beatles tunes reached his ears from one house to another. Midday, Eddie encountered a group of people gathered outside a record shop, where they huddled together, listening to *Rubber Soul* through the open door. "This record is my favorite," one said. Eddie ventured inside the shop, which was packed with people all listening to the music and talking about John Lennon. It was as if he'd burst in upon a wake. He lingered behind the checkout counter above the proprietor who flipped the record, then when it ended, he put on another. One by one, people bought every Beatles record the man had in stock, and those without put their names on the list for albums he would order. Eddie felt their collective sorrow and knew it held them there, in that little shop. Not one among them wanted to break away to go home and feel his sadness alone.

When Eddie ventured outside again, the afternoon sky was burnished in the deep violet wine typical of December. It was late enough for Amanda to be starting supper soon. He ought to head home to check on her. As he turned, he saw a car speed up and a woman in the crosswalk in its way. In seconds he was there to push her safely to the curb. It had been a long time since he had truly saved someone, and it felt good.

Chapter 68
July 1986

After years of trying, after years of heart-wrenching failure, Galen and Amanda's baby girl was born on April 1, 1981. They named her Karin Ann. She was six weeks premature and weighed just four pounds, but she already had a strong will, and everyone assured the Bennetts that very soon, they'd be taking their daughter home. For the time being though, Karin remained in the neonatal ICU, where Eddie kept watch over her. When Amanda and Galen came to hold her and feed her, Eddie could feel the child's spirit respond with joy.

Eddie's time in the neonatal ward brought him a new sense of purpose, and he enjoyed being in the presence of all those babies. He even felt, at times, fatherly. He knew he dared not lift Karin up to hold her, but the desire to do so was so strong, that when he went away, he felt his soul ache like it had not ached in a long, long time. It was, he concluded later, not so much that he couldn't hold Karin now, but that he would never hold a human baby, feel its soft perfect skin against his, breathe in its sweet breath. He would never be a father, and now, he thought, he might have been a good one.

Despite her slow start in life, Karin caught up quickly, and by the time she started toddling about the house, there were no signs she had ever been underdeveloped. In fact, she was such a vivacious child that Galen sometimes grew exasperated with her inexhaustible energy. In bed one night he made the mistake of complaining to Amanda that Karin wore him out. She barked back. "How can you say that? We waited too long for her. She's healthy, curious, and beautiful." And now, as if time had passed in a blink of an eye, Karin was five.

Yesterday afternoon, Amanda had made an emergency trip to Milwaukee where her mother was hospitalized after a fall that had fractured her femur. She had been hesitant to leave. "Go," Galen said. "We will be fine. Your mom needs you."

It was simple enough, Galen realized, to get Karin fed, bathed, and tucked into bed, but when it came to keeping the girl occupied during the day, he had a harder time of it. Though she was far less rambunctious than she had been when she was three, Karin still had an insatiable curiosity about everything in the world, and her constant questions could be overwhelming.

On the other hand, Galen loved pondering his answers. She tested his creativity. He would never lie to her, but telling his daughter where babies came from was a subject he wanted to save for the future. Other subjects were easier. "Thunder happens when cold air and warm air collide," he explained once, "but I have a book about a god named Thor who made thunder with his hammer if you want to hear about that." And so, Galen found that being his daughter's teacher was the most rewarding job of all.

"Will Grammy get well," Karin asked at the dinner table one night. Galen had made hot dogs and baked beans. Karin had poured so much ketchup on her hot dog that her little hands were slick with red.

"I am sure she will. Mommy is doing her best to help. Right now, the doctors in the hospital are taking very good care of her."

"I was in the hospital, too," she said.

They had told her about being premature and about her time in the NICU. "Yes you were. But just once when you were very small. You don't remember it?" Galen asked, handing Karin another napkin.

She shook her head.

"I remember and Mommy remembers. You were so tiny, but you were very beautiful."

Karin giggled. "I love you Daddy. It's fun with Mommy gone."

Galen rubbed his daughter's blonde head and told her he loved her too.

The next day after breakfast Galen told Karin he had some work to do in his office and suggested she play with her dolls for a while.

"I don't want to be upstairs alone," she said. "There's a ghost up there."

Galen frowned. "What makes you say that?"

Karin shrugged. "I just think there is."

Galen went upstairs with Karin to get her doll basket. In the hallway he peeked around, went into every room. "Coast is clear," he said. "No ghosts."

"You know," Galen said as Karin turned the basket of naked dolls and all their clothing onto the carpeted floor of his office, "Mommy and I don't believe in ghosts." He hoped just saying so would convince his daughter to feel the same way. "I have never seen one anywhere and certainly never in our house."

Galen got the feeling that Karin didn't quite believe him.

For about half an hour, Karin played quietly, and Galen got lost in a new translation of Dante's *Inferno.*

"What's that book, Daddy?" Karin asked a short time later.

"Where'd you sneak up from?"

She looked at him quizzically. "I've been here the whole time."

Galen invited Karin to sit on his lap. "It's a very old story that Daddy teaches. It's got monsters and famous people and they all live in a strange underground world with eerie rivers, scary trees, and dark, evil ditches."

"Isn't that like ghosts?" she asked.

Galen wasn't quite sure how to respond. Beings in an afterlife were technically ghosts. "I guess you're right, but honey, this is just a story. Make believe. It's not a real place."

"Can we read my favorite book, Daddy?"

Galen nodded. "Yes. Go and get it." He was grateful for the opportunity to put the thoughts of ghosts out of her mind.

When she returned, Karin had a book called *My Friend Mac* about a French-Canadian boy named Little Baptiste who lived with his parents in a cabin in the woods. One day Little Baptiste brought home a new friend, a baby moose he called Mac, whom he'd met in the woods. Amanda had read the book to Karin many times, and though Galen knew the basic story, he had never read it to his daughter. They sat on the couch in his office, and Karin opened the book and pointed to the first word. Then she looked up at him with an implicit order to begin.

The story was wonderful, Galen thought, and he was glad his daughter found it amusing. When Galen turned the page, Karin picked up reading where he left off.

Then she laughed. "Mommy would be so mad if Mac made that mess in our kitchen."

"Karin," Galen said, astonished by what he had just witnessed. "You read that page. You read it all by yourself."

She looked down at the book, then up at her father. Then she began to cry.

He felt her little chest heave inconsolably. "Oh, sweetheart, what's wrong?"

"I don't want to read," she sniffed, catching each word in a sob.

"Of course, you do. Reading is a wonderful thing."

She shook her head fiercely. "If I can read by myself, then you and Mommy will stop."

Galen understood then, and it made his heart ache. If he could have any power in the world, he thought, it would be to keep his darling daughter from ever feeling such hurt ever again. But of course, she would. Far greater than this, and that knowledge filled his eyes with tears.

"Oh, Karin. Never. I will never stop reading to you, no matter how old I get, no matter how old you get. I will read to you forever if that's what you want."

"Mommy, too?"

"Mommy, too."

Chapter 69

April 1989

Before long, Karin's anguish over learning to read vanished and she became a voracious reader, often tackling books well beyond her grade level. When her teacher suggested Karin might be spending too much time "with her nose in a book," Amanda scoffed. "Her father and I have a different view," she said. "And based on her grades, reading doesn't seem to have had any adverse effects." Amanda left the parent-teacher conference wondering if they ought to investigate other options for Karin's education.

That night in bed, Galen convinced her to abandon the idea. "It wouldn't be worth it, and I think it would be hard on Karin to have to adapt to a new school and new classmates."

Amanda conceded the point. Then moments later she laughed.

"What?" Galen said. "You sounded a bit sinister."

"I'll bet that teacher is worried that Karin is too smart for her to handle. Maybe she's more comfortable planning lessons for dull children."

Eddie laughed as well. "She is one smart little girl," he said. But how could anyone ever read too much? How could anyone ever learn too much? Eddie could not have been prouder of *his* little Karin. She was about the only thing that made it worth waking up each day.

Lately Eddie had been feeling lost, as if the trajectory of his afterlife had tilted off its axis. While daily life with the Bennetts was comforting and pleasant, he had stopped going to classes and to the library. While there was still a whole world of knowledge for Karin to learn, Eddie felt there was very little left for him to discover about human life, at least what he could learn through books. Only the future was new. History was the same as it always was.

What he craved now was experience. Actual human interaction. Out of duty, Eddie still helped those in need, but none were aware of his kindness or caring, so there was never any heartfelt expression of gratitude. No hugs. Not even a squeeze of his hand, as there would have been if he'd done those same deeds as a human being.

Eddie transported himself out of the house into the back yard and settled into the seat of the rope swing Doc Mason had put up. He looked up to where the slender hemp rope was lashed around the maple tree's strongest limb and was dismayed to see one of the tethers looked frayed.

"I better say something," Eddie said. Then he shrugged. "Why? He won't hear me. Nothing I say makes any difference."

With a sigh, Eddie rocked back and forth on the swing, watching ants near his feet scurry over a new-made hill.

An unexpected event forced Eddie out of his malaise. For Karin's eighth birthday, Galen and Amanda gave her a puppy. He was a scruffy terrier mutt with wiry gray hair and a cropped tail, and Karin named him Lucky because she said he came to her on a lucky day.

"Why is it a lucky day?" Amanda asked.

"Because I got a dog," Karin said, as if the reason were obvious.

Eddie could see that for Karin it was love at first sight. He felt almost the same way himself about the new puppy. There had been no pets in Eddie's childhood. Despite his mother's soft heart for any stray dog the boys found, Eddie's father always put his foot down. No animals in the house.

He remembered the summer he was thirteen, when he and Johnny Petrovic worked alongside Johnny's dad one weekend to build a pigeon coop. Mr. Petrovic let Eddie drive a few nails, and Eddie imagined how great it would be if that scene were taking place in his own back yard—his dad poring over a blueprint, sawing two by fours, hammering boards together, tacking down chicken wire. Eddie was so animated with the idea that he came home that afternoon and presented it to his father. He was certain that since the project met the rule about no animals "in the house," Delmar would consider the pigeon coop a fine solution to his desire for a pet. When Eddie's arguments failed, he felt so hurt and angry that he swore he would never talk to his father again.

The next weekend Delmar took the family to the Lincoln Park Zoo. Eddie figured his mother must have suggested the outing as a way to make Eddie happy. She was right in one way. Eddie could not help but be fascinated by the animals in the zoo, extremely so, but he also knew the trip to was meant to be a replacement for his interest in birds or stray dogs or any animal he might encounter in the future, and that knowledge simmered resentfully within him for many years.

Eddie hadn't thought about that trip to the zoo in a long time. How was it that those rifts with his father were still so much a part of his soul?

Pain like that should die with you, Eddie thought.

This afternoon the Bennetts were in the living room with Karin as she played with her puppy. At first Eddie watched through the windows from the front porch, but he did not like feeling so isolated, so he came inside and stood in the foyer between the living room and Galen's office. He laughed with the family as Lucky became interested in a slanted beam of light on the carpet, pouncing his paws as if trying to trap it.

"You silly dog," Karin said. She picked her puppy up and held him to her chest, his head near her shoulder.

At that moment, Eddie zoomed in for a closer look, but when he got near the dog, Lucky whined. Eddie reached out his hand to calm the dog but that only made things worse. The whine intensified, and Lucky wriggled out of Karin's grasp.

Lucky was at Eddie's feet now, rising on his back legs, barking wildly. "What is it boy?" Amanda asked. "What's wrong?" She picked up the puppy, but he resisted her efforts to soothe him.

Immediately Eddie fled to the attic. This situation was bad, Eddie realized. If Lucky reacted to his presence like this all the time, the Bennetts would think something was wrong with the dog. But Eddie also did not want to have to vanish from the family's lives either. Somehow there had to be a solution.

Eddie had been told that animals were more perceptive of spirits than humans were. Lucky proved that to be true. He remembered that rabid dog, the one that had wandered into the yard when Mattie and Gigi were outside playing. That poor thing had been comforted by Eddie's presence, not alarmed. And he had encountered dogs now and then in his afterlife without mishap, so what was the trouble with Lucky?

Eddie's first impulse was to summon Adi to ask his advice, but he put that option off. Eddie wanted to try to figure this problem out by himself. Since there were no manuals on how to get a dog accustomed to the presence of a spiritual being, Eddie turned to ordinary books on training dogs. Nearly all of them involved the use of bits of kibble to reinforce compliant behavior. Eddie thought that method might work if he could train the dog surreptitiously, but if anyone ever walked in on him offering Lucky his reward, they would see only Lucky taking a tidbit from the air. He could not risk anything so ridiculous. For weeks Eddie did the only thing he could do. He stayed out of sight.

Then one morning Eddie was struck with an inspired idea. How did humans gain the trust of a dog? Why couldn't he do the same? When the Bennetts were away, Eddie began to visit Lucky and talk to him. At first Lucky barked when Eddie said hello, but before long he responded calmly to simple phrases like "Hello, Lucky" and "You're a good fella." Eddie soon realized his voice now had a soothing effect on the excitable puppy. But would it work when the Bennetts were around?

Eddie decided to see what would happen one afternoon when Amanda and Karin were struggling to give Lucky his first bath. They had him in a galvanized steel wash tub in the back yard. Amanda was trying to hold him still and Karin was using a large metal pitcher to pour water over the puppy's sudsy back.

"Stop your barking, Lucky. It's just water," Karin said. She dropped the pitcher in the water and petted Lucky's head. "Water won't hurt you."

Eddie could see the child's chest heaving in exasperation. He knelt next to Amanda and looked directly at Lucky. "Shh," he whispered. "You are all right. A bath is a good thing. You want to be clean. Karin wants you to be clean."

Then, whether from the tranquil tone of Eddie's voice or the words themselves, Lucky stopped his fretful barking and stood still while Karin finished rinsing him.

"My goodness, Karin," Amanda said. "You've got the magic touch."

Eddie smiled. "See?" he said to the dog. "You have made them happy."

From then on, Eddie spent more and more time with Lucky, and eventually the dog accepted Eddie's presence alongside his human counterparts as normal. Beyond teaching Lucky not to fear bath time, there were other things Eddie helped with. When Lucky started barking at the mailman, Eddie told him that his behavior annoyed everyone. When Lucky whined before mealtime, Eddie told him to be patient and assured Lucky that Karin would never forget to feed him.

Eddie even took credit for training Lucky to lie down on command, though it happened unintentionally. Now and then when Eddie told Lucky tales from his own life and afterlife, he first instructed the dog to "lie down." It amused Eddie how quickly the dog obeyed, as if he were a child eager to hear a story. Eddie felt finally, he had a friend. Someone besides Adi who knew him.

That summer Karin took her puppy everywhere, so on the day he was at pet hospital for his "special surgery," Karin felt lost without him.

"The operation will prevent him from making babies all over the neighborhood, in case he escapes and goes roaming on his own," Amanda explained. Karin was still perplexed. "All dogs get this operation. He will be home before you know it," she said. "Now go out and play."

Amanda watched Karin from the kitchen window. She wished there were girls Karin's age living nearby. There were many boys, but they were older and not suitable playmates. While Karin never complained, Amanda knew she got lonely in the summer, away from school and her classmates. The smell of cake drew Amanda to the oven. She drew the toothpick out. Completely dry. She'd almost let it overbake. *Buy a new timer*, she wrote on her shopping list.

Just then a shadow passed over her eyes and she looked back out the window to see her daughter rising high on the swing. Panic pricked the back of her neck. Karin had been told to stay off the swing until Galen replaced the rope. Had he done so and not told her? She laid the hot pads down and went out to check. Amanda was barely out the door when she saw the frayed rope tear away.

"No!" she cried, seeing Karin begin to wobble, but then, instead of falling, Karin returned to the ground in a slow arc, where somewhat dazed, she set her feet on the ground.

"Oh, baby," cried Amanda, clutching her daughter to her. "You could have been hurt."

"The swing stopped up there," Karin said. "It stopped all by itself and then I came back real slow."

What Karin described was exactly what Amanda had seen, but it made no sense. "I think the rope held," Amanda said, "just enough for you to swing back safely. It must have been the wind that slowed you down, don't you think?"

"Maybe the ghost saved me," Karin said.

"What ghost?"

"The one I see upstairs sometimes."

"Oh, honey," Amanda gasped. "There is no such thing as ghosts."

Karin shrugged and looked down at her feet, where the snapped length of rope lay in a curl on the grass.

Amanda picked up the frayed end, then tossed it back to the ground.

"I think your father has to buy a new rope now, doesn't he? Or get a real swingset."

Inside Karin told her father the story, repeating her theory that a ghost had saved her.

Galen shot Amanda a look of alarm before holding his daughter close. "You're safe, baby girl. That's all that matters."

A while later, when Karin was on the living room floor with Lucky watching television, Galen pulled Amanda aside. "This thing about a ghost has me worried. She said something once before about seeing something upstairs."

"What? When was that? You never mentioned it to me."

Galen shook his head. "I don't remember exactly. I figured it was just the effect of all the fairy stories we read. But today, for her to imagine there really was a ghost—"

"She didn't imagine it. I saw something I can't explain any other way."

"Amanda, don't—"

"No, don't you. Someone or something kept your daughter from falling. It's so weird, I know. But I saw it, Galen. I saw it."

Galen sighed. "I'll leave it. It's just," he hesitated, "how can it be possible? I don't understand."

I don't understand either, Eddie thought. I was so careful when I lowered Karin to the ground. I tried to make it look like the rope broke after she was on the ground. At least I think I did. I don't know now. What if I've gotten too close. What if I've done something wrong?

In the end, Eddie decided to keep this incident from Adi, if possible, in case he had done something that would keep him in his afterlife even longer.

Chapter 70

September 1989

"Doctor Frederick Mason, formerly of Chicago, died Tuesday, September 9, 1989, at his home in Los Angeles, California," the obituary in the *Tribune* read. "He was 90."

Eddie read the rest with sadness and disappointment. It said nothing about the man's selfless service. Whether folks had money to pay or not, Frederick Mason did what he could for them, and for her part, Anne Mason often emptied her pantry for those in need. Even when most folks began going to the new clinics and the big hospitals out in the suburbs, there were still some in the neighborhood who relied on Doc. Obituaries rarely captured a person's life.

Eddie had missed the funeral, but he went to California that afternoon and stood by the doctor's grave. The girls had given him a nice headstone, and the cemetery was shaded by big trees. Only Eddie, from his vantage point, could see the ocean from there, but he was certain that those who paid attention could smell the salt air when the Pacific winds blew east.

"If you can hear me, Doc," Eddie said, "I hope you will rest in peace. Maybe your next life will be easier." Immediately Eddie retracted his wish. Not easier, but one less sad? An easy life, Eddie now knew was often an unfulfilling life. How much better had Anne's life been than her mother's. Sybil Henry's pampered life would never have suited Anne. She and Frederick were both happiest when they were thrust into the activity of serving others.

Adi had it right the time he'd called the Masons saints. Eddie was certain they were up there now, perhaps somewhere near his parents, and if he could hurry up and get there, he could gather them together for a festive reunion. He almost couldn't wait. And boy, did he have a story to tell.

Chapter 71

April 1990

At first Galen considered his job at Sawyer College as a stepping stone to a position at a more well-known school, maybe even Northwestern or his own University of Wisconsin. But Sawyer had turned out to be a blessing for Galen. The small school nurtured his innovative ideas. At a larger school, he probably wouldn't have had as much academic freedom, and at Sawyer, they didn't obsess over whether their teachers published papers or wrote books, though he was working on both. Sawyer cared more about their professors being good teachers.

When he came to realize what a gem Sawyer was, he put everything he had into the job, and in 1982 he was selected as the college's teacher of the year. The following year he was granted tenure. After a recent meeting with the dean, Galen learned two of his colleagues were retiring that spring, and they wanted him as the new department head. The added position meant a salary boost as well.

He went home that day eager to tell Amanda the news. She'd been wanting to redecorate the house, and now they'd have the money to do it. Not only that, but with a busy summer ahead, if they were going to take that vacation they had been talking about, it needed to happen as soon as Karin was out of school for the summer.

After dinner that night, they told Karin about the vacation and that they'd decided to let her choose the destination. When she shouted out Disney World, they were hardly surprised.

"Epcot could be interesting," Amanda said that night in bed. They both laughed.

"We asked for it," Galen said. "And no way are we going to let on that we're not as excited as she is."

"Agreed. But next time, I choose."

In the morning, Karin had a hundred questions. What states would they drive through? What did Florida look like? How big was Cinderella's castle? Then she showed her mom and dad a list of things they could do in the car to entertain themselves on the way.

"But honey," Amanda said. "We're going to fly in a plane."

Karin squealed with delight and stomped her feet in a crazed dance.

Lucky barked and did his own little spin. It was all Eddie could do to keep from joining them.

"All right, then," Galen said when the commotion was over. "You've still got six weeks of school left, but before you know it, we'll be up in the clouds on our way to Florida."

They say bad news comes in threes.

First, Karin broke her arm at recess. She was pushed to the ground by a group of boys playing rough. Several hours later, Amanda buckled her daughter in the car, taking extra care not to jar the girl's plastered arm.

"It still hurts," Karin said.

"I know, honey. It's going to hurt for a couple of days, but then little by little, it won't hurt at all."

"Will I have to fly on the plane with it?"

"Afraid so, but maybe we can get Goofy to sign your cast for you."

That thought brought a smile to Karin's face.

Eddie hated to see Karin hurt. As boisterous as he and his childhood friends had sometimes been, not one of them had ever broken a bone. He wished he'd been there to stop the injury in the first place, but at least good old Lucky was a sympathetic little soul. All afternoon and the next day, he curled on the couch next to Karin while she watched Nickelodeon.

Next was a bad break of a different kind for Amanda, something she'd kept from her husband until she could no longer keep it. Her doctor had found a lump in her left breast. She had gone quietly to the oncologist a week later. Now the biopsy results were in, and she wanted Galen by her side to hear the news. It was a cancerous tumor, the doctor said, but her prognosis was good, as good as one could hope for. They scheduled her treatment to begin the Monday after they returned from Florida, which her oncologist only agreed to because he also had a nine-year-old daughter.

But it was an incident at Sawyer only a week before their trip that shook Galen so badly that Amanda feared he'd call the whole thing off. And it all had to do with Carson Smith.

Carson Smith was Galen's newest colleague, and like Galen, a Vietnam veteran. In fact, Carson's experiences in the war were one of the reasons they had hired him the previous year. Carson had written a memoir, a collection of stories that had been shortlisted for the National Book Award. In addition to teaching American Lit I and II, Carson was told they wanted him to use his book as the foundational text in a new memoir writing class.

Carson had come late to teaching. He had drifted without purpose after his discharge from the army in 1972. He came home, found it hard to adjust, argued constantly with his wife, and didn't put up a fight when she said she was divorcing him. He could see it. They had only been married nine months before he was drafted, and now what should have been happy times for them was nothing but strife. He quit job after job after job. His employers called him morose and argumentative. It hadn't helped his marriage.

Nearly two years after he'd flown his last helicopter mission, Carson Smith found himself homeless. His drinking, which had been under control up to then, worsened, and every cent he scraped together went not for food, but for the cheapest booze he could find. Then one night he had nearly been stabbed by a man hoping to rob him, and in that moment of lucky escape, Carson told himself that if he could make it out of Vietnam in one piece, he could make it out of whatever current hell this was.

So, he sought help at the VA center, got a job at a warehouse unloading trucks, and on the advice of one of his counselors, he started writing. It would be good therapy, he said. It was one of the men at the halfway house who suggested Carson finish college.

Carson was a gifted teacher, in Galen's eyes, and an instant friend. They met often in the faculty lounge between their offices and spoke about their war experiences, writing, and how times were changing. While Carson could sometimes be withdrawn, on the whole he was a congenial colleague.

Amanda knew she owed Carson nothing but generosity, especially after all he'd been through, but she couldn't help resenting how much time Galen spent with him. It was almost as if her husband had a girlfriend on the side.

It was the last Friday of May, one week before the Bennetts were to leave for their vacation. At 6:20 p.m. Amanda told Karin to go ahead and start eating her dinner. Amanda was annoyed. Galen usually called if he knew he were going to be late. If he and Carson were out at a bar, she thought,

Galen was going to have a lot to explain. Before the end of the previous school year, he and Carson had started going out with a few other teachers on Friday nights after work, but when Galen had come home after seven more than a few times, Amanda let him know it had to stop. And it had. Now most Friday nights Galen was home early enough to help Karin with her homework or to go with her on a walk with Lucky.

So where was he? Several calls to Galen's office went unanswered.

By eight, Karin was washed and ready for bed.

"Is Daddy all right?" Karin asked.

"I'm sure he's fine, sweetheart," Amanda said without conviction. Nevertheless, she hoped Karin believed her. "Want to read a while before you turn off the light?"

"No," Karin said.

Amanda heard the anxiety in her daughter's voice. "Try not to worry. I'm sure Daddy will be home soon. Then I'll send him up to say goodnight."

Karin nodded. "Come, Lucky," she said. And as he did every night, Lucky jumped up on the bed, circled several times, then nestled himself as close as possible along Karin's side.

Amanda went back downstairs and out onto the front porch. It was a warm night, and the bugs were bad, so she went back in to turn off the lamps. When she went back out, Eddie was with her.

He had already been over to the campus and found Galen's office dark. After a fruitless search of nearby bars, he went back to Sawyer College where he found Galen and Carson in Dean Ryerson's office with campus security.

Carson was slumped in a chair, drunk and disoriented. Galen and the dean stood along the wall. Moments later, two police officers arrived.

"They're going to arrest you now, Carson," Ryerson said. "You understand?"

Carson looked up at Galen, as if pleading for help.

"Just do what they say, okay?" Galen said.

Seconds later Eddie went back home. When Amanda rose to go inside, he followed her and sat with her in the kitchen and waited.

"He'll be home soon," Eddie said. "He's all right." But Eddie's attempt to lessen Amanda's anxiety had no effect.

Galen walked through the back door at 8:25 p.m. looking tired and a bit disheveled, and Amanda's first thought was that he had been hurt.

"Are you okay?"

He nodded.

"Then where the hell have you been? What is going—"

Galen pulled her to him.

She could hear his ragged breath, but he hadn't been drinking.

"It's Carson. He killed a student. Driving drunk."

Amanda gasped. "What?"

Galen sunk his face in her neck. "It's bad, Mandy. I don't—"

"Were you with him?"

Galen straightened up and shook his head. "I was working late on that scholarship award and just packing up to come home when Ryerson called me." He moved to the fridge and took out a beer. Instead of opening it, he set it on the counter. His eyes tightened and closed, then he slumped into a chair and rested his head in his hands.

"Oh, Galen," Amanda said. She stood next to him and bent to kiss the top of his head. "I'm so sorry."

Two days later, guards found Carson dead in his jail cell. He had torn his shirt into strips and hanged himself. On the flight to Florida, Galen tried hard, for his daughter's sake, to be happy, but the wound Carson had inflicted upon him, upon all of them, was still raw. The very last place he wanted to be was somewhere called The Magic Kingdom.

Chapter 72

Summer 1990

By mid-July, the incident with Carson was still the main topic among the Sawyer College staff, particularly the English Department who had been interviewing for Smith's replacement. Galen was grateful they found someone early in the process. He realized he wanted to be on campus less and less. Carson had taken more than just that young girl's life. The formerly easy-going spirit of their department was also torn. The new hire was a young woman with an MFA from Iowa who had absolutely no ties to Vietnam. Galen gave the job of mentoring her to their senior composition professor, and he went home for the rest of the summer. September would arrive before he was ready. He'd be teaching the Dante seminar again. Any other year, he would be eager for fall classes to begin.

One Saturday morning, Galen took out the drawing he had been working on for a new project, an illustrated version of Dante's *Commedia* for children. Not that he had any illusion his illustrations would be comparable to Gustave Doré's or Blake's, but Amanda claimed his drawings were delightful. And where those artists, especially Blake, captured *Inferno's* horror, Galen took a gentler mythological approach. Minos and Cerberus were pictured as fantastical beasts, their edges and true purposes softened somewhat. But how does one soften a level of hell like The Wood of Suicides? And following Carson's own suicide, how does one even understand? Galen decided then to scrap the project. Children did not need to be subjected to the worst aspects of the human condition. If he wanted to write a children's book, he decided, he should start with Lucky as the main character, for that dog did cheer him up. He crumpled the paper and dropped it in the wastebasket before going to find Karin.

One evening in late August, Galen sat at his desk. He could no longer put off preparation for his Dante class. He would use the same approach as he had four years earlier, the last time he'd taught the seminar. Using his new Macintosh computer, he revised the syllabus. He'd take the floppy disk into the office on Monday to print out copies. He turned the computer off and started to reorganize the materials that were strewn across his desk.

The last thing to go in the box was his copy of Gustave Doré's illustrations.

He took the book with him to the couch and looked through it. Such detail. Galen never ceased to marvel at how much the pictures had influenced his reading. In fact, he purposefully didn't show students Doré's art until after they'd already formed their own image of Dante and Virgil. For him, Dante would always look like Dore's depiction, the figure with the hawkish nose, safely behind Virgil as they watched Farinata rising from his burning tomb.

And of course, it was not only Gustave Doré's illustrations that colored his reading of *Inferno*. Carson Smith was never far from his mind. Where, he wondered, would Carson be if he were among Alighieri's wracked souls? With those who were violent against neighbors? It hadn't been done with malice though. Carson had been blind drunk when he got in his car, but never had he meant to kill that poor girl. Most certainly he would be among those violent against themselves.

Eddie felt Galen's emotion turn dark and sat down beside his dear companion. If only I could make this all easier, Eddie thought. If only I could turn back time, stop Carson—. "It is not up to you to save the whole world," Adi had once told him. Eddie's impotence to make any difference in the human world had never been more clear.

Galen turned the page to the drawing of the winged harpies in "The Wood of The Suicides." He traced his fingers over the page. Doré had faithfully shown the naked souls of the suicides as Dante described them, encased in the limbs of trees—woody new skins for the ones they had destroyed on earth.

The harpies were integral to the writer's objective: symbolic retribution, or as Galen explained to his students, the punishment fits the crime. The harpies ate the leaves and limbs of the trees, destroying them. Even more cruelly, once the suffering souls were torn to shreds, they were condemned to heal and go through the process all over again, throughout eternity.

"Most pitiable of all, though aren't they, Dante?" Galen spoke as if the man were there beside him. "I think you were too hard on those who took their own lives. I get it. In your eyes, they destroyed the ultimate gift from God, the life that was given to them. They say life is suffering. Seems this is something you should have taken into consideration. You did get something right, Signore Alighieri, and it makes me wonder what you knew. Limbs snapping and reforming only to break again. This was not their punishment in the afterlife. This was their life."

Galen tossed the book to the floor and lay on the couch. He wondered how he would ever face a room full of students. They all knew what Carson had done. They knew that Galen was Carson's friend. That girl was their friend. He imagined the speech he'd have to make on the first day, getting that conversation out in the open. They'd have questions. Didn't he see it coming? Of course, he saw it coming. For months. Carson had started drinking heavily, sometimes even before class. The only time Galen confronted him, he did so in a casual manner, not with the authority of a department head. "Can't be doing that before class, Carson," he'd said. And Carson had waived him off, saying he had everything under control.

"You didn't make him do any of this" Eddie said loudly. "None of it."

"They're going to say I should have stopped him."

A tree had been planted in the girl's memory, near where the accident occurred. Accident, Galen thought. Hardly an accident. Behind the wheel like that, he was bound to hurt someone.

Eddie looked down upon Galen who faced the back of the couch, and he laid his hands on the man's shoulders. When Galen jumped at his touch, Eddie fled to the farthest corner of the ceiling and wound himself into a small gas ball. "You felt me!" Eddie cried.

Galen was sitting now. "Amanda?" he called. He got up and looked for her. The living room was empty, one lamp left on as she regularly did when she left Galen alone in his office before going up to bed.

Eddie had unwound himself now and shadowed Galen as he searched the kitchen and the back porch. The August night was as still as could be. Crickets had ceased their chirping. Galen, certain now he was alone, went back to his office.

"You felt me," Eddie said again, not as a question but as a statement of fact. He hadn't pushed forecefully. Hadn't meant to be felt. He had only used the softest touch in an attempt to console. Such a thing had never happened before. What have I done, Eddie cried out. Surely Adi would not like this at all.

"Carson?" Galen had been too deep in the *Inferno's* afterlife to be immune to the possibility that beings could be sentient after death, no matter what he had told Karin the time she reported a ghost in the house, or that time with the swing. He had not admitted to Amanda that day that he thought it was entirely possible that the dead walked among us. And now he had felt a pressure on his shoulders and then a voice, a faraway voice that was definitely in the room with him.

"Is that you, Carson?" Galen spoke softly. "Come to say— Come back to tell me— What?"

Eddie saw the opportunity. He could let Galen believe he was Carson and in doing so, maybe he could vanquish Galen's feelings of guilt.

"You couldn't have helped me Galen, though you tried. You and Sawyer were the best things in my life, but I was messed up long before you met me." Eddie paused and let his words linger. "You didn't do anything wrong, so stop thinking otherwise. Let me go. I'm just one of life's tragedies, after all. A life for a life, right. Mine for hers."

Galen felt a force surround him, as if he were being sucked into an eddy of air. He closed his eyes and a loud rush of sound pounded his ears.

"You hear me, Galen? Let me go."

When Galen woke the next morning, still in his office, the haunting words from the night before were sharp in his memory. He must have dreamed it all. Dream or not, imagined or not, the words stayed with him throughout the day and gradually an ease came over him.

Mid-morning, he took Karin and Lucky to the park to play with a Frisbee. It was good to see Karin laughing when Lucky leapt up to catch the disc in his mouth. Carson's action hadn't impacted the two of them at all. Galen planned to keep it that way.

An errant toss sent the Frisbee into a row of shrubs along the edge of the creek. "I'll get it," Karin said. She took off running, Lucky at her heels.

"Be careful!" On his way to where Karin was searching, Galen passed a couple of young women sunbathing on a blanket. He thought he recognized one of them, but he was careful not to stare.

"Hi, Professor Bennett," one said.

Now he had to engage. "Hi. Marcy, right?"

"Yeah. This is my friend, Tanya."

"Hello."

"Your daughter is so cute," Marcy said. "The dog too."

Galen was not sure what to say. He imagined they had been talking about the girl who'd been killed and he hoped they would not bring it up. "Thanks. They're having a blast."

"Daddy!" Karin cried out. "I can't find it!"

"I better go help," Galen said.

"Professor Bennett," Marcy said, with hesitation in her voice. "We know it wasn't your fault. What Professor Smith did. We know you were friends, but you didn't make him do what he did."

Galen shook his head. "I—" What should he say? We will get through this together. She's in a better place. How idiotic that sounded. He sighed and said only, "I appreciate you saying so. It was an awful thing."

"See you in a few weeks. I'm in your seminar class."

"Daddy!"

Galen laughed. "I'm being summoned. "See you soon."

That night in bed, Amanda asked him if he were going to be all right.

"Yes," he said. "I've put you through a lot."

"He put you through a lot."

"I know that now. He was ill, I think. Beyond what I could have helped."

"I'm glad you see that," she said. "Come here." She drew him into her, and he laid his head upon her chest.

Amanda had another treatment in the morning, and Galen realized his recent obsession had taken him away from her. She needed him. "Worried about tomorrow?"

"Well, it's never good, is it, afterwards."

"I'll be right there with you. Promise. I'm here now."

She guided his hands to where she needed them, and he did not turn away as he had so often before now.

AFTERLIFE

Chapter 73

January 1992

"Where do you want me to go?" Eddie asked, sounding tired.

"It is not so much that I want you to travel for its own sake," Adi said, "but perhaps there is still something to be learned? He spoke as if there were something specific on his mind. "I know you have read thousands of books, listened to lectures, even debated me." Adi chuckled. "But you have spent most of your afterlife in Chicago, too much time, perhaps. I see now I may have made things too comfortable for you in your house, which is why I want you to leave here."

Eddie looked stunned. "Permanently?"

"You must know, or at least sense, that you are nearing the end of your atonement. I am only suggesting that now is the time to see what else this world can teach you."

"Should I go see the Seven Wonders a third time?" Eddie said facetiously.

"Do you want to see the Seven Wonders again?"

"Have the great pyramids changed?"

"Certainly. A slight alteration of angles due to the abrasion of wind-blown sand—"

Eddie fled from his mentor mid-thought and went outside where Galen and Karin were rolling snow into a big ball for the base of a snowman.

"Do you remember that child as a baby?" Adi asked.

"Of course I remember."

"But can you conjure her face? Can you really see her as a toddler, or as a six-year-old, or as anyone other than the girl she is this moment?"

Eddie thought hard about that and realized he could not. "What is your point, Adi?"

"Life means change. But that is good, is it not? Your entire existence for the past sixty-five years has been in the service of change. Your own. If we did not believe you could change—learn—evolve, you would never have met me. You would certainly not be here experiencing life through these mortal beings you have been privileged to know."

He had been blessed, Eddie realized. And it was also true that life was full of changes. Amanda was in remission and growing stronger by the day. Last May, she had told Galen and Karin that she wanted to go back to work. So with their support, she began sending out her resume. On the morning she was called into Acorn Hills High School for an interview, Karin threw her arms around her mother and said, "show 'em, Mom!"

The only one unhappy about Amanda's new job was Lucky. As much as he could, Eddie did his best to keep the dog entertained, but all the silly pooch wanted to do was sleep until 3:45 each afternoon when Karin burst in the house, eager to see him.

This Christmas, as the Bennetts celebrated their good fortune, Eddie could see that this family that he loved so much, no longer really needed him. He felt like a parent who had raised them, and now that they were off on their own, there was little left for him to do.

And now Adi was kicking him out of the house that had been his since the day he was born. At least it felt that way, and Eddie didn't want to go. What he wanted more than anything was to help Galen and Karin build that snowman. But things like this, these little moments, would never really be his to enjoy. He had learned that fact. If he could somehow have a second chance, he would try to remember that a good life is made of little moments of love, just like this.

Chapter 74

January 1992

Eddie's first full journey around the world in 1965 had been with Adi as his guide. They visited ancient ruins and sites of cultural and historical importance.

"What good is all this sight seeing," Eddie had asked as they stood on the Salsbury Plain looking up at Stonehenge.

"Do you remember when I showed you the Boulder Dam?"

"They've renamed it now, after President Hoover."

"Yes. Yes. The point is, do you remember?"

"Of course I do. I haven't lost my mind. I'm not that old."

Adi smirked. "I wanted you to see what human beings are capable of."

"All right, but I've seen the other side too. The pain and suffering. The greed. The destructive lust for power."

"No one is suggesting you sweep that under the rug, but sometimes a soul needs a bit of majesty. And hope."

So they had spent that year taking in the world's art, monuments, and architechtural and engineering feats.

"Before we go back to Chicago, how would you like to see a bit of my history?" Adi had asked.

Eddie said that would be fine, even though he was ready to be back in his attic. It was evening when they arrived in Rimini, Adi's home on the Adriatic coast of Italy. They sat at a little table at a café, where they watched tourists drink wine. A waiter brought out baskets of bread, which the patrons dipped in olive oil. Later, they dined on seafood and pasta.

"It wasn't like this when I lived here," Adi said, wistfully. "I wish it had been. Life in the 14th century was a bit more tooth and nail."

The next day, Adi took Eddie on a trek up the western coast, into the mountains, first passing over his ancestral farm. "I cannot believe they are still growing grapes," Adi said. "More than we ever had, however."

"It is a beautiful place," Eddie said.

"I have been thinking this is where I would like to retire."

They both laughed, even though they knew it was not meant to be funny. Then Adi said that he longed to return to Celestia, for good.

"As much as I have enjoyed our time together, Edward, I am ready for my duty to end. Besides, there is someone in Celestia I miss terribly. I am only starting to realize how much."

Eddie was speechless. Never before had Adi revealed anything so personal about himself. He had only ever been a dutiful mentor. Now Eddie understood that Adi was more than a spirit. He had been a man.

That was twenty-seven years ago, and now Eddie was sorry that Adi was not tagging along. It was much nicer to follow a knowledgeable guide than deciding on your own where you would go next. Particularly since Eddie really had no real yearning to go anywhere. The only place that had been calling was Florida. So that's the first place he went.

Mick Sheridan's old La Paz had been torn down and rebuilt into a high-rise condominium, with no traces of the Art Deco elegance Eddie admired. He wondered what ever became of the two brass sculptures that had stood as sentinels on each side of La Paz's grand staircase. Sheridan had called them his goddesses. He hoped they were in a museum somewhere and had not been melted down.

While Eddie didn't expect the Palmetto Motor Court and the Pelican Perch diner to still be standing, he was nevertheless disappointed to discover more high-rise condos in place of the little motel and several chain restaurants where he and the boys had eaten red snapper sandwiches and sipped Carribean lemonades. All of it gone. He was overcome with tremendous melancholy, so he left Miami and traveled up the coastline, where he was met with an endless vista of concrete.

Architecture did this Pop, he said, alighting street level in West Palm Beach, where he weaved through clumps of wealthy shoppers, who had nothing better to do than spend even more money, it seemed.

A gusty sea breeze lifted up a crumpled pamphlet from the pavement and sent it in a swirl toward's Eddie's knees. He picked it up to toss in the nearest bin, not caring if any of these sun-tanned men and women saw the paper appear to wave mid air. It was a travel brochure for a Carribean cruise called "Island Escape."

"Why not?" Eddie said. "I could use an escape." So he joined a trail of passengers one morning as they boarded the ship. It did not escape Eddie's notice that the ship's fourteen decks made the vessel appear like a high-rise condominum at sea. He was determined to not let that fact bother him.

It turned out that Eddie's presence on the ship was very lucky for an

Ohio woman named Becky Newsome, for on their very first night at sea, Eddie kept Becky's husband from pitching her overboard. A security officer had seen the whole thing and was quickly there to help rescue the poor woman.

The next day, as her husband was escorted off the ship in handcuffs, Becky shouted from the railing that she hoped he would rot in hell. Eddie found the woman so amusing, he kept her company for the rest of the cruise. When she got home, Becky told her next-door neighbor she had an incredible time, well after they took Ron away. And the most miraculous thing of all was how her daiquiri glass was somehow always full.

After the cruise, Eddie thought any other destination would seem dull by comparison. But he assumed Adi had not intended this sojourn to be a vacation, so he took himself to Asia, where he had gone only once before, that time in '65 with Adi.

Walking once again along the Great Wall of China, Eddie could feel the history he had read about. Now this was some feat of engineering, he thought. Over 13,000 miles long. He traversed its length several times before moving on.

India was a disheartening place for Eddie. It was at once beautiful and sad. On one hand there was the Taj Mahal, which reminded him of Chicago's White City, the one designed by Daniel Burnham for the 1893 World's Columbian Exposition that his father had been so enchanted with. And there were other beautiful places in India too, the rivers, and mountains, but too many poor people lived in wretched slums.

When Eddie thought more clearly, he conceded there were slums in every country. He had walked through the poorest neighborhoods in Chicago in both his life and his afterlife. Seeing poverty up close focused one's thinking like little else.

He had been lucky, he conceded. Always a warm bed. Always a meal. Love. Things he hadn't appreciated. If Eddie were honest, this world tour, in many ways, too many ways, brought his father to mind. It was as if everything he encountered now he was seeing through Pop's eyes.

In Nepal, Eddie sat for a while with the Buddhists. He had never been religious, but he thought if he could start all over, he'd be a Buddhist by choice. The world's major religions, it seemed to him, were too entangled with history, and a warped history at that. They'd all lost sight of what a religion should be—a path to enlightenment. At least that's how he saw it.

He stayed at the monastery until the old monk, who had recognized

Eddie's presence immediately, finally sent him away. Almost nothing surprised Eddie anymore, but he had been astonished when the monk had first spoken to him. The old man explained he was able to be in the same sphere after achieving a high meditative state. Afterwards he and Eddie had lively conversations about the meaning of life. On the day Eddie left, the monk told him he was grateful to have met another wise being from the afterlife. Eddie got a kick out of that. Being called wise. He didn't think he was wise, although he had learned a thing or two since his death.

In June, Eddie went to Finland at midsummer to join a solstice celebration. He had read about such festivities in northern countries and had never been to Finland before. He joined a growing throng of people on the sloped shore of a quiet lake. Hundreds had gathered and had spread their blankets and baskets of food. In some ways it reminded him of his family's Fourth of July excursions to the park. Earlier that day, a tall crown of dense branches had been built upon a raft. It was stacked and bound tightly and resembled a shock of wheat. When daylight dimmed, they set it afire and pushed the raft out onto the lake.

There was something immensely spiritual in all of this—people gathered to revel in the light on the longest day of the year. In six months, it would be the exact opposite. Cheers arose as the flames grew, and before long the bonfire blazed and spewed golden sparks into the violet sky.

Eddie ventured out onto the water near the raft and peered into the bluest part of the fire. He could think of no other blue like it in the world. He reached up to touch the sparks, hot glowing fireflies. Then he remembered something the old monk said, and it filled him with melancholy.

"The world is made up of everything all at once," he had said. "When we die, we burst into a million sparks and rise up into the ether until we become part of one great thing."

"If that's true," Eddie had said, "then you and will cease to exist."

And the old monk nodded.

Chapter 75

December 31, 1993

Adi loved fireworks shows, particularly on New Year's Eve. He called them "excesses of exuberance." Humans needed such things, in Adi's opinion. They needed events that forced them to look outside themselves. He and Eddie had gone to New York many times to watch the big ball drop, but this year they stayed in Chicago, where they joined a cruise to watch the bombs burst high over Lake Michigan. Eddie had heard the mayor was on board, though that fact did not impress him. He had lost faith in politicians long ago.

"One other way spiritual beings have it made," Adi said as they boarded the boat. "You do not have to fight the crowds."

Soon the first burst filled the sky, a cluster of red, white, and blue sparkled like metallic rain until it faded into a gray-blue haze. When the chorus of appreciation quieted, Eddie heard the clinking of champagne glasses before the next mortar fired and the cheers erupted once again.

"Ma would have loved this. The boat ride. All of it." He did not say it out loud, but Eddie realized that Delmar Reed would have loved it even more. It had taken Eddie a long time to understand that his father had been a dreamer, not unlike his immigrant ancestors who had left the old country with their eyes on something better. It's why Pop was so fascinated with architecture. Architects imagined a future that did not exist and they built it. Delmar Reed had wanted more out of life, more for himself, more for his children. His aspirations for Richie's future came from those dreams.

"All my father wanted was to build something better, and he wanted it for me, too," Eddie cried into the sky.

"And now you know," Adi said with great satisfaction. Moments later, amid the "oohs and ahhs," he said, "It is time to go home."

They lay on the floor in the attic and did not speak for hours. Eddie's mind reeled with the memories of his father that had been ever present the past year, memories he had not fully understood until now. Throughout his life Eddie had let little nagging moments build into resentment. An accumulation of injustices, Eddie believed.

The worst injustice of all was that morning Pop had hauled him to the hiring office at the stock yards, made him stand among all those desperate men, made him face that Mr. Overton, who had looked down on him, as if he weren't worthy. And Eddie had to take it, not just the job, but the humiliation too. To admit he was afraid was something Eddie would never have done. So of all the imagined offenses, that morning was the one Eddie had not been able to let go of. Had not been able to forget or forgive.

Only now did Eddie put himself in his father's shoes and understand that he had been the one who pushed Pop to that moment. As a father trying to keep his son out of trouble, Delmar Reed had seen no other way through Eddie's problems. He wanted to teach me responsibility, Eddie thought. It must have been so hard for him, and I hated him for it.

The pain in Eddie's chest felt alive, radiating throughout his being, clutching at his throat, and it intensified as he spoke within himself, "I am sorry, Pop. I am so sorry."

Come with me, Adi said moments later. There is something I want to show you. Moments later, they alit on the roof of a barn outside of Peoria.

"Where are we?" Eddie asked. The scene reminded him of that time he had willed himself to Rome and had ended up in a place just like this.

"It is the old Joshua Roberts farm, where your father grew up," Adi said.

Eddie's eyes opened wide in surprise. "He told us about Mr. Roberts, what a nice man he was, but Pop never took us here when we were kids."

"This is where your father and his brother chose different paths, is it not? And not long after, Richard died in an accident."

"That is probably why he never wanted to come back here."

"And you were not curious to see it for yourself?"

Eddie shrugged. "I guess not. No."

"Your mother and your uncle Stanley grew up in Peoria. And your parents were married in a country church not far from here. This is where their history began. In a way, this is your ancestral land."

"I never thought about it like that, but I don't feel like it belongs to me, this place I mean. Or that I belong to it."

"Hmm," Adi mused. "I felt that way about Rimini, the last time we were there together. I had always considered it my home, but now I wonder what home is. I seem to exist everywhere and nowhere all at once."

"It's nice here," Eddie said. "You can't really see stars like this in Chicago.

Too many trees. Too many lights. They were like this in Finland though." A few moments later, Eddie spoke into the vastness that spread before him.

> *... gliding out I wander'd off by myself,*
> *In the mystical moist night-air, and from time to time,*
> *Look'd up in perfect silence at the stars.*

"Are you reciting poetry, Edward?"

"It's from a poem by Walt Whitman. Always makes me think."

"About what?"

"Mainly how hard it is to know anything. The universe is just so huge."

It is bigger than you can imagine, Adi thought, though he did not say so. Instead he reclined on the slope of the roof and stared up into the Milky Way. He thought of Soraya who would be in her bed looking up at the stars, seeing exactly what he was seeing. Would she be thinking of him at all, or was that only a vain hope?

"I see now," Eddie said, "that I am just one tiny speck in a vast galaxy of— Of possibility, maybe. And that I am the one who determines whether or not I remain small, or, if through the way I live my life, I become part of it all."

"Part of the stars?"

"No. Human life. The galaxy of human life. Look at all of that. One star isn't the show. It's a billion stars that are glorious."

Chapter 76

August 1994

It had been hot day. The Bennetts were in northern Wisconsin at a lake cottage. Life in Eddie's neighborhood was almost lifeless, with most people indoors in their air conditioning. Even after sundown, it was still so hot no one came out to sit on the porch like they often did on summer nights.

"It's the dog days," Eddie said. "Ma always said that about August."

"Do you know why they call it that?" asked Adi.

"No, but I'm sure you are going to tell me."

"It is after Sirius, the Dog Star, the brightest star in the constellation Canis Major, which can be seen this time of year. I can show you, if you would like to see it."

"Why not," Eddie said.

So Adi took him to the observatory.

"I wonder who made up all the names?" Eddie said. "Dog Star." Squinting through the telescope, he said, "I guess it kind of looks like a dog, if you connect the dots." Eddie's eyes wandered across the sky. "What's that one?" he asked, pointing to another bright star.

"That's Vega. One of three stars that make up the Summer Triangle: Vega, Deneb, and Altair—the lyre, the swan, and the eagle."

"They look close enough to touch," Eddie said. "If you could only—" Then before Eddie had a second to know what was happening, he was up in the celestial heavens.

"How?" Eddie said, astonished.

"You said you wanted to touch the stars. Here they are."

Eddie was still eons away from where the stars themselves resided, but he and Adi were amid light so intensified, Eddie felt like he could reach out and hold it all in his hands. And below him Chicago was lit up like a galaxy of stars on its own.

"Beautiful, isn't it?" Adi said.

Eddie did not know what to say. He felt himself about to burst with emotion. "Is this what it feels like?"

"Is this what what feels like?"

Eddie remembered his conversation with the old monk. "Does it feel like this when we enter heaven? Do we burst into a million sparks and rise up into all of this and become part of one great thing?"

Adi lifted his arm and brushed his hand against his vision of the lyre. "Nothing is lost, nothing is created, all is transformed," he said to himself. To Eddie he said, "there are things even I do not know."

Eddie only sighed.

Take him to see the stars, Adi had told himself that morning. He is enchanted with stars. But with all the foresight of a god, he could not have orchestrated a moment as perfect as this one. It was almost as if with his "dog days" comment, Eddie knew where he was meant to go.

I am going to miss you Edward, Adi thought, but there is nothing left to teach you, nothing left for you to learn.

"It is time," Adi said soon after.

"Can't we stay a while longer? Just a—"

"I mean—" Adi said, resting his hand on Eddie's shoulder. "It is time to let go."

Then in a spark of recognition, Eddie understood, so he closed his eyes and let himself be pulled wherever the force would take him.

PART SIX

Chapter 77

AUGUST 23, 1927

Eddie checked his watch again. Quarter to twelve. Late enough, he thought. He had to get out now. Waiting any longer put him in danger, so he made his way down the stairs and just before reaching the bottom step, he heard the distinctive croaky voice of Moose Loughlin and almost froze.

"We know you're in there, Cowboy," Moose said.

Luck occurred in slivers of time, Eddie thought, as he made his way through the kitchen and out the back door as quietly as he could. He fumbled for his rucksack under the edge of the porch and walked quickly across the yard and through the back gate. In minutes he was blocks away.

He stuck to the alleys behind houses, whose lights were almost always out. He moved forward, trying to not go north or south unless he hit an impasse. Right now, distance was his only concern, although he could not stop thinking about how close he had cut it.

At the first hint of daylight, Eddie found cover in a dilapidated garage down a steep hill behind a row of shops of some kind. It was filled with old crates, a Model-T missing all its tires, and rusty gas cans. It was not the ideal place to spend the day, but if anyone came near, there was a canvas tarp over the car he could hide under.

When his heart slowed, Eddie realized just how sore he was. Everything ached. He was exhausted, and all he wanted to do was sleep, but if he got careless, someone would find him. He fumbled for one of the sandwiches and ate it as if he hadn't eaten in weeks. The water he sipped. He had no way of knowing where he would find more if he emptied the canteen too soon. Besides his own breathing, he heard only the sound of a creek or a river nearby. He sat for a long time, peering through a busted out knothole in the door. Later he found a spot in the back of the garage to urinate.

Just after 4:00 p.m., a boy on a bike rode by leaving a cloud of dust from his tires. Not a single car though. A bee thought about entering through the hole, but lit on its jagged edge instead. Eddie watched it until he could no longer keep his eyes open. It was close to dusk when he woke. It was no use chastising himself for falling asleep. He needed it. It would be a long night ahead.

At 1:30 a.m., Eddie left the garage. He took the alley west, where he had seen the boy ride by on his bike, and walked up its long slope until it opened onto a street. There was not a soul in sight, but halfway down the block the neon light of a restaurant cast a red glow across the street. He veered south until he found another alley, then turned west.

Eddie now paid closer attention to street signs. Forty minutes later, almost by instinct, Eddie found his way to the railroad tracks. He had learned from his father that small towns were often built near railway depots. He took the tracks then, taking care not to step into a space between the ties and twist his ankle or cause a fall.

He thought about the summer he and Pop had driven over to Freeport to get his brother. Richie had gone there after his sophomore year in high school with his friend Glenn to work on Glenn's uncle's farm. Delmar had agreed to the arrangement, saying it would be good experience and would show Richie how unsuited he was to that kind of work. Eddie laughed about that. Richie had loved it.

That summer Eddie was thirteen, and he was not looking forward to the start of school a week later. The drive would be a good diversion, Ma had said, and she had sent them on their way with a paper sack of fresh donuts. Looking back now, Eddie realized it was one of the rare times he and his father had got on well.

He and Pop had left home before eight that morning, and by nine the day had grown stifling hot. When they got to the farm, they were both covered in dust from the road, but it had been a lot of fun to tag along with Pop. Eddie was almost sorry they had to bring Richie back with them.

On the way home, Richie spotted a tramp walking along the road and said someone ought to do something about people like that.

Pop was kinder. "That poor fellow," he said, "probably doesn't have a dime to his name."

"We could give him a ride," Eddie said. Richie had kicked him in the shin for that.

"I am pretty sure he will hop a freight before too long."

"What's hop a freight mean?" Eddie asked.

"It means take a ride on a train with nobody knowing about it," Richie said, as if everyone knew what hop a freight meant.

The man was far behind them when Delmar explained that he had read all about it in a paperback novel. "What they do is they go out a ways from the depot, to where the incoming trains slow to a creep. When the eastbound and westbound trains cluster up, it makes it easier to go between them and not be seen. Empty box cars is what they're looking for."

"You still got that book, Pop?" Richie had asked. "Sounds like a good story."

Eddie remembered thinking his father knew an awful lot. The rest of the way home he had thought about that hobo, imagining him leaping up into a boxcar, hoping he was going to make it okay. And now Eddie was the hobo. He crossed the fat ties into the space between the east and westbound tracks and hunched down near a coal crate where he waited. The sky was just beginning to brighten when two trains slowed as they approached each other—one eastbound and one westbound. Just as his father had said.

When the two trains eclipsed him, Eddie stood and hurried to the open door of the westbound freight car. As he reached for a handhold, he slipped and felt the rough wood gouge the palm of his right hand. It stung, but there was no time to worry about that now. On his second try, Eddie pulled himself into car. In the dim expanse, he saw he was alone. The floor of the boxcar was littered with clean hay. It smelled sweet and would make for pleasant sleeping if he dared to close his eyes. He presumed that at some point the train would stop, and there would be men at the door hoisting new bales inside. Eddie hoped to be long gone before then.

His hand throbbed, but tending to it would have to wait. For now, tucked in a dark corner, he was safe. When the train began to pick up speed, Eddie looked at the ceiling and spoke quietly. "Thanks, Pop!"

At the moment, putting distance between him and his old life was the only thing he cared about. The idea had come to him in a flash the night he had packed his rucksack—he'd go to California and find work at an orchard. All the way out in California he would be just another guy. There hadn't been a second thought since. Eddie had known for a while he was finished with the gangster life, had known it even before Bear and Nelson were killed, knew it as deeply as he had known the slaughterhouse was not for him. He just couldn't stomach all the blood anymore.

Eddie knew nothing about picking oranges, but he figured it would be clean work, and at the moment, he looked forward to being out of doors in the California sun. He remembered the magazine photographs of orange groves Richie had shown him—crisp blue skies and deep green citrus trees. Even in pictures, the air seemed light and easy. It would have been a good life for Richie, Eddie thought. He should have had a chance at it.

Just then a sting of guilt struck Eddie. Why had he been saved from it all—the influenza, the bullets, Moose? He didn't deserve this. He choked down a ragged breath and closed his eyes. "I've done a lot I'm not proud of," Eddie shouted into the emptiness. His chest heaved with the weight of his confession. "But I swear, if you let me get away, I will never take another life."

Chapter 78
August 26

A few hours before dawn, the train stopped at a watering station two miles outside of Cedar Falls in eastern Iowa, and Eddie decided it was time to leave the cover of his free ride behind. He waited until the train began to move again, then looking in all directions, seeing no cops or other free-loaders, he jumped out, hitting the ground in a soft roll. To the west of him lay cornfields and silos. Eddie took a deep breath and felt for the first time, that he was on his way now.

He hid behind the wooden shed near the water tower, and waited for daylight. It did not take long for him to doze off. A train whistle jerked him awake, and he left the tracks, climbing quickly up a sloping hill covered in long grass. Behind its ridge, he would be out of sight, and he hunkered down and waited for the approaching train to stop, take on water, then be on its way.

When the train was a blur in the distance, Eddie splashed the last of his water on his face and hands, rinsing away at least a bit of the grime of the past two days. He took off his jacket and shirt and wadded those into a bundle, tossing it as far behind him into the grass as he could. After removing the sliver from his hand, Eddie tossed his knife. He had brought it for protection, but he felt he was no longer under that kind of threat and it was too impractical to carry around. In town he'd buy a pocket knife.

Eddie unpacked his rucksack, then shook it free of dust and straw. After freeing his cash bundles from the sleeve of his clean shirt, grateful that they too were safe, he took one bill and put it in his wallet. Then he packed the bankrolls back in his bag and got dressed. Eddie looked at his watch. Nearly seven. He hoped the town would be awake when he arrived. He would walk slowly, purposefully. No one was chasing him. Then, orienting himself by the rising sun, Eddie climbed down the little knoll and made his way towards Cedar Falls.

The hotel desk clerk had not given Eddie a suspicious look as he had feared. Instead the fellow was nothing but courteous as he handed Eddie the key to his room, which, he said, was up the stairs and to the left.

The room was clean and well-appointed. If Eddie had not desperately needed to eat, he would have flopped down on the bed and gone to sleep.

Instead he washed his face well. The canteen splash had not been enough. He also shaved away the past two days, but decided he would leave a mustache. He shrugged. Why not? A bit of disguise just in case. Before going back downstairs, Eddie stowed his rucksack out of sight. His one worry was his money.

At a nearby cafe, Eddie was seated at a table overlooking the street. He ordered eggs and bacon and pancakes instead of toast. The waitress returned with a pot of coffee. It was hot and much needed. His head was not yet clear, and the voices of other diners hummed as general background noise around him. There was no need to isolate conversations, no need to worry about what someone was up to. It might take a while, he thought, to stop eyeing everyone he saw with suspicion. For now, Eddie stared at a jar of orange marmalade on the white tablecloth, mesmerized by how the rays of sun lit it up like a jewel.

He walked around town, nodding to those who greeted him first. Two men standing outside a land office were discussing the price of hogs. I am in the origin spot, Eddie thought. The place where those pigs I gutted were born. It was a moment of mental clarity that would stick with him for days. He had been, as each pig was, as each steer was, just one cog in a great machine, and his worth had been little more than theirs had been. But now, unlike the poor beasts who could not control their destiny, he was finally doing just that.

At the department store, he bought a pair of trousers, another shirt, socks and underwear, and a casual jacket. He also found a nice traveling bag to replace the rucksack, which said hobo, not gentleman. It was not entirely unlike the bag his mother had once had, just a bit larger. He chose a bone-handled pocket knife, a miniature version of the knife that had once defined him. On a whim, he also purchased a leather bound, unruled notebook and a set of pencils.

Eddie studied the western routes at the train depot. He was in no real hurry to get to California, and he thought it would be good to see a bit of the country first. A meandering route out west would also make him harder to track. This morning he bought a ticket for Omaha. Once he was there, he would plan the second leg of his journey.

"Departs at 7:00 a.m. sharp," the ticket clerk said.

Eddie thanked the man then made his way back to the hotel. After checking that his rucksack and money were still where he had left them, he ran water in the bath. He had been looking forward to it all morning.

Longer even. He had not had a real bath for days. Then he soaked until the water turned cold.

That afternoon, looking out his hotel window, across the river and over the rolling hills beyond the town, Eddie felt a desire he had not felt in a long time. Using his new pocket knife, he sharpened a pencil and began to draw.

Chapter 79

August 27

It felt good to board the train as a modest gentleman. The car filled with men, women, and children, and as Eddie made his way to the rear of the car, to a set of open seats, he breathed a sigh of contentment. He was among ordinary people, the kind he had grown up with, the kind he had left behind when he had joined up with Morrie Nelson. Those days with Nelson and Bear, hobnobbing with well-to-do crowds that frequented Sheridan's club, Eddie had considered himself something of a hot shot, a dandy. But now it felt right to be nothing more than a common man.

"Find your seats, folks," the conductor said. "Departure imminent."

Eddie stowed his bag and settled into his seat, the last one before the passage to the connecting car. His view would be of the miles ahead. No looking back, he thought. He had no idea what tomorrow would bring, but it did not matter. Not one iota.

Unlike when he had kept himself hidden in the freight car, he could mark the time now with places. Signs marking their arrival at small country depots. Des Moines, twenty miles. Council Bluffs. Beyond that was Omaha, and Eddie would be two states away from home.

He sketched the vistas beyond his window, made note of odd sightings, like the little man in a buckboard wagon being pulled by a goat. As the hours passed, Eddie's sketches grew more detailed. And when his eyes drooped from fatigue, he closed them.

At noon, he sat alone in the dining car and ate a simple meal. Eddie spoke kindly to those who engaged him, but did not go out of his way to make acquaintances. Not being unfriendly, just solitary, a man alone.

At the station in Omaha, Eddie bought a newspaper and a ticket to Denver, upgrading to a sleeping compartment. From then on, the porter brought his meals to him, and his last two nights on the train were more comfortable. Gratefully, Eddie saw no reports of a fugitive Chicago gangster called "The Cowboy," so he checked the baseball box scores, and laid the paper aside.

Eddie retrieved the little tin soldier he had put in his rucksack the moment he knew he was going to leave Chicago. He set it on the table in front of his window seat. It reminded him of so much, some of it difficult to think about, but not all. He kept it to remind him of Joe and what a good guy he was. It also reminded Eddie of what a bad friend he had been. *I will do better, now, Joe. I promise.*

Picking up his notebook, Eddie began to sketch, not the prairie and cattle outside his window, but a scene from the past. He had been thinking about Nelson and Bear and about their time in Florida. He closed his eyes and saw the Palmetto Motor Court, that strip of beach, and the ocean beyond that always seemed to be his alone. He drew a trio of ibis on the shore and a lone pelican silhouetted against a thin streak of cloud. As the sketch materialized, Eddie saw it through the lens of memory, so that instead of gray graphite, the azure sea, caramel sand, and bright blue sky appeared under the point of his pencil.

Chapter 80

August 29

From the train depot, Eddie hired a cab to take him to the hotel. He chose the Armstrong Hotel because the porter had recommended it to him. "Best steaks west of the Mississippi," he'd said.

Eddie's room faced the street, giving him a view of the city. Chicago was not the only modern place, Eddie thought. That evening, an overflowing dining room was proof of the hotel's popularity. Before long he was seated at a table for two near the front windows. A quick glance at the menu card, reinforced his choice. Porterhouse with mashed potatoes and peas. He smiled. It was the Sheridan Special. While Eddie waited for service, he gazed out the window. Dusk was beginning to fade into night. Outside the window a streetlight went on as if someone had flipped a switch.

"May I join you?" A tall man with a protruding belly stood at Eddie's table. "The only seat left, I'm afraid."

Eddie nodded and gestured to the open chair opposite him.

Before sitting down, the man offered his hand. "Name's Henry Bloom," he said. "They've put you at my table."

The comment confused Eddie, almost making him forget his false name. "Stanley," Eddie said. "Stanley Nolan."

"I am somewhat of a regular," Henry said, responding to Eddie's confused look, as if it were a well-known fact. "This is my usual table, and they normally reserve it for me."

"I didn't mean to—"

"Don't give it another thought," Henry said. "When the hotel prospers, I prosper."

Eddie pondered the comment. It echoed the kinds of things he and Nelson sometimes told the businesses under their protection. Moments later when the waitress brought Henry's food even though he hadn't ordered, Eddie thought again of Mick Sheridan and how they always just brought him his "usual." Who was this guy? Eddie wondered.

"Do you stay at the Armstrong often," Henry asked.

Eddie shook his head. "This is my first visit to Denver. I'm headed to San Francisco, but I'll be here for a few days." San Francisco was a fiction. Not telling the exact truth was a buffer just in case one day those he met were shown a photo of a fugitive Chicago gangster. If they remembered him at all they'd say "last I heard he was headed to San Francisco." Or whatever place he used as cover. The trick to maintaining a believable tale was to not say too much. And the trick to saying little was to simply listen to others. If you let them gab on about themselves, they often forgot to ask about you.

Right now, Henry Bloom was the curious type.

"What's your line of work, Stanley?"

"Mercantile supply."

"Ah," Henry said, as if Eddie's answer explained everything. "A commerce man. Did you know Denver was built on gold mining, railroads, and prostitution," he said.

"I did not," replied Eddie, somewhat dubious, but he was not about to question the man.

"My father was a prospector. I was a lad when he left us," Henry said.

"Did he strike it rich?"

Henry's guffaw drew the attention of everyone in the dining room. "Hell no. But he had the good sense to die of consumption, allowing my mother to remarry a sensible man. It's to him I owe my good fortune." Henry raised his glass of water, "Here's to good fortune."

Eddie lifted his glass and heartily echoed the sentiment.

Then Henry leaned over the table. "Finish that steak and we'll retire to my room for a proper toast."

Henry Bloom was in a large two-room suite overlooking a courtyard at the rear of the hotel. Two large windows in each room gave Henry a view of the mountains. Inside the door was a valet stand, where Henry hung his suit coat. The room smelled faintly of pipe tobacco. A writing desk contained a neat stack of papers on a dark green blotter. A large mahogany armoire sat along the wall dividing the sitting room from the bedroom. Henry opened the door of the armoire, revealing an interior compartment from which he took two glasses and a bottle of whiskey.

He motioned for Eddie to sit on the settee.

"This is a comfortable set of rooms," Eddie observed.

"My home," Henry said. "That is, I live here."

"In the hotel?"

"Why not? It is perfect for the single man. Dining room, maids, everything one needs. It suits me."

Sheridan had his private suite at La Paz, but he did not live there. "Never considered all of that," Eddie said. "You are a smart man, Henry."

At the compliment, Henry filled Eddie's glass. Then Henry sat in the deep red leather arm chair next to the settee and put his feet up on the matching ottoman.

Eddie had every intention of leaving after one drink, but as he had so easily done before when Nelson twisted his arm, he accepted another one, then later another. The two men talked in general terms for a time. Eddie wanted to know more about prospecting. Later the conversation moved towards prohibition. "Not unlike prospecting times."

"In what way?" Eddie wondered.

"In order to get ahead, a man sometimes has to twist the rules."

And that was the comment that convinced Eddie that Henry might know exactly what he needed. He had intended to find a lawyer in California, but here was a man who just might be on the same side of the law Eddie had been. So Eddie asked Henry if he knew of a lawyer willing to work with an itinerant traveler of some means.

"Oliver Dewey is your man," Henry said without hesitation. "He won't pry too hard into things. That is what you are asking, is it not?"

Eddie raised his glass. "To discretion."

Henry Bloom winked and clinked his glass against Eddie's in a way that made Eddie think that if times were different, he and Henry might find a way of doing business together.

The next morning, Eddie bathed and shaved, leaving the mustache he'd begun growing in Cedar Falls. It was filling out nicely, and he hoped to eventually achieve a western flair. The other advantage to having a mustache, besides the fact that Eddie Reed had never worn one, was that it drew attention away from the scar on his lower lip. At least he hoped that was the case.

After breakfast, with no sighting of Henry, whom Eddie thought might be sleeping off the night, Eddie found a haberdasher and bought a new suit. That afternoon, he took a cab to the address Henry had given him and met with Oliver Dewey. It was the only time since leaving Chicago that Eddie used his own name, and he didn't plan on doing so again.

Dewey set up a bank account for Eddie in his new name, assuring him that it would be no problem transacting withdrawals and deposits via wire from anywhere in the country. After that, they drafted the other documents Eddie wanted sent to Chicago in three weeks time. Eddie handed over the money to cover it all, including, of course, a substantial payment for legal fees. He had expected nothing less. He kept only enough to sustain him until he secured work as a ranch hand.

Eddie's second task was to write letter to Joe Crandall, which after a hearty meal at a cafe near the lawyer's office, he did back in his room on hotel stationary.

Dear Joe,

You have probably heard a few stories about me, and I am not going to lie to you. Some of it is true. But a lot of it was made up to sell papers. I did work for Mick Sheridan. And once in a while we had to get a little rough, but most of the time, I was just trying to keep my hide in one piece. The man you knew is gone. You will never see him again.

Sometime soon, you will be getting a package from a Mr. Oliver Dewey, Esq. In it will be some documents that I need you to take care of for me.

He will be sending you the following:

1. *A bank cheque in the amount of $1,000, payable Jakub Dvorak, or in the case of his demise to his son Arno to divide among the Dvorak children.*
2. *A bank cheque in the amount of $1,000, payable to James Nolan.*
3. *The last one is for you Joe. I hope you can use $3,000.*

Except for yours, of course, I ask that you deliver these gifts in person. I figure if they just arrived in the mail, both men would think it was some kind of joke. I need you to assure them that these gifts, from me, are real. Mr. Dvorak may not know me, but he will remember my father. So tell him, from Delmar Reed's son.

My house will be up for sale soon. I hope you get some nice neighbors.

I also hope you will not worry about me. I have everything I need. I can only say that I have set my feet upon a new path. If anyone shows up at your door looking for me, you can honestly say that the last you heard, I had died. You won't be too far from the truth on that.

Your old friend, Eddie

Two weeks later, after his interlude in Denver, which included a journey by horseback up into the mountains with Henry Bloom, Eddie bought his train ticket to the San Fernando Valley. If a stint in the orange groves proved unsatisfactory, there would be something else on the horizon. This past week under western skies had given Eddie a great feeling of optimism.

As he had in Omaha, Eddie booked a private compartment. Before long, Eddie was settled in and the train whistle blew.

Just as it had before, the countryside became a movie, scene after scene flickering past. Pop would have loved it out here, Eddie thought. Especially the mountains. On the trip with Bloom, Eddie had done several sketches of the Rockies, prompting Henry to say of Eddie that he was a Renaissance man. Eddie had snickered, mostly because he had no idea what that meant.

"Not at all," he had replied. "Just a tinkerer." Looking at the drawings later, Eddie found them lacking. But he'd keep at it. Drawing, even the frustrating attempts, gave him peace.

Delmar would have enjoyed every moment on the train too. Eddie had once asked his father, who was so enamored of trains that he would sometimes take the boys to Union Station or to the freight yards, just to watch the locomotives and listen to the steam and whistles. "Why do you work at the post office? Why didn't you pick a job on a train?"

Eddie had never forgotten his father's answer.

"We cannot always have the life that excites us."

Eddie shook his head. All I wanted was a normal life, though, Pop. Just wanted to be a guy someone like Ma would be proud of. An ordinary guy like Charlie Alford. An ordinary guy like you. But you pushed me into the stockyards. You forced me to—.

No, Eddie admitted, miles later. Pop had not made Eddie take the job with Nelson. He had done that on his own, but he had not done it because he was looking for excitement. All he wanted was a way out of a life that sent men far too soon to their graves.

Chapter 81

September 14

When Eddie got to California, he stepped off the train at the Glendale station in the trousers and a shirt he had bought in Iowa, his new suit folded neatly in his bag. He chose a small hotel on the outskirts of town with a view of the Verdugo Mountains. As much as Eddie had wanted to buy a cowboy hat, especially to honor Bear, most of the men on the streets were hatless or wore fedoras. Any working men he saw wore weathered pork pie hats, so he decided he would buy one of those instead.

He spoke to the hotel desk clerk about orange groves in the area.

"Got plenty of them," the man said. "Peaches and apricots too."

"Would you know if any of them might be looking to hire?" Eddie asked, realizing he probably looked nothing like someone usually asking for that kind of work.

The clerk eyed Eddie up and down. "Figured with your looks, you were hoping to be a movie star. We get a lot of fellas like that through here."

"Not the acting type," Eddie said. "I'm hoping to learn the ranching business."

This answer seemed to placate the clerk. "Closest one's out on Johnsville Road. Gus Magnusson's the owner. He might be lookin' to hire."

In his room, his new hat in hand, Eddie realized that despite what he had said to the desk clerk, he was in the acting job of his life. Passing himself off as an itinerant worker at the moment, he'd played a mercantile agent on his travels. An artist too. In Chicago, he had played so many roles. Life was like that. Trying out parts. So far, he had not found the one that fit him, but he would keep trying.

That afternoon he bought two sets of work clothes and a pair of brown leather work boots. After dinner in the hotel dining room, he went up to his room, bathed, and turned in early.

The next morning, dressed as a working man, Eddie checked out of the hotel and boarded a bus that took him to the main gate of Oro del Sol Ranch. The long lane to the main house was over a mile long. He was in no hurry as he walked toward the ranch. When he presented himself to the overseer, he gave his name—William Fletcher. Will.

"Picking season is a ways off," the man said, "but it's planting time, and one of our crew took off on us last week."

"I don't suppose you have any experience planting trees? Those hands look cleaner than a preacher's."

"No, but back home in Ohio, I worked in my grandparents' garden. They've passed. The influenza. I am willing to learn."

The man nodded as if he too had experience with the great epidemic of 1918. "I can see you're strong," he said. "All right then. I'll take you on."

Eddie inhaled and slowly let out his relief.

"My name's Magnusson, and this is my place." The man held his fingers to his mouth and whistled. The man Eddie had seen standing off to the side of the porch when he'd arrived was inside now. He tipped his hat to the boss.

"Richard, here, we call him Rich, which he is not, but anyway, Rich will show you around. He will tell you we expect hard work and clean living here."

"Yes, sir," Eddie said.

"No liquor in the bunk house. And no gals, ever." Magnusson stood and arched his back. "Go on now. Rich'll get you settled."

Eddie nodded and turned to follow Rich out the door.

"Payday is Saturday—if you are still here," the boss called out from the edge of the porch.

Rich showed Eddie his bunk and said the missus would be out presently with clean bedding. "The others will be back in time for supper," Rich said. "I'm only here on account of you."

"My apologies."

"No need. Good to be out of the sun for a time," Rich said. Then he craned his neck towards Eddie. "It just came to me, who you look like. That movie star."

Eddie shook his head. "I don't know who you mean."

"The cowboy," Rich laughed. "Yeah. Just like him."

That night Eddie lay awake listening to the snorts and snores of his bunkmates and thought of how improbable the past few weeks had been. Getting away from Chicago had been easier than he thought it would be. Along the way, he had continued to put distance between his old life and who he wanted to become. Edward Reed continued to fade. He liked to think of himself as William, Will, and wondered if somewhere his grandfather might be looking down in approval. After all, hadn't the man left home to make a new life? And who knew. Maybe like his grandfather, he would find a nice woman one day too. William Fletcher could certainly see that possibility. A quiet life. A family life. Before long Eddie fell into a hard, unperturbed sleep.

Chapter 82

September 16

In the morning Will hopped the wagon out to the grove and took his cue for how to behave from the others. They were a quiet crew in the morning, unlike how they'd been in the hours before lights out when they'd paired up for horseshoes or card games. One with a guitar had plunked out country songs. Now they stared off into the morning as if they had not a care in the world.

Rich and Will partnered up to plant trees at the furthest edge of the orchard. Will confessed that this was his first time on a ranch, but he wasn't going to let any of them down. He was ready to work hard.

"I thought you looked a little too neat," Rich said with a wink. "Long as you pull your weight, I won't have a problem."

The two fell into a rhythm before long—Will on the spade, Rich setting the saplings in the holes before Will back-filled with sandy soil. Then each tamped the earth with the sole of his boot. Later a watering truck would come along and soak the ground.

"Oh, it takes years," Rich said when Will asked how long until the trees were grown and full of fruit. "Meantime, there's plenty of work to keep these tiny trees going."

"Are those oranges over there?" Will pointed to a tall field of green.

"Yep. When we start picking, you'll feel it in muscles you never knew you had."

Will realized he was looking forward to that too. Feeling the work in every ounce of him, the way he had once felt the slaughterhouse. But this time, it would be in a life he had chosen for himself.

The morning passed pleasantly, and when the wagon came back with their lunch, Will was hungrier than he had been his entire life. He remarked about the fact to Rich.

"It's all this fresh air and sunshine," Rich said. "It's why we sleep so good too."

Rich and Will took their sack lunches to a shady spot under a southern live oak at the edge of the new grove. As Will bit into the thick bread of his sandwich, a breeze rustled the glossy leaves overhead. On the ground a small lizard scampered near his boots. The guitar player from last night took a harmonica from his shirt pocket and blew a blissful tune.

When Will finished his sandwich, he leaned his head back against the trunk of the tree and closed his eyes. No, he didn't deserve this life, not yet anyway. It might take him a while, just like those baby trees. But he'd get there, he thought with a sigh. He would get there in the end.

Notes and Acknowledgments

When I began this story during the autumn of 2020 we were in the middle of the COVID pandemic, and I had just lost my sister, Candace. Her death was not pandemic related, but it was just as unfathomable. I will admit that I am not a spiritual person, but as Candy lay in the hospital, her brain waves flat, I nevertheless felt she was still with me in our last quiet moments together. Where though? Hovering above me? Or already gone?

I have often wondered if she was the one who sent me the germ of this story about a man who dies young without ever realizing what his life could have been? My sister's life, rich in many ways, was also filled with longing and regret. Did she send me the questions that spurred me to write? What if we could have a glimpse of ourselves in a different life, one where we are at our best? What if somehow we could have a second chance to get things right?

However it happened, with Candy in my heart and mind, my tale began to write itself, almost. Then in 2023, I read Robin Hemley's wonderful story, *Oblivion*, and I knew a contemporary writer could dabble in the afterlife. Hemley's muse was Franz Kafka; mine, to some degree, was Dante Alighieri.

As a high school English teacher, I was introduced to Dante's *Inferno* by a colleague; then a summer seminar on *Inferno* at U.W. Madison had me hooked. For years, my AP English students and I traveled with Virgil and Dante on their journey. And each time through, I was struck by the profound truth that our greatest sin as human beings is failing to live up to our potential.

The fact that this novel began during COVID times accounts for my integration of the 1918 pandemic. There were obvious crossovers—masks, mistrust of government, lives lost because we just didn't understand the disease. Taking it back even further, placing Adi Fattoré in Italy at the time of The Black Death was also an obvious choice. But this book is not about three plagues. It's about a boy who can't find his way and won't find it even as a young man. He won't find his way until many years after his untimely death. I hope Eddie Reed is a person with something to teach us all. He certainly taught me a thing or two.

Writing a novel with supernatural elements posed challenges, but I am grateful to have a wide network of teachers and willing advisers. Unlike many television ghosts, in my imagining spirits are gaseous beings, invisible to the human eye. I wanted Eddie and Adi's "lives" to be realistic, but I had no idea how that would work. I am grateful to physicist Hassan Sahouani, PhD, JD for teaching me about the principle of conservation of matter and entropy and for suggesting how spirit Eddie would learn to move and act.

As for illogical elements, I beg my readers to honor Coleridge and give this book their "willing suspension of disbelief." This novel with one foot in fantasy and the other in reality does bend logic.

Edward Reed's life and afterlife intersected with many, many people over the years, and I wanted those characters to reflect reality at each stage of Eddie's journey, which meant that they would be impacted by the events of their time. As some of those folks were immigrants, it was important to me to present them honorably.

I am grateful to my old friend Loretta (Lori Dvorak) Sandhoefner. When she and I were nineteen, we attended a career college for women in Omaha, Nebraska. I was a fish out of water, but during the year we were in school together, she welcomed me into her big farm family and proudly introduced me to her Czech culture and the "Bohemian Alps" near her home town of Verdigre, Nebraska. Verdigre is the self-proclaimed *Kolache Capital of the World*, and Lori's family kolache recipe is my favorite.

At a time in my life when I often felt rudderless, the Dvoraks gave me everything. Like so many characters in this novel, Lori's parents were hard-working, generous people. I never forgot their kindness.

It was Loretta and her friend Peterson Brink who helped me with Czech phrases. Brink, former Assistant Archivist for the University-Lincoln Libraries (Czech Heritage Collections), is now Head of Archives and Special Collections at Creighton University in Omaha.

Bernie McKichan, German teacher and my former colleague at Sheboygan Falls High School helped me put words into Otto Fuchs' mouth.

Valérie Elzinga donated my French phrases.

I relied on my own research beyond that, so those instances where I have erred fall on me.

My friends Donnah and Bill Whitaker were my first beta readers, and I doubt they will recognize this version of the book from the one they first read in 2022. It was a much smaller book then, more of a fable than a magical epic, but their kind encouragement kept me going.

Lois Baer Barr read a fuller version, and her pointed questions steered me straight when I most needed it. Marilyn Zelke Windau helped me with details of the Chicago she grew up in. Lisa Vihos, my art historian friend, helped me with details of the artists and paintings featured in the novel.

Jeff Elzinga and I have been bartering editing tasks for many years. He got me to think about the ultimate reason Eddie was on his journey. I know Jeff was hoping Eddie and Adi would do more to answer our questions about God and the afterlife, but there are certain things even a fiction writer making up her own world can only guess at. In the end, I have no more answers than I did at the beginning.

Peggy Weiner Smith, my long-time friend and faithful reader always finds something I missed. She got me to the finish line.

Some may wonder about my concept of heaven and the afterlife. I wanted this novel to be about a man who was given a second chance. I was less interested in creating a heaven of my own, but at some point I could see no way around it. And also, Adi could not just appear out of thin air (I mean he does, but he has to *exist* somewhere). My apologies to Dante, wherever he is, for how ordinary my Celestia sometimes is. Whereas his *Paradiso* is magnificent, my "heaven" is rather more of a bureaucratic office space. It was a fun place to create, nevertheless.

Earth is a place I know better, and its people, and our failures. In the end, I wanted to wrestle with the questions I think are most important to us while we are living. What makes us human? What gives life meaning? How ought we to live?

I'm afraid as much as it is lovely to speculate that we might have more, I think it is likely we have just this one life. So to not make the most of it is not right. On the other hand, it would drive us insane to be constantly striving for meaning. Sometimes it is just fine to fritter a day away.

For me, I can't think of a better way to pass time than to immerse myself in a really good book. So I must thank all the authors I have read, loved, and learned from.

I'd like to thank Ray Bradbury for a particular writing lesson. "List ten things you love, and ten things you hate," he said. "Then write about the former, and "kill" the latter—also by writing about them."

I hadn't known about this advice from Bradbury until I was in the final revisions of this novel. But it hit like an eternal truth, and I realized that unconsciously I had already been doing something of the sort. This novel is filled with things I love—books, learning, art, family, gardens, kindness, and light, and I have included them in a variety of ways, hopefully in ways that make my characters more human, more relatable.

In whatever way possible, I have killed the things I hate—greed, selfishness, laziness, impatience, willful ignorance. It is easy to create a stereotypical bad guy—black hat, evil sneer—but that's a cartoon. It is not as easy to create your own complex human beings.

My good guy is a bad guy. My bad guys are good. Some of my good guys do bad things and vice versa. And that's at the heart of this novel because I wanted to write about something else I believe in: change, redemption, atonement. For if we are not allowed to change, there is not much point in living.

I'd like say a bit about books in general, because in many ways, they have been my life's saviors. Beginning when I was a child, stories meant everything to me. One afternoon when I was five, I ran away from home for a few hours. In the little suitcase my mother helped me pack were many of my books. During the tumultuous time of my parents' divorce, nine-year-old me found a life net in books. As a thirty-something going to college to become an English teacher, books at a higher level truly transported me into a life I had never imagined for myself. I haven't been without a book since, often reading one after another in a chain.

Maybe you recognized the explicit and implicit references to books (and poems and plays) throughout this novel. If you are interested, a detailed list of literary works follows the book club discussion questions.

Finally, to you, my readers, I am eternally grateful.

Book Club Discussion Questions

1. Eddie's apparent dyslexia causes him to see himself in negative ways. If you could talk to Eddie during his childhood years, what would you say to help him feel more positive about himself?
2. Thoroughout the novel, Edward Reed had more than one father figure. Who would you say had the greatest positive influence on Eddie?
3. Discuss the role of teaching and education in the novel.
4. Who was your favorite character and why?
5. Which scenes stick with you and why?
6. Besides Eddie's infatuation with Belinda and later on his interest in nightclub "dames," Eddie never really develops a love interest. Was that a dissapointment to you? Explain.
7. Books play an important role in this novel, *The Adventures of Huckleberry Finn* in particular. If you are familiar with that novel, discuss the ways Huck's life compares with Eddie's. What do you think Joe hoped Eddie would take away from reading that book?
8. Was Delmar Reed right to force Eddie to work at the slaughterhouse? In what ways did Eddie benefit from that job?
9. At one point, Eddie wishes he could stay in Florida forever. What was it about his time in Florida that had such an effect on Eddie?
10. The "Reed House" had several occupants over the course of the novel. Which family were you most drawn to and why?
11. Which was more important for Eddie: making amends for his criminal life or learning what life could have been if he had made different choices? Explain.
12. Eddie chose to go to California in the end. Were you happy about that, or do you think he would have done better elsewhere?
13. What stories or movies does this novel remind you of?
14. What, in your view, did Eddie leave unfinished? Explain.
15. Extend the ending. What will life be like for Will? Do you think Adi will reunite with Soraya? How do you want the future to unfold for the two of them?

References to Literary Works

Uncle Stanley's little pine bookcase and Joe's bedroom shelves are filled with numerous books a boy of the time might have read.

I was inspired by Gustave Dore's depiction of Dante and his guide, the Roman poet Virgil, as my models for Adi Fattoré. Galen Bennett consults Dore's illustrations of *Inferno* first published in 1861, then later republished by Dover Publications in 1976. Galen Bennett, a Dante scholar, uses the John Ciardi translation of *Inferno.* It is the one I used.

Adi's suggestion to one of his first celestial souls that he might not remember his war experience in his next life alludes to the title of a novel by Mark Helprin, *A Soldier of the Great War* (Harcourt, 1991), a book that suggests that our dead are never really gone as long as we are alive to remember them.

A celestial soul quotes a line from John Donne's "A Valediction Forbidding Mourning." Donne's poem "For Whom the Bell Tolls" is referenced later in the novel.

Eddie remembers his mother reading Andrew Lang's *The Blue Fairy Book* (1889) to him and Richie. Galen Bennett also recalls the book from his childhood. We had a copy of that book in our house as well.

Eddie wandering in search of Belinda is a nod to James Joyce's "Araby," a story from *Dubliners,* in which a young boy imagines himself in love.

Mark Twain's *Adventures of Huckleberry Finn* (illustrated by E.W. Kemble and John Harley) is the book Joe Crandall gives Eddie for his birthday. It was an obvious choice, as Eddie is on an episodic journey like Huck is. However, it is Richie Reed who wants to follow Huck and "light out for the territory." Sadly, it is Twain's *The Adventures of Tom Sawyer* that convinces Eddie he can't read.

The Wonderful Wizard of Oz by Frank L. Baum is referenced first as a book, second as a movie. The two are entirely different entities.

The woman who asks Eddie to haul out a box of books for her is an oblique reference to Mayella Ewell's scene in *To Kill a Mockingbird* where she invites Tom Robinson into to her yard to "bust up a chiffarobe."

Otto Fuchs is a character in *My Àntonia* by Willa Cather, one of the most influential books of my life. The epigraph at the beginning of *My Àntonia* comes from Virgil: "*Optima Dies Prima Fugit,*" the best days are the first to flee. While not overtly mentioned, that "carpe diem" sentiment, which has become my personal mantra, is central to the novel's themes.

When Jimmy Nolan pulls Eddie in and tells him "war is no kind thing," the great Wilfred Owen poem, "Dulce et Decorum Est" (1920) echoed in my mind.

Adi references Upton Sinclair's *The Jungle* (Doubleday, Page & Co., 1906), a book that revealed the ugly truths about the meat packing industry.

Several books by Charles Dickens are mentioned, and one night Joe Crandall imagines he sees Marly's ghost and wonders if he will wake up on Christmas day like Scrooge did, a reformed man.

Thornton Wilder's play *Our Town* was one my American Literature students read each year, and I hope they took away from it some sense that they ought to seize the day.

One day in Galen Bennett's literature class, Eddie provides a lecture of his own on Erich Maria Remarque's *All Quiet on The Western Front* (English translation Little, Brown and Co., 1929), which is a book all high school students should be obliged to read.

The mention of the Victor Appleton book *Tom Swift and His Air Glider* is also in honor of *To Kill a Mockingbird*, as Jem is enamored of Tom Swift books among others. Richie acts out adventure stories, just as Jem does.

Tom Swift and His Air Glider is the book that Rutherford Gage keeps for himself to remind him that boys must eventually grow up.

Women who knit and make things to keep busy and stave off despair like Naomi Reed and Margaret Gage remind me of Odysseus' wife Penelope in *The Odyssey*, who keeps her officious suitors at bay by unmaking and remaking a shroud.

Karin Bennett's favorite book is my favorite childhood book, *My Friend Mac* by May McNeer and Lynd Ward. (Houghton Mifflin, 1961).

The fact that John Lennon's killer stayed at the scene reading *The Catcher in the Rye* is an inexplicable truth, and I agree with Eddie that it was a defilement of good literature.

Eddie recites lines from Walt Whitman's *When I Heard the Learn'd Astronomer*. It is a somewhat subversive poem, suggesting that to learn one only needs to observe the world.

Eddie's brief hobo life and Will Fletcher's long walk up the road to the Oro del Sol Ranch and subsequent bunkhouse scene is a nod to Steinbeck's *Of Mice and Men*.

Lastly, I tucked Joe Crandall's newspaper clipping inside *Great Expectations* purposefully. The Dickens classic is one I resisted reading, then never forgot. It's a story of a boy who rises above his circumstances.

About the Author

Dawn Hogue began writing as a child, a practice she continued throughout her teen, young adult, and college years, but it was not until she retired from teaching high school English in 2015 that Hogue turned her attention to poetry and fiction writing full time. A fuller account of her writing can be found at her website: dawnhogue.com. Hogue's first two novels, *A Hollow Bone* and *Summit Road,* are also available through Water's Edge Press and anywhere books are sold online. A midwestern native, Hogue now lives with her husband Michael and two cavalier spaniels, Mika and Winnie, in Tucson, Arizona.

www.ingramcontent.com/pod-product-compliance
Lightning Source LLC
Jackson TN
JSHW070237040326
98744JS00005B/21
9781952526329